THE END

. . . .

SALVATORE SCIBONA

Graywolf Press

SAINT PAUL, MINNESOTA

Publication of this volume is made possible in part by a grant provided by the Minnesota State Arts Board, through an appropriation by the Minnesota State Legislature; a grant from the Wells Fargo Foundation Minnesota; and a grant from the National Endowment for the Arts, which believes that a great nation deserves great art. Significant support has also been provided by the Bush Foundation; Target; the McKnight Foundation; and other generous contributions from foundations, corporations, and individuals. To these organizations and individuals we offer our heartfelt thanks.

MINNESOTA
STATE ARTS BOARD

NATIONAL
ENDOWMENT
FOR THE ARTS

TARGET.

Special funding for this title has been provided
by the Jerome Foundation.

Published by Graywolf Press
2402 University Avenue, Suite 203
Saint Paul, Minnesota 55114
All rights reserved.

www.graywolfpress.org

Published in the United States of America

Printed in Canada

ISBN 978-1-55597-498-5

2 4 6 8 9 7 5 3 1
First Graywolf Printing, 2008

Library of Congress Control Number: 2007938134

Cover design: Kyle G. Hunter

Cover photo: Jack Delano, Night view of part of Santa Fe R.R. yard, Kansas City, Kansas, 1943. Library of Congress, Prints & Photographs Division, FSA-OWI Collection, LC-USW36-656.

To Helen, Stanley, Barbara, and Big Sam

. . .

Contents

I Know That My Redeemer Lives

1913 – 1953

. . . .

I

He was five feet one inch tall in street shoes, bearlike in his round and jowly face, hulking in his chest and shoulders, nearly just as stout around the middle, but hollow in the hips, and lacking a proper can to sit on (though he was hardly ever known to sit), and wee at the ankles, and girlish at his tiny feet, a man in the shape of a lightbulb. He was faintly green-skinned, psoriatic about the elbows and the backs of the knees, his shaven cheeks untouched by scars of any sort, faithful to a fault to his daily labors, grudgeless against the wicked world, thankful for it, even; a baker of breads with and without seeds, modest cakes, seasonal frosted treats; supplier to all the neighborhood and occasional passers-through; a reader of the p.m. papers, as all of his vocation are, born on the feast of Saint Lucy, 1895; a prideful Ohioan; a sucker of caramel candies when cigarettes he forbade himself from eight o'clock to two; possessor of a broad and seamless brow and a head of sleek black undulant hair, the eyes goonish, unnaturally pale and blue, set deep in the skull in swollen rain-cloud pouches, the eyes of one poisoned with lead, who had not in all his days addressed a piece of speech to more than two persons at once; a looker-right-through-you if he pleased, as old cats look, accustomed to suffering the company of others but always in need of privacy; the baker of Elephant Park; an unambitious businessman; a soul liberated from worry by luck and self-conquest; a weakhearted sparer of the rod with his boys; a measured drinker of spirits who prayed daily for the salvation of his sons and wife; a smoker nevertheless immune to colds and grippes; an ignorer of the weather; a lover of streaks, content and merciful; an unremarkable Christian.

The day's fifteen hours of labor he divided into three parts: six in the kitchen, solitary; six at the register in front, where he experienced the slow wringing-out of self exacted by the company of others not his own; three again in back, solitary once more unless one of his boys attended him. He was the father of three sons.

Of these it was never the first or last who pried open the back-alley bakery door, the hickory-dickory-dock door, it was called, and came inside to sit postschool with his father while he worked. It was the middle one, unfriended, while the others were lost to the streets. It was Mimmo only ever who came and kept company with him, a boy mute, imperious, sweetly piss-smelling, stool-top observer of things spectral and material, who instead of football and coal-thieving from the rail yards opened the alley-oop door, as it was also called (there wasn't any handle and the lock was long busted, but a stick wedged in the bottom right corner would send it swinging), and unlonesomed the hottest hours in the back of the bakery afternoons, when the ovens smoldered for the night and the glass doors that opened for the public were locked and blinded. In truth the baker wished his first or last would come instead, the two that owned their mother's talent for flattery, chin-wagging, exuberant high-pitched singing of patriotic songs, not to say of scrubbing and sweeping.

Despite all his thrift and toil, he had failed throughout the boys' younger years to lay up enough treasure in this world to provide a private room for their sleeping—all three shared a Murphy bed in the parlor—or, in truth, at times, to furnish the Sunday table with meat or poultry; or to purchase decorator items to enliven the parlor walls, or flounces for the curtain hems, or a sign of any kind to label the bakery storefront; or to pay an assistant's wage, so that all the bakery's many chores he did himself. The boys he kept in school. Their mother rolled counterfeit Cuban cigars at the kitchen table.

D'Agostino, the usurer that owned the consignment store, one of his clientele, told him it was the superstition that you couldn't spend what you didn't yet have that had kept the serfs in the fields. "You can't even afford a spinster to punch the till buttons and shell your almonds, which goes to show," he argued.

No, but it went to show instead the limit of what the baker should

hope to own. He understood that America had become great by extending the right to earn money even to money itself, but this was to his
mind a practice of the uttermost corruption, since out of whose hands
was the first money taking the second money but those of the man who
had made it in the sweat of his brow? And therefore no account at any
bank bore his name, since where would the interest have come from?
Usury! Although he otherwise felt toward his chosen country a tenderness only such as he had seen young girls struggle to conceal for their
fathers.

His hopes instead were unpurchasable and plain. He knew what
they were—well, he knew what one of them was, he could describe it
in words but wouldn't tell you if you asked because it was not for your
ears. He was only a modest person, was not eminent in any way, and his
clientele, even the children among them, did not use his family name
but called him Rocco, as though he were their servant or cousin.

He was susceptible to dread.

At the least expected time of sweet lonesomeness, in the earliest of
morning hours, while he bumbled down the bepuddled alleys beneath
the tenement balconettes, where in summer months the caged-in children snored beneath the washing, under the yellow-dark clouds of coal
smoke, dread leapt from the shadows and pounded him in his face.
Or later, at four in the a.m., while he filled the proofing shelves with
the day's 180 oblong loaves, slowly but slowly rising all around him, all
white (picture a colossus in a mausoleum of innocents); or while he was
coaling the oven, the dread descended and clocked him. At such times,
what could he do to protect himself but name the dread and hope that
that would sap its force? So he spoke inwardly the Biblical warning that
described it so much better than he could on his own and described as
well what his role was in the universal scheme and the consequences of
failing in that role. The first time he heard it was at the mass for the last
one's baptism. Monsignor read it in Latin, and he didn't follow; then
in Italian, and he wasn't paying any attention; then in English, and it
did its terrible work: *"Behold, I will send you Elijah the prophet before the
coming of the great and dreadful day of the Lord: And he shall turn the heart*

*of the fathers to the children, and the heart of the children to their fathers, lest
I come and smite the earth with a curse."*

He was the father of three sons. He loved them so, as the Lord required. Mrs. Loveypants, their mother, also called Luigina, was be-
loved of him, too, but collaterally, as the vessel by which his boys had
blessed him.

They were boys, and therefore their souls were unfinished and their
habits impressible. The first discovered the eating of salt with water-
melon, and the middle and last took the habit up shamelessly, imitat-
ing also the first's wincing and puckering, and shot the seeds off their
tongues like savages at passing dogs. They ran away from home and yet
came back. They were innocent of resolve. They were as vulnerable to
their surroundings as mold. For this he might have congratulated them:
They were Americans after all, who felt nerves where older nations felt
fear, and a million possible nervous selves crowded around them, clam-
oring to be chosen, and his eager boys looked perpetually in all directions for the one they most desired to be, always in a state of becoming.
He himself, on the other hand, had long since finished becoming and
therefore faced fewer, more concentrated, and infinitely more terrifying uncertainties—the hour of his death, the resilience of his faith in
the Lord. He might have congratulated them if only he could have assured himself that all of their becoming would at some point in early
adulthood *conclude* and they would experience the benefits of having
become: the ease of physical comportment, the directness of gaze and
speech, the freedom from the desire to seem, also the ability to pray
without requesting something for oneself. His own father had a word
that described this, and here was Rocco's hope, the thing he wouldn't
have told you because it wasn't yours and he didn't want to dishonor it
by explaining. It was something he wanted for his boys, whom he loved
as himself—he hoped that the boys, once men, would *harden.* Think of
a brick in a kiln. His father had achieved this, his grandfather more so,
and it was evinced by the rain-cloud pouches about their eyes. "Don't
associate with people who touch their faces while they talk to you," said
his father. "That's not what the hands are for."

Now, take his boys. He did not understand why they must always be smiling! They were taught in the schools to shake hands with strangers while widely showing the teeth, as if they were horses offered for inspection. They were not horses! They were Christian persons, but they laughed at what wasn't funny because they desired above all things not to become hard but to become liked, and it made Rocco's blood boil because they were putting themselves up for sale. And in his eyes, as in the eyes of the Lord, they were beyond price.

Three boys, one two three, and him their father, and Loveypants.

One of his cousins had had a cousin he wanted Rocco to meet, and that was Loveypants (although yet to acquire the name), and they had gotten married. All right, it was marginally more complicated than that. This was in the city of Omaha, in the Nebraska, where he had immigrated at first and found work goading steers onto and off the trains. Woodrow Wilson had just had his stroke, and Rocco was in grief on account of Edith, the young bride who had rescued Wilson from his widowerhood. Furthermore, as the Spanish flu plagued the wider world, where was Rocco's place of work but a rail yard, among trains that had come from far-off infected ports in the east, south, and west. It was like the heat of a furnace, this dread, like the hot breath of the Lord blowing on him, saying, *Harden.* So he said to Loveypants, with whom he'd been sharing insufficiently reserved boxcar liaisons, "I guess we'd better get married." To which she responded, "We agree." And due to his already having shamed her, he received no dowry, which was not unjust.

Loveypants, Luigina, drove a spear through the heart of the Rocco of becoming and watched it beat its last. Once he was hardened, his father had prophesied, the things of his softness would look shameful to him, and so they did. And he abandoned salooning, urinating from high windows, weekly letters home to Mother in Catania, and finally the Nebraska itself, and bought two train tickets eastward and two sets of new underclothes. What remained of the life of the Rocco of becoming was little else but Loveypants, who herself had hardened admirably, and to whom the name Loveypants (her boxcar name, her own invention, which she preferred) did not apply anymore in the same degree, but a word is a harder thing to spear and kill than a person.

In December 1919, Loveypants and Rocco reached their destination and disembarked from the train. Her hair was in tangles. Snow caught in the fuzz of her limp cloth coat. The tin reinforcing cups on the corners of her trunk hissed on the ice as she dragged it by a belt tied to its handle, while the other baggage she carried in a tarpaulin bundle on her back. Down the Ohio road she pulled her things, pregnant, singing to him.

Four and a half years later, which would be three years into his apprenticeship under the baker Modiano, the old man, anticipating retirement, offered to lease the bakery to Rocco until he had the cash to buy it outright. How was he to raise the money? For a day, he considered, and then, in a flash, his plan came to him: He would simply open the store every day. Without exception. The Sabbath be damned, and Christmas and Pentecost. Loveypants was not the only one to express skepticism about this plan, but he proceeded in the teeth of doubting Thomases and Tomasinas.

Therefore his streak began, and his fidelity to it was absolute down the many years, and labor coursed continually over his willing shoulders as though he had determined to build his house under a waterfall.

"But now begins a journey in my head, to work my mind, when body's work's expired," recited the green-eyed first one, standing atop the downfolded Murphy bed in the parlor while Loveypants prompted him from a school reader; and Rocco, despite his own best efforts, saw his focus go slack, and splayed himself on the rug, the bag-of-bones last one that would not eat his father's bread tucked inside Rocco's night coat, the middle one, the Buddha, his legs crossed, watching from his accustomed perch within the armoire. From Rocco consciousness began to take its nightly four-hour leave. What he would give to forswear sleep! If God was good, on the other side he'd give Rocco back such hours that sleeping took, postsupper in the parlor, the spit of the papoose on his sleeve.

Loveypants applauded. The armoire hinges complained as the middle one shut himself inside. And Rocco slept.

And trouble came.

No sooner had he finally bought the old man out, after fifty-two months of leasing, than the store began to sink. It was the beginning of the panic. Free enterprise was bunk after all. For example: A child needs milk for his bones but his father can't afford any; a certain Swede of the father's acquaintance, a dairy farmer on the South Side, dumps fifty gallons daily of whole cow's milk that nobody can afford to buy into the swill for his hogs. There is supply, there is demand, but there is no money. And yet money doesn't exist, really; it's more a theory; and so the root cause of so much waste was the lack of something that did not exist. For example: The loaf that Rocco slides from his peel onto the cooling rack has a splendidly chewy crumb, holes of many sizes and shapes, a light crust that shatters against the teeth. It has, at the moment he opens his store, just reached room temperature and is at its peak of texture and taste. In comes his clutch of clients who neglect entirely this living object of his art for yesterday's dead leavings, available to them at half price. Today's will sell tomorrow. God bless us.

He had no debts but his boys weren't fed so his streak endured.

With Roosevelt came relief, and Rocco was nearly ruined. Bread they gave for free to anybody willing to wait in line. Cotton wool, he should say. Soap foam. Fermented for only an hour and a half (he asked one of the miserable scabs employed to bake it) and cooked in a luke-warm gas-fired oven. Now the bread that issued from Rocco's oven on a Wednesday morning was the fulfillment of dough he'd started Sunday night. Look at the blistery, barklike surface of the thing he made. Put it in your mouth and press it with your tongue. He asked the Lord what had become of shame. Meantime, agents of the federal government were buying piglets and sows and incinerating them in a starving nation because they were not expensive enough. In the winter, to save on coal, Rocco and the boys and Loveypants slept in cots in the bakery kitchen. The last boy got scurvy. Briefly, Loveypants believed that she was pregnant again, but malnutrition had merely made her monthly irregular. Then her mother, living in the New Jersey now and widowed, wrote on a postcard that through the intercession of a certain Alfred, stepbrother of the deceased father, Loveypants could obtain full-time employment there in a union candy bar factory. This uncle offered as well a bed in his home—there, in the New Jersey—that could sleep two in one direction and perhaps a third crosswise at the foot, if this third, the postcard concluded, was shorter than four feet tall.

This is the tale of the man whose bucket leaked on his way home from the well.

Here is what they did. She took the first and last with her and the middle stayed with Rocco. Once the store prospered again they would regroup themselves.

Mimmo, the middle one, Mimmino, now the baron unchallenged of all the parlor, was no longer called upon to share the water in his bath. When a chicken could be found, both drumsticks were his, and the fat gleamed on his great teeth. Within a year he overgrew his father. He undressed himself while standing on the furnace grate, a suit of white flesh, immaculate, grown from Rocco's meager seed, and Rocco pulled the bed down from the wall and threw the blankets on the boy, and doused the light. He could not bake or add or sew or read and would not learn. Mornings, five hours after Rocco had left him midsleep in the house, he stumbled into the bakery for his breakfast. He sat and ate an egg and ate a roll. Rocco dripped some oil upon his comb and pulled it through the boy's unruly, nigrous hair.

It had long been claimed by Mimmo that bearded spirits visited him, and not in nighttime merely. He could be seen to follow them with his gaze at supper and attend to their conversations—they did not speak with him but with each other, in a language that he did not understand. But he did not fear them anymore, he said, they were older than before and frail, and he now believed that they were on his side.

Rocco had not known that they had been against him. "You should have told me," he said, extending his hand toward the boy and with the backs of his fingers tapping Mimmo's chest, three times, mirthfully, on the buttons. "I would have driven them off for you."

"But they're on my side now," repeated his one remaining.

"Whose were they on in days gone by?"

"Yours," he said.

Early evening. October. Mimmo slouched, boneless, on his stool. The first and last and Loveypants had decamped sixteen months and five days before. The bold and simple pennant flag of Ohio hung from curtain rings in the doorway between the front of the store and the kitchen and billowed with the heat convecting from the oven in the rear. The numbers sixteen, five, twenty-four, stitched by Rocco into the central stripe of the flag, attested to the date of the initiation of his streak. The dough in his grip, leavened by a colony of yeasts he'd founded and daily fed and daily taxed so as to save on brewer's yeast, was folded by him, rolled, thrust, folded, rolled, swung through the air behind him, thrashed against the surface of the worktable, rolled again, all at terrific speed (he was not ungifted at this) until it was as tight as a mattress and wondrous to touch, even this late in the day its charms unlost on him. "Strike it with your open hand, Mimmino," he murmured, hoisting it under the melting boy's unsubmitting eyes. "Spank it. Look, I am a little god. I make flesh out of dust and water. Look, it weighs more than you. Why, it feels more like your ass than your ass does." His voice was soft, rasping, tired, a soft bass voice, the soft voice of a hardened man. "Give it a roundhouse punch, it won't mind." He sniffled, as did the boy. The Buddha wore a forlorn look today. His posture made Rocco worry he wasn't feeding him enough cheese. "Go on, close your fist and give it what you have," he said. "Feel how silky and warm like your skin it is. Sit up and touch it, why don't you, talk to it, stick your nose in it and take it in."

That was when the boy asked, if it was all the same to him, and if room could be found on the floor, maybe, if he could go live with his mother. He had the merest beginnings of yellow-orange whiskers at the corners of his mouth.

Rocco put him on the train and watched him go.

The bucket leaked. The water dripped on his shoes. And yet he didn't run home but continued walking at the same pace.

She didn't come back. She stayed there. Even when he had a little money and wrote postcards saying, *Now is the time; Steak for breakfast; I will take you dancing; I will close the store on Sundays; What therefore God hath joined together let no man put asunder.* And the boys stayed with her. They visited their wanting father seldom, then less, then not anymore. One married. One enrolled in a taxicab-driving class. One volunteered to fight the nation's enemies in the Far East.

Like anyone else, he struggled to keep the commandments and to be steadfast in his faith. He confessed on Saturday afternoons that, notwithstanding the threat of the scriptures, he had as yet failed to turn the hearts of his children to their father. He took a break from work at six thirty Sunday mornings to hustle up the street and receive Communion and made it back in time to open the store at the wonted hour. Regarding his neglect of the day of rest, he recalled that the Lord had once asked, If you had a sheep that fell into a pit on the Sabbath, wouldn't you lay hold of it and lift it out?

His streak endured.

He desired for himself solitude, which was to say the company of his own.

Late afternoon. August 14. Yesterday. Seventeen years unwifed. Dog days. The days the Dog Star rose with the sun. Attempting to nap on the Murphy bed in his work pants. The judgments of the Lord are true and righteous altogether. Drip, said the ice in the icebox on the pan. Something to slow his heart down, gin maybe, of which there was alas not a spoonful in the house. Ice cubes in a dishrag on his eyes.

When they knocked on his door he thought it was time already for D'Agostino and the Friday card game. Why, hello. Brush kitty from the door with the foot. They were wearing impractical woolen outfits but were unsweating and tucked their hats under their arms as they entered, and then they made their outlandish pronouncement.

Pursuant to the terms of the recent armistice, all United Nations prisoners of war in North Korea were to be let go, Mimmo among them. (Rocco read the news, thank you, he was aware, he had awaited the day.) However, Mimmo, they declared to him, in words that really did not allow air to get in between, had contracted tuberculosis and, by the date of the exchange of prisoners, had died. This was only last week that this had happened. The navy was soon to return the body to the New Jersey, where Loveypants intended to bury it. The secretary of defense wished to express the regret of a grateful nation.

Rocco had no shirt. His nipples looked uncertainly at his knees.

Well, this was stated in such a way as not to allow for another person's way of looking at things. Obviously they had received training in theatricals and elocution. So it was not really any use to argue the case. Because they were committed to their view. Which was their right because in America we have liberty of talking as we please. Thank you, good-bye.

A moment to consider how he would proceed. Bending deeply, he poured a teacup of cod liver oil into the cat's bowl.

On straightening again, his resolution was complete:

He would physically transport himself, finally, to the New Jersey, to the dwelling place of Loveypants and the boys, and confess to them his own sin in having permitted them to live separately from him these many years, leaving them exposed to the Lord's righteous anger. He would not plead weakly via post. He would go and see their faces, not only in the mind's eye but in blood and skin. Once they perceived the earnestness of his confession, they would return with him to Ohio to live.

Outside the screen door, a woodpecker with flaming red plumage about the head glided past, and the cat flattened herself watchfully to the floor. Rocco cracked the door, and out she slunk.

All at once his blood went thick with fatigue. He reached his bed just as he lost the strength in his knees to stand. The streak was nearly as old as the middle one himself, if memory served, and now had seen its completion. Sleep, real sleep, lusty, murderous, fell on him at last in all its smothering weight.

In the middle of the night, not far from his house, the Russians exploded an atomic bomb.

No, sorry, it was only the risen sun. He was a little disoriented. He had slept clear through the dark part of the morning for the first time in 10,685 days.

2

War at last! Again! It was the beginning of the atomic apocalypse, or so he surmised.

Rocco was abed, alone, striving mightily to be stouthearted. The flood of light had broken his sleep, and now a boom was going to come, and he would be finished off. Everything was white and ablaze—his sheets, his Skivvies on the chair, his blameless knees. Would he hear the boom, or would it split his eardrums first? He waited for the fabled shock wave, a naked man in his brilliantly illuminated bedroom on a sheet. All of mankind would be annihilated this time for sure.

The cat fastened her claws to the doorjamb and stretched herself. He had time to note that outside a jay was shrieking. He waited to go deaf and then to disintegrate. He waited in the famous interval between the flash and the noise. Assuming their aim was good, the Russians had bombed the steel mills downtown. That was what Rocco would have hit if he were running their show. He waited—liking himself a little because he wasn't afraid—for the boom and then the nothing. He commanded kitty to come keep Papa warm, but she refused him and refused him until, acquiescing, she levitated onto the bed and gave Rocco a kiss on his chin. "Here it comes," he told her. Nothing in reality was as terrible as in his nightmares.

And wouldn't you know. No boom. Why, it wasn't any atomical cataclysm.

Outside, the paper-rags man bawled his plea that Vermilion Avenue bring out its old paper and old rags. His nag clip-clopped. His nag clip-clopped. The dray wheels rasped along the sandy pavement bricks.

Rocco pissed, he showered, he shaved, he boiled his coffee, he toasted his toast. His brood would not recognize the toaster once they returned, but he hoped they would appreciate that he had otherwise maintained the furnishings they knew.

Mindful of the August daytime heat, he decided to defer the start of his drive until the cool of the evening. In the meanwhile he put on his good duds—a coal-colored, faintly pinstriped three-piece suit and shiny brogues—folded a square of toilet paper for his breast pocket, and went out.

Hair swept back and tonicked, cup and saucer in hand, he now made his way toward the bakery to take in the mob scene that, he was confident, awaited him there. A seething pile of shoppers was what he had in mind, all of them deep in perplexity as to why the Lord was visiting upon them this particular deprivation on this unexceptional morning. Rocco was always, but always, open, such that they seldom thought of Rocco, did they? They presumed that there was ever Rocco with anise cookies at Christmastime, and in February with the glazed sugar mounds that have the red candies on top and are supposed to recall Saint Agatha's tits.

He made the turn off Thirtieth onto the Eleventh and, look, indeed, below him down the slope the crowd had amassed. The reality of what he'd incited was far worse than what he'd hoped for. Sixty in total had been his thought. This was easily two hundred.

He changed his mind. He was almost out of coffee already, and he wanted to go to the bathroom, and he decided to go home.

Yet his body continued its forward progress down the hill toward the squirming horde. Nobody had seen him, or at least nobody had recognized him yet. Already he missed his own company. He wanted deeply to go home and to sit on the can and for nobody to know he was there.

A boy on roller skates flew by on his right. The head was lowered like he was a halfback charging the line. The skate key on a string around his neck bounced on his back. He was wailing nonsense. His acceleration was impressive. He was aimed straight for the horde, on a collision course, perhaps randomly, with Lenny Tomaro.

Rocco was almost part of them now.

The boy hit Lenny from behind and fell backward onto the blacktop.

Lenny kicked him a few times, tappingly, sort of motheringly, in his ribs, but the crowd paid no notice. Rocco was among them, but they didn't know it. He heard himself humming "Bye Bye Blackbird" as he sauntered through their midst. On their knees on the sidewalk, two girls in pinafores played jacks with a yellow rubber ball. Next to them twin boys worked a jigsaw puzzle on the concrete. Radios chirped from shops with their doors propped open. Nobody, maybe, recognized him with the nice duds and no flour in the mustache and no paper hat over the hair. He heard his name spoken but not in such a way that anyone was calling out for him.

Somebody said, "I only let them stay because the girl got bit by rats, plural, at the other place." Somebody said, "I can tell you this, I can tell you this, he begged me. And I can tell you also the words which I used when I gave him his answer." Somebody said, "We saw there was a line, so we got in." Somebody said, "It says *Continued on B-twenty-four,* but you didn't bring B-twenty-four, did you?" From light post to light post across the narrow avenue, banners flapped with red lettering that wished long life to the Holy Mother. It was Assumption Day. He'd forgotten. The feast would start in a few hours, and how many of them would go crustless and crumbless at this feast because Rocco hadn't opened the store?

The bell in the belfry of the church began to toll.

Somebody said, "She has that sunglasses that she rips them off her face, like now I'm supposed to be scared."

"Oh, oh, oh," somebody said. "Here he is!" A woman with tightly bobbed red hair—her name was Testaquadra—pointed at Rocco like he was a criminal, and two by two the eyes began to seek him out and fix their gaze.

It was eight o'clock in the morning.

The woman Testaquadra approached him, kissed the sides of his face, muttered something he failed to hear amid the chatter of the others, and walked off down the hill.

"The store is closed," he softly told a buxom young lady with maybe sympathetic eyes, but she chose to look away from him, pretending it wasn't her he meant to address. She was one of the many, faithful to the host that desired a leader who would speak to them collectively and explain why no bread today. He himself was not such a person; there are those whose greatness of spirit only the Lord sees; he could not speak in a loud voice to the all. He was a simple believer. He turned and went in under the tattered canvas awning of his store and sat on the steps.

The others were still talking among themselves, watching him closely but averting their eyes whenever he looked back, and awaiting his address.

Near him in the crowd stood a very young girl, towheaded, slit-eyed, with sharp teeth (her name was Chiara), and he beckoned her with his finger, and she approached him bravely.

He made a sandwich of her little hand between his hands and said, "Rocco doesn't work at the moment. He's taking a holiday. A week, perhaps. Tell them. Afterward, things will rearrange themselves nicely." He picked up his cup and saucer from the concrete step, and sipped, and flapped his hand toward the others that she might run off now and explain for him.

Instead she sat on the step. She petted his biceps, scanning the crowd, vigorous, wrathful.

When D'Agostino poked through the front of the crowd, Chiara leapt in front of him, folding her arms as if to forbid his approach, and clicked her heels.

Sidestepping the girl and bending himself double, D'Agostino kissed the air on either side of Rocco's ears. "You suffer, and so I bless you," he said.

"There's something maybe you can explain to them for me, and then they'll shove off," Rocco said.

"Yesterday evening I came and knocked, but there was no answer," D'Agostino said. "So unlike you. But now it's already understood." He added, "Most likely you've already seen this," and unfolded the newspaper he had stowed in his vest.

In order to hold the paper and still leave one hand in the care of Chiara, who had resumed her seated position beside him, Rocco was obliged to balance his saucer in his lap.

The main headline, with a gruesome photo, read QUADRUPLE AMPUTEE HEADED HOME, PLANS TO RELAX. D'Agostino stooped, seizing the paper, and flipped it upside down. Under the fold, next to an ad for a carpet-cleaning service, five inches of a single column began with the heading REMAINS OF ELEPHANT PARK NATIVE INCLUDED IN OPERATION BIG SWITCH.

Chiara's stockings were powder blue and stitched higgledy-piggledy with little fishes. He wondered what he had done to deserve her at this time.

Then, with alarming conviction, a reckless laugh sprung from Rocco's stomach. He held the newspaper aloft. "You have misunderstood, Joseph. All of youse have misunderstood. This isn't Mimmo. There was an error at the highest levels."

He laughed again, wickedly.

"There has been a *misidentification*."

D'Agostino, the side of his nose twitching as he spoke, asked him what did he mean; what was going to happen?

What was going to happen was that Rocco and his wife were going to have to go to the government and look at the face of the body of this unlucky person and explain that it wasn't Mimmo.

A cement truck tooted its horn, and the crowd, which now occupied the breadth of the street, contracted toward the sidewalk. Some version of what he was saying to D'Agostino spread among them. The general volume ebbed. He felt, like a swollen sinus, the pressure of their attention on the workings of his private mind.

D'Agostino said, So he would have to inconvenience himself, that was to say, he would have to keep the bakery closed while he traveled all the way to New Jersey and then back, only because they had failed to keep their records in order?

"Exactly that," Rocco said.

Chiara looked at him, compressing her lips so that the blood left them. "Thou hast borne false witness," said the resolute expression of her arch, white mouth.

He mustered all the charity and patience within himself and whispered, "You must understand, my dear. They're trying to stick their filthy fingers in my mouth and look inside."

D'Agostino leaned back on his heels, out of the shadow of the awning, raised his face to the sky, then glanced behind himself, then turned again to Rocco. You would think, he said, that the government could at least read the identification tags that, like everybody knows, you wear in the service at all times, wouldn't you?

In a sense, Rocco had to acknowledge, he could understand where the government was coming from, seeing as this boy they'd found was, according to the gentlemen from yesterday, in fact wearing the god tags of a Mimmo LaGrassa, and the serial number matched the one Rocco'd kept in his wallet since Mimmo had enlisted, which he kept the number for just such an occasion—rather *dog tags* he meant to say—and the height was the same.

He turned to the girl and said, "Satisfied?"

"I would very much enjoy an apple fritter," she entreated.

He looked at the newspaper. He was full of rage and shame. He was saddened that Chiara should see him this way.

So the gentlemen from the Marine Corps, D'Agostino pursued, just to make clear, had said to him, "We need you to come identify"—like they were confused and they didn't know—and here the paper made it out like this information was *confirmed?*

Why ask him about the newspaper? He didn't write it.

D'Agostino looked up again, and back again, and forward. And how tragic, really, because the gentlemen from the Marine Corps had never used any words like, for example, *We are sure* or *We confirm?*

"Or a marmalade crescent?" said the girl.

Well, you might say, "I confirm that the moon is made of green cheese," said Rocco, but if the moon isn't in fact made of green cheese then you haven't confirmed anything, because how could you be sure of a statement that was false? And so on and so forth.

Chiara flitted off on tiptoes, as little girls will do, or else she could not abide his sin.

Somewhere a bicycle bell was rung.

Or else it was a desk bell somebody was beating to demand service. A version of what he'd said to D'Agostino, mangled, doubtless, had permeated the host, and they didn't like it. They maybe disbelieved him.

D'Agostino excused himself and peeled off in the direction of the bell. Others followed. Soon there was a wholesale dispersal of the verminous crowd. A few wished him courage, told him to keep his eye alive, and disappeared. Probably they were ashamed at having been so mistaken—probably.

In short order, all of the faces were facing away from him but one. They scattered into the side streets and the places of business along the Eleventh Avenue, but for one old woman who was making her way through the tangle of bodies in his direction. She was in the widow's uniform—the black shoes, the black dress, the black purse. She came closer.

She said, "Mr. LaGrassa, you will come please to my house for lunch at one o'clock." She held a clothespin, which she methodically snapped.

"I have to go to—"

"They told me where you have to go." She held up a hand. Her name was Marini.

"I have to change my oil."

"Change your oil. Wash your hands thoroughly. Climb onto my front porch. Knock on my door. Et cetera."

In truth, he was starving. He said, "I guess I'll come, then."

"What is that, 'I guess I'll come'? What is that?"

He was standing now, in the sunlight. He looked up. He saw what it was that had snagged D'Agostino's eye when he had looked up. A girl in a ratty yellow sun hat had ascended, by means not readily discernible, to the top of a telephone pole, where on a small plank she sat reading.

How long do you have to live in a place before you notice it? The whole morning was a dream. Around every corner was a view that should have been same old, same old, but today impressed itself on his mind as for the first time and for all time. As in, Look, there's a kid licking the streetcar tracks, wearing short pants—only it seemed to Rocco that he'd never seen the tracks or a child in short pants before and he was never going to forget this. As on a day when the ruler dies and everybody, without even trying, holds on to the slightest speck of mental lint from that day for years. As in, I was squirting blue sugar roses on a wedding cake when Loveypants popped the alley-oop door and whispered, "Harding went to Alaska, and now he's dead." And she had a tiny bit of snot dangling from her one nostril. And right away he knew it was going to be that dangling bit of snot he would remember. Today, with no apparent excuse, the neighborhood was full of these bits of snot, so to speak. A boy alone, eating a banana on the steps of the church. It must have been not going to work that did this. He had a bird's-eye view of the forest for the trees. He went to Bastianazzo's and got his cup refilled with the watery coffee available at that establishment. Bastianazzo himself pretended to be too busy ironing his aprons behind the counter to talk to him. He drifted about the streets awhile, noticing so much and considering the city itself, which he was about to depart for the first time in so many decades.

He liked to go up onto his roof in the summer and look at the city. He would straddle the peak and use the chimney crown as a table for his gin glass and his ashtray. Up there you could count on a breeze in the summertime, and when you are the baker and it's summertime you will pay dearly for a cooling breeze. The house was on the tippy-top of Elephant Park, and from there he could see the thousand glittering lamps above the highway, the spires of the many churches, the mills expiring their sulfurous clouds, the rim of the lake to his right. The city was a mammoth trash heap—even the lake was brown—but it was an honorable place. It put pretty to one side. Nobody ever came here to have a good time. It was a place for people who had quit being children. It was a place to be employed for a period of a half century and thence to pass out of this life. That nobody regarded it as anything else made it unique in his limited experience and sacred.

At home, he put on raggedy clothes. He drained and refilled the oil in the crankcase of his car, rubbed his hands with turpentine, washed them with soap, got back into his good duds, and walked to his luncheon appointment.

The woman Marini's house stood directly behind his store and shared his alley, but he had never been inside. She was not of his class. Her husband had been a small-scale manufacturer of women's shoes and evidently had left her with enough to live in a certain elegance as long as she pleased. There was a rumor that she earned other income from an illicit source, but Rocco didn't need to believe it. Wasn't the magic of compound interest illicit enough? Her own shoes, as it happened, were strictly plain Jane. She had been living in this very house for at least ten years by the time Rocco himself was born. She was ninety-three years old.

She came from Lazio; however, her enunciation of the Italian language was barren of regional influence and pitiless, as though each word were a butterfly she was shooting out of the air with a pistol. One could hear that she had learned her English from the German people who had lived here years ago. Today it was the Sicilians, such as Rocco himself, who prevailed. Then it would be somebody else. God is great.

On one occasion, in his store, while searching her change purse for pennies, Mrs. Marini had asked him, "Why don't you close up for Easter or Flag Day or whatever the occasion?" He was used to questions like these, but not from her, and he blurted something he regretted. "What in the world would I do all day?" he said. She responded, counting off each word on her fingers, "Entertain, read, garden, pray, converse."

He knocked at the door. A boy showed him in. The boy was more than a foot taller than he was, and while they spoke, Rocco found himself looking up into the dark cavities of the boy's long and listing nose. The lips were fat, contorted, the eyes far too big, the ears too pointed; the gaze—which never fails to reveal too much—was suspicious, ashamed, exalted, pious, self-consumed, attractive, and mean. The boy was a picture of becoming that had gone awry. Rocco had met his like at the yards, where he had been paid to chase the vainglorious transients from the boxcars.

I know your fate, but I won't tell it to you, he thought, shaking the boy's hand, although he knew nothing of his past.

There were too many kids around here. He could never place which mother and father with which kid, or which name with which kid, irregardless of how many times they were introduced, but this boy was no relation of Mrs. Marini's, as she had no relations in this country. Her one child, said the legend, had died in infancy. Recently the woman Testaquadra had started to tell him the whole tangle of events that had led to a boy of sixteen living with the old lady, but Rocco held up a hand and said solemnly, "I am disconcerned with this information."

The dining room lacked fancy woodwork and porcelain figurines, but the walls were hung with silk paper that showed a pattern of white and yellow flowers, and the exposed floorboards were waxed, the furniture was upholstered tightly. There was only one decorative item on the wall: It was a china dish painted with the face of Bess Truman, and it was upside down. Plainly she was a witch, as were all women of a certain age. The boy took his derby and asked after his health and led Rocco to a chair, which he pulled out for him. When, during the uncommon visits of his boys during their adolescent years, had he witnessed the slightest evidence that Loveypants had instilled in them any basic training in class, such as pulling out the chair for a guest? Not once, never.

Mrs. Marini appeared in the kitchen doorway. "How do?" she said, and, paying no mind to his response, served the first course.

Once she was seated, it was evident that her spine was straighter than his own. Her hair was not genuine but her teeth appeared to be. She asked perfunctorily after his comfort before the boy said the blessing and they fell to.

The table would have sat fifteen but their places were set companionably together at one corner. All the windows were open, and an orchestra played on the radio from the parlor. He perceived that the boy was on orders to keep up his share of the conversation, which was informal and was concerned at first with the gardening of wax beans. The boy took the dishes to the kitchen and returned with the meat course. While chewing and listening to Rocco, Mrs. Marini periodically extended her hand toward the boy and tapped the tablecloth twice with her fingertips, whereupon the boy put down his knife and fork and refilled Rocco's wineglass. The boy did none of the things you are not supposed to do with regard to eating at a table except that at one point he inclined his head very slightly toward his fork as it approached his mouth; she observed this and, without taking her eyes from Rocco, said, "Ciccio will kindly remove his snout from the trough."

"Beg your pardon," he said, straightening. Like a dog, it pleased him to obey—but why expend judgment? A boy needs someone to obey. Ciccio was the name; Rocco made a note.

The boy took the plates away again and came back with the salad. The meal was progressing with extreme slowness. Rocco couldn't remember the last time he'd sat down to eat with other people, with a tablecloth and gravy boat and the whole shebang. Ciccio took the plates away and came back with cheese and some peaches. A breeze came through the window. Gratitude was expressed for the last night's thunderstorm, which had broken four days of stupor, although more storms were predicted for that night.

"But it's such a long way, Mr. LaGrassa, and all by your lonesome," she said. "Take the train."

"I want to see the big happy country as I go."

"The obvious thing that I have to tell you is, Buy a window seat."

"I want to look at the pretty flowers and then stop my car and pick the flowers."

"But you've never driven such a distance, I expect."

"I meant to tell you," Ciccio said, "the other day you were turning by the bridge—"

"I saw you," said Rocco. The boy had been among the usual miscreants throwing junked auto parts and rubble into the river.

"Yeah, you were turning, and I heard a sort of jingle-jangle from the car."

"The car will break in the wilderness, and then where are you with your flowers?" she said.

"Yeah, my thought was one of your motor mounts broke," Ciccio said. "And you were making a turn, and maybe the engine torqued up to the other side, and the fan pooched forward, and it was maybe grinding on the shroud and the radiator."

Rocco chewed a peach, his hands folded on the table, and looked at the boy. Finally he swallowed. "A fair guess, but no," he said. He extended his hand and deposited the pit on the boy's plate.

"So I'm mistaken?"

"It's a trick I do. Do you want to know what it is?"

"Yeah, I would."

"It's a device I've devised," Rocco said. He inquired of himself why he had presumed to dispose of his own waste on the boy's plate. His self responded, This is one of the gestures of which a man may avail himself to say to a boy or a younger man, I am the boss, but I like you.

"Here we go. Let me have it."

"If you want to know, I'll tell you."

"Faster, please," the old lady said, stabbing a knife in the cheese.

"The man fills my tank with gasoline. I keep the change in my pocket. When I get home I slip the silver down there into the tank. When eventually the car is defunct, I drop the tank, I cut a hole, I collect my change. Here is the money for the next car."

"You sit down," Mrs. Marini said, unscrewing the pit from her peach, "you take a nap, you go to the dining car and you buy a sandwich. Isn't that a good time?"

Rocco begged leave to smoke. The boy was dispatched in search of an ashtray.

The conversation turned to the war and the recent cease-fire and then to a curious story that he was surprised to find she had failed to notice in the *Voice of the People* and the *Reserve Gazette:* Immediately after the armistice, the North Koreans had agreed to release a number of United Nations captives in advance of the general prisoner exchange. (Rocco had had no way of knowing if Mimmo would be among them.) But once the initial exchange was actually carried out, about a dozen prisoners of the promised number were unaccounted for—

The boy, having delivered the ashtray and a box of matches, pulled out his chair, whereupon he was regarded by the old lady, who adjusted her eyeglasses.

"What? I'm interested," he said.

She lifted a hand.

"I have something to add."

She lifted the hand another inch, and the big boy plodded to the kitchen, from where Rocco then heard the washing of the dishes.

A week had followed with no further news. Then recently they'd published interviews with the first round of released prisoners, who described the conditions in the camps: to eat, cracked corn, one cup daily; men kept for weeks in underground cells too small to stand up or lie down in; death from untreated wounds, malnutrition, dysentery. The North Koreans and Chinese had forced them to smoke marijuana and tried to brainwash them with respect to thieving imperialists, glorious revolution, inevitable victory of the proletariat. There were colored and white soldiers together in the same huts in subzero temperatures without firewood, but it was with the colored prisoners that they had made a special reeducational effort. For example, the colored soldiers had been made to watch news footage that depicted how the police at home were handling certain crowds of colored people involved in political demonstrations.

Some of the colored prisoners finally capitulated. They were offered houses, young wives, and jobs in Red China, where they could live out their lives in a workers' paradise, and they accepted. And this handful of individuals represented, it would appear, the prisoners missing from the original exchange. Wasn't that something.

The funk of August midafternoon now permeated the dining room. From outside, the beginnings of the feast crowd in the avenue rumbled.

How sad, Rocco concluded, and it just went to show that, unfortunately, it was true what one heard so often repeated, that a Negro did not have the patriotic feelings of a white person.

"You or I," she said, "would never think of leaving our native soil for a home, a spouse, an occupation on the other side of the world. The idea would never enter our heads."

"Well, now."

"Not on pain of death."

"Wait, wait. You misunderstand me. I have two points. My first point is that there is moving away, and then there is to defect, to make treason against the home country, and so on and so forth."

"I contributed cheerfully with my tax dollars to the destruction of Cassino not ten years ago, which is in my home province."

"That's different. That's not the same, and that's different."

"Two points you said you had."

"It's not the same, and I move on in any event to my second point, which is that these people were brought, but you and I came. Which there's a difference. If I'm a colored person, do I salute the flag? Who knows."

"In fact, the importation of slaves to this country was outlawed in 1808," she said, sucking her teeth.

"I'm having a day today where I can see the big picture," he said. He was not in control of his mouth in the usual way. The uncooked contents of his brain were transported so quickly out of his mouth that he had to listen to himself to find out what he was saying. There was one Rocco outside, in the world, holding forth. And there was another one down in here, observing the proceedings, feeling awake and asleep at once, and feeling—what was the word, how could you say it?—joy. However, he did not feel it at this precise moment. He'd been feeling it a couple of seconds ago, before he'd noticed. And he wanted to not notice it again, the joy, if that could be done, to not know it, to lose it and thus to get it back again, like a Christian does with his dignity when he puts his faith in the Lord.

"Let me say politely that you are seeing the little picture," he said, "such as picking nits over somebody that was brought versus somebody that his grandfather was brought. In the big picture, let me say politely that you are just talking like certain people."

"Which people?"

"The people who say, Let the sparrow mate with the crow, and so forth."

Ciccio came back into the dining room with a dish towel around his neck like a scarf.

"Ciccio has been listening?" she said.

"More or less," said the boy.

"Ciccio may now describe his opinion."

"Yesterday," he said, "in the early paper I saw an update, like, how that most of the ones that defected were white guys. One of them who got out said the ones who stayed were sure there was going to be a Communistical revolution worldwide, even right here in our own country, like, in a few months. So they figured they'd just cool their heels in China and wait for America to go socialist."

"Your conclusions?" she said.

"They want to betray the government of the USA but not the place of the USA."

"Very good. Now then"—she turned to Rocco—"my reading tells me that the sparrow and the crow cannot mate, as they are different species. However, mulattos, such as in the Caribbean they have many, demonstrate that black can mate with white and produce offspring. Therefore black and white are the same species and your metaphor has collapsed." When the boy had come in she'd stopped speaking in English, but now she was switching from Italian to English and back again from one sentence to the next. "You are confusing *physically impossible* with *morally repugnant*. What you really meant to say when you said 'mate' was 'live side by side with,' which is distasteful enough." A corner of the tablecloth was pulled taut by her twisted fingers.

"All this time, you know, I've never been inside your house," Rocco said abruptly.

"Oh, that can't be!" she said. "Oh, Mr. LaGrassa, I'm so ashamed. I thought at least—it can't be!"

"On the porch and in the garden a few times but not inside."

"I'm full to my eyes with regret," she said. "I've never been in your house either."

The only untidiness about this room was that the window looked out on the peeling, mud-splattered eyesore that was the rear of his bakery. He had looked at his own reflection in the other side of these windows—while he had the day's first smoke, early in the morning, when all her lights were out and the blinds were pulled—maybe each day for the last thirty years.

"So what's all this about, just curiously? What's the occasion that today I am asked to come in?"

There was a silence while she probably tried to put together the words of an apology for having believed at first what the newspaper had said about Mimmo. Rocco wanted to say it was a case of no harm, no foul.

"The occasion?" she said, brightening. "Why, it's your day off, naturally!"

His streak was over. His secondhand suit was forty years old. He wore it carefully so that he could be buried in it.

She refilled the glasses. "You're in a position to judge, Rocco. Which is better, work or play?"

He had assumed his visit was concluding, but now his glass was full again. His back eased into his chair. A band in the street could be heard amassing. Horns blared. Somebody was banging cymbals. Ciccio started playing a game with them before they knew what he was doing, and before they knew it they were playing along. Rocco recollected from his bottommost depths the pleasure of company, of talking when it didn't matter what the topic was. Behind how many windows for how many years had others laughed and talked of nothing while he had organized his life to avoid them? He had been wasteful of himself—he had drained himself down the drain.

"Hail," Ciccio said, "bombs, volcanic ash."

"What is this?" Mrs. Marini said.

"Birds that have heart attacks."

"Objects descending from the clouds!" Rocco said.

"Oh, good, a game. My turn now," she said. "The sun. A pumpkin. A twenty-dollar gold coin."

"Things that are orange," Ciccio said.

"You can do better than that, Costanza," she said, slapping the back of her hand.

"Gather pennies and nickels," Ciccio said. "Look up from a place of darkness to a tiny circle of light."

She said, "Things that little underprivileged children do."

"Wrong," Ciccio said. "Cry for help. Play with the rope and the bucket."

Rocco said, "Things to do in a well."

3

The opposite of to die is to have a family. Therefore to have no family is to be dead.

Rocco detected a stink of turpentine and excused himself to Mrs. Marini's lavatory, where, with her cold cream and nailbrush, he scoured his hands. He had awoken this morning convinced that his death was upon him; he'd impressed himself by being unafraid; but had he been unafraid only because, having no family, he was already dead?

No. The name of Loveypants was Luigina. The names of his boys were Bobo, Mimmo, and Jimmy. He had a cousin Benedict still in Omaha.

At home, he kept the door of the medicine cabinet open while he washed his hands so as not to see his image in the mirror, but Mrs. Marini's mirror was affixed to the wall. He turned his back to it while he abraded his fingers. Then, lest he splatter cold cream on the tile, he knelt and continued his work over the commode. The three of them had carried on the whole of the afternoon, and now it was the supper hour, and the racket outside was beckoning them toward the bedlam of the feast.

He flushed. While turning to face the sink, he regarded a grommet on his right shoe, and then, while rinsing his hands, he watched the chrome flange of the drain. But this did not keep him from seeing his arms and stomach at the edge of his vision in the mirror. What did it matter if his hands weren't clean? It would be four days at least before he touched anybody else's food. (Oh, but there was all that bread and the onion pastries that were rising in the walk-in at his store; the whole place would smell like a brewery by the time he got back in town; he'd have to go back and throw them out; labor, treasure, purpose—wasted;

gloom.) He touched the bathroom doorknob and then turned it coura-
geously. A firecracker exploded in the alley.

Who was this man he became when he emerged from solitude into
the company of other people? The hallway smelled of mothballs and was
dark, and he felt his private self recede as he approached the bickering
in the kitchen.

Ciccio said, "Fine, but if we'd only focused the whole invasion on
Montreal in 1812 the continent would have been ours."

Rocco wanted to turn around, to turn in. He paused in the hallway, solitude at his back, society ahead, feeling ensnared in this middle
place, feeling he'd spent his whole life in this hallway and wishing at
least for the next couple of hours to be all in the bathroom or all in the
street wholeheartedly. I can't go into the one place, I can't go into the
other, he said to his heart. A sneeze began to overtake him, and he succumbed to it.

Here it was—*bam bam bam*—the smoke in the streets, ninety-one de-
grees on the Fahrenheit scale, a boy in a window throwing an egg down
at the masses and then a goldfish and then ice cubes. Every half block
a man was bent over a box of coals as the sweat dripped and hissed on
the pig flesh on the grill, and a woman at his side with cockeyed brown
teeth took the money and rolled from time to time a pop bottle over his
face. A Rican-looking kid falling out of a tree. There was the stench
of animal flesh on fire and human flesh expelling salt and toxins from
its pores. A kid climbing a gutter pipe attached to the façade of the
church. Everywhere you looked there were children trying to climb
things, maybe hoping to get out by way of up, then falling or sliding
down like when an earwig is trapped in a bathtub. Kids climbing the
backstop of the ball field behind the convent where the carnival rides
were parked, kids on the roof of the new pet store scaling the gigantic
birdcage that housed a man-sized fiberglass parakeet. The pavement in
places was not visible for the bingo cards, prayer cards, matchbooks,
eggshells. The men wore ties, but their hats were off. A woman kissed a
heel of bread and tossed it into a puddle.

Speculations, threats, and scoldings littered the air, slurred and shouted.

"If it was the present day," said a woman, "I already would have left you fifty times and a half."

"Once we get home, young man," said a man, "I got a big stick waiting for you."

Somebody said, "No, just a friend from Oskaloosa Reformatory. Wanted to give him courage, but they wouldn't let me."

"The Amish can take buses, but they can't drive them, that's all."

"Everything is in place and nothing is in order."

"I don't remember it very clearly, you see," someone said, "because it didn't happen."

A priest pointing with a slow and curving finger at the asphalt insisted, "It doesn't live here."

A human skull was immured in a niche bordering the courtyard of the convent, and various other bones—ribs and fingers and clavicles—were mortared around it in a pattern that resembled a chrysanthemum, and beneath it was an inscription in a copper plate reading: *Let us perform works of justice and mercy while we are still in time.* Someone said, "Now, you shut up and listen to me." Someone else: "In the part of the brain where the rest of us have common sense they have money."

Children were climbing sweet-gum trees and telephone poles and ginkgo trees and Papa's back. Were they trying to climb out? And what were they escaping from, exactly, and where were they escaping to?

A man in a gas mask wearing black shorts and a white tank top and suspenders dragged a love seat onto a third-floor balcony and reclined on it, and observed the crowds, and unbuckled his mask to take a sip on his lemonade.

A couple of police observed on horseback, as still as statuettes on the corners of Sixteenth and of Twenty-eighth. Also, pigeons and rats and alley cats.

Somebody said, "What is that, Stanley? It looks like pie."

Hungarian was spoken, and Slovak, Rumanian, Polish, German, Russian, Croat, Greek, Lithuanian, Spanish, Bohemian; and if you looked closely you saw a couple of Japanese, army brides, it appeared. And there were multitudes of Italians from the crosstown neighborhoods and from the suburbs. And some colored were there, and they were being given what you call a wide berth, such as could be managed in the press. It was a neighborhood outside of which outsiders stayed except for once a year, on the fifteenth of August, when they descended in their tens of thousands. And there were the carny games where you paid a nickel to throw a softball at a pyramid of soup cans in the hope of winning a salami sandwich. In the central event, the Virgin was paraded out of the church and through the streets by men in white robes accompanied by torchbearers who until recently had covered their heads with pointed white hoods. However, the police, careful to prevent miscommunications and slanders, forbade them to wear the hoods anymore.

At times you could not fully expand your chest to take in breath, such was the push of the bodies on your body. And the kids in the trees throwing spiny sweet-gum monkey balls at your head. There were moments you felt you might be crushed. It had happened, in 1947. A Slovak woman and her babe in arms were crushed right here. Imagine killing somebody with your chest, a pair of hot corpses borne along by the pressing of your body and other people's bodies—and still you came, out of this instinct to cram into the streets, because the body, despite reason, insisted on satisfying an urge that nothing in your brittle, private, homebound individual interior could satisfy. What you felt was primitive—a grasshopper becoming a locust, a yard dog becoming a pack dog. The mind of the throng became your mind the way a whale takes on the desire of its pod to feel the sand of the beach under its belly.

Europe was happening, right here, and it didn't fit. This wasn't the continent of the group, socialism, a million jam-packed cities. This was the country of the particular person, private enterprise, vast and empty grassland counties, the Protestant Jesus who went by his first name and saved souls one by one, depending on Do you believe, in your private heart, or don't you? This crowd did not belong in this place.

And the kids hunched in the windows and straddled the exposed I beams.

The doors of the church swung open, and three boys in red cassock and white surplice were first down the steps: Two carried candles as tall as themselves; the other bore a staff. At the top of the staff, of course, was the golden, emaciated figure, stretched and pinned, either dying or dead, of an individual man who had been tortured and executed by a mob. And night was falling.

Rocco was alone in the crowd, trying to make it to the bakery. He wanted a cigarette, but there wasn't enough room between his mouth and the hair of the woman in front of him. He might have enjoyed a sausage sandwich and some peppers, but the buns these people were using were beneath the honor of the swine that had died to stuff them. He wanted to get a move on, there was the New Jersey to reach in two days' time, the face of Loveypants, a commandment he was shaping. There was the need while in a crowd to seek out a darkened corner where nobody could get at him with their paws. He also knew that to escape from the crowd was to rip off and kill the part of himself that was attached to it. You had to gnaw off the leg that was trapped in the trap. And once in fact you left you felt as lonely as you were ever likely to feel.

While fording the human current in the direction of the alley behind the Twenty-fourth Street nickelodeon, he inadvertently stepped on the foot of a white-haired boy of perhaps three years in denim coveralls and brought him screaming to the ground, but Rocco kept forcing his way through the crowd. He made a right and a right and a left through the labyrinth of alleys that led to the alley between his store and Mrs. Marini's house. Half a dozen boys in linen blazers, their hair in uniform flattops, were shooting off fizgigs in his alley and paid him no mind as he pretended to use his key to unlock the alley-oop door.

Immediately he heard a shrill, unbroken keen, as if from an ailing electrical device, the residue that tremendous noise leaves in the skull upon one's entering a quiet place. He put his head under the tap and drank. The ventilator was off, and the air in here, even with the coal burned out, even to Rocco, felt tropical and oppressive. He hung his hat atop the pile of springform pans, verified that the deep fryer was off, pulled aside the flag of the state of Ohio, slouched into the front room, and sat on the floor in the crawl space of relative cool. On the other side of the storefront windows he beheld the arms and hips and wilting hairdos of the masses squishing against the glass, smearing it with sweat and pomade. The crowd had stopped moving along the street as, just above head level, the Virgin hovered slowly up the hill. He was safe from them in his little box in here. Half of the moon had risen over the tenement roof across the street. The balconies and fire escapes abounded with onlookers whose faces were indistinct in the twilight. Did he have any friends? No, not really.

He dumped fifty pounds of serviceable, if oversour, sponge dough into the rubbish because the Lord had called him to more crucial work in the days ahead. The pastries were in the walk-in cooler at the rear of the kitchen. Maybe he'd stay in there for a minute, in the walk-in, and collect himself. He sprung the walk-in latch and had gone so far as to lift a tray of crescent rolls from the wire shelf, when he turned his head and was stricken to discover that he wasn't alone in here, either.

A lime white man facing the rear of the cooler was seated on a box of vegetable shortening. But for a fedora with a peacock feather under the band and white knee socks, he was naked.

Rocco stood there and looked at him.

The man started and got up, his back still turned. He inserted a foot into a leg of his trousers and stuffed his underpants in a trouser pocket. A smoldering cigar was on the floor. His furry back was turned to Rocco and was rippled with fat, gray-bluish white, deathly under the fluorescent tubes that had come on when Rocco opened the walk-in door. His arms and neck, however, were brown—a man who made his living out of doors. Judging from the fur, which was gray and patchy, he was roughly Rocco's age. The man yanked at his shirt, though it was much too large for a shirt, part of which was stuck under the shortening box, and mashed his shoe with his foot, unable to find the hole where the toes were intended to go.

A cloud billowed in from the moist outside, and a switch was tripped in Rocco's head that made him shut the cooler door. It was an economic impulse, but the man let out a yip, puppylike, and fumbled at his shoes (it was a sound Rocco had heard himself make when he'd had too much coffee and it hurt him to piss). And Rocco sensed weakness in the enemy and a sudden blood thirst in himself. Murder him, said a voice. The cooler smelled of dried-out cigar, as would the doomed pastries have smelled. Use the pan, said the voice of the beast inside him.

The man had liberated his shirt and was tying it over his head, the back still turned.

It was unlikely that Rocco could bludgeon to death with an aluminum baking pan an adult male as thickly built as he himself, but so ordered the voice, and he raised the pan, somewhat higher than you hold a ball bat before swinging. The pastries cascaded down on his head.

At last, the man turned. The capacious shirt enshrouded his face. The breathing was loud and distressed. The fabric over the mouth went convex and concave. His pink tits hung there. He held his hat in hand, and the sleeves of the shirt fell around his shoulders like white, bedraggled hair. Without a face. The fabric containing the head like a hangman's hood.

Did he know this man? He had no idea if he did. A man who was not he, was not Rocco, unless he was Rocco, only he couldn't be.

"What did you steal?" Rocco said in dialect.

The head shook no vigorously.

"Did you piss on my floor or do yourself like a saw in here?"

No again, as the hands reached up and tightened the mask.

There was an outsider, a member of the public, or rather an insider, a member of Rocco himself, who hadn't only intruded into the bakery kitchen, Rocco's private citadel, but had violated even the cooler, the holy of holies, the place where Rocco closeted himself when his need to be alone was at its bleakest.

"Get that thing away from your face!" Rocco said, swatting the air.

Look, a grown man disguised as a figment of his imagination. Unless . . .

The head didn't move.

Then, inside Rocco's brain, the spinning tumblers of a lock seemed to align, and the door of a vault swung open.

"Oh," he said softly. "It's you." He lowered the pan. "You've been hiding from me in here all along."

The head didn't respond, but still Rocco felt a bracing pang of belief.

"You thought you could hoodwink me, my boy," Rocco said, grinning and pointing his finger. "Don't you think I know my own when I see him?"

And yet the figure only cocked its head.

Rocco called on his courage. He took a step, his heel sinking into a pastry, and moved to embrace the large and devilish child.

There was a timer attached to the hinge of the walk-in door, an ingenious device. The overhead light came on automatically when you entered, and then, sixty seconds after the door had closed, the light switched off again on its own.

Now the light went off.

The figure struck him in the dark, a full-body collision, and Rocco fell against the pastry shelves, and the door opened, and the interloper barreled out.

Rocco got to his feet. He heard the din from outside briefly and heard the alley-oop door slam. There was a snot rag on the tile.

Across the ball field a sister scampered, her habit hovering in the infield dust, waving her downturned hands with emphasis at the begrimed men who operated the carnival rides. The Matterhorn and the Witch's Wheel were spinning, and the Dipsy-Doo was dipping, all of them festooned with lights that blinked ever more quickly as the cars approached maximum velocity, each blaring its own tinkle-tinkle melody. Stop the machines, she commanded; the Holy Mother was out of the church and in the street. The men, sometime vagrants, sometime elementary school janitors whose clothes emitted the musk of pencil shavings even in August, opened the gates, and the dizzy children stumbled into the outfield.

There were kids even on the roof of the convent, one climbing a flagpole by its cord.

The altar boys were preceded down the avenue by twelve prodigious men of early middle age: slow on their feet, oxen-stout, contemptuous, in white muslin cassocks and white gloves and brimless black felt hats. They forced a channel through the masses by prodding them with the blunt ends of brooms and packing them into the stalls of the vendors, against the storefront windows, unspeaking, a hard element parting a soft element in two, like the keel of a ship cutting the water.

Somebody said, "Do you have a time yet as to what time you will come to see us?"

On the roof of the Twenty-fourth Street nickelodeon, the men who had readied the fireworks display passed a bottle of beer among themselves and spat on the tar, lethargic, cursing.

Following the altar boys was a troop of priests from various parishes, some in long skirts and birettas. And the bishop of the city, a German, was among them, in a green miter and cope, a scowling, ancient man walking with a shepherd's crook and leaning on it to balance himself.

Behind the clergy came the Virgin, smirking, her porcelain skin dark like an Arab's, the nose upturned, English, her stature dwarflike, her clothes and hands stuck with specks of diamond donated over many years by women who had had them pried from their engagement rings. She stood on a stone platform, four spiral wooden columns supporting the gilt roof over her head. The rails undergirding the platform were borne on the shoulders of sixteen men in white albs. Ribbons hung from the columns and the people pinned money to the ribbons as they dragged by. And white-robed men with hoods hanging down their backs guarded the platform, holding bull-rib torches, singing plainsong.

It was darkening but the heat was the same.

Several hundred women in black followed the Virgin, praying rosaries, their feet naked to the pebbles and the cigarette butts and the soiled napkins and the spilled pop on the pavement. A band brought up the rear, making vehement noise. The brass played a waltz and the clarinets a two-step and the violins something else you could only barely make out. And behind the band, in the wake of the procession, was a half block of empty space where maybe it was cooler, maybe you could breathe freely.

All the bells in the church were tolling.

Rocco needed some air.

In the ceiling over one of the coal bins was a pasteboard scuttle he'd painted many years ago to match the surrounding plaster. He climbed atop the bins, popped the scuttle from its frame, and, with considerable effort, hoisted himself into the bakery attic. The heat was nauseous. He was blind until, with his hat, he screened from his eyes the hole of light emanating from below. The source of light thus obscured, a cloud of airborne dust appeared, thick and twinkling. As he caught his breath, he saw the dust stream into his mouth and swirl out of him. Wood shavings and what appeared to be dry lumps of chewing tobacco covered the attic floor, the leavings of a roofing crew from the 1890s who had never bothered to clean up the job. It was damn hot up here. His skull vibrated in sympathy with the noise from outside.

Crouching, and careful to balance himself on the joists, he made his way to a ladder in the attic wall. It was flaked with rust, and the mooring bolts were loose in the blocks, and the ladder shook as he climbed to the trapdoor in the rafters.

He emerged in the rooftop twilight and breathed. The music, if you could call it music, was close by and deafening. He twisted his head around, and wouldn't you know, peering over the wall that formed the top of the façade stood five girls and a little boy. He held out hope that Chiara was among them.

"How did you get up here?" he called to them, brushing the spider-webs and sawdust from his pants.

"We climbed," one of them said. There was a run in her stocking and a fresh, bloody scratch down her leg. She didn't turn to address him.

"What did you climb?"

"I don't know."

"You don't know."

"The wall, I guess."

"You have a cut, little miss, on your leg there," he said, pointing, but she didn't answer him.

He approached the ledge and observed the tumult below. He was wet with exhaustion and defeat. One two three four five. No Chiara. Sigh. And the boy.

"It's always the same," another said, disconsolate. "Why is it always the same?"

"It's opposed to be the same," said the boy.

They meant that year in, year out, the procession was always the same.

Then one of them jolted upright. Then the others. The first poked the air. "Look!" she said. "Look at the shines!"

All told, the procession was five blocks long. The Virgin now tee-tered at Eleventh Avenue and Thirtieth Street. An empty space of half a block, which people had historically enjoined themselves from entering, followed the band. At the edge of this space, a colored woman and a colored man were dancing.

Shortly, they were joined by some other colored men and colored women, not too many, about seven. They were clapping, he could see, and doing a slow-stepping, herky-jerky dance, invisible, as one is in a crowd, so they surely believed, while the fevered, dissonant music kept playing. Funny. They weren't in the conventional man-to-woman, two-by-two embrace, nor even holding hands. They were nine, now, out of maybe twenty thousand, pretty inconspicuous even from up here, and upon more careful observation they were all young people, even teenagers, although one more, a girl younger than the girls on his roof, tried to wrest herself from the grip of a white-haired, squat colored lady and join them.

The children, renewed in their boredom, commented wearily in phrases of forced adult courtliness on the multitude. "Maria, Maria, but we are in so many," one said.

Rocco had to envy the colored kids down there, dancing with the herd and by themselves at the same time as though they weren't obliged to pick one or the other. Either they were naïve, or he had made a needless choice. If he were ever put in jail, he hoped they wouldn't let him have a window.

A white-haired colored man in a tan suit and black tie was hissing, it looked like, beside the squat lady and pointing at the dancers and then back at his feet, furious. And Rocco had to shake his head at this poor, forbidding fellow so much like himself.

Somebody smacked the lone tuba player on the back, Rocco saw this, and the mighty instrument turned around like a stag in the brush.

Then—he could see this happening, he actually watched it happen—the remainder of the back row of the brass turned as one man, saw the Negroes dancing, and turned forward again. They in turn tapped the shoulders of the drummers, who turned and craned to see. And this smacking of the back and craning to see progressed row by row up the band at terrific speed. As you watch, from high banks above, a stick make its way down a river. And the band kept playing—they saw, they passed on the news, and kept playing. And he could see this news, this stick, passing up the procession into the pack of barefooted, black-clad women, where it splintered and spread radially through the procession and the wider crowd.

It struck him that the original tuba player had seen what was taking place and then had kept on playing. The man was flattered. But it struck him also that the barefooted women couldn't see through the band to see what he saw. It struck him that the news worming its way through their midst was seventh-hand, eighth-hand, ninth-hand, tenth-hand.

As though he stood outside of time with the children on the bakery roof and saw, all at once, the past (at Twenty-second Street, where the Negroes were dancing); the present (right beneath him at Twenty-sixth, where the men in the band were telling one another what they had seen); and the distant future (farther up the avenue, where no one could be trusted and the original moment was lost).

He saw it progress to the Virgin, and he saw the Virgin stop and the rest of the procession stop. And the clergy conferring in the distance. And the altar boys milling, confused. Then another message appeared to pass back down the hill, this time by means of yelling with the hands cupping the mouth. Everybody having stopped. And finally the music stopped. Only by now there was no dancing, either. The Negroes had vanished.

And the violinists tucking their bows under their arms, wiping their foreheads with their neck towels.

The parade then did an unprecedented thing. It lurched backward down the hill. The old ladies sat on the curb and reshod themselves and got up and followed the musicians back into the church. And the Virgin was carried into the church as well, none too slowly. And the men on the roof of the movie theater were packing the fireworks, unexploded, back into the crates and handing the crates down a ladder and into a truck in the alley.

Wait, wait. The feast was over. Something had happened and the feast was called off. How did they all know it was called off? What had happened? Had everybody seen it but him?

The kids on Rocco's roof were crying because, he supposed, no fireworks. The generators in the ball field coughed and fell silent. The lights on the carnival rides disappeared. There was a frenzied commotion at the streetcar stop way down on Sixteenth Street. To his right, on Twenty-sixth, he saw that woman Testaquadra drag two children by their hair into a house and throw the door shut behind her.

As though time were moving in reverse. The procession was supposed to go to the top of the hill, veer toward the cemetery, circle back all the way down the hill by way of Chagrin to Eighteenth Street, and return uphill toward the church. Instead, it moved from one moment

(Thirtieth Street) backward in time down the hill on Eleventh, backward to the church again, hurriedly, in disarray.

No, no. Wait. Something had happened, and nobody had seen it *but* him—and the children. There were some Negroes; they heard music and saw a band; they started to dance. But the men up front, the priests and the sweepers and the men carrying the platform, and all the many thousands in the crowd who did not see what Rocco saw must have heard a thousand differently contorted versions of what had happened—like, Some Negroes are smoking dope in the parade; Some sacrilegious niggers have mistaken the holy procession for a roadhouse. And the only part that all the versions had in common was the end—off with the lights, everybody get out, everybody go home.

The girls were crying on the roof, and the boy stood apart from them at a corner looking down at the street and looking back at them in spasms, and Rocco could see the boy was crying, too—the welched-on promise of a fireworks display was to them the height of betrayal. The Eleventh Avenue bled people into all its tributary streets. This terrible quiet everywhere, even the smoke having cleared out, the avenue open enough that cars might pass, only no cars were passing. The people made their way on foot, murmuring or dumb.

The children were gasping. He was wrong. It wasn't that they'd been cheated. They were frightened.

"Now, listen, my little ones," he began, but he couldn't think of anything to say.

It was the quiet that frightened them, he knew this emphatically, and he wanted to reassure them but didn't know how he could do this, could not invent a single lighthearted word to distract them. If only he could put together a few words that could help them.

He made one backward step on the tacky tar of the roof. Then paused. Not one of them so much as glanced in his direction. The children had forgotten he was there.

4

Rocco crossed into the Pennsylvania at one a.m. and spent the night in his car in a wayside. Half a dozen times he awoke as cargo trains screeched across the bridge overhead.

When the sun rose, his arm was wrapped around the gearshift and was numb, his undershirt was pasted to his back with sweat, and his ribs were squeezing his kidneys. His glasses had migrated to the backseat in the night. He shook out his dead arm. Having located at last his cigarettes under the brake pedal, he walked into the slag-littered field under the railroad bridge and pissed and smoked a cigarette and blew his nose. Between the piles of the bridge, a stream dribbled, and on its surface many-colored swirls of oil glinted in the sunlight. He got to his knees on the sandy bank to say his rosary. Afterward, he asked the Lord to grant him safe passage to the New Jersey and to restore to Loveypants her long-lost sense of reason and decency. Again, overhead, a train passed, but in the other direction. He climbed the bluff toward the highway and drove into the next town for breakfast.

All he asked the lady to bring him was coffee and toast. You might have thought toast was a simple enough dish, but you'd have been mistaken. He was made to pay fifteen cents for two pale squares of baize soaked in margarine. He washed his hands and face in the café lavatory. He looked like hell. Warm water and soap were evidently too much to ask. He'd heard of a pretty meager level of civilization in the state of Pennsylvania, and so far he wasn't disappointed.

He found a barbershop down the block from the miserable café and went inside. (How reassuring that wherever you went in the wide world a barbershop smelled of talc and ethyl alcohol.) He sat on the bench, awaiting his time, turning the pages of a lawn and garden magazine.

The barber and the client in the chair were discussing white meat versus dark meat, it sounded like. Rocco wasn't paying attention because it wasn't his business.

When the barber tucked the collar of tissue paper around Rocco's neck and asked what he could do for Rocco this morning, Rocco said he wanted a trim and a shave.

"Speak up."

"Just a trim all around the sides, the ears especially, and a shave, thank you," he expounded.

"Just a trim and an alla-something and a something else," said the barber.

He didn't mind repeating himself. There was an autographed photo taped to the wall of Rogers Hornsby with the barber as a younger man.

At this moment, from Leningrad to Buenos Aires, the barber was tucking the tissue paper around the client's neck, throwing the oilcloth shroud over the clothes, and fastening it at the shoulder. All over the world—Ohio, the Pennsylvania, irregardless—this unique mode of conversation was taking place in which the barber and the client addressed not the face of the other, but the face of the other in the mirror opposite. If the client was a stranger, the barber, by rights, adopted a superior tone. But Rocco's sense today of being right with his God, of having embarked on an enterprise that aimed to make straight what spite and cowardice had conspired to make crooked, a mystic hopefulness this morning, inspired a charity in him that exposed petty complaints—his meager breakfast, a spleeny barber—as petty complaints.

With the handle of a comb the barber artfully elevated the tip of Rocco's nose and snipped the hair growing from his nostrils into his mustache.

"I don't go in for the hunting of waterfowl with dogs, do you?" the barber said. "I don't think it's right to train a predator to put food in its mouth and not eat it. I wonder what you think."

"I don't follow," Rocco tried to say without moving his lips, on which the barber pressed with a finger.

"I'll give you a for-instance. You take a woman to a store that sells fine linen sheets and tablecloths and what have you." He turned to rummage a drawer. "You roll up a hundred dollars in her fist and tell her to walk through the aisles for an afternoon and then to give you the money back. Why, that's cruelty! Tell me what you think while I'm stirring this here."

"I thought they had that type of training in the breed."

"That's a good point. I never thought of that. It's an important insight."

"Thank you."

"And let me ask you something else. I think about this here in my store when it rains and nobody thinks of coming to be groomed. Say you could go to any city in the world for a week's vacation. Which city would it be? My answer is Perth, Australia."

"The boat trip would be longest," Rocco surmised.

"Just so. I would take the eastern route, following the coast of Africa as the Portuguese traders did. Which country do you come from that you talk like that?"

"Ohio," Rocco said.

"Where's that, in Russia somewhere?"

"Ohio," he said. "Next door. The mother of presidents. The land of Thomas Edison and the buckeye tree."

"Frankly, I don't have the first idea what you're saying," the barber said lightly.

Rocco's eyes were closed; the chair reclined; the barber piled a hot towel on his face. Rocco drew the letters in the air.

"I see," said the barber. "Condolences."

"Warren Harding, Orville Wright, the vice president's father, all from Ohio," Rocco said into the towel.

The barber laughed with a snort.

"You think the invention of the airplane is trivia. It's a circus act to you."

"Okay. I'll tell you what. I knew what you were saying. I'm just a frolicsome kind of a person. I like to give the foreigners a hard time. I was a foreigner once myself," he said, removing the towel. "Guadalcanal.

I wasn't received so kindly by the natives as you were here, I'm sure. Everywhere you stepped on the sand, a dead marine."

"I have a boy in the marines," Rocco said. "There are those who believe he is no longer among us. They were taken in by a mountebank writing in the newspaper." He inhaled profoundly, and the mentholated vapor of the shaving foam beneath his nose submerged his nasal passages and soaked his brain. "But I know that my redeemer lives," he said.

"Is that so? They bring your body back to this country, they do. Give them that. The other services have more important work, I suppose. And you're married, then."

"As it happens. I am married these thirty-three years. However, she has been living at a distance from me, which I regret. And tomorrow I will see her again for the first time in so long. So make me up nice. She doesn't know it yet, but I have had my full of her desertment. And I'm putting a stop to it. When I come back through here in a few days' time, I will have her with me, and the boys, first, middle, and last, if I have to cut them in pieces."

In Libya and in Sweden there was the hot towel and the rasp of the stropping of the razor, a sound that sent aged men into dim boyhood afternoons sitting on the bench, swinging the feet that did not yet reach the floor, while Papa, the master of the universe, reclined and another man scraped a blade over his gullet. There was a figure of speech in dialect, a phrase his own boys wouldn't know since they hardly spoke dialect (their mother had forbidden Rocco to teach them): *to search for the dead father*, which meant "to desire the impossible."

Rocco said slowly, "I have never been to the Pennsylvania before, don't you know."

"This ain't Pennsylvania, pally. This is New York."

The barber's breathing smelled of mustard.

"You're joking."

"You are one half hour's motoring time south-southwest of Buffalo, New York."

He had swerved north of his planned trajectory on account of having decided that to buy a road atlas was to betray Providence. He knew he was headed east, essentially. In the fullness of time, the Lord would lead him to his destination.

The barber had progressed to the back of Rocco's neck. "Listen, there isn't any natural place for me to stop here." He swiveled the chair and positioned a hand mirror so as Rocco could see in the mirror on the wall where he was pointing his razor. "What do you say?" he asked.

Rocco pouted indifferently.

The mug in which the barber agitated the shaving brush was embossed with a swirling blue design, and a barrel, and the words *I went over Niagara Falls.*

"Put your head down."

A speck of dandruff landed on the oilcloth. The barber folded Rocco's ear over itself and slid the warm steel over a mole on his neck.

Niagara Falls.

But wait. But he was a half hour from Buffalo. But Buffalo was, was it not, only a half hour from Niagara Falls.

He inclined his head, too quickly, feeling a gleeful stress, an elation of childhood—of climbing the lava columns in the bay at Aci Trezza, naked at night, and leaping into the sea. The razor sliced into his neck.

"Aw, hell," the barber said, reaching for a towel. "Look what you made me do."

It was 11:42 in the morning on the sixteenth of August, 1953. The republic, so vast and beautiful, the heir of tremendous technological and political genius and of thousands of millions of hours of the working man's work across the centuries, had yet, as of this moment, to be destroyed. It was a tyrant killer, a vendor of grain and typewriter ribbons. Nothing could be more self-evident than that it meant well by the world, and still the world was threatening at any moment to transform us, its people, into ash and bone shards. Our belief in the justness of our cause was being tested.

In the meantime, said the Lord to Rocco, consider the gorge I have scooped out, and the steaming cliffs of falling water that I have made to fall so that you might come here and feel your heart being drawn out of your throat.

Canada was right over there, across the canyon. If he squinted, Canadians could be seen moving along a Canadian street in midday Canadian summer sunshine.

The titanic physical dimensions of this place gave to the movement of any small thing, any merely human-life-sized thing, an illusion of supernatural slowness. The Canadian cars on the opposite lip of the canyon seemed at best to be creeping. Any splash, any arbitrarily chosen patch of water you followed into the cloud below, appeared not to fall (since what could take so long falling?) but to drift leisurely down the face of the cataract. A few clouds overhead and these other clouds, what a shock, drifting up into the sky. And down by the base of the falls the clouds were so thick as to obscure completely his view of where the falling water made impact with the river itself, giving him the impression that the water wasn't descending into the river at all but into a befogged chasm, where it was swallowed up and annihilated. Raw senses were not to be believed in this place. And he had to ask himself if the unchanging physical rules that governed small things in fact changed radically in the face of a really big thing. As in, if he dropped a newspaper into the river up here it might turn into a flamingo by the time it got to the bottom of the falls. Next to him the river was clean, green, fat, and fast. Down there, postfall, it was blue and teemed with hills of brown scum. A knee-high sycamore sapling, very still, only one leaf ashiver, grew not six inches from a current that could have thrown a truck over the cliff's edge. Somehow, a little upstream of the falls, these brave, industrious people had managed to build a bridge over this arm of the river, had managed to sink the pylons into the rapids, and couples were walking hand in hand in yellow rubber rain slicks over the bridge toward Goat Island, which split the Niagara River into two arms, one falling over the Horseshoe Falls, the other over the American. A mile off to his right, downriver of the falls, another, far longer bridge spanned the gulf, hundreds of feet above the water, connecting the second- and fourth-largest nations in the world. He put a nickel in a binocular telescope and aimed it at the bridge and saw a kid throw—was it popcorn?—into the wind and hang his head over the rail to watch it fall.

Why was she not once in her rotten, betrayed life to be taken by her spouse to see Niagara Falls? Loveypants had lamented. She made the preposterous allegation, so it seemed, that you could board the six o'clock train and arrive there by lunchtime. Rocco invented a tune, a chipper five-note sort of birdsong to sing at her, the words to which— *I don't believe you, I don't believe you, I don't believe you*—sent her into a fit of catlike violence. There was the spitting, and there were the fingernails attacking his eyes, and the threats to smother his children, until, sorrowfully but with no more delicate tools at his disposal, he leveled one clean, close-fisted blow at her nose to settle her down. Truth be told, he would've loved to have come here, he still owned at the present day several picture postcards of the place, which postcards a cousin had sent his mother when he was a boy; but how was he supposed to keep his offspring in a row if they didn't fear him, and how were they going to learn to fear him if he demonstrated, by giving in to their mother, that persistent mutiny paid off in the long run?

This cousin, Tata (his mother's niece and goddaughter), had been shipped away by her father to marry a corn miller in Buffalo. She sent the twice-a-year letter or postcard home to Sicily, and young, literate Rocco was made to read it aloud for the diversion of anyone who stopped in—a shameful chore, since it was clear to him even as a seven-year-old that his mother had been Tata's confessor and that the letters were intended only for her and, out of necessity, for whomever she could find to read them to her. His mother didn't care, she was a traitor. They had in Buffalo a house of their own with plumbing indoors, Tata reported, and meat was easy to come by. But she had many babies, eleven at the final count, three of whom died, and her husband, on whom she had not laid eyes before the men involved concluded their agreement through the mails and she was packed like a white slave, alone at sixteen, onto a steamer to Genoa and then to New York, was middle-aged and clubfooted; bathed rarely; had more than once taken their older boys with him to bordellos. The uncle or the neighbor to whom Rocco was reading shrugged and said, "Well, so it is," and then made him re-read the cheerfuller parts concerning the occasional trips to see Niagara Falls and the tulip gardens in the boulevards. When he was fourteen the letters stopped. Two years later a note arrived from one of her daughters relating that Tata had died in childbirth. It was with one of Tata's sons who'd moved to Omaha that Rocco went to live when he was eighteen. And when, six years later, he'd moved to Ohio with a cousin's cousin's guarantee of a steel-mill job, which was never to materialize, he'd promised himself this single luxury, once two or three years of careful saving had passed: to go to Niagara Falls. To see this celebrated place. But he got sidetracked.

A sense like revelation here, that the worry and the useless chaos he experienced in his little coffin world, in his pomade-smearing-the-window, mildew-on-the-bathroom-tile, fungus-in-the-toenails world—that all the mess surrounding him was a delusion brought about by the accident of being a small man with small eyes in a small room, and that all he'd needed all along was to get to Niagara Falls and view an immense thing from an immense distance and the delusion would be dispelled. He would see the sublime order with which the Lord had composed his work. Up close, up here on the lip of the canyon, he saw a tree branch rush down the river and slip over the crest. But when he tried to follow it down the curtain of water, it vanished. The particular mess was lost in the grand design. A sense of significance in all things that he could feel only once he felt the insignificance of any one thing.

One night, after cards, D'Agostino had spread on Rocco's kitchen floor a map of the earth and pointed out that Norway was shaped suspiciously like Sweden, and Sweden like Finland. Was this an accident? Ohio was shaped suspiciously like the United States, with Port Clinton sticking up there into the lake like a stunted Michigan, and Ashtabula pointing up toward the northeast like a little Maine, and a wart growing out of the bottom in the middle, by Ironton, like a Texas. When D'Agostino flipped Australia upside down, it, too, resembled a little USA, with a swayback and a gulf in the underside. And, look at it, the upside-down Australia bore a remarkable resemblance to Red China.

Repeated shapes, order, the existence of an afterlife, were all obvious to anybody who looked for them from a frontier. The way so often he saw Europe in the clouds.

As a boy he'd understood this instinctively. As a man, somehow he'd forgotten. And now it was coming back to him.

Distinctly he recalled the white alb and the black felt hat he wore when he was a boy of nine pulling with thousands of other boys and men the ropes that bore, up Via Etnea, a massive carriage that harbored the undecayed remains of Saint Agatha, the patroness of his hometown. The ropes spanned seven city blocks. He was supposed to be pulling them, but with so many of the devoted participating, he was lucky to get a hand on one of the ropes. Nowhere could he see actual pulling taking place, and yet the carriage was impelled up the street. And as they passed into Piazza Stesicoro, he saw the most incredible thing: From the parapet of a fourth-story balcony, a brick, with no visible cause, fell, just fell off the front of the building and smashed to the street.

And young Rocco thought, If I could understand one moment I would understand all moments.

The Canadian side, the Horseshoe Falls, was supposed to be larger and more majestic, but he could see only a corner of it from here. If he crossed the bridge over the gorge to the Canadian side, he'd heard, the view was unobstructed except by mist. And that required leaving the country, an act that represented, yes, the terminus of the path along which Providence had been leading him. He had entered the United States one morning forty years before and had yet to leave. The pattern of these last two days, the instruction he was receiving, was to take the long view, and longer. The next step, yes, was to get out of the country altogether and turn around and see it for what it was.

What a pleasure, how strangely reassuring, to listen to the tinkle of the keys on his key chain, as he bounced them in his hand, and to the roar of the water.

The music of his keys and the unlikely sycamore sapling sending down its baby roots into the earth at this suicidal proximity to the crashing river (it was Liechtenstein clinging to the side of Switzerland, hoping Germany wouldn't notice) and these flimsy-looking tour boats down in the gorge, stuffed with raincoats, speeding toward the base of the falls, all served to reassure and reassure him that his middle one had not finished becoming only at last to turn into a nothingness. That Loveypants and Bobo and Jimmy would be swayed and return to their rightful places.

Because there is *no such thing* as a nothingness, said the falls.

He knew what D'Agostino and those devils at the newspaper wanted, and the crone across his alley and her sidekick and the faithless feast crowd—they all wanted him to deny three times that he knew his own boy, and then the cock would crow. They wanted him to declare submitfully that this thing had been destroyed while he wasn't looking. They had the height, they had the serial number and the dog tags, they had the full faith and credit of the United States Marine Corps. But those were vanities. Those were nothing compared with the authority of Niagara Falls and of one man's faith. I have only changed his shape, said the falls. The voice of the roaring river told him to cast his bread upon the water, for he would find it after many days. The branch was lost to the viewer in the curtain of water going down, but it wasn't lost to the falls.

He was full of the fear of God, and happy.

Here was the bridge, saying, as all bridges say, Cross me. Beseeching. And a leftward-heading white arrow on a green metal sign that made the remarkable claim *Canada This Way.*

Go ahead, Rocco, cross the bridge, it's pretty over there, they have a little Union Jack in the corner of their flag, and a wax museum.

He searched his clothing for cigarettes and, finding them in his left hip pocket, said, "There you are, little friends!" And he mounted the bridge.

He could see at the far end a customhouse and men in red uniforms, not, alas, wearing bearskin hats. The head of state was a twenty-seven-year-old woman—a truck driver and skilled mechanic when she was a teenager, during the war—whose coronation was just two months ago, and who, perversely, lived in a different country.

He could almost see the Horseshoe now. The river was blue and rushing beneath him. A sign approaching on the bridge sidewalk came into focus; it said *International Boundary Line*. And under that: *Now Entering the Dominion of Canada*. He paused and threw his cigarette butt over the rail and the wind tossed it under the bridge before he could see it hit the water, and with significant twisting of the body to shield the match from the wind, he lit another.

He'd forgotten to leave kitty sufficient Chow Chow Bits for his absence, but she'd survive, he assured himself, she was an intrepid little monster.

Go ahead, Rocco, cross the border. What's this shilly-shallying?

Foreboding, an itch in the brain.

Across the sidewalk ran a stripe of paint, which yet another sign alleged was the actual location of the border, although it was, he now was, the bridge was, according to the sign, two hundred feet above the surface of the river. Evidently, absurdly, an unseen wall reached into the sky. How far into outer space was Canada supposed to extend?

Shall I? Shall I? Dillydally.

In an average minute, six billion pounds of water passed under this bridge, called the Rainbow Bridge, completed in 1941. It was the fourth bridge to be constructed on this site. The first, a suspension, had collapsed in a windstorm in January 1889. The second, also a suspension, had been taken apart and put back together some miles downriver. The third, a steel arch, was destroyed by Lake Erie ice floes that had tumbled over the falls, crashed into the moorings, and collapsed them at 4:20 p.m. on January 27, 1938. The remains of the two destroyed structures lay on the riverbed even at the present day, 175 feet below the surface, one on top of the other.

Blue, yellow, red American cars, voluptuous and shiny, passed on his right, northwest-bound and southeast-bound, Ontario-bound and New York State–bound, oblivious, unslowing, as they traversed the cartographer's invisible wall, the bodies of the people inside them cut in two for a split second, half-republic and half-dominion, one legal code and expanse of history constraining one half of the body, another the other.

Why this itch? A surveyor had calculated that rising through this stripe of paint was an invisible plane. Why this belief that the plane existed, that there were two places and not one? The border didn't demonstrate a separation, it only asserted a separation. He was too old not to know this. He had disembarked from the steamer *Natalie of Tunis* in New Orleans in 1913 a stupid child, telling himself the same nonsense people had been telling themselves since the beginning of the spoken word: There is another place promised to you and to your children. There is a solution in this other place.

On either side of the paint stripe two Oriental girls of about seven, in identical periwinkle skirts and white sandals, bounced a tennis ball across the border to each other, back and forth against the pavement, deadly serious, aiming the ball and aiming again and throwing very softly lest the wind catch it.

Don't tell lies to yourself, Rocco. Turn around.

We have in the American language a stouthearted expression, Rocco, that doesn't mean what you'd think, it doesn't mean, Enjoy yourself, it means, Tell the truth about what you did.

The tennis ball, having again been aimed very carefully, nevertheless caromed to the north and was exploded under the wheel of a late-model Pontiac.

Face the music, Rocco.

The guard back at the American customhouse demanded his driving papers and inquired after his citizenship.

"U.S.," Rocco said.

"How long were you in Canada?" the man said, coughing into his documents.

"I didn't go in Canada."

"That's Canada over there where you were, Jack-o."

"I . . . I like to read the signs. I saw there were signs, so I wanted to read them," he said weakly. He wanted an ice cream. It was hot, and he wasn't hungry, and he wanted to stick something colorful into his face.

He was so confused.

"It's a bridge. You can go one way or the other way. You can go to our side or their side. Seeing as you are now here, Jack, the onliest place you're coming from is there, which is Canada."

He wanted an ice cream. "I went far enough to read the signs, that's it. I didn't cross the border. I wanted to read the signs and learn the history of the place and so . . . and so . . . and so . . ."

He was so confused. He didn't understand the meanings of things. The feeling of wanting very strongly to be in love could sometimes resemble the feeling of love itself.

The sun, reflected in the windshield of a car veering onto the bridge, flashed momentarily in Rocco's eyes.

"I'm so confused," he said to the guard.

Briefly, he was convinced that there was no God after all. The falls weren't speaking to him anymore; only the bridge and the cars, artifacts of a country married to mathematics and ferroconcrete, were speaking to him, or rather were screeching meaninglessly.

The guard handed him back his moist papers. "Answer me, did you buy anything over there?"

"No, I didn't."

The guard let him pass. He retraced his steps along the edge of the gorge, slowly, having lost hold of all the many convictions to which his first few minutes of observing the falls had led him. He didn't understand the meaning of anything except the stripe painted across the pavement of the bridge. He tramped the crisscrossing sidewalks in the little park abutting the gorge, in search of ice cream. He felt profoundly unhappy and alone. The meaning of the stripe of paint was, You have been behaving as if imaginary things were real.

Certain nights at home, he felt his spirits lift upon hearing the *toc, toc* of the pilot in the new furnace and the gas catching and making its *whoosh*. His spirits lifting as a knock on the door would make them lift. He regarded the furnace as company, as a human being. The regularity of the furnace lighting itself, *toc-tocking* every half hour in the winter nights, was the suggestion of a permanent alleviation of aloneness. He called the furnace Harry, as in, Give 'em hell.

The cigarettes were making his heart slam away at his rib cage, and experience told him the only way to address this was to smoke another.

The ice cream man, once he had been located under the heavy cover of a sugar maple twenty feet from the pre-fall, crashing Niagara, wore a white paper hat in the conventional military shape, the same model Rocco wore when he was on the job; also, a white and blue polka-dotted shirt and a black bow tie. A lipless, unholy grin was frozen to his face. He sat atop the steel cage of a milk crate behind his refrigerated cart, his back against the trunk of the tree. The light all around was splendorous, but the shade afforded beneath this tree was so complete that no patches of sunlight whatsoever fell on the grass.

Such a complicated device just to catch light with. So many thousands of leaves. There was a leaf for every angle of sun coming down. The tree was a cistern for light.

The ice cream man had nothing he was reading, no oddments to fiddle with. Each of his hands rested on the knob of one of the freezer hatches as though he were manning the gate to a passage underground. He stood up with some effort in the strange shadow of the leaves. He was aged significantly. He began speaking before Rocco had completed his approach.

"I have strawberry. I have chocolate. I have pistachio. I have a sugar cone. I have a regular cone. I have no vanilla. One napkin, please." He cleared his throat. A grasshopper landed on Rocco's shoulder and the ice cream man leaned smoothly toward him and flicked it off. "I have no sandwiches, drumsticks, or novelties of any kind. I have paper cups and wood spoons. One scoop, twelve cents. Two scoops, nineteen cents. Three scoops, a quarter. I have no nuts. I have no cherries. Sixty feet in that direction one finds a public water fountain. Thirty feet to the left of that is a public latrine. I don't know what time it is."

There was a pause while the two men took in each other's faces. Rocco thought he saw a shiver of recognition pass across the man's features, and then the man stifle it. There was unquestionably the too-longness of the pause and of the looking at each other before the man set himself to opening the freezer hatches and exposing his wares. The paper hat was cockeyed—a cheerful angle, the way Rocco himself wore his—and liver spots were visible on the exposed portion of the scalp, beneath what remained of the glossy, pallid hair.

"I know you," Rocco said.

"No, you don't."

"We know each other. If you give me a second—"

"Whoops! There it goes! Now then, to summarize, your choices are three in number—"

"I hope you'll forgive me. For two days, I've been beside myself."

"—flavor, vessel, number of scoops."

"I've been under a cloud. I'm having trouble thinking with a high degree of clearness. Whenever I think it's lifting, or thinning out—the cloud, I'm saying—suddenly everything gets darker than before."

"You think you're unique. You think the newlyweds don't give me this. I am their uncle that died. I am Grandma's former milkman. They leave the confines of Mother's home to get married, and they come here and get a motel for the night, and the next morning, snap—"

"No no no."

"—suddenly I am the long-lost. I am Mark Twain. One night with their husband and they have second thoughts. They want a return to normalcy, Grandma, the butter churn."

"No, but—"

"Pull yourself together, for Chrissake."

"I'm in some very delicate business these days. Let me not hang details around your neck. It's enough to know that at the very heart of this business is something that I have to have all my powers about me."

"I'm plain of face. I could be anybody."

A tabby cat with a live swallow in its jaws sprung from a rock below them onto the sill of the cliff, squeezed itself under the rail, and padded away across the bright grass.

"I am a man of firm beliefs," Rocco said. "Such as love of my country; the power of prayer; the belongingness of wife with husband, and children with their father."

"And now you're corrupted. That's the confession you feel compelled to make. Like as though it hasn't ever occurred to anybody before to open their heart to the old man under the tree and pretend he is the dearly departed whatever-the-relation."

Rocco peered into the gaping mouth of the freezer, but he saw only what was promised—three tubs, brown, pink, and green, in a shallow, frosted box.

"I am not corrupt," Rocco said.

"And yet you think corrupt thoughts."

"I'm very, very faithful, sir. What I'm trying to explain is, I *have* to know you. If you have the face of the person, that means you *are* the person."

The ice cream man closed the freezer hatches, turned aside, and made four neatly spaced and phlegmy sneezes into his handkerchief. Rocco blessed him.

"Something in my face—thank you—evidently expresses, Please come over here and unfold your regrets," he said wearily. The sneezes had taken something out of him, a reserve of spiritual force necessary to maintain the cocksure veneer. There was a suggestion of pleadingness in the voice. Rocco felt certain now that he was faking.

"And you know me. We know each other. If you give me a second."

"No . . . ," the man said, trying to sound lackadaisical, making a grandly dismissive gesture in the air, a shoo-fly gesture in which the hand, at the top of the arc, snapped to one side as if only barely tied to the wrist, a move Rocco had no doubt he'd seen before.

Unless the feeling of wanting very deeply to have no doubts could resemble the feeling of having no doubts itself.

"At least once, we've seen one another. I think."

"Jesus Christ, this fucking ragweed over here."

"Unless our Lord has led me astray."

"They actually planted it, if you can believe that. It's part of the landscaping, is what they told me, the park rangers, when I asked them why not mow it down."

In the moss beneath the hedges, the cat stood with its forepaws on the swallow's neck and tail and bit into a bunch of feathers and ripped them off, while one of the wings methodically slapped its face.

"You never lived in Ohio anywhere, or in the Nebraska?"

"I'm going to sneak in here at night with a can of turpentine and a match, is what I'm going to do."

"Unless I'm deceived this whole time," Rocco said.

"All summer it's the grass pollens, the windblown corn rusts." He sneezed four times more, fluid leaking out of every opening in his face. "And the fungus spores."

"The things that I absorbed for so long," Rocco sputtered, "for I don't know why." The sun was on his back, and a caddis fly alighted on his belly. *Thumpety-thump* went his heart.

It didn't matter what he had done or failed to do. He didn't see what he saw. He was not where he was. He felt so hungry and light-headed and confused that he wasn't hungry.

And yet I have my pink scoop on top of my green scoop on top of my cone, he considered, licking them, as he crossed the grass and then the pavement again and stood at the rail on the lip of the gorge and watched again the falls falling, the shapeless mists rising up.

His streak was over. He had no possessions worthy of note. His parents had long since gone to their long home.

He was fifty-seven years old.

PART TWO

All the Daughters of Musick
Shall Be Brought Low

1928 – 1936

. . . .

5

For thirteen years after the death of her husband, Costanza Marini had lived alone. She was now sixty-eight. Death beckoned. And that was really too bad, because, having been anxious in her youth, disappointed in maturity, and then desolate in middle age, she had recently made a conspicuous turn: In what she expected were her final years, she found herself in possession of powers she had long ago given up hope of acquiring. It was a windfall. She had become happy—no, exuberant. While she slept, a storm had knocked the fruit out of the trees.

In retrospect, the turn's success had depended on her failure to notice it until it was complete. Consciousness had sabotaged her past efforts at reform so consistently that she didn't bother to blame it anymore. It couldn't help itself. Surgery required that the surgeon be awake and the subject etherized; operating on her own mind, she only woke herself up halfway through and made matters worse. Reform, she had slowly become convinced, was impossible. Fatalism was true. These were the tenets of a religion to which she had every intention of staying faithful. But the religion had a flaw that would prove its undoing.

It was so all-embracing that it used her every observation as evidence for its claim: Her pudding wouldn't thicken—why? Because it had always been the fate of this pudding to be thin. Therefore, eventually, why observe? Why be conscious? Why not sleep? And at last, she slept, firm in her faith in misery, finding nothing new to contradict it, and envisioning her death with a growing interest and fear.

For the turn that then ensued and changed so much, she had to take at least some credit. Although she'd been asleep, yes, and hadn't *done* anything to herself, she still had had the absence of mind to stay asleep and not to take heart until whatever force was acting on her had finished its work. She was like Saint Peter walking on the sea, only the moral of the story was upside down. She could do it so long as she believed she couldn't do it and was afraid.

Her expression at social gatherings during married life was one of regal dispassion, the face of a sleepy predator. In fact, she was abashed and so let the men talk, congratulating herself for being bored by them. She was impervious to the suffering of others and did not weep at the theater or at funerals. She did not pity the poor, the halt, or her husband, Nico, as he declined. "You are cold, cold, cold," he said. Maybe so. She took his word for it. She could hardly feel the lack of what she had never known in the first place.

The question arose after he died whether she was naturally ill formed in these ways or had learned her, her—the word was *callousness*—over a long marriage and might unlearn it. An intractable widow she knew, a muleteer's wife, still treated herself and guests at lunch to raisin cake, for which she professed a passion while from her own piece she picked all the raisins; she disliked raisins; it was her Angelo who had liked the raisins. Those women were so stupid! But when Costanza Marini did the same things they did, she was no more forgiving than before, of them or herself. Where was her nerve? The ability to speak the truth to ourselves must have been the advantage that the adaptation called consciousness evolved to exploit. But the truth, over and over and over—that she was a sneerer and a scold, heartless, timid, fated to die alone—wasn't only bleak, it was fatiguing. Where was her pride?

Four years into her widowhood, Satan visited her in her garden. She was on her knees, yanking the quack grass out of the spinach. Iridescent flies dappled the carcass of a bass in the furrow. "Egoist!" said the tempter. "Despair!" To despair is a sin. But, true enough, she had no hope. She could not remember having hoped. "Die!" said the devil. She was never to speak of this episode to another soul, but she really saw him there. He was dressed like Young Werther, in a blue jacket, yellow vest and pants, and tricorn hat, and he spoke with a German accent. Her transformation was in fact slow and continuous, but if she'd had to point to an emblematic moment, a swerve, it would have been that morning with Satan in her garden. For she had straightened up her back, quaking, as he tried to lay her low, and she surveyed him head to foot in his absurd outfit; her eyelids peeled back into her head; her chest jumped with a gush of air; the skin under her hackles itched piercingly—and she laughed at him. "Don't laugh at me!" he snapped. But he was ridiculous. What he was saying was ridiculous. She herself was ridiculous. She was fifty-nine. Her health was sound. The hem of her skirt was in the mud. "I am a fool!" she said aloud, and tightened the laces of her shoe.

In conversation she became an interrupter. Her brows swelled. The wizening of her neck she emphasized with tight-fitting collars, the better to show the glazen skin of her cheeks, jaw, forehead, and nose. In a daguerreotype—of her husband and herself in the 1880s—that presided over her bedroom, her bones were already asserting their ownership of the face. The eyes were dull and recessed. (In fairness to the goose in the picture, her infant son, Alessio, had lately died; however, your pity did her no good; she would lay other eggs—except, as it happened, she would lay no other eggs at all.) Look at the eyes now! Black globes, protuberant, fat. There was another animal in the mask than before. Why, she wondered, do we always look to the eyes? *Windows of the soul,* she disregarded as fanciful. No, it's the eyes themselves, to be exact, that look to the eyes. They are as competitive in their vanity as we are.

She read hysterical murder stories, and history, and the Bible itself, which in her youth was a sin to read, and English literature, untranslated, deep into the night, so that sometimes she slept until noon. Now, Nico had let her read. In fact, he bought her texts on diseases of the blood, anatomy, nutrition, tokology, and hygiene. And he used his acquaintance with the dean of laboratories at the university across the bridge to procure a seat for her in the back row of lecture halls, where ladies were invited to sit and take in, if not comprehend. It was hardly pure husbandly kindness for him to do all these things, since he profited from her industry as much as she did. Still, if she wasn't in bed with her hair up and books closed by nine o'clock, he moped, and what a disgrace to see that, how it wounded her pride to watch her husband debase himself by entreating her. The surplus from her income he would not let her spend, so as not to call attention. But she spent it now, damn him, and his hoarded treasure, on cheese and the opera.

A gull encountering a fish on the beach, she considered, will first dig out its eyes, which are softest and easiest of access and provide a clean route to the brains, which are soft, too. Is that why we look to the eyes? If I look you in your eye and you flinch, do you suspect me of plotting where to aim my spoon?

It was akin to Protestant conversion, this swerve, seeing the light and so on, only in her case she saw the darkness. She did not say, I will die in hopes of being reborn. She said, I am dying! She was vain, and exaggerated, and let her arms swing around her while she talked, and was too up-to-date American to stay in her mourning clothes longer than four or five years (she'd graduated from peasant to petty bourgeois the first time she took money for her services), but by 1928, thirteen years after Nico died, she hadn't changed them yet, and why should she? They were a becoming badge. She looked good in black. She was both the genuine article and a fake. A European wouldn't understand how to pull that off. To a European you were either wearing the clothes that belonged on your body or the clothes that belonged on someone else's. But an American—yes, she was an American now; you couldn't touch her, not with your scruples or your history or your handwoven stockings—went to a masquerade ball wearing her own linsey-woolsey housecoat as a costume. You have not become an American until you have learned to impersonate yourself in a crowd.

Ice water did not curdle the juices of the stomach, she discovered, by drinking it nervily and waiting. Why, that was only a prejudice, common among those of her nationality and insisted on by Nico for all his days. To think that for centuries Aristotle had peddled the canard that women had fewer teeth than men—and they bought what he was selling! she was mad!—when anybody might have opened up and counted. Thus false doctrines were impaled by her and—even at this late date, for sixty-five, sixty-six, sixty-seven, were so old, were so much older than she'd planned to live, should have been deep into the intransigence of the downward slope—were trampled under her feet, along with false likes and dislikes, raisin cakes and their kind.

Honor is for those who hold themselves responsible to a kernel of unchanging self. Alas. None of that for her.

While dressing she considered her fattening but still meager breasts, which Nico had only half-playfully jeered. They were like what? Like miserable, withered medlars (yes, *medlars;* he'd missed out, good): a medlar, which is only a small, spotted, unlovely orb, yes, but is perhaps unique among fruits in that it is inedible until it starts to rot.

Soon, said Death. And she began to sum up, to tie contrary judgments together with a phrase and put them to one side. In this way she discarded old remorses and confusions and made way for last things. The phrases ranged from promulgation of a settled rule to abstraction, code, euphemism, sophistry, baby talk. As to sin: *There is no such thing, and yet I will pay;* alcohol: *whenever you please, but no liquor before five o'clock;* how her dead would receive her in paradise: *not bearing fruit baskets;* the significance of the tower far in the distance, across an ocean of grain, that recurred in her dreams: *Avert your eyes, look at the grass;* her vanity: *"Ye have the poor always with you, but me ye have not always";* the past: *Strictly speaking, it does not exist;* her means of income: *to the good, sweets, to the others, mutton.* She needed one for the cause of the swerve. A phrase. All this had happened over ten years. And she was so grateful. Character wasn't fate. No one else, in her experience, had demonstrated such a shift so late in life. She needed a phrase.

She waited for the humiliation and incapacity of old age, but the curse had passed her by. A Hebrew had mistakenly stricken the posts of her door with lamb's blood and the Lord had skipped her house. Against any part of her did not a dog move its tongue. Oh, well. Probably she would fall down the cellar stairs and smash her skull. The good fortune of her new life suggested that death, though soon, would be only a swift blackening of mind. Fine. When Nico died, she had believed she would be trapped forever in the past. Only she could no longer sympathize with the self who'd felt this way. She laughed at it. She laughed!

How about: *I laughed at myself, with scorn?*

Midwinter. When all the autumn fruits have been consumed, and everything you eat is cooked or caked in salt, and all the world is dead. A pulpy something sweet would mean so much. Only a little. You find the medlars in the root cellar in a box of sawdust. Finally gone to mush. They were no good for anything before—he'd missed out. Too bad.

Now, about summing up: Not everything can be accomplished with a phrase. It would have been self-defeating and anyway impossible to condense into a few words all the refinements she had produced over forty years of study and practice in her trade. She had elaborated her methods from crude hand-me-downs (her grandmother's tools were a root broth, heavily salted, and a bellows), to a precise, well-tried, and sterile science. The prospect that all her advances would evaporate at her death was a poison she tried to absorb stoically, with the help of a palliative phrase: *"All the daughters of musick shall be brought low,"* she said, but was dissatisfied. Her stoicism finally failed her, or she failed it, as more and more her pride prevailed and she began to change her view. Resignation wasn't worth the effort; the right phrase existed but might take years to find; action, in this case showing someone what she knew while her brain still worked, was easier than inaction.

Therefore I shall seek an apprentice and heir, she said. But the *an* was misleading. There was only one person she wished to ask. She had long intended to pass all her wealth to one special girl, and if she was going to give away her expertise as well, she saw no one else to whom she'd rather give it. The wet human feelings this implied were repulsive enough that to keep herself from being made sick by them she screwed herself to her more selfish motives.

Envy, for example. For this particular girl and for no one else she felt the species of envy, rare except among the old, that expresses itself in the desire to be replaced by someone and consequently improved by him. Here she discovered herself on the farthest frontier of egoism, which was funny, because egoism was the very vice that the girl, in replacing her, would best have corrected.

This was not to say that the girl in question had no *I* or wasn't, like the rest of us, in constant conversation with it, but rather that, in a trait Mrs. Marini had coveted since before the girl had lost her milk teeth and which she'd somehow maintained through her adolescence, she didn't seem to know it was her *I* with whom she was speaking. Birds of prey, horses, snakes, bears, and elephants all give one this impression; dogs, bugs, fish, squirrels, chickens, and human beings, in general, do not.

Anyway, practically speaking, the choice as it currently appeared was to ask Lina, the Montaneros' daughter from Eighteenth Street, or to drink the poison and be forgotten.

A phrase?

She was hale, flat chested, inward. All things, perhaps not coincidentally, that were less and less true of Mrs. Marini herself.

She was the elder of two girls, of whom there would have been many more and sons besides, no doubt, starvelings all, had Patrizia, the mother, not availed herself of Mrs. Marini's counsel some decades ago. The younger, Antonietta, or Toni, had lately married and moved to California.

So long.

They knew better, her mother and Mrs. Marini both, than to trust in oaths like *I will return to pay visits, I am not lost to the deep.* America is the deep. Elsewise, why did you come? Lina, on the other hand, already twenty years old and beaten to the finish by her younger sister, faced dimming prospects of marriage. The parents had made a sloppy error to let Toni marry first, and Mrs. Marini told Patrizia so, who agreed; however, the father . . . the father—but over him Mrs. Marini preferred to pass without comment. Not that Lina seemed to mind or make any effort to vend herself. There are compromises we make in the authenticity of our expressions for the sake of attracting men to us, Mrs. Marini argued. Men did not notice Lina, but whose fault was that? One needn't give oneself over to the licentious fashions of the day. One might simply train one's bodiless hair in curls. Lina's flannel skirts might keep her warm, but flannel did not describe the leg to the viewer, and she had many long years ahead to be warm.

Well, but Lina was not going to be moved by argument, as Mrs. Marini knew. Lina was not modest out of commitment to modesty, she was naturally, mulishly modest. Deliberation did not cause, precede, or otherwise clutter her deeds; this was what you admired her for. Her mind was not a chamber in which a crowd of lawyers competed to direct and obstruct her will; it was a forest, and deep inside, alone, in a cool pond, her *I* swam freely on its back and scrutinized the tangled canopy of thought overhead.

She did piecework in the overcoat shop behind the theater on Twenty-fourth Street. She was irregular in her attendance at mass, as the Sicilians were wont to be. She had finished school but didn't read. She spoke good Ohio English and court Italian, as Mrs. Marini had coached her to do from her early girlhood over school-day suppers (the parents were at their dreary jobs; Mrs. Marini's husband was newly dead). She had had only one unmitigated success in bending the girl to her will over the many years she'd auntied her: She had peeled the dialect right off Lina's tongue. Lina was only an immigrant seamstress from the backward South who'd received all her education in this country, but were you to hear her over a radio, she could have passed for a Savoy. Hear how crisp and comprehensible? We say all the letters in the word because otherwise, why are the letters there? Jefferson, proving that Negroes could reason, had taught his slave to do calculus. Or so Mrs. Marini had heard tell. But she didn't believe it. That was going too far.

To summarize, Carmelina Montanero was a work of art she had made. True, Mrs. Marini had failed to carry out her original ambition (Lina was not going to seduce the emperor), but a professional man or a merchant were still fair expectations. And anyhow, it must have been in the nature of an artist to consider his finished work a failure, inasmuch as his original idea looked amorously toward the prospect of its execution without admitting that the prospect itself was another idea, which the finished work, being composed of different stuff, had to consume in order to come into existence. Disappointment was the result of an idea's attempt to miscegenate with the visible world. Even God experienced this, as all but the first two pages of the Old Testament attested.

She supposed that an artist's foremost joy was to see a real thing come into existence through his effort, and that it was in his starkest failures to carry out the program of his idea that he most felt the resistance of the visible world and knew that the thing he'd made had broken from its home in the mind and made it to dry land. Likewise, she may have gloated over Lina's splendid Italian; but she never felt more tenderly toward her than on the days when Lina was so rumpled, poorly painted, remote, and unhappy that anyone could see Mrs. Marini had bungled her, and it was incredible anyone would ever volunteer to be her husband.

A pause to observe the sweet melancholy of discouragement. Of maybe having failed.

Okay. Nevertheless. Bungle or no. She must be vigilant. Left in the state of her own nature, Lina was likely to tighten all the strings Mrs. Marini had loosened in her and loosen all the ones she'd tightened.

Some women were unfit *not* to marry. That one who stood too close behind you at the bakery, humming, audibly sucking a cherry coughing lozenge; the stranger who asked you to hold her bag while she boarded the streetcar and as you handed it back began to chant the litany of relations to whom she'd given her money and her faith, only to be hunted and stripped and ridiculed by them—in other words, the women (there were men, but the men were incurables from the beginning) who did not seem convinced that you, an other person, distinct from themselves, were quite there. On meeting these people she knew immediately, in a leap of intuition over science's head, that they were spinsters—who might have been saved if only in their youths someone had imposed a man on what was at the time merely their contented self-dependence and wasn't yet their brainsickness. She was well aware. She might have been one of their number, but marriage had cracked her in the necessary way.

6

She speculated and spied and picked and plotted. She was trying to find a way of carrying out her new ambition, that Lina should succeed her, without dooming her old ambition, that Lina should marry someone, but in each of her plots she at last foresaw the same mistake and threw them one by one wrathfully into the trash. The mistake was that if Lina should take over the business, she would become self-sustaining, and thus the last reliable lever that could still press marriage upon her—that she was penniless, and so was her family—would be removed. It was for this same reason that Lina didn't know she stood to inherit Mrs. Marini's house and money.

She had one further misgiving about making the girl her apprentice. It was that Lina was a child. She lacked the natural cruelty that a conversance with the marital act encouraged one to refine.

Anyway, Mrs. Marini was short for this world. She was sick of sitting around. Her brain had a rash from scratching. It was sometimes necessary to commence doing before the plan of action was drawn. One must lay one's faith in one's native power of striking a thing, of whacking it with all one's force the moment instinct says go. And. And, and, and, the plan existed, it must have, but in a dark corner of her undermind, where it was wisely protecting itself from her.

She went out into the street in search of Lina. It was a Thursday.

She aimed herself through the postwork commerce that clogged Eleventh Avenue, in which the city was opening a trench, half a mile long, for the fitting of sewer pipe. She peeked down into the moat as she made her precipitate way. Behind a single-file team of jackasses, a man down there was plowing up the clay and rocks.

Otherwise, she hardly observed. She was equal to motion plus thought. When the gears of the intellect began to click, sensation was a waste of time, and time did not pertain to her. She was attentive only that she not pay too close attention to what she was going to propose. The crucial elements of her plan must not make each other's acquaintance up in the conscious mind until the latest possible moment, when they must be thrown together in a fit of resolve, as when, making a dough for pastry, one combines the ice water and the shortened flour with a few quick turns of the cold hand.

The sun went down. She kicked perhaps unnecessarily at a pigeon that kept an annoying pace a foot in front of her. She might have gone first to Eighteenth Street and called for Lina at home, but Umberto was out of work once more, the father, and therefore was certainly holed up in the house awaiting an audience for his grief, while his women, just two now, thanks to him, were at this hour in the street going pushcart to pushcart looking for the cheapest lemon, or else in somebody's kitchen helping put up the last of the beans. A peasant woman is never alone.

She raked the streets, peeking in certain likely windows, not finding them.

She should have said a peasant woman is never solitary, because others are always with her. To be alone is to have no thoughts to keep one company. She herself, conversely, was quite unalone.

"What will become of that girl is so sad to ask, so you'd better meddle some more—I mean, fix everything," said Nico from his moldering place.

"You shut up," she said. She knew it was not really him because Nico was never sarcastic. It was only her own brain generating phantasmal senators to impede the exercise of her imperial rights. The style was wrong but the tone of voice was flawless.

"You're all mealy-mouthed pitiation and no pity, Costanza. You don't want to assist anybody. You have been unfitting that child for female kindliness since I exited the scene. Witch. You only want to ready her for witchdom. Twenty is so many years to have. You can't be serious! See how you conduct yourself, with the lies and the twistings. Twenty is the bloom of youth, hag. You don't want to make her rich; you want to erect a monument to yourself. You don't want her to get married; you—"

"Who will marry her? Give me his name!"

The girl wasn't in any of the back gardens along Vermilion Avenue, nor in the church.

"You don't want her to get married. You don't want some bumpkin digging up your treasure. You only suspect that you ought to desire her benefit above your own, but you're completely insincere. If you make her a witch, like yourself, all the boys will know and no one will call for her. This is your plan. And, by the way, you won't be any good at it, the witching instruction. You'll hector her and embarrass her. It won't be like teaching somebody to read a newspaper in your boudoir. There will be the matter of your conscious subjects lying there. But I know what you'll do. You'll just give them some gas."

"You are so wicked!" she said.

"No, you are!"

"What entitles you of all people to dress yourself up as my conscience?"

"Introspect and you will observe your incapacity to do a genuine kindness," he said.

"Stop abusing me, Nicolo!"

But it wasn't really him, as she had already decided. It was never really him. She might have her silly hopes, but in all honesty if the ghost of the true Nico should ever visit her, she wondered if she could bear to speak with it without ruining all the gains of her later years and turning back into her former, wretched self. There were certain things she dearly longed to say to him—things that had come to her only while she was pushing the gelatinous food between his teeth during his last days, while his kidneys were failing and after his mind was already destroyed—but they could only be said in the past.

She was sure Lina had never indulged any sniping ghosts like this one; however, even if she had indulged them, she would have been able, as Mrs. Marini rarely was, to declare herself innocent at the last, or innocent enough, and march out into the cold autumn air.

There was a bench under the consignment-store awning where the girl and her mother sometimes sat and watched Joseph D'Agostino's cockatoo through the plate glass and made doilies out of the bleached threads from a burlap bag, but neither Lina nor Patrizia was there.

There was a scent—she passed a woman in the intersection, a mother of nine but slender, clean-complected, the name was, the name was; but she must not *try* to remember, lest she fail—a smell of soap, hair, and something bitter besides, and it dropped her into a crevasse many ages old, accessible only via the nose and only if the scent was lost again at once: I have opened my sister's carpetbag to see that she does not take my leggings with her when she leaves us forever tomorrow.

Such was her recent distraction that she'd allowed three days of newspapers to accumulate on her sideboard, a dereliction only of what she owed herself, since no one remained whose conversation demanded a knowledge of the news. The Prussians were departed, and Nico. Her peers were dead. And the age of gripping public events was over. Once women had been allowed to exert their influence at the polls, the nation had been beset by eerie calm. Consider aeroplanes and the Great War and the influenza and the headlong rush to outlaw good times (booze, she meant) that had preceded this, the republic's least interesting decade. And, as though to emphasize the point, Elephant Park, where until recently a variety of peoples had lived (mostly Germans, agreed, but they were literate, they spent some money now and then on a pretty object that had no use, didn't they?), had been narcotized over the last ten years by an injection of the unwashed from her own home country. Consequently, the Germans, the Danes, the Croats, and the Magyars had been driven off. One-family houses were divided into threes and fours. The refuse in the streets, the crowds, the rickety children, and barnyard animals tied to mailboxes—she was not pleased. She was like a Jew who had transferred herself to an obscure island in the outer Venetian lagoon and found, to her amazement, once she had grown old, that all her coreligionists had been moved out of the city and into her garden.

The new people had no politics. When Plato had gone to Sicily, hoping to put his political ideas into practice, the locals had sold him into slavery. As far as the new people cared, the body politic included their blood relations and nobody else. Equally and oppositely depressing: The *individual* also included the blood relations. *I* was *we*. The notion that you might sacrifice the good of your sister for the good of the commune was absurd, likewise that you might eat a whole chicken by yourself. She used to be more like them, in her peasant days. But she used to be a wretch.

She was in the street wearing a scowl to keep would-be chatters at bay. Now, if she wanted solitude, why not stay at home? Because she did not want solitude, she wanted the life of the mind, which was best lived in the street. Politics, or the life of others as lived by oneself, was the mind's natural subject. Conversation was its natural sport. And the dearth these days, which seemed permanent, of interlocutors made her want to spit on—on everybody, on her own shoes!

And the fog gradually thickened into a swarming drizzle under the gas lamps overhead and the girl could not be found.

Mrs. Marini had voted for the first time at age sixty, for Warren Gamaliel Harding and the rest of the Republican ballot, thank you, bearing dearly the memory of T.R., dead almost two years, we would not look upon his like again. Harding seemed okay. Being himself an Ohioan, it would have pressed her loyalty to reject him. Let's leave Europe to its feckless wars, he implied. Let's stay at home and grow our corn. "Hear! Hear!" she said. This from a man born in the tall-corn town of Corsica, Napoleonic in name only, between Mansfield and Columbus, so he must have had a sense of humor, too, to advocate such a platform. She pardoned his vote for the Volstead Act, since he was one of tens of millions to have been swept away in the hysteria for temperance, the backward bacchanal, and she ignored Prohibition anyway. If she'd known they would be so boring, the twenties, she would have voted for Cox—

No, she wouldn't have. What was she saying? She was determined to get to work finally, but her material was somewhere among the fruit carts, evading her.

"Or else Providence is hiding her from you," said the voice of one of her dead who lived in the crevasse, "because she is a child."

She didn't understand why the Democratic party was allowed to exist; a war had been fought and half a million men killed to expose the Democrats, and still they were among us.

Finally she permitted herself a snoop down Eighteenth Street. But no light glowed in the Montaneros' hut (formerly a stable), and she paced back up the hill.

That woman's name was so common, the woman she'd smelled in the intersection, and her plight was so common, and the cut of her coat, and the syncopated bleating of her accent, that Mrs. Marini presumed insipidness in her every particular, which was always unfair, as Mrs. Marini's profession never failed to remind her, checking her tendency to assume that no other houses enclosed so many mansions as hers did. The woman's name was Giacoma. The file card had fallen into the bottom of the brain's drawer, but, here, she'd found it: a syphilitic, from her husband's dalliances; the last two children were stillborn and blind, respectively; from her adolescent years in Brazil, she had learned to sing sweetly mournful songs in Portuguese.

Where was her quarry, her lamb, her pot to put her gold in?

There she was.

See her? A girl flitting over a bridge of bowed planks that spanned the sewer trench. Lina waved wildly, as though she also had come into the street in search of someone and it was Mrs. Marini she hoped to find.

"Here I am!" Mrs. Marini called in an ecstasy of self-esteem.

"Narcissus," said Nico's voice. "Sun Queen."

Not to be abject in concession to him, but a phrase was in order, something to redirect her feelings outward and focus her wits. She said aloud, but softly: *"Make a fist and show me where your brains are."*

Lina waved again with her hat, vigorously, so that its pheasant feather was knocked askew.

Gray in her dowdy flannels. One misstep would send her ten feet down into the muck.

Here, kitty, kitty, beckoned the deep underneath, as the planks bounced.

Let her turn today to the happiness that all existing things share, dead or living. The chimney flues and the blinders on the dray horses, and the great pipes, wide enough to walk through, that were stacked in the avenue waiting to be buried, and she herself, a girl in the street, all shared the fate of existing in this time and place. She had waited at the door of the someone else she was sure to become for so long, like a dog under the porch while it snows. But this afternoon at last the past and the future coincided in the present moment. Her completion, which had lived behind this door from the beginning of beginnings, would at last, at last, impose itself, and the footfalls inside were audible and approached the door where she was waiting. The somebody else who she would become had eyes that would meet her eyes and claim Lina as her own and obliterate her at last. You, Lina would tell her once the door opened, have always been the only one—and now we have met: because Father has found someone to marry us.

Things were moving quickly now.

She was in the street, in search of Donna Costanza, who would help slow the things down and point to each one and explain it.

Along the sidewalk, the men talked closer to one another than the women because the brims of their hats didn't get in the way, as hers did.

In the trench in the street, six men in coveralls were having their picture taken while they ate their working supper—though it was late and the light was poor; and the meat was stuck in their whiskers; and on the great timbers, which were like a parlor wall in the great trench where the pipes would go, they had tacked drawings of girls in the nude.

Boys in striped breeches showed their ribs through their thin shirts as they swung from the tree branches. It was too cold to go around without a coat, but the boys did as they pleased. They might swim in the creek bare-ass, daring her to watch. She didn't watch anymore, openly from the bridge, with her legs dangling under the rail. Nowadays, she worked.

The man her father had found had already seen her photograph, for which she had borrowed her sister's wedding dress. It was a piece of ingenuity of her father's, so that no one could mistake the photograph for the kind men pass in trenches at suppertime. But she had not believed that the picture would work until today, when her father revealed that it had achieved its purpose. The man was two years in the union, could read and write, although not yet in English. A bricklayer from the countryside east of Naples whose one eye lazed. Fear not the mother, her father said, meaning the man's mother. The mother would stay in Europe. Lina would be the mistress of her own house.

Someone in a double-breasted coat, with the flag of America stuck in his hatband and in his horse's harness bells, drove past and told the street it must try his brand of soda pop. And a thin-lipped girl slouched on the seat next to him, dourly waving to the crowd that did not pay her any mind.

A woman stood on a plow while a man behind the wheel of a flivver dragged it through the remains of the charity vegetable garden.

A man sold potatoes from a steam cart in front of the pharmacy. Lina had never needed to enter the pharmacy, because her health was excellent. All her pieces worked, her father had told the man, whose name was Vinciuzzo—but she shouldn't use dialect names or presume affections.

Her husband-in-waiting was a latecomer. Her father said that when he showed the man proof of her penmanship and her addition and subtraction, the man had noted that she didn't draw a line across her sevens, as Europeans did. In other words, her skills would be her dowry. Her father would not have to pay him to have her married, as he had Mr. Schaeffer to take Antonietta off his hands. He had sold her by not having to pay, so now he and Mother could go and live on a grape farm in the country, as he had always wanted. And in this respect, Lina was proud.

She hoped the new man would let her wear her skirts above her shoes so that the hems didn't need so often to be mended. She wasn't finicky, but she hoped his teeth were sound. She wondered which language they would speak in the house and with the children.

Her life had been like the clay that she and her mother and her sister dug out of the creek bed and molded around a turkey or a capon at Christmastime, careful to make the mold in the shape of the bird inside, like a sarcophagus; and they baked it all slowly, and took it out to cool, and painted feathers on it with whitewash—and eyes with shoe polish, and its wattle with her mother's lipstick—and waited for her father to come to the table and say that he blessed it, and the three of them, and Saint Joseph, his patron, and for him to hold the hammer and smash it. While they cheered and the steam came out.

She would meet the man-in-waiting on Saturday. And if she accepted him—she could not see why she would not accept him—then he would be the one, a month from now, for whose sake she would paint the case around herself and let him smash her.

Everything was going to commence at one time with a smash. It was fitting, it seemed impossible and right, that she would be introduced to her completion by something that otherwise was a crime.

Donna Costanza was not at home and so could only be making the passage in the street, pacing monkishly, as she did. Lina's feelings were so severe now, and she knew there were some disclosures Donna Costanza had held back, waiting for today, about what she must do for her husband and what she mustn't ever do to him. Her mother wouldn't do that. Her mother watched more and spoke with her face. But sometimes Lina was betwixt and between, and Donna Costanza could be trusted to explain.

Her father had met with this man, and even kissed the sides of his face, as he must have done to seal the agreement—even though the man was saying in so many words that he was going to lift her clothes off her and touch her underneath. Her mother had given a look that said, It is this way. And nothing else. As though for her father to have to watch as people greeted her on the arm of this man with the horrible laughing knowingness in their eyes, as though her father's simply agreeing to it because it was this way, because it had always been this way, would alleviate his shame.

She could move about freely only because everyone knew to whom she belonged, like a bicycle you might leave unchained anywhere you pleased because a thief would have no place to ride it without being called a thief by everyone who saw him. But now there was a middle time that Donna Costanza, she hoped, might help her with, when her father had relinquished his claim to her and she didn't belong to her father or yet to anyone else.

The married women shouting to each other in the street, and the ratty laundry flapping over her head, and the spoiling fruit in the carts, were all so filthy and pure and perfected because they had all met now. And her mother had shown with her face today that now all of Lina's parts would come suddenly into order, as though a rope was pulled tight.

Once, when she was a child, her mother had sent her to Donna Costanza's garden to pick some leaves off the laurel tree for a stew, but she had misunderstood and had come back with a branch as long as her arm, saying she had been asked for only a little, but, look, she had found so much. And her father had scolded her mercilessly and held her by the scruff of her neck as he conveyed her along Chagrin Avenue with a brush and a pot of tar and showed her how to graft the branch onto the tree again. His intention was to instruct her that as much as possible she must strive to keep things from going to pieces.

On this corner the smoke of coal in a furnace was predominant, on this next corner the smoke of nuts being cooked on a charcoal grill, on this next one the smoke of a barrel of rubbish that the leather-faced madman named Pierangellini was burning to warm himself.

The air was dank and stimulating, and the smallest pellets of water darted through it and pricked her face.

That woman there, hawking a cage of puling piglets from the back of an ice wagon, carried her fat in front of her, in the middle, like a man.

He would put his fingers, washed or unwashed, on whatever part of her he pleased, whenever it pleased him to do it, for the rest of her life, until he should die. Despised by her or no. The fingers intolerable, while she made a face for him to see of something sweet in her mouth. Her body filth-smeared, the body she had scrubbed and polished and hidden away to give only to him.

She needed to say to Donna Costanza, as her mother would, with her face, Everything is coming together at once, yes; but also, Everything has gone to shameful pieces.

Once Lina had explained what had happened and explained her feelings with her face, then Donna Costanza's lips began to twist as though she was struggling to smother a rising sneeze, and her gray and mottled teeth were exposed to the air. It was a face of hatred. But for whom?

Lina wanted to go inside, but Donna Costanza made her stay out, although it had become dark and was cold, and told her to walk along the trench, where the men continued digging in the muck, now by the light of hurricane lamps.

With a look, Lina said she was frightened and ashamed.

But Donna Costanza said that, even so, she must walk along the trench, where the men looked up at her, a pretty young thing at night, accompanied only by a widow carrying a purse and a string of songbirds, tied together at their necks, that she had bought from a boy in the street for their supper.

Now, as she did this, Lina felt no less frightened or ashamed, and with her face she said so. And Donna Costanza, who always spoke aloud and rarely needed to speak with her face, nonetheless this time seemed to say with only the slightest raising of the lids of her eyes: Carmelina, it is this way. You must break. He will recline, perhaps even stinking of alcohol through his skin, and point to a piece of clothing you will be wearing. And you will take it off.

Then, once it had become very cold, Donna Costanza led her away to her house. But she didn't hold Lina's arm, as she otherwise would have done; instead, she walked at a distance off to her right as though in some way Lina had failed her.

The birds were already plucked and singed. It was difficult to say what kind they were. Grackles, she supposed. Donna Costanza roasted them over the fire while Lina chased a housefly around the dining room with a clump of scarf in her fist.

The baker Rocco was in the alley. She saw him in the window. He was holding in place a clapboard that had fallen off the rear of his building, and one of his young sons held a nail while another hammered it with brisk, confident strokes. Snow fell on them.

On the floor of the fireplace, the blackened fat of the birds smoked.

The two women also ate chicory from the yard.

Mrs. Marini was careful to cut away the meat from the legs and breasts of the birds on her plate. However, the distress of spite and the reversal of her hopes had made her ravenous, and she finally ate the ribs, too, cracking them between her jaws and swallowing them, hoping to quell her rioting stomach. They were Umberto's bones, she imagined.

"Father will buy that farm now," Lina said.

Mrs. Marini made a Victrola-cranking motion in the air, meaning it had been many times that she had heard this distasteful song before.

"He can use the dowry money to buy the oxes he needs," Lina said.

"Oxen."

"Oxen. He'll make it up to me. You misunderstand him. He's faithful to us." Lina was terribly overexcited. Her arms had gone white, and the green veins were visible through the skin. Her look was dreamy, but the dream was perhaps the kind in which one does disgusting things and then tries to hide them from the police.

"I find this whole arrangement medieval, frankly," Mrs. Marini said.

Lina looked at her.

"I had hoped you would marry above your station, which the promise of this country makes a reasonable goal," she said. "It's as though I had some priceless stamp and he mailed it."

The fly landed on the table, and Lina at last killed it with her hand.

Mrs. Marini said, "He's sold you cheap, aren't you proud of him?"

"No, please."

"What's its name, your peasant master?"

"Mazzone, Vincenzo. Please don't."

"Your children will misspell your name on your grave now." Mrs. Marini had organized all of the heads of the birds on the lip of her plate so that their beaks hung over the edge, as though straining to peck at the crumbs of bread on the tablecloth.

Her stomach appealed for more.

She knew that soon she would say something indiscreet, unnecessary, and hateful and that later she would feel a modicum of remorse, which she would truss and dispose of like this: *Fatti maschii, parole femine* ("manly deeds, womanly words," the motto of the state of Maryland).

"I expected you would be loud and make a scene but later on you'd be kinder to me," said Lina.

"In fact, I am too disgruntled to raise my voice," Mrs. Marini said. Cattishly she smoothed her thinning hair. "Did you know that two years ago he had it in mind to buy a different farm? But your mother said he must wait until you and your sister were married so that you wouldn't have to be spinsters on a croft once they died. And did you know that he said he intended to go, with you three or without you? That those were his very words? And that your mother and I had to hide the money in another bank to foil him? There's your 'faithful' for you."

The uneaten bird on Lina's plate bathed in its cold juice, on which a skin had formed. "Yes, I did know that," Lina said impatiently.

"And, and, he'd already bought the bell for the cow!"

"No, it was a gift." Lina pulled on a hank of her shapeless hair.

Mrs. Marini was extremely annoyed.

"I know all about that," Lina said. "But it's finished now. And he'll be happy. But I hoped you would say something else. I hoped you . . ." She flushed and her little ears flared.

Two or three more nasty, discrediting revelations percolated against the lid of Mrs. Marini's brain. "Oh, what do you want out of me?" she asked.

The girl's face was open, charming, perfect, utterly stupid, and loving.

"Please don't be disgusted by me," Lina said.

"Why in heavens not?"

Lina rubbed a piece of the fly off her hand with her napkin. She said, in a burst, "Won't you come with me, at least?"

"When?"

"Saturday. When I meet him."

Umberto would be outraged.

"Certainly!" she exclaimed.

As regards making Lina her apprentice, only an hour before Mrs. Marini had believed in the idea passionately, but having thrown herself into action after many months of brooding, only to see competing events turn her intentions awry at the last moment, her resolve, being passionate, cooled and, once Lina had been married for several years, no longer seemed so pressing. For the time being, it even seemed in poor taste, because Lina and Vincenzo were unable to conceive a child.

"Sophist," Nico said in an undertone, but again it was not really him.

Mrs. Marini had lowered herself by a long rope to the floor of the crevasse in her mind. Fungi sprouted from the viscous cavern walls. A yeasty ooze enveloped the feet of her dead, who paced away down here, along with a few unappeasable, carping previous selves. One of them wore a Nico mask, but Nico never came.

"*You're* the child," said the one in the Nico mask. "You're a child, and you've always been a child. You wanted to be the one who prepared the marriage, but you were upstaged. Then you threw a tantrum."

"Impostor," she replied. "Don't think I'm fooled. He was not so smug."

It was really her self of about 1920 who was talking to her, from the period after he had died but before the swerve. It ably wore the dangling jowls of the Nico mask and hoisted up the shaggy brows in mock surprise to emphasize a word as he would do; however, her hair of that time (thick still, but colorless) overflowed the edges of the mask like a frizzled mane.

"She was a glabrous, faithful, sexless thing, which offended you. So as punishment you made her walk where the goons could look up her slip, and then you tried to rake muck about the father. When that didn't satisfy you, you took away the job she didn't know she was about to get."

"You always had to be the one and only," her sister sneered, in a linen smock and *her* leggings, kicking the ooze.

"Why not simply say you changed your mind? I know why. Because you lacked rationale," said the voice in the mask. It was such a compelling impersonation that she wished she were taken in by it. "You insist on rationale. Then your disappointment over the shabby groom presented itself as a distraction you might twist into an excuse."

"You are a petty cuss," her mother said in the dialect of the town of her youth, which Mrs. Marini had had no occasion to speak in fifty years.

Here is how she met her husband.

In her town, in Lazio in 1876, a platoon of soldiers under the new king was squatting in the palace of the duke, who had lately been expelled. The local boys challenged them to a footracing tournament. She was sixteen. Her mother forbade her to go and watch, but she defied her.

The boys and the soldiers ran one-on-one sprints from the palace steps across the weed-ridden square. They were stripped to their undershirts, barefoot for fairness because the soldiers had only their boots and the boys wore light sandals. At the end they ducked their heads in the spray of the fountain. There was a crowd. She would be seen. That someone in the crowd should betray her to her mother may have been her preeminent aim, but no one seemed to notice her.

Two officers—lean, redheaded brothers from Bologna named Marini—faced each other in the championship round. She carried in her pocket a deck of laminated playing cards, a gift from her father's mother that she resolved to present to the winner. However, as it happened, the victor was carried off on the shoulders of his comrades, and instead she gave the cards to his brother.

7

Sixty years later, Mrs. Marini was riding in the rear of a car that crested the last of many gradual slopes and began its descent into the murky predawn countryside of the Cuyahoga River valley. She had not traveled outside the city limits since the summer of 1905, when Nico had taken her on a train to a resort hotel in Sandusky. A quartet had played on a dais in the hotel dining room. All of the better restaurants still employed real musicians at that time. The two of them ate the most succulent galantine of duck, and waded in the lake, and slept under a silk coverlet in a light, airy room.

The old car in which she now rode had once ineptly aspired to the middle class (the imitation marble of the footboards was actually linoleum), but, judging from the racket inside and the indefatigable jolting of the machine at every speed, it had long ago learned its place. However she was not an authority. Lina sat in front, and her Vincenzo guided the car through the mud and gravel of the uneven road. They had been married for seven years.

The car suffered the inclines terribly: The engine made pitiful screams and repented the affectations of its youth and begged Enzo's forgiveness; but he was immune and pressed it onward. Nico, Mrs. Marini recalled, had always treated their horses with humanity and grace.

She wished one of them would turn around and talk to her. Her throat emitted a harsh noise to no avail. The car was a 1924 Buick Roadster. She had tried to forget this useless datum and therefore had failed. In general she considered it extravagant that urban working people should own cars, but this was only a clamorous old thing with rubber patching in the canopy, and Enzo did the repairs to it himself. The young couple lived in a two-bedroom hot-water apartment, a clean place of recent construction in Elephant Park, five blocks from her house. The three of them often went on excursions to hear live music played or so that Mrs. Marini could buy Lina something pretty downtown, while Enzo smoked in the department store lounge and studied the newspaper. Enzo offered to drive but always eventually deferred to her preference for the trolley.

Since Lina and Enzo had no children still, their expenses were modest. Lina maintained her position at the overcoat shop on Twenty-fourth Street, and Enzo's talent for staying employed in the present time of hardship, which had produced a boomlet in Mrs. Marini's own business, was remarkable.

They were heading to the wretched grape farm so that Enzo and Lina could help Lina's father trim the wretched vines and Mrs. Marini could confer with Patrizia, who had sent so many invitations through Lina for Mrs. Marini to pay a visit that she had begun to disregard them, with continually greater ease, until the previous week, when Lina implied (it not being her practice to speak directly of interesting things) that an urgent matter had arisen and her mother, who had no telephone, required Mrs. Marini's advising right away. Her egoism thus engaged, Mrs. Marini agreed at once. Lina did not, on examination, seem to know what the matter was.

Mrs. Marini tilted her eyeglasses so that the stems pinched her temples and the image outside came into focus. She had hoped that a hardy agricultural scene would alleviate her present cynicism, but what she beheld was not agriculture. Agriculture was the domination of a landscape by the hand of man. What she saw were budding woods that crowded to the edges of every open place as though a barricade held them back from the orchards and the shorn acres of pale, busted stalks and mud. (It was April.) Every meadow, in its squareness, manifested a persistent human attention. It was evident out here that Ohio had recently been a single, dense forest, open only where the rivers drained it, and would rather be so again. Even from the faces of the bluffs, the trees protruded, laterally. She was living in a barely domesticated country. Certainly there were those who found, in the same scene, a grid of cornfields plundering the poor, wild trees, but her priorities were the other way around. Savages and sylvan paradises did not interest her, even in literature. She was a city girl. She wanted to read about civilized people corrupting one another. She did not want your Zane Grey. Give her a swimming pool, and it's poisoned. Setting was ancillary. Who poisoned the swimming pool? That was what she wanted to know.

Yet as the trip wore on she perceived in spite of herself a more and more powerful intuition of, of—what was the word? she was unsure there was a word—of here-ness. Providence had brought us here, to this of all places, to our remote country. No, but it had nothing to do with the Constitution or the Battle of Bull Run. History, politics, culture, those were her mind's milieus, and they could not have been more impertinent to this queer intuition, which was neither purely a product of her thoughts nor of the place itself. Fog rose from an anfractuous river that flickered through the beams of a covered bridge they crossed. The spirit of the place pressed itself against her senses, but she was not the kind of creature that was capable of letting it in, of becoming an unconscious part of a vast, unconscious whole. The result was a feeling of sharp physical pain at the base of her neck that rose up the back of her skull, as though a malignant hand were petting her. She was separated, by virtue of being a conscious animal, from the rest of creation, which was unknowing and therefore complete, and therefore irrevocably real. The trees were both in the place and of it. But to *know* that one was *here* was to be an awareness amid the limitless unaware; it was to be in a place but never of it, like a pearl in a cake.

"Enzo!" she said. It was nearly impossible to make oneself heard over the engine.

"Here I am for you," he said.

"Enzo, stop the machine. I want to be sick."

There was only one lane and no shoulder, but he stopped the car immediately, obstructing the road. No one approached from either direction. He opened the door, but she did not let him help her out. Lina pulled down her window, making mewling syllables of concern.

Mrs. Marini walked in the clover toward a fence where some sheep were feeding. The cold and the pervasive, brisk smell of manure re-freshed her. The morning had broken completely, and the sun shone all over the sprouting grass in the sheepfold and over the sheep, three of whom trotted out to regard her more closely. Then the rest of them followed. There were about twenty. Enzo stood nearby, his one hand hovering trepidatiously in case a part of her clothes should need to be pulled away from her vomit. In the other hand, he held the strap of her purse, which he had brought from the car.

"What may I do?" he said. He wore a stiff jacket Lina had made for him out of the stuffing of an old chair and a piece of canvas. The collar was half turned up in a rakish way, but it was his only vanity.

Across the meadow, at the edge of the trees, three men in heavy clothes tore the mossy shingles from the roof of a barn.

In fact, Mrs. Marini did not feel nausea and had not felt it before, but it would have been inefficient to explain herself, so she didn't answer him. The pain in the back of her head left her.

"Hello, you little thing," she said to a lamb with a black face.

One of the men wrenched a portion of the old tin flashing from the bottom of the chimney and threw it to the ground.

The lamb quivered on its tiny legs; it couldn't have been a month old. It ducked its head under a ewe's stomach and nursed while it and the mother both looked upon her with the agreeable, crazed eyes of sheep.

"Little Molly," she said. "Aw."

The lamb fell to its knees, then got up again and faced her and spoke its brief word.

Lina said, "She isn't sick."

"Yes, I am," Mrs. Marini protested.

"Oh, not so badly. Let's get a move on." Marriage had tapped the honey from Lina's blood, which was gratifying to see.

Mrs. Marini was not, of course, under the delusion that she had communicated with the lamb, who was only a lamb, after all, whereas she was an old person, from whom so many of those who were once close to her were now absent that it was arguable whether they were all alive and she was the dead one.

She gripped a rail of the fence and made herself laugh.

"See?" Lina said. "Here we go. Chop chop."

They got back into the car.

"I'm starved. I could have eaten that one you were talking to," Lina said. She had grown flatteringly thicker, too.

"Your mother will have some coffee and oats, I expect."

Enzo made a shiver. His bowels did not tolerate whole grains.

Soon they arrived.

Umberto Montanero had grown a dense and handsome beard. The rigid hairs were black, brown, gray, white, and red, and extended to his breast pockets. The whiskers about his mouth were not stained by tobacco or food and did not hide his lips. The flanks were combed, the bottom corners neatly rounded; a cleavage ran up the middle (the chin whiskers were shorter than the rest). It was as though he wore an elegant jacket about his face. He had welded a miniature sickle for cutting twine to a steel ring that he wore on his thumb. He accepted Lina's and Enzo's kisses and greeted Mrs. Marini in formal language, making the slightest inclination of his torso in her direction—a satirical bow, a masterpiece of contempt. He took a drink from the pump, and blessed his groundwater, and the morning, and his own good health, and Saint Joseph, and his sound old boots that kept his socks dry.

Lina said they would be out to help him once they had changed their clothes.

"That's all very well," he said. His pruning shears were fitted with a spring; he snapped them shut and they popped open again with a decisive screech that seemed to give him courage.

They were standing in the mouth of the barn. A rabbit leapt from the open window of a dead car that lay on its side under the dripping hayloft. The vineyards were immaculate, but the house, the barn, the coop, and Patrizia herself—who emerged from behind the car as three more rabbits fled a branch that she methodically wagged over the packed dirt of the floor—were in squalor.

"Close the gate!" she cried.

"And may you be blessed, too, madam, even you!" Umberto said,

indicating Mrs. Marini with his shears and slamming the low gate behind their backs. "And may the Lord sustain me, but only so far as I can
throw my spit. And may he bless even you!"

He swallowed his phlegm.

Patrizia, the indispensable companion of Mrs. Marini's middle age,
whom she had dropped, closed her in her stinking embrace.

Mrs. Marini had never relented in her devotion to the sacraments,
but she was not a Christian.

Umberto stalked into the vineyard. Enzo and Lina followed shortly,
and the two old women were left alone in the house.

The farm was in an unincorporated township on an unpaved state
highway in Ashtabula County, near the border with Pennsylvania. The
northwesterly winds that crossed Lake Erie from Canada moderated
the summer heat and insulated the region from the first autumn cold
snaps, producing a long, temperate growing season conducive to grape
farming. During the first months of winter, the winds became saturated
with moisture as they passed over the comparatively warm surface of
the lake, so that the region received three to four times the early winter
precipitation of the inland towns and the cities to the west and was
nearly always under profound snow by New Year's Day. Then the lake
froze.

Prohibition had compelled many of the farmers there to dig out their
vineyards and turn them over to corn or pastureland. The others had
replanted them with table grapes, principally Concords, as the previous
owner of Umberto and Patrizia's property had done. Umberto sold the
crop to a jelly manufacturer in Geneva, when they had a crop to sell.
Owing to consistent cloud cover the previous summer, the sugar yield
of the grapes wasn't even enough to pay the migrant pickers' wages, so
they had let a year's work rot on the vine.

As soon as the others had gone out, Patrizia retrieved a portfolio
from the cellar. All of the documents in it had been folded many times
sloppily, as though they had been stowed in a pant pocket. Patrizia

had never learned to read. She would like to know precisely what they said, please.

Several hours of deliberate study ensued. Mrs. Marini read aloud and translated. Patrizia tersely paraphrased and asked whether she had the right idea.

Owing to arrears in the payment of their mortgage, the bank owned a lien on the property. Owing to arrears in their taxes, the county owned another one.

Patrizia was unimpressed and unsurprised. In some of the documents she made a series of diagonal folds, a filing code that Mrs. Marini presumed her husband would not notice.

There was a four-year-old auction receipt for a mule, which they had lately butchered and eaten. In this she made a simple lengthwise crease across the middle and flattened it out again.

"What does that one mean?" Mrs. Marini asked.

Patrizia made a gesticulation. It meant, Into the fire, but later.

They broke for a snack.

"We never eat such piquant cheese anymore," Patrizia said, as what Enzo had brought them from the city today. And her happiness in splitting it with her front teeth was an example of the superior power of the senses over the mind.

A decisive period emphasized each of the pores of her nose. Her unglossed fingernails flaked. Few of her molars remained, and she managed to mash the cheese using her tongue and palate, with the lumbering, mute physical dignity that Mrs. Marini had always admired.

To explain her desire to have the portfolio read to her would not have been Patrizia's way, and Mrs. Marini didn't care to know any more than was self-evident—namely, that they were ruined but that Umberto had withheld the details from her. In fact, being occupied with a demonstration of her command of a complex subject (money), Mrs. Marini didn't care to think of anything else and was quite free of sympathy. This was invigorating, as always, but inappropriate. She wished she weren't aware that it was inappropriate, but she was. As recently as two years ago she could have made herself unaware with an act of will, but the worm had turned again.

The unshameable egoism of the years following the swerve had been invented by a woman who had expected to die soon. Naturally, at the time she had believed it was more in the line of a discovery than an invention, but anyway it had restored her. Death was no longer interesting. Through the influence of her current intimates, who were two generations her junior and had immediate, present-day concerns, she had begun again to ask herself what would happen next. The fraudulent Nico voices, spirits of the middle past, squawked at her less incessantly. Instead the further past came calling—seldom, but in terrible blows.

In the deep past, as in the current moment, this exuberant *I* was like a fat person that stood close in front of where she sat, obstructing her view of anything but its own backside.

In the afternoon, the two women went out onto the porch.

Mrs. Marini asked whether Umberto's cousins often came from Youngstown to help with her harvest.

"Yes, sometimes," Patrizia said, suspending a rabbit from a hook in the overhang, its blood dripping into a bowl on the concrete slab of the porch. The porch was the only obviously sound structure of the house. Enzo had poured it. There was not a square angle to be seen anywhere else.

"I suppose there's a crowd," Mrs. Marini said, "a reunion atmosphere, and the latrine gets clogged."

Patrizia sighed.

Mrs. Marini looked at her.

Do not look away from me! said the sigh. You were the closest friend I had in the world, and my husband dragged me out to this godforsaken place, where we don't even have a toilet inside, where you knew I never wanted to come. I liked canasta on a Thursday night, like you. And you have let seven years pass without a single word. You could have said, "Enzo, let me come with you when you visit your mother-in-law. She must be lonely." But you forsook me.

Patrizia cut the animal from its throat to its anus, then around the neck and the ankles, and ripped away its hide.

There's no point in dressing properly, said the woman's face. I have to listen to Berto and his idiotic plans and his raving about the eggs that are an hour out of the hen and the yolks are red, like they're supposed to be. What difference does it make? Eggs all taste the same. Think of what I have for conversation here. Think of all the talking we used to have. Look at this house. Look at the paint coming off. We can't afford paint. We don't have time to paint. See the barn? See how it leans? A stiff breeze could knock it to a heap of boards on the ground. And I wish it would. I pray for that. We are bankrupt, and I am so glad! You thought we were poor before. And you left me here without even a little talking now and again.

"No more," Mrs. Marini said to herself.

The records accompanying the deed showed that the Montaneros were the fifth owners of the property since the state of Connecticut had sold its colonial reserve (a 120-mile-long tract still called the Connecticut Western Reserve that formed the northeast corner of Ohio) to the Connecticut Land Company, in 1796. Why, what an unlikely piece of information! She could read it all right here in the cheery brochure from the real estate company.

Patrizia hacked the rabbit into pieces. Mrs. Marini got up and searched the purlieus of the house for dandelions to eat in the salad.

"The vineyards are so sharp and pretty," she said to Patrizia, who was washing the pieces of the rabbit at the hand pump by the barn.

Patrizia shook off the meat over the grass. Indistinctly she pronounced a single English word.

"Beg pardon?" Mrs. Marini said.

"Herbicide," Patrizia repeated.

Mrs. Marini washed the greens at the pump. It was incredible that water so cold was not frozen.

Patrizia made a pouch of her apron and bounced the rabbit parts in it to dry them, and faced Mrs. Marini as if she were speaking. A kerchief imprecisely contained her nappy hair. She had used to flatten it with an iron. Her face was utterly sad and in conflict. It said, You have not understood at all.

They went into the house. Patrizia browned the meat in grease and covered it in grape vinegar and simmered it on the stove. She went outside and honked the horn on Enzo's car to let them know to come in for supper soon.

Mrs. Marini flattened the morning crossword on the table. Through the window, she saw Patrizia slam the car door and trudge, in unlaced work boots, through a depression of mud. Her body tottered like that of a man carrying a pail of water with one hand. Her breasts hung to her stomach. She was not wearing a brassiere. Mrs. Marini thought, I have committed a crime.

The sun fell into the frame of the window in the opposite wall. The young vineyard leaves were inky blue and still, and she was struck by the resemblance here to the view from her grandmother's pantry, where a single window had overlooked a monotonous repetition of vineyard rows down a hillside. There was even a stump in the foreground, as there had been years ago, where the old woman's lemon tree had grown.

Patrizia came in and slipped on her house shoes. Several sickening minutes passed as they did not speak, and Patrizia clapped a heavy knife resoundingly against the chopping board.

Mrs. Marini put down her pencil. She opened and closed her hands to stretch her creaking fingers. Outside, the hypnotizing rows of vines led straight and shimmering from the house, as neat as a typescript, and seemed even to meet under the sun, at the distant end of the woods.

At the train station in 1879, with one suitcase, with one bottle of water, waiting for the train, looking at the vast country, the terraced hills, the vineyards on the plain. If she had told anyone they would have locked her in a room. Running away to marry a man she had talked to three times, the loser of a footrace. I will never see them again. I will never see this place, ever again. Unable to find Ohio on a map, thinking, Maybe he meant Iowa, Iowa is right here, in the middle. Never having looked at the hills with anything but angry boredom, until today. One suitcase. One bottle of water. Never to see her mother or father again.

The silence went on too long, then continued.

Had they been strangers, if Mrs. Marini were lost on a country road and came in to ask directions, there would have been no disconcerting minutes while she thought of what she might say to ease the moment into familiar idleness or to bring about the crisis of saying the hidden thing out loud. With a stranger, one introduces oneself and transacts one's business plainly.

Waiting at the train station to be a stranger to everyone. Waiting for the train to come and looking at the hills and actually stepping off the platform, back into the weeds. Maybe she could make it home without anyone noticing that she'd left. To have time to linger on the terrace of her father's house and record each detail of the view, the elephantine limbs of the chestnut trees, the missing roof tiles, a view worth recording. Time to consider. Time to keep the promise she'd made to cut her sister's hair. The weeds around the platform bending against her legs. What if this man beat her up? Who was she to go to where there was no one who understood the private language of her town, which even he didn't speak? From inside the station, the eyes of the man who had sold her the ticket peeking out, a man she knew only in passing, who wondered, perhaps, why this girl was standing so still in the weeds around the platform. The expanse of sky. Her sisters would inherit her things. The light sparkling on the slag between the train tracks. With one suitcase.

Maybe Patrizia likes it here. Who knows?

They used to converse with only their eyes, as women will do among young children. Patrizia had had a gift for identifying what Mrs. Marini had eaten last by the way she held her cards during canasta, how often she reorganized her hand.

"You are so exasperating," she complained to the wrecked crossword.

Patrizia stared spiritlessly into a saucepan.

Mrs. Marini stood to set the table. She had given up. She was through.

She opened the cupboard and recognized the gaudy china she had given away. She said, "I forget. Which glasses do you use?"

Eventually to forget the names of the streets. Leaving now meant never coming back. Wanting to keep in her brain the exact words her mother had used in forbidding her to go to the race but having already forgotten them. Wanting to keep the shrillness of the woman's voice; though, remarkably, she could not call it to mind even now. One bottle of water. Phrasing the telegram she would send in New York to the man who'd said that he would wait for her, a man she would never have met if his brother had been ever so minutely slower of foot. Stepping on and then back off the platform. Then turning and seeing that nobody else was waiting there for the train. Nobody else was checking the clock. To her right, the opening in the trees from where the train would come; to her left, the opening where it would go away. To leave now meant that this was the last picture she would have of the place in her mind, that she would always think of it as looking the way it did that afternoon, and her mother, father, sisters, brothers, aunts, as looking just the way they had at lunch that day. None of these people would ever die. They would be fixed in Lazio, in time. She would send no address. She would receive no news. To leave now was to keep them.

"Umberto wants to go home," Patrizia said.

"Marvelous," Mrs. Marini said. "We'll make a party. I'll get all the best things. You can stay with me until you get a house."

"His brother in Sicily died. There weren't any children, so Berto inherited the house. I use the ones with the cherries on them," she said, pointing into the cupboard.

"Which house? In Siracusa? What do you mean?"

"It's like the last time."

"Which last time?"

"With me or without me."

"Oh, I see."

"With me or without me."

"And then?"

"Or the teacups. It doesn't matter."

"But it's not our affair," Enzo said. "It's not our thing to decide."

"It's not, excuse me," Lina said, "it's not his to decide, either."

Umberto cut a leg off the rabbit and passed it to Lina.

Enzo said, "We cannot—"

"You're a married man, who, therefore—what a burden—can't just act like he's eighteen and move to another country because he *feels* that way," Lina said. "Because—what a *weight*, what a *pity*—he has a wife and a family and a house."

"But I have another house," he said.

Mrs. Marini said, "Twenty-four years."

"Because," Lina said, "excuse me, but there is a person at this table who never wanted to come to this country in the first place. But *you* said she was coming, so she came. And who never—Mother never wanted to move out to this paradise of donkey labor in the first place, but you said she was going. And she went without a word of complaint. Not a groan. Nothing."

Enzo stood up and spooned the pasta into the bowls.

"Why don't you say something, Mother?"

"Donna Costanza, do you want more of this sauce?" Enzo asked.

"Don't raise your voice to your father," Patrizia said.

Mrs. Marini put her thumb and forefinger together. She said, "A bit, thank you."

Umberto said, "Where's that cheese?"

"Look at your wife seven years ago," Lina said.

The plate of cheese was passed from hand to hand.

"Things happen between married people that you don't understand them from the outside," Enzo said. "As you know."

"Twenty-four years, Berto," Mrs. Marini said.

Patrizia chewed. Her hands sat in her lap. She looked at her food.

"Look at Mother seven years ago," Lina said, "and look at her now."

Outside, Mrs. Marini could see that the sun had gone down. The vineyard was dim. There was a stripe of pink left in the sky.

"My wife didn't say why she's not coming," Umberto said. "She's welcome to come. Tell them why, Patrizia, go ahead."

"Welcome," Mrs. Marini said, "is a word you use for strangers who want to come into your house."

"Tell them. Speak."

"Will you pass that cheese?" Patrizia asked.

"Answer me."

"I don't want you to go."

"That's it. No other . . . thinking. No 'I like this here,' 'I prefer that here.' Just 'I don't want you to go.'"

"This rabbit came out nice," Patrizia said, "if I say it myself."

"If you like rabbits, we can get rabbits."

"If you prefer for us not to discuss this," Enzo said, "if it's a private thing."

Patrizia swallowed. "It's a little stringy, but it was the biggest one."

"If you want me to drop it, Mother—but no, I won't," Lina said.

"There is room in my house for both of us and rabbits and visitors," Umberto said.

Mrs. Marini said, *"My* is what you call your house when you are an unmarried person or your spouse has died."

"No, go ahead, talk," Patrizia said. "This cheese is beautiful, or else I'm just deprived."

"You see? You see what she does?" Umberto said. "It's good cheese, Vincenzo, thank you."

"Why should she have to give reasons?" Lina said.

Enzo picked up his loin of rabbit and headed toward the door to the back porch.

Umberto addressed his plate with bewilderment. "This is my own child who speaks in such tones to her father."

Enzo stopped in the doorway.

"And who's going to wash your floor," Lina said, "and cook your supper and trim your beard?"

Umberto tapped a thick steel serving spoon against the table and closed his eyes.

Enzo went back to the table and sat down.

"It's a natural thing that when a man is old, he wants to go back to his home. Your aunt will have to find someplace else to go. That house has been my property for a thousand years." He tapped the spoon on the edge of Lina's plate.

Patrizia fixed her eyes on Umberto, and Mrs. Marini could see, for the first time, something icy in her face.

Lina put her hands under the table and pushed her body into the back of her chair, slowly. She moved her tongue across her teeth.

"You'll see," Umberto said. The spoon *tap-tap*ped against Lina's plate. "This Enzo will want to go back, too. Give him some years. He wants the sea, the *la-de-la*"—the *tap, tap, tap* of the spoon—"the songs, his father's house that belongs to him."

Enzo was watching Umberto and his lips disappeared into his mouth. He may have begun to stand up again, because he looked pre-ternaturally tall. He loomed over the table. His right eye strayed to the side. It gave Mrs. Marini the impression that he was watching everything in the room at once.

"Your mother's dead, Berto, and your father, and your brothers," Mrs. Marini said. "There's only your sister-in-law, whom you will un-house. All of your friends are over here."

He adjusted his grip on the spoon.

Enzo's one eye watched Lina's plate while the other leered out the window.

There was something bare but restrained in the way Patrizia was watching her husband.

Lina didn't move.

Enzo picked up the dish in which the carcass of the rabbit was sitting and stalked to Umberto's side of the table. "Say, Papa," he said, "why don't you give me that spoon now. I want to soak it."

It was dark outside. The image in the window had flipped: It was a reflection of the five of them, at the table, waiting.

Waiting for the train, looking behind herself. Thinking that in this way everything would remain as it was on that afternoon, that they would always be there—but knowing that this was a lie and that someday she would admit to it. That she had left her mother and father, that she had allowed them to die or killed them. Then looking at the chestnut trees down the track and around. And, God forgive her, stepping back onto the platform. Then a puff of smoke over the trees, the scream of the train. The train swerving into view.

And later—in her kitchen on Twenty-sixth Street, in the house she'd shared for thirty years with this man who was her consolation, her right arm, her pearl of great price—the timer went off, and she opened the oven door. She called to him in the parlor. She said, "Nico, wheel yourself in here and carve the roast." Waiting a minute, but he didn't answer. She didn't turn to go into the parlor (but she knew he was in there, reading on the sofa). The wet air smelled of cloves and pork. She stood in front of the oven, saying it louder, saying his name, louder, and waiting. From the gaping mouth of the oven, the heat rose to her face.

8

They left the farm.

Everything was radiantly black and oily outside the car. Lina drove, and Enzo directed her incorrectly, and soon they were lost in the southern part of the county, where much of the land was fallow and saplings grew from the gutters of the dark houses. The road was too narrow for the car, which straddled it crookedly, two wheels on the grassy embankment, two in the single rut down its middle. In fact, it was little more than a path fixing the boundary between many miles of adjacent farms. Dung littered it. In places the trees on either side approached so close to it that their branches met in the air overhead, like the arch of a narrow tunnel.

Dogs scattered from the corpse of another dog as the headlights struck them. Lina had no choice but to slow down and run it over.

"Holy Mary, the stench," Enzo said.

A little while later he was sick, and lay down with his head in her lap.

"You only want to drive," she said.

His nose in her skirt, he inhaled deeply.

It was one of his peculiarities that he could break a bone without sentiment but when he was nauseated he demanded comforting from her openly.

She touched his hair.

He muttered an endearment into her clothes.

"All I could hope is that I embarrassed him," she said, meaning her father.

"That spoon," he slurred, picking at his eyes. He was so miserable.

"The spoon was for show," Lina said.

Enzo rolled onto his back, looking up at her wretchedly, and pointed at his mouth and pointed at the window, but she knew that he didn't really want her to stop the car.

He had strained to make his strabismic eye look forward while he ate with her father, and now the muscles needed to be rested. She had learned his system, as Donna Costanza had said she must do. Often she knew what he wanted better than he knew it himself.

She glanced down at him as he wrapped his arms around his shoulders snugly and closed his black eyes.

She knew, for instance, that his desire to have a son was terrible. It was like a wraith that followed close behind him and that he could hear but never see (only she saw it). He would never admit that it was really there. He no longer wrote letters to his parents, having no children to report and no interest in describing himself. Excepting Donna Costanza, he was the only person she knew without a single relative in the United States. She was supposed to have made him one and had failed. She was probably also supposed to be ashamed of having failed, but she was only a little ashamed at feeling so unashamed of it. She thought she must be very cold. Sometimes she thought she should make a show of her regret and beat herself softly with a heavy spoon out of solidarity with him, but his feelings were genuine; she admired them; the wraith was a formidable creature; it remembered his ancestors and feared his death for him. It seemed right to her that he should be haunted this way and stupid that she should ever try to interfere with it by pretending to be haunted herself.

"If your father hadn't kept you out so late, we might have left in the daylight," Mrs. Marini shouted from the rear.

Enzo sat up. "We went there to work," he told her.

"Don't defend him. He's—he's a cannibal!"

"No, he is a farmer," Enzo responded.

"We better find a quicker way to get out there," Lina said. "She won't ever leave now."

"Well, that's so," Mrs. Marini said.

"Why shouldn't she?" Enzo asked.

"Revenge," Lina said.

"Hell hath no fury, and so on," said Mrs. Marini.

In a cynical voice that was unlike him, Enzo said, "Why should he care? How will he know? Will she send him photos?"

"God will know," said Lina.

"God will know," Mrs. Marini repeated.

"That isn't revenge. That's just what-do-you-call."

"Spite—," Mrs. Marini said.

There was a hole in the floor of the car. Enzo had cut it with a hacksaw and planted the gearshift in it when he had replaced the transmission the month before. The hole was overwide for its purpose and exposed the interior, by a circuitous route through the undercarriage, to the open road.

Suddenly a shard of gravel shot up through the hole and ricocheted against two of the windows, cracking them.

Lina felt something formless and gratifying settle over her brain.

"Ooh!" Mrs. Marini shrieked. "What was that?"

"A stone!" Enzo said.

Lina watched the road. She had foreclosed the false hope of having a child. It wasn't hard to do because it was false, and it was false because she had never cared very much to have a child, and she had never cared to have a child because there was a part of her that was supposed to be there and wasn't (she didn't miss it), but it was a hope because Enzo hoped for it, and she felt his feelings.

"I said, what was that?"

"A stone," Enzo repeated.

"He said it was a stone," Lina said.

The cracks in the windows weren't serious, they were nicks. One of them was on the passenger side, the other in the windshield.

Then it came to Lina that the stone was sitting sort of proudly on the dash; and that it had struck her nose, high up near the eye, on the left side, where the others couldn't see it, and a welt was growing, and she was slightly cross-eyed.

She picked up the stone. It was a kind of reward. She started to announce it to the others, but then she changed her mind and put it in her pocket.

Enzo stuffed his scarf and one of his gloves around the gap at the base of the gearshift, cursing the expense of replacing the glass once the cracks spread.

Mrs. Marini poked her face over the seat and jabbed her finger toward the hole in the floor while she shielded her eyes from it with her pocketbook. "We could have been killed! And all because you were too cheap to buy the collar for that thing!"

Lina blinked and blinked again. Her vision corrected itself.

They found the state highway, and she aimed the car at the setting moon.

As they entered the city, they approached a stop sign in front of a boarded-up dry goods store, where a woman sat on a valise on the curb. Her clothes enveloped her so heavily that at first it was impossible to see that she was carrying a baby behind her in a sling. She stood as they reached the stop, rattling a tin can and opening her mouth to let her thick tongue out. Then she smacked Enzo's window with the can. The child was big and asleep, utterly unresponsive to its mother's erratic movements. She did not produce any comprehensible words.

"Slattern!" Mrs. Marini said.

"Go away! You'll break the glass," Enzo said.

"Malingerer!" Mrs. Marini shouted, banging with her knuckles on the window.

Lina sped through the intersection. The momentum carried them to the crest of an incline. She shifted the transmission into neutral, and the car sailed down the Eleventh Avenue hill, into Elephant Park.

They saw Mrs. Marini to her door and went home.

Enzo had left the apartment windows open in the morning, and now all the rooms were cool and damp, but they left the windows as they were; it was the first spring night that year warm enough for sleeping in the fresh air. They took off their clothes and pulled back the linens of the bed and lay down. The mattress was new and hard. The starch in the sheets and pillow slips was fresh.

She was alone with him at last.

Soon after Lina was married, she had put on fifteen pounds. She had done it deliberately—with a boiled egg before bedtime and a sweet pastry from Rocco's every afternoon—in an unsuccessful effort to become pregnant. She had been indifferent to eating for so long that she had wrecked her ovaries, it seemed. Donna Costanza said that was probably what she had done. "Or else you bought a faulty stag," she chortled.

Anyway, Lina was pretty now. She really was. She had had the luck to collect her new weight where it was most in need: in her hips, backside, bust, fingers, and cheeks—which had always been depressed before but now were convex, as though the heads of two spoons were turned upside down.

Marriage had exposed her true figure, but this was only the most obvious of many unexpected changes, some of them quite abstruse, that it had brought about and that she herself didn't notice until events made them self-evident.

She damned her father to hell, and felt the rightness of this deeply, and would have said it to his face if she had gone to see him again—which she refused to do—before he left for Siracusa that summer.

She was cheerful, attentive, direct, nervous only regarding her hair, which was too fine to hold a permanent wave and was prone to knots and wrinkling. Her signature on a check was compact, loopless, leftward slanting, distinctive but illegible. Her command of the cursive zs was poor, so that no two of them were identical, the first always improved upon by the second, which pleased her.

The overcoat shop went under. These days she did piecework at home—draperies—for a Jew in Fort Saint Clair. She didn't have to work at the kitchen table, at least, as her mother used to do among the corsets that she would sell to a wholesaler downtown. Instead there was a spare bedroom where Enzo had built dummy rods in all the walls so that she could hang the drapes and see what she was doing. Earlier, he had stenciled the walls with a design that was supposed to be a toy locomotive but looked more like a steaming pot on trivets. The single window looked out on the creek and the trolley stop across the bridge, so she could watch for him coming home. She could also see Bastianazzo's from here, and the men going in for newspapers and coffee. There was no one to talk to in the little room, so she listened to the radio. She had never been alone very often before, and now when she went among other people she felt simultaneously relaxed and invigorated by the contrast with the way she spent her days. Her own income was modest, but Enzo was foreman now, and, anyway, having no children they could afford to eat well and sometimes go to a concert. They were in good stars to have any income at all these days, as Enzo said.

Doors open before you on their own once you have found your true figure, her mother said. She said it in a gesture: They were at the farm a couple of years before her father betrayed them. Her mother brushed her hands down Lina's rounded sides with pleasure as Lina was leaving, and then, although no wind could be heard, the storm door blew open spookily. Her mother pointed at it and said, "See what you can do?" Donna Costanza, on the other hand, was more indelicate and said to her while they were walking in the crowd at the Assumption feast, "You're more striking now that you're someone's meat."

Lina's digestion was magnificent. If she wanted, she could eat fresh curds and then a grapefruit and go ride the trolley.

This, while her Enzo's intestines rebelled against nuts, ice cream, even apple skins. When they went to a show, he bought her a lemonade and a chocolate bar from the concessioner, but nothing for sale there sat well with his stomach, so he smoked throughout the picture to blunt his hunger and bit the heel of his hand with pity at the climax and shouted.

On their way home, at Bastianazzo's, where they would stop, he drank a demitasse of baking-soda water along with his coffee. She loved him. His suffering and shame (he had little schooling, and the accent of his English was inept, and he desired a son with every breath; he was thirty-three) were almost invisible and therefore were to her mysterious, perhaps infinite, and he approached, wanting her and no one else.

She was not a woman in a dream anymore. She was no longer Carmelina, daughter of Montanero, waiting to be the wife of someone and the mother of someone. Her name was Carmelina Mazzone. She was the wife of that man there, Mazzone, Vincenzo. She was definite, like letters on a page. And her mother looked at her as if to say, You are all turned out now, you are completed.

The eyes of others didn't pass over her face obliviously, like before; they stopped, as if caught.

As when a gust blew open her overcoat while she was carrying a heavy bag across a bridge, and the blouse beneath the coat was thin, and her hardened nipples showed through the fabric . . .

Someone loitering on the bridge, looking down at the current, glances up and sees when she passes behind him. His helpless eyes are caught. He is tall, extraordinarily white of face, impeccably shaven. He wears a dark worsted-wool coat, a small red book poking out of the pocket.

She is carrying an onion sack on her back, and he takes notice of this. Snow falls. What a day to be out of doors in a coat that won't stay closed.

She passes him, and his poor eyes are snagged, his neck slightly twisted behind him. She was always hypothetical before to him, a faceless notion, but now she's real, present, irrefragable, distinct. He watches her go. He may elect to follow her.

He does not know her name. But she is right there. There is no missing or mistaking or misgiving.

How it thrills him to think of another person at last, and not of himself. To begin a sentence with *She*. To be awake.

There. A woman with a sack on her back.

She crosses the street. Her coat has come open again. Catch her while she catches you. She won't last.

Before too long Lina would become yet another person, with another name, of her own devising—similar to the current, married one, essentially a translation, more in line with the names of the people among whom she would find herself. However, she was not among them yet, and in the meantime she had every reason to believe that Carmelina Mazzone was permanent. She had no cause to suspect that all of this was only an interlude.

The man on the bridge watches her ascending the hill. She is stooped by the weight of an enormous sack on her back, so touchingly like a mule, like an enduring animal that slowly carries on its back a burden as large as itself.

It would be impossibly sweet and satisfying to follow her. The sweetness of saying "she" is the intimation of somebody else, of something else that's really out there being real, that isn't an idea or a ghost but a person, definite, completed.

But he's watching her now. He can't not. And while he watches her, he is turning her back into an idea, so he must act fast. She has already begun to disappear.

Mrs. Marini proposed to make Lina an apprentice in her business. Lina decided she would do it so long as Enzo didn't disapprove. He did disapprove, however. He believed it would curse their children, it being unclear only to him that they could never have any children. He was rather innocent. He had even believed that Mrs. Marini still made her living off the interest from her husband's shoes. Still, he was within his rights, and Lina turned her down. They might have been rich. Instead she was stuck with her drapes.

That was in November of the year 1936. It was the winter Pierangellini, the madman, was found at the dump in a crypt of newspapers.

The coroner's determination of the cause of death was celebrated: He had eaten the head of a broom.

"You wonder if he cooked it first," Enzo said two days after Christmas, knotting his boot strings on the kitchen floor while Lina hastily fried their breakfast eggs.

"No, the papers would have caught fire," she said authoritatively.

They had slept through the alarm. They ate out of the skillet, standing over the stove and haphazardly pulling on their clothes. They rushed out. At the trolley stop, before Enzo got on the inbound, he reproached her for underdressing.

Lina took a bus to the warehouse in Fort Saint Clair, where she delivered a week of her work wrapped in brown parcel paper and was paid $7.45. The woman who gave her the material for the next job surely didn't sew herself; she had allowed her nails to grow down over the tips of her fingers.

Because Lina had been late, she had no choice of jobs and was saddled for the ride home with fourteen yards of damask and heavy chenille fabric, which she carried away in a big, awkward, burlap, vegetable bag.

The Forest Runner

Decades of insomnia have taught him that when he's tired—and he was up reading past two o'clock this morning, he is terribly tired—the best palliative is to be precise in his appearance. The cowl makes the monk. He shaves along and then against the grain. With tweezers he picks the stray hairs from his coat. He shines his Sunday shoes and threads new laces through the eyelets. He strides soundlessly on the thick carpet of the red stairs, holding the rail firmly while he goes to enforce in his mind this sense of private formality, and he feels the consummateness of one who stands erect although no one sees him. His spirit is a pure, cold gas.

At the breakfast table, his sister pours out his tea. The dining room is suspended in kerosene light and damp heat. It is a redoubt of civilization carved from the barrens of a northern Ohio midwinter morning, hours before sunrise. They live in the house where they were born, on the West Side, on the lakeshore. Great rough-cut, whitewashed stone, four chimneys. He had a gang of Poles in last year to wire it for electric lights, but they haven't caught the habit of using them. Their father is dead, their mother, too.

The date is December 27, 1936. He is fifty-four. His sister is fifty-five. Neither married. They are homely people, and reserved. He still runs the jewelry store downtown that his grandfather opened in 1886; meantime, his sister tends the house. She was created, he has come to believe, to sustain things; he was created, it appears, for something else.

They keep collections in their respective fields of interest. Hers is buried behind the house, a life's accumulation of tulip bulbs, many of them quite valuable. His, on the other hand, occupies a single desk drawer and is materially worthless: a little more than two reams of yellow foolscap, each page covered on one side in the same handwriting. They represent the letters home of the Sixty-fourth Confederate Tennessee Infantry, Company K, wiped out, to a man, on September 20, 1863, at Chickamauga, and all of the letters, regrettably, are copies. Even the eight written by his own maternal grandfather are transcriptions he made long ago in secret in his uncle's cabin in Kentucky while his uncle was out baiting his traps.

Used to be he'd offer to buy the letters themselves once he tracked their owners down, but nobody would part with them, and at last he gave up. You'd think it would be the subject matter they'd want to keep for themselves, but, no, it's the paper they want. And in his heart he understands. He wanted those old scraps from his uncle, but his uncle wouldn't give them up, and eventually the cabin burned down with the originals inside. But by then the jeweler had begun the long campaign of reconciling himself to the idea that what he had, the words, the sense of the thing, was more important.

It isn't so hard to get inside the houses. The offer of one dollar per copied page does all the work. And once he's curled himself over the kitchen table, triple-checking every line, they believe he's a scholar; hence the vertical marginalia in his collection denoting what else they had to say, by way of rounding out the personality of the dead, while he scribbled.

When he himself dies, his collection will go to the public library. In the meanwhile, he is assembling a book—the complete concordance of his collection, every word, every spelling, every occurrence—that he does not intend to finish. We are all terrible, and have sworn never to take safety again in the sweet crime that our nature has chosen to make dear to us, and so we give ourselves some work to do instead, and this is his. What does the scripture say? *And further, by these, my son, be admonished: Of making many books there is no end; and much study is a weariness of the flesh.* What else does it say? *Let us hear the conclusion of the whole matter: Fear God, and keep his commandments: for that is the whole duty of man.* The conclusion of the whole matter—who doesn't long for that? Who, reading a stranger's letters, doesn't finally wish to put the letters away and meet the living stranger himself?

The jeweler finishes his breakfast and drives his car into the frozen city—all deserted at this hour except for the hobos camped in the park. Icicles hang from the drooping trolley wires. The old, narrow mule-cart streets leading to his store are clouded with the steam that leaks from the sewer grates and the manhole covers as though a behemoth is asleep under the pavement.

He is so uncommonly spent this morning that it takes him half an hour to replace a single hairspring in a woman's wristwatch.

At eight, he closes the office and unlocks the showroom. A passerby who happened in here, missing the sign outside, wouldn't know immediately that it was a jewelry store. The walls are hung and the sofa and display cases are stacked with all the bric-a-brac he's picked up in his research. Books, door knockers off dead houses, flintlock rifles in rusted disuse, a twenty-four-carat cocaine straw, an Arapaho headdress. Each of them excites his deep capacity for sentiment in its own way. Their service is not to be materially useful or to speak to him of the past, but to touch him with the past directly, to recall to him the boyhood mind that knew not what a thing was for, nor worth, nor called. They are toys, in the workplace; Father would not have stood for this, but Father is dead.

He seats himself under the bric-a-brac, behind the case of silent watches, and opens a slim red volume that he's read many times before, a novel for young people, *The Forest Runners,* by Joseph A. Altsheler— its subject, dear to his heart, is the Ohio River valley of long ago—and reads:

> Paul stopped in a little open space, and looked around all the circle of the forest. Everywhere it was the same—just the curving wall of red and brown, and beyond, the blue sky, flecked with tiny clouds of white. The wilderness was full of beauty, charged with the glory of peace and silence, and there was naught to indicate that man had ever come. The leaves rippled a little in the gentle west wind, and the crisping grass bowed before it; but Paul saw no living being, save himself, in the vast, empty world.

Later that morning, a soft-spoken young lady needing his aid to remove a ring is standing at his counter, where he has wrapped the swollen finger tightly with sewing thread, first at the tip and then down around the offending knuckle, in a dense coil, forcing the blood back into the hand. With a paper clip he stuffs the thread under the ring, and he's begun unwinding the coil from the underside of the ring, each turn pulling it farther onto the knuckle, when the woman, wanting something to say, her modesty challenged (it's an intimate encounter, alone with him in the gray room), gestures with her free hand at the long row of books above his head.

She says, "You got a whole liberry in here."

His ear did catch that sweet word, yes. And the accent—Kentuckian, eastern. A lot of Company K boys from up around Prestonsburg, where his mother was born. His uncle's property was a little downriver, near Louisa.

The woman has fine yellow hair, freckles all down the fine white arm. Dreema Hannibal, behind the Big Sandy Crick Baptist Church, in Prestonsburg, used to give him her fingers to squeeze after luncheon.

"To think I's askeered you'd have to cut it off," she remarks, watching his work.

Last night he dreamt he went back to Prestonsburg, to Mama's hollar, and he heard the old folks talk again. Prestonsburg. And he feels the weakness, the woundableness, of a bashful man by the noise of common speech just as he has not heard it spoken in so long. Why today instead of any other day to be weak? Because the jeweler is tired; the concordance is failing him; and the woman says those sweet words not as people say them now, here, but as they used to do in Lawrence County, Kentucky, visiting with Mama's people when the jeweler was a boy.

Soon after the woman leaves, he is standing at the counter, playing with the little hammer he keeps lying around to give people the idea that he cuts his own stones. With the head of this hammer, he finds himself tapping the countertop glass, as if idly. Then harder, making a sharp, constant tock, like a metronome.

Then the hand that holds the hammer rises above his head, unbidden.

· · ·

Why does he say it again, aloud this time, but so quietly, hoping to hide behind its skirts like a child, when he is a man?

Prestonsburg.

Glass, many millions of pieces of glass, on the floor, on his shoes, on the watches, on the watch chains in the case.

Look where it comes again. A dog that bit you mercilessly, that you drove deep into the hinterland and kicked onto the snow, that's found its way back to you. Because it loves you. You could never make it understand that you've repudiated it. He has indeed sworn an oath to never, never, never, never again. He wants to be let back into the room in his father's house, where no lamps are lighted. He has grown old since the time he forsook it. Hello, it says. I love you.

A man in a wide-brimmed hat on the porch, knocking. (That man was him.) He has reason to believe you may be able to assist him with his research. He will pay handsomely for the privilege. His teeth gone brown. Don't you nor anybody else know how many times inside the house the woman said, "You want a root beer?" and he said no; "You want to eat some crackers, Professor?" and he said no. How many times he told the dog, "This is my true calling—you stay under the table whilst I copy these down."

The mere finishing stroke is what often appears to create an event which has long been an accomplished thing, wrote Thomas Hardy, of a man who discovered that what he believed was his sanguine nature was never his nature at all.

The jeweler is more afraid of the man in the hat on the porch, wheezing, than you are.

He's two blocks down the street before he remembers he hasn't locked the store, but now he is headed away.

He is brilliantly awake and running. He climbs aboard an eastbound streetcar. All around him people are pressed into one another's shoulders and asses. Two men are arguing in some Slavic language in the rear of the car. A boy wraps his arms around his mother's leg. The jeweler wipes off his shoes with his handkerchief as though it will soothe him. But he doesn't want soothing now.

When the hammer came down, the glass pieces of the countertop sprung up and the case was a bloom of splinters, like the crown of a thistle that's come open.

The brakeman lets go his brake, and the car rolls down the salted rails through the East Side streets.

The jeweler does not know where he is going.

Later. Dusk. He is seated on a stool in the back corner of a café, waiting. He has a foreign newspaper he's pretending to read. In his mind, he sounds out each letter of each meaningless word, each piece of gibberish, like a man tasting marbles one by one. There is a window looking out on the avenue, and it lets in a weak, smoky light, and the passersby tap a nail on the glass to get the man behind the bar to raise his chin and acknowledge them. This could easily be the smallest place of business in North America. Foreigners enter in twos. The jeweler can smell them as they come in. He doesn't try to talk to anybody. The only English words he hears them use are slurs and the names of the makes and models of automobiles. The afternoon progresses into evening.

The jeweler moves his eyes over a string of words beneath a photograph in the newspaper of a kind of demonstration, a strike or a funeral or a Christmas parade—they are carrying a statue of a woman through a street. He has been sitting here for five hours, eating miniature marzipan peaches and watermelons, poisoning himself with sugar, waiting to be found. He's not hiding, he's right down the street, he's right here. And it comforts him to think that the words beneath the photograph, considered as a group, are called a *caption*. He knows that's what these words are called even if he has no idea what they mean.

As a boy, with his uncle in Louisa, every winter for eight years, he walked through the snow and muck, following the trapping line, and into Prestonsburg on Sundays for church. He was meant to attach himself to the place sentimentally. They stayed in a one-room cabin with a potbelly stove to heat the place and cook on and ate opossum stew for

THE END · 123

supper, and turnips. How bored he was in the woods, he complained to his mother when he got home. But one time she told him something that he is reminded of by the caption, by the moment of release it brings to call a thing what it is—she said, "You're bored because you don't know the names of things."

Therefore he has developed the habit, in moments like this—when the din of all his selves recriminating one another is more than he can bear—of picking out the objects in a room and naming them to himself.

That piece of furniture holding the spare china is a sideboard. The lower part of the wall with the paneling on it is the dado, the paneling itself is wainscoting. That's the door.

Some of the men linger. Some of them buy a box of cookies tied up in blue ribbon and throw the silver down and dash out. Some of them are assumed into the others the moment they come in, no greetings exchanged, and the little coffee cups appear on the bar without their even asking. Women knock at the window and call the men by name, but the women don't come inside.

The jeweler turns a page of the inscrutable newspaper.

The woman's blood is under his fingernails. Before he left, he washed his hands in her kitchen sink, then dried them, then washed them again. He washed the water glass he'd used. He left it to dry on the dish rack and went back into the parlor, where the woman lay on the floor. He introduced himself again, it was at least the third time, and asked again what her name was, but again she didn't respond, or even stir, half-naked there under the coffee table. He couldn't find a nailbrush, so there is still some blood under his fingernails. He tries not to look at the blood under his fingernails. He resists the temptation to smell them.

Two ancient foreigners are arguing at the bar, in suits worn pale at the elbows and shoulders and knees.

The jeweler touches the room with his eyes, telling himself the name of each object he settles on in an effort to reattach himself to the material world.

That little beam over the door is a lintel. He says this to himself, and he feels better. *Lintel* has occurred twice so far in the concordance, if memory serves.

His mother's hope was that he would use the names to affix himself to the world. As in, You do not see the mayapple until you know that's what it's called, and then you see it everywhere, the words teaching you to love the things they name. But this isn't why he's telling himself, That's a samovar, that's a pencil sharpener. He never used the words as his mother intended. He uses them to keep material things at bay. And by now, in fact, the words have replaced the things themselves.

But there are moments when his nostalgia for the world of a potbelly stove, bull thistle, Dreema Hannibal behind the church in Prestonsburg, holding his little hand in hers while no one saw, of his mother dipping the comb in the water of the washbasin and parting his hair while the two of them observed in the mirror—moments when his desire to hold a thing, a thing in his hand, to impress himself again with the dumb objectness of it—is so piqued he will do anything his imagination tells him in order to achieve it.

He wants the world and not the name of the world.

But every time he tries to descend on a hammer, or an amethyst, his interior voices start asking him, What is the word for that? What do you think it means to lift an amethyst in your fingers? Telling him, Get back to work. Telling him, Put that hammer down, you'll break something.

And, finally, the private argument is always, always, Should he do this, or shouldn't he?

So that he must ask himself if he dares stir the sugar in his tea.

(He does not.)

If he dares refill the oil in the lamp.

(He does not.)

If he dares lift his head from the pillow and watch his sister depart the room.

(He does not dare lift his head.)

So that every mere wish to hold a key, a thimble, a saw, and to leave it at that, collapses into accusation, counteraccusation, shame, and dread.

So that this morning, with the glass from the watch case glittering on the toes of his shoes, the jeweler's hammer in the jeweler's grip as if this were fitting, and then charging down the street, and then on the streetcar, the old solution—as backward as the problem—presented itself to his mind, once more, sweetly, like the promise of custard after supper.

Does he dare step off the streetcar?

He does step off the streetcar.

Does he dare follow this woman home, a whistling, unlucky woman he has never met before, with a burlap onion sack on her shoulder as she goes up the street now? (We will all have our misfortunes.)

He does follow her.

The old promise, the repudiated dog that loved him. Saying, There is a thing, wrapped in its name. Go on, catch it.

Then, afterward, he wanted something sweet. He walked down the block toward the main avenue. It had begun to snow. In an alley two girls were trying to balance another, much smaller girl on the back of a dalmatian. He paused on the sidewalk in front of a tiny storefront window where pastries were displayed, and intricately decorated cookies in the shapes of summer fruit. It was some kind of café or tavern. Inside, the space between the bar and the wall was just wide enough for a man to walk through if he turned himself sideways. The jeweler bought three of the cookies and a newspaper. He sat at the far end of the bar and waited for them to come find him.

He is waiting for them at the bar, which gleams this way, this beautifully, because of the beautiful name of the substance enveloping it—*shellac*. A word of which records are made, and then music is etched into the records. A word over which he has been compelled to pause before, aghast at how lovely it is, and yet how it shows his own unlovely face back at him. Which word, in one of its verb senses, means "to thrash soundly."

PART THREE

Bogus

1952 – 1953

. . . .

9

A Saturday. Enzo Mazzone was on the job until six o'clock. When he got home, the dishes were still in the sink, a pack of cigarettes was missing from the utility drawer, the radishes were not picked, the peppers were not picked, the beans were not limed, the lettuces were not weeded, the boy was nowhere to be found.

Wood spoon in hand, he prowled the backyards, stalked across the ball field behind the church, down the railroad tracks, under the bridge, over the bridge, down around the perimeter of the Chagrin Avenue woods, whacking his head with the spoon as the mosquitoes fed on him. With the right wind he could have smelled his prey. He sneaked up the alley by the bakery and out in front of Mrs. Marini's house, but the boy wasn't there.

The old lady was sitting on the banquette of her screened front porch in a bushy black wig, shucking corn over a laundry kettle.

"Enzo!" she shouted through the screen. "Come here."

"Give him up," he commanded. He was standing in her begonias, right up at the rail of the porch.

"But I don't have him."

"Habeas corpus," he said.

"He wasn't here earlier. He's not here now."

"I want his head. Do you understand?"

"Come up here. I'm like a judge, where you're pleading your case at the bar. He's a nice boy. Leave him alone."

Enzo went inside the cool, dim, bugless enclosure. He opened a lawn chair and sat down, extending his hand in the direction of the kettle.

"Keep your grubby hands off my corn," she said.

"What's all this? You hate corn."

"Dom LaMana had garden surplus. He thinks he was doing me a favor. This, this enormous basket of chicken feed he carried fifteen blocks in the sun. The sweat on the top of his head, you should have seen, it was like a fountain. I disguised my true feelings out of courtesy." She gave him a wide-eyed look that Enzo took to mean, Please take this corn off my hands.

"I have the colitis. I can't eat corn," he said.

"Perhaps Ciccio—"

"The boy gets nothing," he interrupted. "The boy starves."

She went into the house and brought him half of a salami sandwich, a wilted salad, a fork, and a limp linen napkin.

Enzo surmised it was all left over from the boy's lunch. He insisted she disclose his whereabouts as he pushed the sandwich into his mouth.

"Don't think you can bully me," she said. And then in English, "Go find your fink someplace else."

She suggested that if he were to clean his hands thoroughly she might permit him to help with the corn, so he went inside and scrubbed the grease and mortar out of the cracks in his hands. He had expended the day laying brick for a suburban shopping center, three stories up and as long as a city block, without a single angle or window, like the tomb of a dictator. He worked more slowly than years ago but accomplished twice as much. He was a shining piece of modern engineering these days, fleshless and precise, an unerring machine.

He went back out. The trees overhanging her porch were lush, the sun was not too bright, the wind had a taste in it, a vegetable sweetness. Down the block people were hosing down their driveways and sidewalks. Next door, Larry Lombardi was using an electric gizmo to trim his azaleas.

"Left," Mrs. Marini said.

Enzo offered his hand for her inspection. She pulled the fingers apart, glowered at the cuticles, the stained and swollen eminence that opened and closed the thumb over the palm, the blood blister beneath the nail on the middle finger. She said, "Is this as clean as they get? Did you use the brush?" His left pinky didn't work, it stayed erect when he made a fist. He had been made to register as an alien of enemy nationality during the war; the clerk tried to get his fingerprints, but the tips of his mortar-worn fingers were as blank as glass. He couldn't put a spiral on a football because he couldn't get a purchase on the skin.

He bent himself over the kettle, ripping the corn apart with disgust while begonia pollen breezed through the screen.

"Did he eat here or did you pack his lunch for him?" Enzo said, wagging a shorn ear at her and sneezing into his shoulder.

"Don't you threaten me."

"That Slav was with him, I guess."

"You believe that I am breakable, and you are mistaken."

"He went to downtown, to the ballgame, with the flea Ricky, while my peppers are rotting, and you protect him," Enzo said.

The boy was fifteen years old. He was smarter than his father, but he didn't know it yet. He claimed he couldn't tell the difference between a tomato from the garden and a tomato from the store. He gave up on the accordion, and Enzo wrapped it up in its velvet pall, closed it in its case, and stowed it in the otherwise vacant attic of the house he'd bought the year after the boy was born. All Ciccio wanted to do in what he called his free time was play football and pick fights. As if it mattered what he wanted to do. Enzo made him work all summer in Patrizia's grapes, hoping the lonesome would make him a more formidable person. The boy was too old to be so agreeable.

Ciccio had a sight hound's face. The long, narrow, protruding nose was crooked, and the big eyes were closely set. He had recently pubesced, instantaneously, and the hairs grew even on his pimpled shoulders. His teeth were discolored from coffee and Mars bars. It must have been an illusion created by the comical elongation of his forehead and face that his hairline seemed already to be in regress. His height was excessive, like a vulgar joke.

They finished with the corn. They went inside and she put a loaf of bread on the table, and a bowl of mushrooms. Enzo chewed one of them, then got up, rummaged her kitchen drawers for a pack of cards, and discreetly spit the mushroom into the bucket of scraps for the garden. It was raw.

A knock came from the clatterous screen door that opened onto a path through her garden to the alley gate in back, and she popped up to answer it. He found the cards and poured himself a glass of wine from the pantry, unable to hear what she was saying in the breezeway to these people at the door. He sat down with his glass, snapped the rubber band off the cards, and inspected his shirt pockets for cigarettes.

The pneumatic mechanism that slowly closed the door of the breezeway *siss*ed, long and malicious, as the piston pressed the air out of the cylinder; then it shut with a clap.

The smell reached him, sweet-sour—only momentarily did he fail to recognize what it was—of the fetid feet of an unwashed teenaged boy.

He blinked. He stood up. The chair crashed to the floor behind him.

He shot through the breezeway, down the garden steps, and through the pole beans and chard growing on either side of the narrow garden path. The old lady protested from the house as he fumbled with the latch and finally threw open the back gate into the alley. What he saw there was the accomplice, Ricky, rounding the bakery corner and disappearing onto Twenty-sixth Street.

The closer on the breezeway door repeated its long, insinuating sound.

He listened to it, then pointed himself down the center of the alley and flew.

He was all legs, growling, fleet, and livid.

He ran on top of the puddles. Rounding the bakery corner himself, he caught a glimpse of Ricky, in some old man's plaid pants that had been shorn crookedly at the knees, vanishing at the edge of the dry cleaner's. They were turning onto Eleventh Avenue. A tactical error on Ciccio's part (Ciccio was leading; Enzo hadn't seen him, but he had smelled him well enough). *When being chased, avoid open places.* The boy never listened.

Enzo threw himself across Twenty-sixth Street, leaping into the air. He could not hear his footfalls. Hurdling heaps of garbage, springing right in front of a cruising yellow Oldsmobile. However, they were headed *uphill*. Perhaps he'd underestimated the boy. Exhaust the enemy, the boy was thinking. I am fifteen, he is forty-eight, the boy was thinking. I will not merely escape. I will humiliate my pursuer.

Enzo made the cleaner's and veered up the hill. Eleventh Avenue was a throng of fruit vendors, nut vendors; the armies of the retired, the lame, the blown out and wasted; the philosophers; the poets of the last, lost era; the prophesiers of impending atomic catastrophe; the man who sold his homemade brand of bleach from a wagon painted electric white crying, "Brilliantone! Brilliantone!"; the woman who picked the sidewalk clean while she went; the heartless, the jobless, the shoeless; the man who sharpened your knives with a pedal-operated grindstone while you sat on the stoop, listening.

He swerved into the gap between the lanes, and the boys came into view, both of them at once, toeing the double yellow line between traffic, white knee socks pulled all the way up (they had been in the high grass someplace), on a dead sprint. The cars moved slowly to the edges of the street. Nobody seemed to be taking special notice, because a man chasing two boys up this street was nothing special.

He had forgotten the happiness of running away and of giving chase. Between the ages of five and thirteen, he had spent half his hours crashing through the dark alleys of a desolate hilltop town thick with the odor of molding fruit peels, bathwater, and shit, ducking away from the wider lanes, playing games in which the rules changed without notice, midcareer.

The narrowness of mind and of purpose.

There is the boy. Get him.

The initial burst of desire and power burned off. But then he didn't stop. Going up and up the hill, the cars having parted and made way. He didn't stop, and the thrill turned into something else, a peacefulness of mind he rarely felt anymore.

They were, all three of them, moderate smokers. This couldn't go on forever. Enzo was gaining on them, but he was shorter than they were, so his old legs were working twice as fast. The boy would be taking this into account. Let him wear himself out, the boy was thinking. Exhaust him and humiliate him while I run away in my baseball socks.

A whale of a Studebaker turned left onto Thirtieth Street, blocking his view momentarily, an excuse for the boy to change course. When the middle of the street opened up again, Enzo saw Ciccio's burred head breaking left above the traffic. Ricky had escaped. All the better. Ciccio's scalp was red and peeling. Enzo had found a louse on him and shaved his head two days before and rubbed it with poison and told him he must wear a hat now or the sun would scorch his naked scalp, but the boy had disregarded him.

There is the boy. Bring him to justice.

Enzo wasn't tired. He could run like this forever.

He turned down Thirtieth Street.

He wasn't tired—then a stopcock came open in each of his two flat feet, and the life force was like a liquid draining out of him, into the gutter.

He slowed, and slowed, and finally sat on the curb, crumpled, sucking air.

Someone had removed the classy old egg-and-dart cornices from the façade of the house he was facing and had replaced them with plain white boards. Certainly they were easier to paint.

He stumbled along the downhill blocks back toward Mrs. Marini's house. Maybe it took him three hours to get there. At the fish truck, on the way, on the corner of Twenty-ninth, he bought a walleye. It was the biggest thing, a long silver animal with savage teeth. He was famished.

"Head off, or head on?" said the uneasy, ill-fed, and gray-faced young man as he shook the ice off the fish, which eerily resembled him, onto the avenue pavement.

"On," Enzo said. And the young man wrapped it in white butcher paper and tied it with a length of orange ribbon, poorly.

Also, Enzo bought a bag of licorice and a bag of cherries and some parsley from various men on the street.

His fault was not that he did not beat the boy enough, but that he didn't beat him with a correcting fervor, and so, for the boy, to be beaten was only the cost of a scamp's afternoon and no longer shamed him. Enzo's heart wasn't in it anymore. Look, he'd already bought him some candy.

He entered Mrs. Marini's kitchen still not in control of his breathing. His shins were killing him. She was at the sink shelling peas.

"Go outside and knock," she said.

He went outside. He was a believer in the formalities, in the keeping of customs even after their original intent was exhausted. They sustained him.

She came to the door. "My Enzo!" she said, stretching her sarcastic arms. "What's this package that someone didn't know how to tie?"

He gave her the fish. Then he took off his shoes and went into the front room, where the boy lay asleep on the sofa.

He dropped the licorice on the boy's chest.

The boy woke up. "Hey, Pop," he said.

Enzo sat down, rubbing his shins. The boy's ripe feet repelled him. "You will obey me," he said.

"It's a pleasure to see you. You're a sight for sore eyes." But his sore eyes were closed. He grinned with his thick, chafing, woman's lips.

"Don't get wise in the face," Enzo said. "Now then, my peppers and beans. Speak."

"I forgot."

"He forgot, he says."

"I forgot to do them."

Enzo unbuckled his belt as he stood up, trying to think of something he could say that would penetrate the boy's goodwill and also fend it off. "And the lies," he said desperately.

"Sorry. I meant to say, I made a bad decision. I don't know what's good."

"Stand up so I can beat you."

"Stand up so I can beat you," the boy parroted. It was dead-on. It was incredible. He had a gift, but it was for the circus. And Enzo wagged his weary head at the prospect of this boy turning into a man who had never learned that eventually you have to give up the cheap kick of being interesting to other people, that you can go on eating it, but it won't feed you.

From the kitchen came the solid *thwack* of Mrs. Marini decapitating the walleye.

"I am the king of my house."

"But this isn't your house," the boy pointed out, raising a finger.

"Yes, well," Enzo said, tightening his belt again and snapping it closed. The boy would get his beating later, on a full stomach. Good.

"Have some licorice," said the boy, tearing open the cellophane and breathing in the saccharine chemical aroma his father despised.

Enzo Mazzone was a person of fixed patterns that mostly served him well, such as buying a treat for the boy on weekend afternoons although it might contradict the lesson he was otherwise trying to teach.

"I am the king of you," said Enzo.

"Sure you are," said the boy.

Mrs. Marini made a broth from the fish's head and cooked the rice in it. She boiled them some peas to eat with the fish itself, which she roasted in a pan. Finally, a pear tart she had bought from Rocco's.

Afterward, Ciccio and Mrs. Marini drank coffee while Enzo sipped at a glass of tap water that tinked with a dozen cubes of cocktail ice. He was of the school that abstained from drink until the meal was finished so as not to dilute the acids of the stomach. The ice stank of the freezer, and the water itself was barely potable, compared with the water on his mother-in-law's farm, which he bottled and took home with him. His feelings regarding a drink of bitingly cold water with the merest whiff of sulfur coming off it were sentimental. They had more power over him than he would have liked.

(He had had an uncle, unmarried and abstemious—the name was Gregorio—who leased Enzo from his father at grain-cutting time and who would drink only the water of his own well and only when it was freshly pulled out of the ground. When Enzo was with him, he did likewise and taught himself the pleasure of going without. After the day's work on the hillside plot, without a drop to drink since lunchtime, they trotted back to his uncle's house, under the walls of the town, three miles, shoes in hand, as the dusty sun went down. When at last they arrived, his uncle hoisted the bucket out of the deep cave—and Enzo drank, the nerves inside his teeth throbbing and his esophagus recoiling painfully before it let the water down.)

The three of them—the boy, the old woman, and Enzo—opened walnuts in their chosen ways. Enzo smashed two of them against each other in his fist. The boy laid one seam up on the table and shattered it with the fat of his hand. Mrs. Marini used a mallet. Enzo couldn't eat his and gave them to the boy.

Mrs. Marini said she had a six o'clock appointment. Ciccio wanted to know what kind of an appointment, but Enzo interrupted.

"If she wants you to know something, she'll tell you," Enzo said.

Mrs. Marini pursed her lips, aggrieved as always when she felt the boy was being roughly treated.

Enzo's rolling eyes regarded the crystal light fixture in the ceiling. He would have to make an effort to beat Ciccio once they got home, but more and more of late it slipped his mind.

The boy and the old lady nipped at their little cups and went on talking. It was only local gossip, but it was frank and mean-spirited and smooth. He liked to listen to them. He rarely knew exactly what they were talking about.

He was a very lonely man.

They walked on down the avenue, Enzo and the boy. It was the hour of digestion, and no cars tried to pass through the crowded lanes, and the natty old men went arm in arm among the crowd, talking under their hat brims. What did they talk about? Supper; "Your nephew Anthony with the jungle-bunny music while I'm trying to sleep across the alley"; "That's very nice workmanship on your slacks there, Carmen, who did those for you?" But these were already the dying days of men walking arm in arm down an American street while they digested their food. The young generation preferred to lie down on the sofa and smoke in their underpants.

The boy headed up Twenty-second, and Enzo followed half a step behind, fat, at his ease.

They stopped in for a minute at the DiStefano household so that Enzo could pay his weekly respects to a union brother lately retired.

Eddie DiStefano pulled himself nearly to a standing position and allowed them to shake his hand. Then he settled back into the recline of his lounging chair. It was in this chair that he now expended his summer days as the current of the fan atop his radio cabinet unendingly struck his bristled face—chin up, squinting, serene, like a malamute on a car ride. His obesity was majestic. You shook his hand, rather than shaking hands with him, because he did not swing the thumb down over your hand to grip it.

Did they know, Eddie began as soon as the volume of the radio had been adjusted by one of his little ones and Enzo and the boy were seated, did they know that there were certain cultures now living on Saint John's Avenue, five minutes by foot from the house where they were currently relaxing in safety?

They did, but he continued.

The Slovaks had sold the parish of Saint Bartholomew's. You could count on the fingers of one hand the Caucasian people still living in Fort Saint Clair. "Columbiana Avenue—absolutely lost, Dugansville, New Odessa, Tooley Boulevard. One gigantic plantation. All of them holding hands, singing their songs."

His many young children scurried on the carpeting around and under the mighty leatherette throne where he lived. His wife was at work (a typist in a brewery).

Six months before, lest doubt remain as to the sentiments of the citizens of Elephant Park, Eddie DiStefano and a few of his colleagues had hung a Negro dummy from a streetlamp in front of Holy Assumption Church; then they had called the newspapers and set it on fire. The dummy was made by Eddie's little girls out of pillowcases, grass clippings, and house paint.

Time was, the Slovak kids knew better than to come into Elephant Park, and vice versa for the Italian kids staying out of Fort Saint Clair. If you married into another nationality (like Enzo's sister-in-law, Antonietta, whom he'd never met; her husband was from Austria), it was understood you wanted to move, say, to Chicago or the suburbs. Now they were all concerned, white people. When this had happened, Enzo could not have told you. He himself didn't even prevent the Croat Ricky from sleeping in his house.

With a yardstick, Eddie reached out to the fan on the radio and depressed one of its buttons, whereupon the previously fixed instrument began to turn its head imperiously from side to side, sermonizing them with its cold breath.

Eddie went on about the tizzoons.

They hadn't planned to linger too long. It was more a visit to say, The men of Local 238 salute you and vow to carry your coffin when the day arrives.

Eddie said, "Am I right?"

"I am not political, Edward," Enzo responded. He'd never voted. He was unsure how, physically, voting took place. He wasn't even formally a citizen, he didn't think. During the war, the previous war, with Europe, he wasn't allowed to fly in an airplane, use a shortwave radio, or own a camera. It wasn't any skin off his nose. The restrictions were lifted in 1943, he found out five years later. The boy wasn't really political, either. He could tell you whatever you wanted to know about the Battle of Tippecanoe and how the Constitution was amended but had no interest in the local news.

Now, Enzo did follow the police action in Korea, with the anxious eye of the father of a teenaged boy. It was stalled now, but he was sure another war would start someplace in time to catch Ciccio up in it and blow him to smithereens.

Eddie asked them to stay for the supper that his Phyllis would prepare once she got home from work. The boy said sorry, but they'd already eaten. Coffee, then? Ice cream? A beer? Enzo said no, thanks, but he didn't drink beer.

The boy began to suffer a fit of blinking, the way he did when he knew he was supposed to keep quiet but was about to make some flip comment anyway.

Enzo pointed at the boy. "He doesn't drink beer either," he intervened. And they all laughed. Ha, ha.

They continued toward home. Enzo suggested the width of a single wooden match by holding out his thumb and forefinger before the eyes of the boy. "You are this close," he said. But Ciccio only boxed him on the shoulder like old chums.

They waited at the stoplight on the corner of Chagrin. The boy stood in the street and Enzo on the curb, so that they were nearly the same height and Enzo could see the pores inside the boy's filthy ears.

Ciccio, inserting three fingers between the buttons of his jersey, flapped it to dry his sweat, and his father realized only then that all day long the boy had been flouting another one of the original house rules.

"Hold on," Enzo said, his nostrils flaring as they sucked in the boy's wafting scent. "The law regarding an undershirt at all times. Say it."

"What do you care?" Ciccio said, his head bent into the breeze from below. "I should look like you, that's all you care."

Enzo bit his lip. He raised his hand, rotating it so that the splayed knuckles were oriented at the boy, and swung, cracking him in the face.

From Ciccio's slanting nose a little blood splashed out, like a prize. The boy said quietly, "Fuck."

"Now how do you look?" Enzo said.

Fatherhood was a catalogue of threat, surveillance, legislation, prescription, prohibition, penal retribution, harassment, breaking and entering, assault and battery, cigarettes, meals, Latin, trigonometry, "Do like I say," "Go get the tin snips," "The square root of two divided by x," "I told you to use the shoe trees, but you didn't use the shoes trees." While driving, the left hand is free to smoke with because the boy can shift the gears. Up the highway, down the highway, he washes you dry.

"Stand up so I can beat you." "You don't know what's good." "Close the mouth when chewing." "Close the light when leaving the room." Brilliantone. Laundry.

Boyhood was contempt for the rule and the rule giver, knowing that your every slouching step was surveilled. Lies, capricious and glib. Running flat out. "Someday soon, old man, I'll knock you down."

Carmelina, the boy's mother, had left them sometime between noon and four o'clock on the afternoon of August 8, 1946, when the boy was nine years old.

When Ciccio had finished the eighth grade (this was two years ago), Patrizia had offered to take him off Enzo's hands and put him to work full-time on the farm. Enzo had arranged for an apprenticeship with the laborer's union—Ciccio could have passed for sixteen at the time—but unluckily the union now wanted a birth certificate proving the minimum age had been attained, and Ciccio's career was forestalled. Why not send him to the farm, where he spent much of the summer anyhow and could be of use? Enzo didn't like it, that was why. He had given the boy his name, Mazzone. You see? He had bought, he wasn't renting. They would have to put him in a high school.

He preferred to send the boy to the public vocational school up the road, but Mrs. Marini said that was a half measure and he should go instead to a gymnasium downtown that had been started in the 1880s by a group of Jesuit priests from Munich, who incidentally had bought their shoes from her husband. Ciccio should learn languages and theology, not cabinetmaking. And she would pay for it.

Enzo mistrusted the school's intentions. Specifically, would they try to turn Ciccio into a missionary? Most of the priests who taught at the school were born in Europe, which confirmed Enzo's notion that their aim was to remove boys from their natural home and throw them to the four winds; while for Mrs. Marini it only confirmed that the instruction there would not be very stupid. Neither of them cared to ask the boy's opinion. He would go where they told him. Except where chores were concerned, he was a suggestible person (all the more reason, in Enzo's mind, to keep the Church away from him). They wouldn't let him in anyway, Enzo didn't think, nor should they. This kind of schooling was not for the likes of the sons of him, but for the middle class.

Mrs. Marini scheduled an interview. The three of them rode the trolley into the city, the boy holding a strap in the ceiling while his two elders sat on the bouncing wooden bench arguing over whether he could pass the exam, although neither of them knew on what he would be examined. Ciccio, slick and mirthful, only whistled through his teeth until she shushed him; he was bothering the other patrons.

The examination, so-called, consisted of a five-minute chat in Latin with an old French Canadian monk, who pronounced Ciccio "unacceptable," followed by two hours of timed drills on the football field. At the end of the afternoon, they offered to let Ciccio go to the school, starting the fall term, so long as he made it through the four weeks of double-session practices in August.

"Is this a school or a stable?" Mrs. Marini demanded of the headmaster, a trim and fresh-faced American priest of Irish parents, who had allowed the lime that marked the grid of the football field to color the hem of his cassock. He tried to feed her some nonsense about training the whole boy, but she was supremely uneager to hear it.

She struggled to control her distress. Her original enthusiasm for sending Ciccio to the school was like a pot of milk that had just been too abruptly boiled and in which clots had formed—however, they were only clots, she decided, and might be strained away. Therefore, while the priest intoned his response, she pretended that she suddenly heard a curious buzzing in her inner ear. She gazed vaguely at the solemn oak beams of the ceiling as though she were about to let her head fall back and go to sleep. Thus she convinced herself that she couldn't properly hear him and avoided learning anything that would have made her change her mind.

What the priest said brought Enzo halfway around. The school wasn't so fancy as he'd assumed. He meant it wasn't all prayers and incense, they weren't going to castrate Ciccio for the choir.

On the way home, Ciccio was silent. He looked down at his large duck feet glumly.

"What's wrong with your face?" Mrs. Marini asked.

When addressing her (but never his father) he could still sometimes come out with the sincere eruption of a boy's gelatinous feelings, at which it was difficult for her to keep from laughing, since he was so big. "I'm sort of afraid of those guys," he said, blinking.

"Who guys, precisely?" she said.

"The priests."

That sealed it. Enzo was sold right there.

They were three in a row, seated, on the trolley bench. Mrs. Marini sat between the man and the boy. Enzo twisted himself across her lap, pointing at him. "You are going to go to that school," Enzo said, with equal emphasis on each word.

Ciccio breathed deeply, once, and let the air out.

"It will make you important," she said consolingly.

Enzo had never intended in the first place to let Mrs. Marini foot the bill; he paid it out of his savings. What did he ever need to buy for himself? Buttons. Aspirin. But by the time Ciccio was starting his third year at the school, Enzo was unsure it was doing him any good. Enzo wanted them to teach a class in not being so eager to please, and how to keep your mouth shut if you don't have anything to say. Instead it was algebra and the writings of the saints.

Rather than paying the tuition, Mrs. Marini made him his uniforms. It was Enzo's idea. He considered it an imposition to suggest she use cash to buy them. And she was pleased to make them herself until she realized that Ciccio would outgrow everything but the socks almost as soon as he put it on. (No, she did not make the socks.) In the notebook she kept of his changing measurements, she had recorded an increase of four jacket sizes in the space of a single school year. His inseam was like a stock in which she should have invested. He was six feet two inches and wore size thirteen shoes.

Regarding the present day, it was her need to finish yet another blazer that had made her tell the fib after supper that she had an appointment for six o'clock; in fact, it was for eleven thirty that night. She had only said that so they would go away and let her get the blazer done before starting her next job, which was of a different kind and required different parts of her brain. As much as possible, she did one thing at a time. And she could not sew with anybody else around. She wondered why that should be.

As soon as they left, she nailed herself to the seat in her sewing room. The radio played. It was Wagner, whom she despised. But she must not get up. She must finish.

She drank coffee from a thermos, dribbling some on her chin and dabbing at it with a bit of satin that would remain hidden on the inside of a sleeve of the jacket.

Her arches tortured her. She would have kicked off her shoes, but the floor was strewn with straight pins that would have stuck her bare feet, and she always stayed true to the first article of a seamstress's discipline, taught to her at the convent in Lazio when she was eight years old: You must never clean the floor until the work is done. There will always be another pin.

The dog that lived at the corner of her street bayed and bayed unremittingly.

She must finish.

Her eyes crossed with fatigue. Her glasses slid down her nose when her foot pumped the treadle. The work was beneath her gifts. She might have simply paid for a new blazer and cut out the tag, but it would have humiliated Vincenzo if he should ever find out.

The dog went on ruing its sins and begging forgiveness of the grass, of the trees, of the chain fence at which it flung itself resoundingly when cars passed, of the houses, and of the multifarious and brilliant smells that fill up the universe of a dog.

Wheedle, wheedle, wheedle, went the shaft of the machine as the thread was jabbed through the fabric by the power of her smarting leg. She wanted to comfort the poor, lonesome dog and also to hang it. "Yes, hang it," she said, laying the side of her skull on the cool gabardine for a moment, only a moment now, and slept.

When she awoke the windows were dark. Her face lay in her hair, which she had pulled off and folded in her sleep, mistaking it for a pillow. The only sound was a persistent knocking at the breezeway door. She listened for the bay of the dog, but there was no bay.

Someone had come for the dog! A poisoner! Death! (Or else it had been run over by one of the cars whose tires it nipped when it ran loose, thinking the car was an impudent sheep.) And now it was coming for her, too, Death! The Reaper!

"Murder!" she cried, but not too loudly, in case she had misunderstood. She fluffed her hair and put it back on.

The breezeway door squealed as it came open.

"What did you say?" a voice inquired.

"Murder?" she said again, under her breath.

"I'm coming into the house now," it announced, female, throaty.

Mrs. Marini held the seat of the chair tightly.

A woman's plump and sunburned face appeared in the sewing-room doorway. It was Federica, her assistant, the wife of a friend of Vincenzo's.

"Say, why didn't you come to the door?" she asked.

Mrs. Marini saw no reason to dissimulate. "I thought you were my death coming for me," she said.

"I'm late. Rossie woke up screaming out his brains."

"*Pavor nocturnus*," Mrs. Marini said. "It'll go away when his testicles mature."

"We had to dunk his head in the bathtub."

"Don't worry. I was asleep myself," she said, stretching her arms luxuriantly and closing the sewing-room door behind herself. She would have to go at the infernal jacket again tomorrow.

"She won't be here for another half hour," Mrs. Marini said, looking at her wristwatch.

Federica started the water boiling (for tea; they sterilized chemically) and ran down the cellar stairs to prepare the instruments.

She was a stout lady of forty-five, a mother of six, and a former client. Smoking had abraded her voice, but otherwise her manner was clean and healthful. She was the kind of woman whom other women find it easy to like because, although she was vain, her vanity was hapless: She had acquired the wrinkles of a much older woman by sleeping uncovered in the sun, and she stripped her coarse and wavy hair and dyed it a bright yellow that it was perfectly impossible to believe someone of her complexion could naturally produce.

She had a strange habit of putting her best foot backward. She scolded the children fiercely in public but doted on them and played all their games cheerfully at home. When first introduced, she would look a person up and down, icily judging their looks and class and Were they well bronzed? and say, "Pleasure to know you," in a tone devoid of pleasure. But then she quickly melted (even too quickly, in Mrs. Marini's judgment) and used familiar address with everyone. Her English was wretched. Her Italian was worse; dialect had polluted it irreparably. The Lord was punishing Mrs. Marini for having expected ever more refined company by putting her into friendly association with commoner and commoner persons.

The girl didn't arrive until past one o'clock. She had no discernible accent. She claimed she was a homemaker from Van Buren Heights, although a girl from that neighborhood would never have skulked around here. She looked seventeen. Her brother-in-law, as she clumsily identified him, stayed in the kitchen while the women descended into the basement.

Mrs. Marini had always intended to have brighter lights installed in the dreary stairwell. The open maw of the cellar probably frightened the girls, who rarely believed her when she assured them of how little danger they were in—to an experienced hand, the procedure was straightforward, and in an emergency she could consult with one Dr. Snead of Eastpark; however, she had had no emergencies in many years. Fright was always to be avoided, leading invariably, as it did, to a rigid cervix that submitted only painfully to dilation.

Many years ago, under her direction, Nico had pasted the walls with pale blue silk paper that gave the procedure room, which necessarily had no windows, a lighter affect. She used electric fans to keep it dry in the summer. The cushions on the table were thick and comfortable.

They gave the girl a pair of sterilized rayon hose and underpants from which the crotch was cut away, and arrayed their tools on the linen of the instrument table with their backs turned to her while she undressed.

Mrs. Marini fit the girl's feet into the stirrups and firmly patted at her arm. She did not ask the girl any more questions about herself, having done all her preliminary questioning two nights before. The girl must not have occasion to tell any more inconsequential lies. Lying was the enemy of the physical relaxation that was central to her method. She was convinced that the majority of the injuries inflicted by otherwise competent physicians were caused by their (male) insensibility to the extreme effect that extreme emotions could have on a girl's body. Mrs. Marini herself was a vicious judge of everyone, but she had trained herself to hold her judgment in abeyance and even to feel motherly, though the client might in fact be a despicable little harlot.

Whereas the doctors were ashamed, Mrs. Marini was proud, of her skills, manual and emotional; and the feelings of the practitioner never failed to be directly communicated—yes, through the hand—to the subject. Empathy was only another shiny tool, like the speculum, for opening up and evacuating.

The girl's makeup was fresh and too carefully painted: She had darkened the rings under her eyes in an effort to age herself and had covered her legs with pancake and drawn a line of eyebrow pencil from her heels to the backs of her knees to imitate the seam of a nylon stocking. All this the surgical hose had wrecked by smearing.

Federica scrubbed and scrubbed her hands while Mrs. Marini hung a sanitized pillowcase over each of the girl's legs.

"Now, if you feel your feet falling to sleep, dear," Mrs. Marini said, "then you let me know."

"Do I push?" the girl asked. Her name, she said, was Sophie.

"You must not push," Federica commanded, turning from the sink.

"You don't have to do anything at all, dear," Mrs. Marini said. "Let yourself be limp. You are in a bathtub. The water is just the temperature that you like."

"May I scratch my knee?" she simpered.

"Which one, child?" Federica asked, shaking the water from her hands.

The girl pointed, and then she let out a shriek of laughter; she snorted and spat through her tight lips. It was the laugh of abject silliness that an older child sometimes makes when she plays with a younger one; after which, when Mother shows her contempt, the child wonders why when she used to be smaller and used to laugh in the same way, Mother had smiled and used nice words. The laugh wasn't uncommon in here right at this juncture, when the legs were exposed but nothing had been done to cause the client pain. The idea was to show the girl the fawning mother's face, although it might embarrass one to pretend.

Federica reached under the cloth and scratched and patted down the leg of the girl, breathing deeply, slowly, and audibly, as Mrs. Marini had trained her to do.

The girl wore an inexpressive half smirk, and Mrs. Marini indicated with her eyes that Federica should stall until the smirk abated.

Finally, Federica sat down on a stool between the stirrups. "How do you feel?" she asked. "Do we get you something to drink?"

"Thank you, no," said the girl.

Mrs. Marini continued to slowly rub the papery skin of the side of her hand on the girl's hairless arm. "Now you're going to feel a pinch, and you might want to bear down, but I want you to think of the pinch as a fist you can open up if you please," she said, demonstrating in the air with her knotty hand.

Federica stooped, peering, and inserted a dilating rod with a stab, like a teacher indicating a pupil with her chalk.

The girl hissed.

"If you want to curse, dear, why, that's fine. Nobody will hear you."

"Thank you, no," said the girl with composure.

"Or count, or say a rhyme."

"No. Thank you."

"Or cry, if you like," said Federica, repeating the stab with a thicker rod.

"No," she said, from the back of her throat.

"That's very good," Federica said. "What a good, good girl you are."

Years ago, Mrs. Marini had worn a nurse's costume. It fit her poorly, so she had adjusted it. Nico said it made her look like an iceberg. To be addressed as Nurse when she had for many years allowed her clients to call her Madam Doctor was the cost of a modest advance in her method and a significant new source of referred clients. It was also a penance for a septic case she might have prevented if she had spoken more carefully.

The girl had ratted her out to a tokologist at the Lutheran hospital, who had then tracked her down at Nico's store. Nico attended the register while they talked in the workshop. The doctor knew all about her practice, as did his colleagues, but he had never had occasion to clean up a mess of hers before, which, ironically, had led him to seek this meeting.

"I was struck dumb when she told me you were responsible," he said. "But while I was performing the therapeutic, I recovered a foreign object. That was when I concluded she was lying to me. I suppose she was too proud to say she had tried it herself and failed."

"What did she look like?"

The doctor gave a precise depiction, which she recognized immediately.

"She thought my fee too high," Mrs. Marini said.

"And you turned her out?"

"Of course not. I asked her what she could afford. And that was my error, that word, *afford*. I engaged her shame, and she walked off. What was the object?"

"A pencil tip."

She made a little smile.

"It appears your record is better than mine, which I find difficult to believe, but there it is. You couldn't possibly duplicate the sterility of a professional office, for example."

"All of you were so surprised about germs." In the air, she drew a broad circle around the doctor's head to include the whole of the medical profession. "One does not need a theory of invisible animals to know it is repugnant to eat with a dirty fork."

He proposed an exchange. He was interested in what she knew. She would "assist" him in his surgery with the cases for which he was able to get hospital approval. Most often a father or husband had purchased a determination that the woman's life was threatened. Mrs. Marini learned a little about a topical anesthetic treatment and a slower, less painful means of cervical dilation.

When they parted ways, he gave her an assembly of elegant steel tools.

"I already own all these," she said.

"Anyway, they're spares. *Curette* derives from the Latin for 'to take care of.'"

"I *know*," she said, exasperated, and shook his hand.

10

A letter arrived in October. Enzo read it through in a glance. Then he read it over more slowly, while an invisible figure behind him wrapped its thick arm around his throat, crushing his windpipe, so that he felt the swell of blood in the eyes and the expulsive twisting of the stomach muscles and the strange jubilation of a man who is being strangled.

It was late on a Sunday night after he and the boy had come home from a weekend of fourteen-hour days harvesting the grapes on his mother-in-law's farm, which once again the bank was threatening to take from her. Before he found the letter, he had sent the boy to bed, but he himself couldn't sleep and had lain down on the cruddy floor of the kitchen, screwing one leg over the other so that the vertebrae snapped, and smoking in the dark while the moon came in.

He felt he ought to clean the house, but he didn't have the talent for it. Mildew thrived in his dishrags and left an odor on the water glasses. A pale film, strewn with hairs, accreted to the toilet rim. It was a house, for all the world, a clapboarded three-bedroom with dormers gaping out of either half of its face; the address painted on the porch post was 123. But to him it was less a house than a building. Furniture rambled from room to room. The boy shouldn't have had to live like that, but slovenliness in a household was like contempt between married people, profoundly sinking its roots long before it sprouted.

He got up from the floor and sat at the kitchen table, playing cards awhile by himself and meditating with his nose on a glass of well water from the farm. Then he drank it down. Black ten on a red jack. The motor of the icebox burned natural gas to keep his water cold. All the unusable cards in his hand reappeared, one after another, and he was beaten. It was the lack of aces that did him in. His fingers were stained from the grapes.

Then he went out to look in the mailbox at the curb, having neglected to check it since the week before.

The surfaces of the neighborhood were plated with frost. The grass cracked underfoot, and the air smelled of nothing but cold and the absence of plant life. Everything was lusterless and tinny.

In the mailbox he found a bill from the fire-insurance company and a letter, corrugated as though it had been rained on.

The letter bore an Italian airmail stamp, and when he opened it under the streetlight he discovered to his astonishment that it was from his father—whose last letter had reached him six years ago, not long after the war, a letter, like many others, that Enzo had not answered. The present letter announced that his father would leave Naples for New York on the thirtieth of September, would spend a week with his niece in Yonkers, and would then make his way to the address on this envelope. It was hoped that the receiver of the letter might know where he might locate his only living son, Mazzone, Vincenzo, who had once sent him mail from this address. He would wire with the specifics of his arrival once he reached New York.

His father's name was Francesco. The boy, being a firstborn, had had to be named for him, but they called him by the diminutive, Ciccio, and his name at school was Frank.

Three weeks passed and still Enzo received no further word. He feared his father's ship had sunk while he also hoped for that very thing.

On the twenty-sixth of October, he returned from work to find, inside his storm door, a telegram including the Yonkers, New York, phone number of the niece, his cousin. Enzo had never heard of her; she must have been born after he left. His feet itched inside the threadbare socks he wore, which failed to soak up his sweat, and there was mortar clumped in his hair. Did he call the number? Yes, he did.

A woman answered briskly and put his father on the line.

The engine room of the ship on which his father had been traveling had caught fire in the mid-Atlantic. It was towed back eastward to the Azores, he said. While there, he had eaten exceptionally well and cheaply. The fruit was of the highest quality; however, the wine was rancid. He had then taken the only available United States–bound liner, headed for New Orleans, where on his arrival he found the stench of the city was so foul that he ate nothing for two days but stale salt crackers. Finally, he had taken a train to New York.

He whispered over the line that Enzo's cousin was obese and unwelcoming. He was keen to get out of New York as quickly as possible.

The conversation was clipped, respectful, bureaucratic. Enzo had trouble understanding his father's dialect and spoke it haltingly. He had not talked with a blood relation in twenty-four years.

His father said evenly, "I probably won't recognize your face. I want you to wear the yellow scarf your mother made you."

"I lost it," Enzo said. He had thrown it away he couldn't remember when.

"Very well. Borrow a yellow scarf. I'll be in the backmost car."

Enzo informed him that he was separated from his wife, who lived in Pittsburgh, in the adjoining state of Pennsylvania. Also, he reminded him about the boy and the boy's name.

His father said he certainly did not need to be reminded, as Enzo's very brief letter announcing the splendid news of the birth of the boy, albeit two years after the fact, was the last they had heard from him.

But about his brothers? Enzo inquired.

No, no. His brothers were quite well. They were employed by the state in the northern city of Bergamo—one was an officer of the national police, the other drove a mail truck. Unfortunately, they were so distant that Enzo's father saw them just twice a year, at Christmas and the summer holidays.

"I only indicated they were dead to state my case with more force," he explained. "I assumed it was you who had died. After all, I received no response to my letters of September 1939, November 1940, December 1945, and March 1946."

There was a crack on the line, which began faintly to pick up a radio station playing Caribbean dance music. The effort of declaiming all of the syllables of all of the dates at once had taxed his father's breath. Enzo heard the air filling the old man's lungs again and took the opportunity to slam the receiver down on the carriage.

The telephone table stood just inside the front entrance of his house, underneath the banister of a staircase that led to the three bedrooms on the upper story. Above the telephone, a calendar dangled on an old curtain hook that was strung through one of the spindles of the banister. He had been given the calendar by a family of Jehovah's Witnesses: a blond lady of thirty-five who visited him on his front porch, together with her husband, who wore a synthetic brown suit and held the hand of a boy toddler dressed in just the same fashion as he. The father and the boy stood behind the mother, grimly staring Enzo down while the woman explained to him that soon, very soon, his house and all the people therein and all the material wealth he had saved would be destroyed by the Lord his God.

The calendar page that was now showing depicted four brown-skinned people bent obliviously over a bean field while a volcano erupted in the background. However, it was the page for July.

Enzo looked at the stairs and climbed them, dodging Ciccio's textbooks and the rank pads of his football uniform, which obstructed the steps.

He drew a bath and peeled off his clothes and got in, soaping and rinsing himself expeditiously, shaving his face and combing the mortar out of his hair underneath the water. Carmelina used to whet his razor for him, but now he did it himself.

He tied on his bathrobe and looked into the boy's room, where Ciccio lay on the floor reading a color comic book, on which the ash of his cigarette had fallen. On the writing desk, the teeth of the second-hand typewriter that Enzo had bought for him, and that he had to be forced by threats and beating to use, were jammed together, so that all of them pointed toward the opening that exposed the paper but none of them reached it, like a mob trying to shove its way onto a bus.

"Get your goddamn books off my stairs," Enzo said with fatigue.

"All right," Ciccio said, turning a page, intent while he read the pictures.

Enzo said, "Do like I say: I want you to put some Brilliantone in the utility sink and fill in the water and wash off all that padding you put inside the football clothes."

Before the boy could answer him, Enzo closed the door and descended the stairs, taking each step more slowly than the last. His tongue was swollen as though a bee had stung it.

Did he ring the number again, incautious, while he sweated through his robe and the calendar pages ruffled in the wind from the open window down the hall? Yes.

"What happened?" his father asked.

Somehow the line had broken, Enzo explained, feeling buoyant and sick, like a child in a toy boat. He had been waiting for the last half hour while the long-distance operator tried to reestablish it, he said. In any event, what was the number of his father's train?

Halloween night. Enzo and the boy drove the truck downtown and left it in the parking lot of the cavernous baseball stadium. Nothing protected the stadium from the winds of the lake, which was only a hundred feet away to the north, and the wind blew through its open corners, playing the building like a reed. They walked through Public Square, the boy, as always, two paces ahead—was it the boy who was speeding up, or was Enzo slowing down?—and into the basement of Erie Station Tower. He told Ciccio that if his grandfather learned, by whatever means, even from a little birdie, that Ciccio smoked cigarettes, he would be beaten within a quarter of an inch of his life.

He had made the boy iron their shirts for once, and Ciccio had done a competent job, but he had used too much starch, and it had turned Enzo's sweat to glue. A train pulled into the terminal. People of all colors spilled out of the cars. Ciccio was in front of him. He tucked the boy's tie under the back of his collar. Enzo's lazy eye veered off as he tried to make sense of the timetable.

"He's going to be a big fucking ballbuster," Ciccio was saying despondently.

"And the language," said Enzo.

"And he won't understand anything I say," Ciccio said. "What do I do with this guy when you're not around?"

"'This guy.' What kind of a word is that?"

Ciccio looked at the pavement and spat on it.

What was the boy? What was the word for him? *Careless*. But if Enzo weren't charged with shaping him, if he were somebody else looking at the boy from the side, then the word he might have used instead was *untroubled*.

Once, while Enzo was in the barber's chair, he had seen Ciccio sliding down the sidewalk across the street with his pack of pals. He was the tallest of them by a head. He smoked, like the others, while they passed a basketball by bouncing it against the concrete of the sidewalk. Then one of them bounced it too hard—it was a piece of mock abuse— and the ball flew over the boy being abused and caromed into the street, where the swerving cars dodged it.

Ciccio went after the ball, sideways. He kept on yammering with the boys. Enzo saw it while Pippo the Barber's scissors chirruped at his sideburns.

Ciccio's feet and his hands were looking for the ball, but the senses that lived in the head were pointed back at the conversation he was having.

All this happened very quickly.

The ball still had a bit of bounce, and Ciccio, reaching it in the near lane, tapped, and tapped again, with his cigarette in the fingers of that very hand.

Look at that boy there.

Where were the cars?

What is the name, Mazzone, that you gave to the boy on the other side of the glass?

Where were the cars that would flatten him?

The ball came under the boy's control. But rather than throwing it back to the sidewalk and hustling out of the way, what did he do (while his father watched unseen, wishing he had a god to call on)? He dribbled it, free and easy, right on the street, and the car approaching slowed to a halt in front of him while Ciccio made a half wave at the driver and in due course reached the group again, never having slowed or sped his untroubled step.

On the platform at the station, Ciccio looked down at his spit and stepped on it.

A man in a white uniform sold them some peanuts. There were many colored children. Another car arrived, and the men climbed down to the platform, cigarettes hanging from their mouths.

"Why isn't he bringing his wife?" Ciccio asked.

"Your grandmother, you meant to say—hey, pick those shells up off the floor," Enzo said. "You're in a public place."

Ciccio bent down. "You got a mother, don't you?"

"No, I don't," Enzo said. "She died."

The boy stood upright. The swollen veins that divagated across his forehead gradually reverted into the skin. He said, "I didn't know that. Why don't you tell me why I didn't know that?"

"She died eight years ago," Enzo said, chewing each bean into a paste before he swallowed it.

"When do I get to find out about your secret mob ties?" Ciccio said. "You know, I mean, come on." He wasn't angry. He didn't get angry. He got mouthy.

Enzo inspected the boy's creased and unpolished calfskin shoes. If he had one wish, it would be to get into the boy's dreams and trouble them.

"It's like you think I'm a worm for the Feds, seriously."

"What do you want to know?"

Ciccio adopted an inquisitorial tone. "What's your real name, *Mazzone?*"

They stood over the trash can, dropping in the shells, inhaling the fragrant bacteria.

"Mazzone," Enzo said. Because he could think of nothing else to say, he added, "What's yours?"

Some of the skins of the nuts were tangled in Ciccio's shameful mustache.

"I'm bored. Why do we have to be so goddamn early for everything? This guy is going to squash me. Why am I telling you? You'll laugh."

He liked it when Ciccio talked, sometimes. He wished he had more to say to him. He was more and more the hearing kind.

The trains barreled into the station along half a dozen tracks with the great noise of many tons of iron rolling on steel. The shriek of the brakes deafened him.

He hadn't gotten a scarf. He would know his father's face. But five minutes after the train had arrived, he and the boy split up, looking for an elderly, confused-looking foreigner certain to be dressed to the nines for travel. Enzo hastened toward the front of the platform. By now the train that had allegedly contained his father had already left, and an identical train had taken its place.

He regretted he hadn't worn the scarf. A dozen silent Negro children were being led off the train by an old Negro woman and a young Negro man wearing a clerical collar.

Enzo headed systematically toward the rear of the platform, stopping to check the bathroom and the ticket counter. He took off his hat and smoothed his hair. He put his hat back on.

Shortly, the boy was standing in front of him, holding the arm of a gnomish gentleman with a carnation in his lapel.

Unfortunately, it was not his father. His father was much bigger than this. The boy was distracting him with games.

"He looks lost, but he isn't the right size," Ciccio said.

The man looked Enzo up and down.

Ciccio held a suitcase in his free hand.

"Stop, Cheech, you're just confusing people. Leave him alone."

"I told you to wear the scarf," said the man, in dialect.

"What did he say?" the boy asked.

A boar hunt. His father waited, wearing a black tie and his only coat, at the mouth of a ravine. Enzo chased the crying animal down the slope. He emerged from the trees, and the boar headed south, but he threw a rock that made it veer the other way, and it charged around a copse of fig trees, following the edge of the dried-out bed of the creek. Moments later he heard the report of the shotgun. He heard his father make a call for his brothers and him to come down from the woods. No one knew yet that he had won. He had chased the boar into the trap. He was fastest. He reached the bottom of the ravine in time to see the old man blow his nose into his handkerchief and twist himself around the panting animal's head, gripping the tusks, and cut its throat, and the blood came out. And then the old man looked up. He looked up. He saw that it was Enzo running in the ravine, pulling on the shirt that he had flapped to flush the boar. Now Enzo reached him, and the old man wiped the blood off his hand, and put the hand to Enzo's face.

The man let go of Ciccio's arm and pulled down Enzo's face and kissed his mouth.

Clocks and smoke. The butane perfume of cigarette lighters flipped open. He had last been kissed on the mouth by a prostitute in the summer of 1950. It was the only time. Later, he regretted the expense.

The old man had had an old man's riven, misleadingly hard and dour face even in Enzo's youth. It seemed like a cunning disguise that he had since grown a layer of fat that had transformed the face into a rough pile of fleshy pouches, like a dilapidated stone wall from which the mortar in the joints has washed away.

"Oh, Vincenzo," he said courteously, "how long it's been since I've seen you."

Enzo thought he saw all the many lights in the station diminish and go bright again, as though the shadow of death had raced across his eyes. "Hello, Pop," he said.

"What did you say?" asked the boy.

Enzo's father let go of his face and turned to the boy. "Mazzone Francesco," he said, indicating for the boy to incline his head, and then kissing his cheeks, "I am called Mazzone Francesco as well."

It was 7:14 in the evening, said the great clock suspended from the ceiling of the vaulted vestibule.

"Tell him to stop kissing me," Ciccio said.

"Doesn't he understand anything I'm saying?" said Francesco Mazzone.

"Sometimes," Enzo said. "He doesn't know how to speak. He understands when he tries."

"You're talking about me, but what are you saying?" said the boy.

Outside, Francesco wanted to know if it was customary for children to dress in such dramatic fashion. Witches, ballerinas, ghosts, and hobos entered and departed the storefronts.

"He's confused about the costumes," Enzo explained.

"How disgraceful," Francesco said.

"This is our Public Square," the boy said pleasantly.

"This is the square, he says," Enzo translated.

"I see that for myself, thank you."

They walked down Coshocton Street toward the water.

Francesco Mazzone shook a couple of Camel cigarettes from a pack inside his coat and handed one to Enzo and one to the boy. "I bought these in Yonkers. They are of the very highest quality." His head was a well-cut block on which the trim white hair was meticulously arranged.

Ciccio was wide-eyed with awe and gratitude.

The old man had taken Ciccio's arm.

"Enzo, translate."

"What did he say?"

"I'm dying from cold," Francesco said, addressing the boy. "Is it always like this? I've never been so cold in my life."

Enzo started to translate, but the boy waved him off. They managed to communicate through pointing and nods. As they approached the truck on the dark side of the stadium, the boy started using Italian words he had always refused to admit he knew how to pronounce.

They drove east down Maumee Avenue, Francesco in the window seat, the boy with the gearshift between his legs, shifting when Enzo engaged the clutch. Francesco and the boy were holding a more or less regular discussion, with only occasional recourse to Enzo for translation.

They drove through niggertown.

"This is where the moolies live," the boy said.

"Hey."

"What? I thought that was the word."

"What did he say?" Francesco said.

"This is where the tizzoons live," Ciccio said.

"I *told* you what to call them."

"Is there a law?" his father asked. He meant a law about who could live where.

"No," Enzo said. "Maybe. I don't know, honestly."

They passed through a series of green lights. Snow fell. Francesco held up a finger, pointed at himself, indicated the truck, and then spoke briefly.

The boy said, "He's never been in a car before?"

"That can't be," Enzo said.

"Buses, of course. All the time. When we go to see your brothers in Bergamo. Never once in a private car. This is a strange kind of car. What kind of car is this?"

"A pickup," the boy said.

Francesco repeated the word.

The boy said, in Italian, with nary an accent, "Your voyage, how it was? You am comfortable on it?"

"Where did you learn to talk like that?" Enzo demanded.

"I can't. I don't know," the boy said, downshifting. "It just comes out." That was the boy. Opening his mouth for anything that knocked on his rotten teeth.

And here was their church, the boy explained.

Enzo had been married in it twenty-three years before, with his union pin holding the boutonniere to his jacket and the boys from Local 238 standing in for relatives. Carmelina wore a satin suit and a small hat with a veil on it. He used to wake up in the morning with her sweet rose soap on his breath and a loose strand of her hair stuck in his throat.

Something was slowing Enzo down. It had been slowing him down for a long time. Eventually, like a ball thrown straight up that slows and slows, he would come to a stop for a moment, in midair, and begin his descent.

Francesco Mazzone, throwing one leg over the other and turning himself suavely, gripped Ciccio's chin, turning the head from side to side, examining it skeptically, like a rancher at a livestock auction. "Such a good-looking boy," he said, staccato, in dialect. "You should do something about these teeth, however, Enzo. Lemon juice and bicarbonate. Morning and afternoon."

"What did he say?" the boy asked.

Enzo didn't answer.

Tomorrow was All Saints' Day, and after that All Souls', but he had forgotten to buy candles to light in his house for his dead.

II

Some kid caught hold of Ciccio's hair, a rassler from the public school who smelled of Munster cheese, sort of a dude, with his corduroy collar up—never mind how the fight got started. They were downtown, at the New Odessa rail yard. Ciccio had the usual advantage of his height and reach. But this individual went for the hair, no self-respect, and bounced Ciccio's face on a railroad tie.

Now Ciccio was leaking blood from a gash on the high bone of the cheek, limp with fear of what Mrs. Marini was going to do to him. But he'd allowed a wound of similar depth to go unattended in the past—it was on his forearm, he kept his sleeves rolled down—and it got so fouled up he'd had to dig out the pus with a spoon.

It was the Wednesday night before Thanksgiving, a holiday they hadn't kept since his mother went away, six years previous. Nobody ever told him what the reason was.

Mrs. Marini probed indifferently at the swollen mess under his eye before changing her glasses to scrutinize the clothes, sniffing at a creosote blotch in the elbow of his jacket and then, with heartfelt scorn, smacking his face on the clean side. "When you die your father will have no heirs, don't you realize that?" she said. "Go to the bathroom."

There was a pot on the stove and the kitchen smelled of boiling poultry, but Ciccio's appetite had just now left him. She hobbled down the cellar stairs.

Francesco Mazzone, the earlier model, lay on his back on the floor of the sewing room tinkering with the chassis of the desk. He had found an electric motor in the trash on someone's curb and was trying to substitute it for the pedal-action drive of Mrs. Marini's sewing machine, which excited the rheumatism in her hip. Or so Ciccio gathered from the two dialect words he recognized, *machine* and *trash*, and from the looks of things. The rubber pedal and the frayed belt that turned the flywheel had been tossed behind the dressmaker's dummy into the heap she set aside for the paper-rags man, who would also take copper, tin, and bicycle tires. Earlier in the month, the old man had retiled the bathroom back at home with scavengings and rehabilitated her coffee percolator, a device he had never met before, the product of which disappointed him.

"Did you win?" asked Francesco Mazzone, taking Ciccio's arm and leading him down the hall.

"Yes, I win," Ciccio said. But he hadn't won in any respect.

He sat on the lid of the commode. The disembodied heads of three young plaster ladies wearing Mrs. Marini's other hairdos observed him with their remote, sexual, pouting looks from a shelf over the toilet paper. There was a fourth, but it was bald. His grandfather sat on the lip of the bathtub marveling at what you could find in this country's rubbish and handling Ciccio's skull in such a way as to position his thumbs on either side of the wound, pulling it apart and peering inside with one eye gaping and the other twisted shut. He exhaled tobacco, oranges, and tooth decay. His arms and his hands were so big and his grip on Ciccio's head was so secure that he might have twisted the head off Ciccio's shoulders like a squash.

"How did you get these little sticks in here?" the old man said, shiningly proud and slack-jawed, so that Ciccio could see all the way back to where his yellow tongue disappeared down his throat. The eroded molars put Ciccio in mind of the Black Hills of South Dakota, where he had never been. He had never been anyplace but the farm, and here.

"I turn him piss, shit, blood. I make nothing. The stars makes circles at his head. I rise. I come home. The victorious," Ciccio said carefully.

The old man contorted his lips to dislodge a seed in his gums, and succeeded, and swallowed heavily.

Mrs. Marini supervised Ciccio's washing of his hands with disinfectant soap and let him proceed straight through rinsing before she made him do it all over again with the brush. Only then did she allow him to handle the tweezers she had soaked in alcohol. His grandfather held the mirror while Ciccio picked the splinters out of his face. She dabbed the wound with peroxide and smeared it with iodine. He was saddened to hear that stitches weren't called for but held out hope for a little scarring. A faint, permanent change in coloration was all he wanted, something to observe in later years, when he'd be able to think better, nothing that would make him look retarded, or more so, rather, just a historical marker, a chip in the favored plate.

Ciccio Mazzone took no pride in his looks. Something was amiss in his face, but he didn't know what it was. The scientific thing would have been to monitor the changes of his features over time by comparing Ciccio Mazzone (or Frank, as nobody at home would call him) with his baby pictures, but none existed. Pop, when asked why not, only cut the crusts off his sandwich, carried it on the cutting board to the ottoman in the front room, crashed softly to the carpet, and ate.

Mrs. Marini snipped some gauze and taped it to Ciccio's face, all the time slugging him with abuse. If Pop had said the same things to him he would have felt backwardly joyful, but coming from her—he wanted to pull his shirt over his eyes in shame.

The trick with the sewing machine had worked. Mrs. Marini even applauded, which Ciccio had never seen her do except to be nasty. The screaming motor made a smell of ozone. She sent them back to number 123 with a pot of chicken stew and some changes of the bandage. Pop was working time and a half, so supper would have to wait.

Ciccio and Francesco Mazzone made their way down the hill, quiet. All the stores were closed in preparation for the holiday that nobody understood. Due to recent petty theft, the church was chained shut. A thin rain came down. All day the city had been leaking dark fluids down its curbsides, prone in its dress grays, like a dead Confederate soldier.

He had had to wear his good shoes to school for a debate in Western Civilization. Then he had slunk with the fellows for two hours in the drizzle, and the leather had shrunk around his feet, which now tormented him. He guessed it might be all right to have some Sally or

Susan-Anne, to tell her, Aw, baby, my feets hurt bad. And she'd be soft with him. Probably. But then she'd want to come visit at home.

His grandfather handed him the umbrella they were sharing and hiked up his pants like a dainty chick at the beach so the bottoms wouldn't drag in the runoff.

It was a strange day. Ciccio was feeling unlike himself. He was fifteen, restive, aggravated. During similar moods when he was a little kid, he would climb onto a chair in front of the calendar over the telephone table, flip ahead a few months, and write, in a square that indicated a very distant date, *This day will never come.*

He suspected that he missed his mother. He turned the suspicion over in his brain and poked under its folds and did some timeworn experiments to test it, and he was embarrassed when he concluded that it wasn't true. For example, two years ago she had sent his father a telegram saying she wanted to come stay with them, but Ciccio had intercepted the shitty thing, the telegram, and disposed of it. Did he regret that? Nope.

They passed the darkened pork store and made the turn onto Twenty-second Street, a turn he had made one hundred thousand times. He confessed to Francesco Mazzone that his shoes were ruined and his feet were in pain. Anyway, that was what he was trying to get across. And the old man only sniffed, so that the hair growing from his nose fluttered, and the rain went *tap tap* on the umbrella.

Francesco Mazzone had made a practice of rousing Ciccio at five a.m. by sopping a dishtowel in cold water and slathering Ciccio's face with it. Then he walked Ciccio to school—a four-mile slog down Saint Ambrose Boulevard, the road thick with smoke under the sinister light of the streetlamps while the trolleys sped down the median. Ciccio had always ridden the trolley before, dozing through the jolts and rattles, and had stumbled into morning chapel with the rheum still clogging his eyes. Now he'd come to count on this long exertion in raw weather to grease his mental and bodily wheels. They didn't have much to say to each other while they walked, and there was a generosity in this, a roominess. It left him free to watch the street and think. So long as he didn't fall into the trap of thinking about himself, he enjoyed it.

The old man would shuffle along, tying and retying his scarf and yanking at his pants as they went. How he managed to walk all the way into the city and back again on his ruined feet, Ciccio didn't know. The only complaint his grandfather ever made was that his feet hurt. At the same time the old man was convinced that all his foot trouble came from poor circulation and that unless he walked for at least three hours a day, his feet would dry up and fall apart. Ciccio had seen him take off his socks, exposing the dried-out flecks of sponge that were his toenails, and the many corns, and the purple-blotched and bloated insteps. The bones were contorted in such a way that you wondered how he could walk at all.

The two of them and their chicken supper arrived at home. Ciccio climbed the stairs and threw his books on the floor in his room. He lit a cigarette and stumbled down to the kitchen, faint under the effect of the noxious chemicals he'd introduced into his bloodstream. He felt trapped and crippled, thinking, Ciccio Mazzone, Ciccio Mazzone, Ciccio Mazzone. He felt at a permanent remove from everything he saw. Hard to say what had brought this on. He hated this house. He hated the smell of the house.

He wished he had somebody to talk to.

At the sink, the old man was drawing hot water into their stockpot. He indicated with a movement of the hand like the dribbling of an invisible basketball that Ciccio should sit down.

Ciccio got an ashtray from the counter and seated himself, observing the square and determined back of this figure he resembled in no way but in name.

The old man heaved and pivoted, bending deeply, and dropped the steaming pot on the floor at Ciccio's feet. He knelt strainingly. Then he began to unlace Ciccio's shoes.

The mind of Ciccio Mazzone was an unruly animal. He could not explain why it would buck or leap or chase some innocent creature that wasn't truly there at moments when the world outside the brainpan gave it no clear impetus for doing these things. In any case, here were the events being recounted in his mind at the present moment:

At the siege of Yorktown, in 1781, when the Americans were trying to free themselves from the British, Lafayette and a French army had come to the Americans' aid. One hundred thirty-six years then elapsed. Lafayette, Washington, George III, Cornwallis, all had died. Their children and grandchildren had died. The Germans were beating up on the French, and the Americans decided to get into the Great War and defend them. John Joseph "Black Jack" Pershing, the American general, landed in France. The story was that he then traveled to Paris and visited the crypt where the old hero was buried in soil brought from the United States, and one of his aides, Colonel C. E. Stanton, said aloud, "Lafayette, we are here."

To Ciccio Mazzone the significance of this was that we may perceive ourselves to be careening aimlessly through space, when in fact distant events have thrown us into long, elliptical, cometlike orbits, far from our origins, and eventually we will circle back on people whose lives preceded and gave rise to our own. We may recognize them immediately. Or else we may meet a stranger for the first time and, while shaking his hand, feel vividly that an ancient obligation has finally been kept.

"I'm going to show you how to take care of your feet," the old man said. "Pay attention and don't forget how I'm doing this."

His glasses were fogged. He took them off, inserted one of the stems between his teeth, and rolled up the sleeves of his shirt. He stripped Ciccio of his sodden socks and cuffed his pants. Then he seized Ciccio's feet and plunged them, with his own hands, into the stinging water.

The old man shifted his weight from knee to knee, the lenses dangling from his jaw while his white hands and Ciccio's white feet reddened in the pot. Hands and feet were then pulled from the water, and the old man began his work.

Each of the toes was pinched individually and rolled between the meaty fingers. He scrubbed the dead skin from Ciccio's heels with a brush and picked the rot from between the toes, flicking it into the water. The webbing between the toes was cracked, and the old man's fingers were crooked.

He dropped the feet back into the water for a minute and stretched his hands. Then he lifted the feet out again and jammed his thumbs into the arches. He squeezed and stretched, kneading the balls of the feet, and isolated a long tendon, the existence of which Ciccio had been unaware, and rubbed it down and pulled it straight.

Ciccio hadn't realized how stiff and cold his feet were until they began to loosen and warm. His foot was held in both of the old man's hands, was wrung by them, then released suddenly, and he could feel the blood go.

Meanwhile, in a distant quarter, the mind of Ciccio Mazzone was chasing Lafayette. Marie-Joseph-Paul-Yves-Roch-Gilbert du Motier, marquis de Lafayette. Some decades after the Revolution he'd taken a tour of the states and everywhere he went they named towns for him that persisted to the present. From this trip, he took home to France a box of American dirt so he could be buried under it.

Now, Ciccio would have liked to talk to Lafayette. Maybe Lafayette could have answered some questions he had. Because this thing of taking the American dirt home but still wanting to be buried in France, this was the act of a man who was really cut in half, like Ciccio was cut in half (but what were his halves?), and had found a way—the shipping of the dirt—of turning an idea into a real thing. Like these pods at the bottoms of Ciccio's legs were only ideas to him, they were kind of unlikely locomotive machines that translated electrical impulses and muscle contractions and logarithms into swift forward motion, but the old man was saying, They are feet, they are feet.

12

The new road to Ashtabula was freshly, soundly paved, a four-lane superhighway, white with salt, that shortened the trip to the farm from two hours to one and led them along the lakeshore, through the ashy manufacturing and port towns, rather than through the corn and hog tent counties to the south, as the old roads did. As the truck flew over the surface, the frigid air whiffled into the vents, through the simmering foils of the radiator under the dash, and out over the shoes of the two men inside, saturating the cab agreeably with warmth. The younger man, Enzo, who drove, resembled his father in the slight flatness of his crown, in the furrows that had begun to show at the corners of his fleshy mouth, and in his thick, mangled hands, on which the skin was too scabrous for hair to grow. However, both his father's eyes looked squarely forward, unlike his own, and the nails of the fingers were better cared for.

The old man thrilled at any chance to ride in the truck. Likewise, he adored the machine itself and kept watch over it in spare hours lest passing children molest it in the driveway. He touched its body only with gloved hands. It was the most valuable piece of merchandise anyone in his family had ever owned. The vibrations from the floorboards, he said, did more for his feet than any previous therapy he had devised.

It was the twenty-third of December. They were going to have another working Christmas, but Enzo preferred it that way. The boy had been at the farm a week already, paring vines. Patrizia had driven her wreck into the city to retrieve him the day school let out. But there was plenty of work that still needed doing. All the vineyard posts had to be repounded and the rotting ones replaced before the ground froze.

The truck glided across Painesville and Perry without stopping while Francesco Mazzone gnawed an apple core and likened it to the mealy ration apples he had eaten at the end of the war, which led him to the broader topic of wartime shortages, and finally to wartime losses, a subject Enzo had taken pains to evade. The old man, once launched on his narration, enunciated it definitively, as though he had given it many times before to strangers on buses, ships, and trains. He was an easy talker and had no secrets.

Enzo already knew from one of the letters that, due to the Allied invasion and the shelling of Naples and the surrounding towns, the civilian population of his village had abandoned it and spent four months living in caves in the hills. The occupying Germans, aware they couldn't hold the village, busied themselves booby-trapping doorknobs, irons, bidets, light switches, kitchen gardens, shoes, corpses, mansard doors, birdcages, and jewelry boxes, hoping to slow the Allied advance. The chapel where Enzo had been confirmed was destroyed when, upon the arrival of the Allied troops, a boy ascended the belfry stairs and set the bell ringing. The letter, sent in early 1945, neglected all but the most critical pieces of personal news. It was addressed *To the Bearer of This Letter* and had been dictated, like all the others, to Enzo's sister Giulia, who wrote it on faded blue paper dating from the early years of the Fascist government. Enzo knew the paper well; it had been given to him by a teacher in school, and he'd left it behind. *It would be profoundly appreciated,* read his sister's handwriting, *if the gentle bearer of this letter would be so good as to pass it on to Mazzone Vincenzo, if such a person is known to him.* Enzo remembered the letter in detail, although he had read it only once and thrown it immediately in the trash.

"All winter we ate walnuts," the old man said. "Nothing but walnuts. Your nephew Filipo, who you never met, stole about ten bushels of walnuts from the German commissary. He was discovered and executed, with a shot, here, in the spine. But, see, they didn't know where he'd hidden the walnuts. There were six of us. Your mother, Gregorio, your sister, her husband, her daughter, and me. Filipo was the seventh, Giulia's boy. We all had terrible coughs, we were cold. Moreover, there had been seven of us and then there were six.

"We would sit on the lip of the cave, truly like savages, filthy, with nothing to do. The boredom was worse than the fear. From the mouth of the cave you could see Giuseppina Fiorentina's orange grove. But we had heard that there were bombs in the branches of the trees, and mines in the grass. We watched the fruit become fat, and then dry, and then fall to the ground. And we ate nothing but the walnuts. And after the war we learned that it was Fiorentina herself who had led everyone to believe the grove was mined, so nobody would steal her precious mandarins and clementines. I don't think the Germans even knew it was there. She made everybody believe this, and then she went back into town to save her music box, and they found her afterward in her bedroom with her arms blown away. It was boxes where valuables could be kept that were the first things—that is, the first things in which they installed the traps. They started to do it even before we left our houses. The first things were jewelry boxes and music boxes and armoires.

"In any case, later it was March and the wild asparagus was in season. Our house had been cleared of traps by an Australian who was working with the Allies. There were five bombs just in our little house, which I'm sure you recall. We were all very poorly nourished. But your mother had somehow acquired a cup of cream. This was, I can't tell you, a feast, just to have a cup of cream, and the Americans had given us this cheap pasta, and so your mother went out in the morning to look for asparagus to complete the meal. The zone was supposed to be clear, where they found her, but obviously it wasn't clear.

"She had come home with this cream in an aluminum can and she was, truly, wailing with happiness, you know as she would do. We put it in the pantry to keep it cool. We felt like having a celebration, and I had two cigarettes. I can't remember how I got my hands on them. I can't remember, either, why we smoked them this way, but in any case we didn't smoke them one to each, we smoked the one together—we passed it between us, very romantic—and then we smoked the second one the same way. She departed. I smoke a lot now. I didn't used to. I enjoy these American cigarettes very much.

"Close your window a minute while I light this."

Enzo slid his window up and the old man struck his match.

"An American soldier came to our door. Someone told him where to find our house. I had never seen an American up close before. I thought he would be much taller than he was. I didn't know what he was saying but it was late in the afternoon and your mother had been gone for many more hours than I had expected, and I knew in my bones what had happened. I went to the bedroom to get my good shoes. Then I left the house with the American. He led me to a small room at the school. There were a lot of Americans there drinking that thin coffee you have and painting all the tables and chairs in the room with green paint. The fumes of the paint made me light-headed, but perhaps I was already unwell. They must have known who I was, because they stopped talking when they saw me. One of the soldiers could speak a little of some kind of Calabrese. I understood him enough to know what they were taking me to see. He led me down the corridor.

"I was outraged that they had not cleaned her face. I simply couldn't believe it. Her face was painted with mud. They didn't even put a blanket or a sheet on her body. Her leg was missing. The whole leg. I remember I looked about the room, but I couldn't find it. It was as confusing as if my own leg were missing. The American from Calabria offered me a cigarette and I told him to get me some water and a towel for her face, but he just pointed the cigarette at me. I told him very clearly to get me a water bucket and a towel, and he left the room. Then I sat down and waited for him to come back. I looked underneath the table for the leg, but of course it wasn't there. After perhaps half an hour, he returned—with a cup of tea. That was when I left and went home. I got what I needed from the house and went back to the school."

When they arrived at the farm, Francesco Mazzone answered a question that had puzzled Enzo for twenty years: Why was no one able to grow respectable wine grapes in Ashtabula County? The soil was too good. It was evident even in December that the summer vegetation was rife and the topsoil must be very dark and rich. The old man assumed they had plenty of rain, which they did. These plants would hardly have to work for their livelihoods and would throw off an abundance of use-less foliage. What you needed was rocky soil, poor precipitation. The plants had to feel they were in danger of dying off so that they would put all of their energies into producing fruit. No amount of pruning could correct for the soil, and no grape with any depth of flavor would be produced unless the root was made to suffer. He allowed it was suit-able terrain for table grapes.

He listened with interest while Patrizia described the myriad pests that yearly afflicted her crop and the expense of the sprays she had to buy to destroy them.

The strain of carrying her big, unequal breasts had begun to twist her back, and her neck was bowed like a stalk holding up a heavy flower, but still her step was long and quick. Her white braids were tied with locks of her own trimmed-off hair and pinned to the back of her head under a heavy bonnet. She wore a widow's black dress, although she had no way of knowing what had become of Umberto, whom she referred to using the term that described his relationship to the person with whom she was speaking: "your father-in-law," "your grandfather," or even "your old acquaintance." She did not refer to Carmelina or Toni at all.

It snowed Christmas Eve, while the boy slept on a cot in the kitchen and the two men went to bed on straw mattresses spread over the floor of the parlor, by the stove. Enzo was conscious all night long; the straw blades pierced his nightshirt, and his father's raucous snores abused him like a harangue. He rarely slept through the night in his mother-in-law's house, anyway, although usually it was the quiet that disturbed him.

Eventually he crept outside wearing his rubbers and the brown me-rino coat he kept at the farm—an elegant garment, a hand-me-down, belonging originally to Mrs. Marini's husband, that Enzo had misused by allowing the dander of Patrizia's rabbits to penetrate it. The air was still and nearly warm, and the thick snow traversed it cautiously, as if trying to escape notice, although it covered everything and rose to his knees. He dipped his hand in it and brought it to his mouth and ate, and felt the cold course in his veins.

On Christmas morning, oranges, grapefruit, and cheese were exchanged as gifts. Patrizia had crocheted an afghan for Ciccio out of a drab yarn she had bought for a nickel at an estate sale.

After breakfast, they dressed and went out. Patrizia drove the tractor at a crawl through the snow, while Enzo and the boy stood in the high wagon it pulled, each swinging behind him an enormous oak mallet that he brought down on the tops of the posts as they passed them. The old man followed on foot in the rut of one of the wagon wheels, delighting in the snow, the like of which in depth he had never seen.

The vineyard under snowfall looked like a sheet of paper on which a single word had been typed, and typed again, and again, and again; until the ink in the ribbon failed and the word, at first so distinct, could hardly be read.

What was the word? For Ciccio Mazzone, to whose bored and erratic mind it occurred that the vineyard under the snow looked like a page and the identical rootstocks and locust posts like the same letters endlessly repeated, the word was a phony Latinism, an American invention meant to sound like it came from the noble Romans, although it probably came from a West Virginia riverboat pilot or an itinerant preacher; the word meant "to flee" or "to abscond," but he would rather not speak it until he was on his way out of this fucking place, if you don't mind.

For his father, on the other hand—who watched the boy with satisfaction as the great hammerhead sailed behind him, twisting his back as it went, until with a little upward heave the boy pitched it over his head—the word, if there was a word that repeated itself across the white page of his mind, uninvited and unremitting, was not, in fact, *bastard*, not anymore, not for ten years, at least; nor *Carmelina*, sorry to say, he had given up on that; but *sleep*.

Sleep, said the posts when he pounded them, as he inhaled the sulfurous fumes of the diesel engine and tore a frozen shoot off one of the vines and chewed it.

Two nights later, Enzo and his father headed back to the city. Ciccio stayed at the farm. The old man's return train for New York was to leave early the next morning, and Enzo thought of the soft springs of his bed at home with love and hope.

The roads had been cleared after the Christmas Eve snow shower, but now it was snowing again. Shortly after the men drove away from the farm, the snow turned to rain. The highway was black and shimmered under the headlights. After tomorrow, it was unlikely Enzo would ever meet Francesco Mazzone again.

The windshield wipers were beating like mad. Enzo saw the road less distinctly than the rain itself—the glowing atoms that emerged from obscurity in the near distance, hung there for a fraction of a second, and then shot at him by the millions.

"Now, about the boy, there's something I should explain—," he began, and turned his head.

His father's posture was rigid, as always, and his heavy arms were folded tightly against his ribs. But the rumpled eyes were shut, and the head was bowed in sleep.

Enzo could faintly make out the white stripe on the side of the road, along which he was guiding the truck.

He had parked the old Buick by the curb, he had climbed the stairs. His socks had been soaked through since lunch. He was never to forget that he had gone into the apartment—right through the front room, and then directly to the bedroom—opened the bureau, and changed his socks. Only then had he strayed back into the front room and found her on the floor behind the coffee table, her face pressed against the ottoman. Somehow she had fallen, evidently, and somehow, in falling, her dress had been hiked up over her behind. Which for some reason was naked. And somehow, evidently, she had hit her head, because she was unconscious, on the floor there, with the bleeding, although he could locate no bruise on the head. She had fallen and had been bleeding seriously, the blood was on the Oriental, and she was unconscious. He had carried her to the bathroom, her little legs were limp and slick, and put her in the tub, bending the knees so the feet would fit inside. He stood up, scanning the room, for what? A hairbrush—her hair was a mess—and didn't find one. He ran to the kitchen, looking, for what? A rag. He had been utterly at a loss as to what had taken place. There had been a water glass, strange, a single water glass drying on the rack by the kitchen sink. It wasn't Lina's way to leave glasses out; she dried them and returned them to the cupboard. He had filled the glass with water from the tap and had drunk it down.

He was so tired.

Something warm and analgesic was suffusing his brain. The effect was like the stuporous, chemical ease that follows sexual release, and it led him toward the fathomless sleep of early marriage. The sleep of the thousand years.

Nine years passed.

He had come home from work. How many times had he come home from work? He had told the boy to run him a bath. He had asked the boy where his mother was, and the boy had said he didn't know.

In the corner of Enzo's vision, his father's sleeping head jerked upright. "My God, wake up!" the old man cried.

Enzo looked again for the white stripe along the right side of the road and found it. But it was two stripes, and they were yellow. He was driving in the wrong lane.

Brilliantone.

Stand up so I can beat you.

Ad astra per aspera.

Momentum? Momentum is easy. Momentum, on a perfectly frictionless surface, is equal to the mass of the object times the speed.

He engaged the brake, and yet the truck continued its forward motion. Headlights growing brighter by the millisecond. The wheel was turned from side to side, and yet the truck kept on going, straight as the road, and struck the opposing vehicle face on face in an exclamation of shrieking metal and glass.

Sleep.

Up the highway, down the highway. He washes, you dry. Close the mouth when chewing. Close the light when leaving the room.

I was eleven. There was an uncle, the name was Gregorio, who leased me from my father at grain-cutting time, and who I loved better than all the others. He had left to fight in the war against Turkey and returned with a collection of postcards depicting the cities of the north in painted colors, one for each of us. But for me, secretly, there was another gift, a silver cutlass taken from the Turk he killed in Libya, my finest possession. I used to keep it in a hole in the ground in a wooden box, under a medlar tree.

Today, the two of us were walking home. We had been out from sunup taking in his wheat. The scythes, we left in a shack by the field. Our feet were bare. The heat, even now, at twilight, was incredible. We were starved and thirsty when we reached the final slope and the bell tower in town came into view, far off. Then we were hopping downhill, along the path, going faster, then faster.

Then we were running, both of us. The stones pricked my feet but it didn't matter, we were running. When at the foot of the hill we hit the main road, we were at a sprint, the both of us, shoulder-to-shoulder. It was impossible to go any faster. But then I did.

I pulled away, breathing in the dust. I was young and fast. I was alone in front. My determined feet were small and weightless. The ground gave out under me.

13

Mrs. Marini and Patrizia drove downtown to pick up Lina at the train station on New Year's Eve. They walked across Public Square and into Erie Station Tower and rode the elevator to the secondary basement, where toilet paper and butterscotch candy were stuck to the concrete and everywhere they looked, colored people of every age and tint crowded the platform, making them both anxious to get out of there. The block signals down the track turned green, and a locomotive arrived from Youngstown with what seemed to be actual blood and animal parts on the cowcatcher. Another train pulled in, from Baltimore, and an aged colored woman stepped into the gangway, holding her hat to her head. Then she seemed to see it was not the way out, went back inside the car, and emerged a minute later at the side door, goggling at the throng on the platform, tremulously touching her hat as though to reassure herself it was still there, until another old colored woman called to her and rushed to her and took her bag. A tall white woman, biting her lip, wearing a blue coat with a mink-neck collar, was engrossed in a movie magazine, on the back cover of which a grinning, mustachioed Western actor testified that Luckies Taste Better. Somebody tried to sell them a chocolate bar. What appeared to be a perfectly good man's boot stood upright, shiny, in a rubbish can.

Earlier that day. Mrs. Marini paid the undertaker and bought herself a Danish pastry at Rocco's on the way home. Once inside, she kept her long johns on and wore a stocking hat in place of her hair. She couldn't remember a chill that had lingered so long and defied so many means of throwing it off. She made herself wear a shawl—and she despised shawls. The urge to wear a shawl is the body's advice that you had better get your paperwork in order and unhide the petty cash so your heirs won't miss it. She drank half a gallon of steaming water with lemon, but it passed through her too quickly to do its work.

She wrapped an afghan over the shawl. (Abjection; serfdom.) She exercised by pacing from the kitchen to the parlor to the bedroom to the parlor to the pantry, up the stairs, down the stairs, down again into the cellar to shovel more coal into the furnace. Back upstairs. (Her hip! Suffering!) Her face was gray and her fingers were blue. She was determined not to let a certain party see her like this.

She positioned a chair over the register in the kitchen floor. She opened the dictionary on the credenza. She rubber-banded the crossword to the cutting board in her lap. The pen was in hand. The clock said 10:17. She gave herself twenty minutes.

Work fast. Scan for capital letters in the middle of clues, indicating facts, indicating only one possible answer. *Capital of Yemen. Dog of Thin Man. Joseph of Gori.* No loafing now—*Sanaa, Asta, Stalin*—or you missed the point.

An enchanted moment came, an erotic flash, at fourteen across: eight letters; second-to-last letter an *a*; the clue, *Baloney.*

She was a naked woman reaching into a tree, plucking a plum from the branch.

Claptrap.

She had trouble with thirteen down: ten letters, *An image that bleeds through.* She had *nti* in the middle. Last letter, *o.* What were they talking about? Then *pe* at the beginning. Was it *pentimento?* She consulted the dictionary. She had not known it counted as an English word.

On filling in the last letter, with two minutes to spare, she felt the familiar triumph. She had defeated the puzzle writer. But triumph was succeeded immediately by hopelessness. She often felt this when the puzzle was done. The paint repented and gave up the image it was hiding. The crossword faded, and underneath was the day's agenda. None of this was helping her color.

She needed a plan.

It came to her.

She would stew herself. She left her hat on the hair of one of the plaster heads in the lavatory downstairs. She took a detective novel with her to the bath and sunk into the tub. She refreshed the water every ten minutes, draining a little and refilling, reading the book cover to cover, until she could have peeled her toenails out of their slots. Sweat stung her eyes.

She tossed the book onto the toilet seat and pulled herself to a standing position with the rails Vincenzo had, to her zealous and futile protestations, bolted into the tile. Microscopic machinists had tunneled into the flesh of her leg, filed the ball and socket of her hip to a glassy finish, and painted them with Vaseline. She could've run a marathon, but she had more pressing business. Her wristwatch on the toilet seat said it was 3:03. She toweled off the mirror and observed her moist, bald head. Her victory over the cold was absolute. She could've fried an egg in her palm, but she had business.

She dried herself. She had to get a move on. Patrizia and Ciccio were due any minute to pick her up and go to the station.

She pinned her wig, an extravagant black pouf, to what was left of her hair. She had the smallest possible moment of regret while putting in her earrings. What with so many years of metal dragging at her earlobes, the holes weren't piercings anymore, they were dragged-down gashes in the cartilage. Had she known she would live this long, she would've waited to pierce her ears until she was fifty. But, then, if she'd waited to pierce her ears, Nico would never have had occasion to buy her all these earrings to begin with.

Very good. Her hair was on straight, her taupe rayon stockings were clipped up, her color was high. The image in the mirror showed its teeth. She saw a spark at the edge of her mind. It was an idea, at first distant and indistinct, and it was shooting toward her like an arrow in a dream. It was a hideous idea, but she was not culpable for having conceived it, because it had attacked her from the outside. She hadn't thought it up, it had thought itself onto her; however, she could not help but recognize that it was indisputably true. The idea was that she would outlive them all.

Her purse was black. Her dress, of course, was black; all of her dresses were black. The open-toed mules she picked from the closet—she was impervious to cold now, she wanted to look harum-scarum and regal at the same time, the queen of Hell—were black. She hadn't set foot outside of her house in any other color since 1915. She hadn't set eyes on Lina, her lamb, her little lover Lina, since 1946. She painted her face up strikingly. She sharpened her cheekbones into scimitars. She didn't want to look good. She wasn't vain, merely. She wanted to look terrifying. She practiced the countenance with which she would greet Lina on the platform. Was she more frightening with her arms folded or at her sides? The sneer, she found, was less effective than closing the lips tight and dilating the nostrils. Don't show the teeth until you are moving in for the kill.

The senses in which Lina was at fault were too many to list, but that didn't stop her. There was the disappearing with no trace and no word for days and days. There was thereafter the word every couple of years communicating little more than that she was alive and in a lunar Western outpost working in the kitchen of a school, and then, of all places, in Pittsburgh. There was the reasonable if not demonstrable hypothesis that, Enzo and his father having reportedly been dead tired before they left the farm, they may both have fallen asleep, if only for a second, which never would have happened if Lina had been in the car. She never fell asleep in cars. She would have kept Enzo awake or driven them home herself, because she wasn't proud and careless behind the wheel like he was. There was the little matter of leaving her boy with no mother. There was the husband who said, Thick or thin. There was the mother whom everybody else had already abandoned. There was the man in the other car, who was also killed, and Lina would have talked Enzo awake or driven herself. There was the no reason ever given, to anybody, not in a letter, not in a phone call, for leaving. There was Mrs. Marini's own theory that there never had been a reason, only a decision, made and executed in a single deft, unmeditated stroke. There was Costanza Marini. There was, What about her? There was, I gave you my heart every day for thirty years. There was, Even when you pass a dead dog on the road, you pay it the courtesy of a backward glance. There was, I drove you from my thoughts, I did not say your name while you were away.

She may have reserved her severest judgment for the sins, committed by someone else, of which she happened to consider herself most guilty, but that wasn't the point. She wasn't interested in extenuating circumstances or Christian psychology or petty tolerance. She was interested in driving a stake of fear into Lina's heart. The Lord would have his opportunity for retribution in due course. Meantime, there was a price to be paid down here, at home.

She was plucking her eyebrows before the bedroom mirror when Patrizia and the boy arrived. Ciccio came in and sat on the bed, expressing curiosity as to what she was doing to her face.

"I don't come out of the package like this, you know," she said.

He said, "What do I know about cosmetology?"

"Did you tramp snow on my rugs?"

In the mirror, she saw him lift his stocking feet for her approval.

He said, "Are you sick or something?"

"No," she responded.

"You look sick. Pardon me saying it."

Patrizia shuffled into the bedroom, tinkling her keys. Her face was swollen and splotched. Mrs. Marini checked Ciccio's face in the mirror, but it was a weird and peachy mask of health and goodwill. Then he left the room. Patrizia looked at her sideways as she continued to lay siege to her brows. From the other side of the house she heard Ciccio repeatedly opening and closing the icebox.

"Are you hungry?" Patrizia yelled toward the doorway.

"No," he called back.

"Are you playing with my icebox door?" Mrs. Marini asked.

"Yes," he said.

"Do you like the noise? The clicking noise?"

"Yeah," he said feebly.

He did that before church, when she made him go, and before

returning home when his father had a list of chores waiting for him, and before the penmanship practice to which she used to subject him in the afternoons. It was his way of asking to be left alone.

She faced Patrizia and made a coquettish smile.

"Don't start, Costanza," Patrizia hissed. "You be nice."

"I'm nice," she whispered, leering. "I'm always nice. I'm so very, very nice. Don't you think I look nice?"

Come to think of it, her strategy would come off much more smoothly if Ciccio were left at home. Too bad Patrizia insisted on driving. She wanted Lina to herself.

"Let him stay here," she said.

"He'll go," said Patrizia. "He wants to go."

"We'll have to smoosh together in the cab, which will be hot and disaccommodating."

"He likes trains," Patrizia insisted.

"We'll smoosh and think of the trouble with the shifter."

"When he was a baby, he had the toy trains that he pushed on the sofa and the driveway, and he made the train noises. Remember? He had the stripy hat I made him."

"A passenger car. A sedan."

"We'll buy him peanuts that he likes."

Mrs. Marini and the boy were connected temperamentally. She had a keen sense of justice, as did he. She had the snapping of a clothespin; he had the opening and closing of the icebox door, a waste of gas she would not have indulged for anyone else. The connection antedated his birth and had its source in events and confidences of the kind that her profession had taught her to inter in deep caverns, so far out of day-to-day reach that it required no effort to keep them there.

(The events that had led to Lina becoming pregnant with the boy were such a confidence; however, Lina's specific reasons for refusing to dispose of him when he was still only a germ were not. It had seemed to both Enzo and Mrs. Marini the only unobjectionable course. If Lina had run away in shame at that time, no explanation would have been expected of her. Instead it was as though she had waited to disappear until no one could have imputed to her any motive other than supreme egoism.

"Aw, Coco," said the glib ghost that pretended it was her husband, "takes one to know one."

"How about you give me a whisper of fellow feeling for once?" she exclaimed. "Will you never understand me? Carmelina was my heir. She wrote *herself* out of *my* will. On a whim. How absurd.")

"If you had the sort of car in which it's appropriate for four people to ride at the same time," Mrs. Marini said, "I admit I would have no quibble. But you have the truck."

"I'm going to eat one of these bananas," Ciccio yelled from the kitchen.

Patrizia lowered her voice further. "I want your best behavior," she said.

"I have mortadella in the drawer on the right on the bottom," Mrs. Marini yelled back.

"Save your rotten-egg throwing for at least a month. As a favor to me."

"I don't see the bread," he said.

"A month?" said Mrs. Marini. "A month from now she'll be hunting seals in Norway."

The train waddled north out of the soot-smeared green dells above Pittsburgh into the familiar flatland, in the direction of Erie, Pennsylvania, where the woman would transfer to a two-and-a-half-hour westbound into Ohio.

She asked a cadaverous young man who was reading the Book of Mormon across the aisle if he had any cigarettes, but he said he didn't. She tottered into the next car, scanning the seats for a prematurely wrinkled face. The other passengers glanced at her and looked aside. Finally, an army private gave her a Chesterfield but claimed to have no matches.

Her husband, from whom she was estranged, detested Chesterfields. He would indiscreetly leave a room in which Chesterfields were being smoked. In the dining car, she got a light from a girl behind the counter. The canteen was closed for business. They were only a few miles from Erie. Nobody was in the car but the two of them. The girl was perhaps twenty-five years old and wore a golden yellow turban tied in front with a knot that was like a French crescent pastry. She wheeled a bucket from behind the counter and then pressed with her foot on the lever of one of the castors and locked it in place.

"Missus, don't you have a handkerchief?" She sighed.

The woman was sitting at a table by the window. She shook her head no.

The girl yanked a handkerchief from her pocket—it was clear the embroidery on the edges had been done by hand—and waved it at her. "Now, that's fresh from my iron this morning," she said, "but I guess you'll keep it."

The woman said, "Thank you," and wiped her eyes and nose, preparing to be softly but aggressively pitied and then to be evangelized.

The girl only commenced mopping the floor.

Later, in the station in Erie, the girl came up to her again and asked passingly if she had a while to wait. The woman said she had two hours, yes.

The girl sunk her fists into her coat pockets and blew a long breath through her teeth. The turban had gone a little crooked. They both stared up at the estimated times of arrival and departure, the platform numbers, the destinations. The girl, keeping her eyes on the timetable, cocked her head and asked under her breath, "Missus, don't you know you got that dress on backwards?"

He opened the icebox. He closed the icebox. He was alone in the old lady's house. He listened to the noises when he (a) pulled back the handle, releasing the latch; (b) broke the airtight seal that the weather stripping around the door formed; (c) pushed the handle forward again, lowering the latch; (d) tossed the whole apparatus away from him, the latch relatching and the seal resealing simultaneously.

He allowed the mind to unravel. He allowed it to think whatever it wanted. Then he pierced it with the sound of the icebox door. He tried to synchronize the noises with the ticks of the clock. He watched as the mind organized itself around these sounds, *click* by *whomp* by *click* by *whomp*, until all other thoughts became inaudible.

It wasn't really working. Usually it was a surefire strategy for quieting the interior clamor, but not today. Now Ciccio had blown so much time working on his head that he had just two hours left.

He picked up Mrs. Marini's phone and called Ricky.

Shortly thereafter, the two of them were coasting down Chagrin, Ricky steering, Ciccio on the rack behind the seat with his feet out to the sides for balance. It started snowing again—great clumps of snow flopped onto the street.

"You were at the farm this whole time?" Ricky said.

"I told you, ass."

They dropped the bike in Ciccio's driveway and went in through the back door.

"Off with the shoes," Ciccio said.

They took off their shoes.

"Now," Ciccio said, "you're going to keep your mouth shut about this, got me?"

"Yeah, okay."

"I'm serious here," he said, although Ricky was to be trusted.

"I said okay, fine."

"The train's supposed to get in at five forty-seven. Give them till quarter after six to make it back. We have ninety-two minutes to clean this dump up."

When the conductor called out "Erie Station Tower," the woman got off the train. She could see them out of the corner of her eye, two old ladies in black scampering toward her like ants, from two o'clock, about fifty feet distant. She looked away to the left. She pretended to search the faces where she knew they weren't, pretended, for about five seconds, not to hear that one of them was calling her name, and held tight to these last moments of strangerhood.

The fear of being called by name in a crowded place.

She stood fast until it was no longer plausible that she couldn't hear them, and then for one second longer. The dread of the faces that knew her face. Then the faces themselves, taking her in.

There she is. The hair is different, it's faded. You expected that. Mercy is to be resisted at all costs. Make the face. Just like that. Freeze your jaw in exactly that position. Do not lift the eyebrows, your wrinkles will show. Giddyup. Don't let Patrizia get ahead of you. It's not faded, of course, her hair (she's coming into focus); it's part black and part white.

Hold the face.

There she is.

Here she is.

She's skinny. Outside it's New Year's Eve, with the snow squalls aswirl and the bone-chilling temperatures, and yet she has no coat or hat or earmuffs. Her dress, which she isn't wearing so much as it's hanging off her, is yellow with blue stripes and is hideous and unironed. Her shoelaces, however, are double knotted the way you showed her. The skin of the face is the color of an undershirt that needs bleaching. The skin of the neck has begun to pucker like a sock that's fallen below the calf. You fail to detect remorse in the eyes, in the mouth, or in the posture.

But now here she is, face-to-face. You take her hands. You feel the presence of sex in yourself as an infected organ, and you want to open up your flesh and cut it out.

You struggle to steel your resolve. You struggle to keep at the forefront of your mind the senses in which she is at fault, but here she is, face-to-face, and you are forgetting all of them but one, that you are a *me*. And I have a face, too, see it? And I was left behind.

One thing.

One enormous thing that had included her but didn't now. It broke apart and came together again in a smash and broke apart continually.

Each time it came together again, a small part of it wrenched itself away.

What became of the part? It traveled through empty space. It was not aware of any trajectory.

What had become of her poor father? No one had even heard a word.

What had become of her?

The woman had redepicted in her mind certain moments from the past so many times that it was impossible to distinguish the moments as they had happened from her remembering of them: Imagine a house repainted with a hundred thousand coats, under which the original wood has rotted away; and yet the house still stands, composed now entirely of paint. The moment itself may not have mattered anymore. It may have been trivial to begin with, but the act of redepicting the scene for herself, changing it each time over decades, had trained her thoughts around a central mystery in it.

In one such scene she was a girl standing under the laundry line on the packed dirt of their yard, a clothespin between her teeth and her father's wet undershirts hanging from her arm, when suddenly the projectionist of the film of which she was the subject changed the reels. There were two projectors, the second standing at the ready for the proper moment, and the change was seamless, but she had noticed it. She had entered an infinitely precise model of her own backyard, but she knew all the same that she was not in the same *place*. Whatever underlay seeing, hearing, smelling, whatever people meant when they said the laundry basket was "over there," whatever they meant by *there,* had changed.

And then again, behind the wood shop at a missionary school where she had worked until two years ago—it had looked like Wyoming and smelled like Wyoming, but she knew she wasn't in Wyoming, she was in a place not far from where she was standing right now on the platform, in this city.

The way people didn't mean the same thing when they said "location" as when they said "place." They said "place" meaning the self of the location.

The present scene risked someday becoming one of those scenes. It was moving too fast, she wanted to slow it down. She had exactly one chance to witness it as it was taking place. Not even one. Her painting of it would become all it was.

The women approached, and Lina turned and looked at them. Her mother's eyes were so hidden behind the bloated lids that it was doubtful whether she could see anything. Mrs. Marini's eyes were enormous behind new, thicker glasses, her cheeks and lips and eyelids and eyebrows made up in a way that made her look like a grim clown, her mouth quivering. Lina was astounded at how old they were. She was astounded that she even knew who they were, because they looked so different now.

The way people said, "she," "you," "I," and they didn't mean only bodies or faces, they meant *her self, your self, my self.*

And she could tell they were doing the same thing she was doing. They were looking for the self behind her changed face, as she was looking for the selves behind their changed faces.

"You look like disaster," her mother said.

Mrs. Marini took Lina's hands in her hands and then took Lina's head in her hands. The old woman's little nostrils opened wider; her lips flared, disclosing the gray teeth. Lina watched the eyes go opener, everything open, the face unmasked and savage. The old woman pulled Lina's face to her face still closer. Maybe Lina was about to be bitten on the face. The wet breath of this woman on her skin. Lina's own eyes going crossed. Then trying to pull away and the old woman yanking her face back closer still, to the face that belonged to the self of this person she had gone away from.

14

They walked out of the station. A crowd of smartly dressed Negroes was milling in Public Square under the candy-cane Christmas lights and the plastic holly boughs that were stapled to the trees. Snow was falling. In the center of the square stood a greenish black monument in which life-sized soldiers were carved wearing the garb of the last century. Some held rifles and some torches; others appeared to be tearing up a railroad. Perched atop the monument's pedestal, a woman in stone, dwarfing the soldiers and the people in the square, gripped a sword in one hand, while in the other, the palm upturned and limp, a clump of snow had amassed; one of her breasts was exposed. At a corner of the square was a dais and banner that Lina couldn't read through the darkness and the snowfall. They turned onto Coshocton Street, which led to the lake several blocks below, and the wind crashed into them, and the snow fell harder and laterally.

She was clothed for springtime and it was snowing, but she did not feel cold. The cloud cover was complete and low and orange with city light. Her mother was wearing a translucent plastic babushka. Mrs. Marini wore nothing on her head but a huge nimbus of a wig, which was snow speckled. Lina felt the snow melting on her shoulders. It stuck in her eyelashes. Her nose began to run. They walked in the street, using parked cars to steady themselves. The wind fell off momentarily. The snow continued to come down. She was going to have to see the boy soon.

Her mother drove them east, out of downtown, pulled into the parking lot of a VFW post, put the truck in neutral, and stomped down the parking brake, waiting for a snowplow to tail home. She asked some desultory questions concerning Had the trip been very long, Was it warmer in Pittsburgh than here, How about a little lip gloss on that kisser.

Mrs. Marini sat dumbly between them, crouching, sucking her teeth. The inquisition was coming, the target was within range. Lina perceived this as you perceive an invisible pursuer hunting you through woods in a dream. She was to be peeled and butchered; her parts would be arrayed, trimmed of fat, spitted, roasted, and consumed.

She could hear her blood rushing behind her eyes. She pressed her face against the window to cool it. She had made a purse to put herself in out of rag patches and chewing gum, and now they were going to try to spill her out.

A plow rumbled past, and her mother popped the brake and sped behind it. Twenty blocks of churchlike silence ensued.

Mrs. Marini twisted her knees to the passenger side of the gearshift so that they were pointed at Lina's legs. Likewise, she dangled her right elbow behind the seat and turned her shoulders toward her. She took at least a minute to assume this position. Patrizia shifted the truck into third. Then, with the meat of her left hand, Mrs. Marini rapped the dashboard. "Now is the time when I am going to ask some questions and you are going to give some answers," she said.

Lina said, "All right."

"Where are your clothes."

"In the back of the truck in my suitcase."

"Where are the clothes that a rational person would wear in hostile weather such as this, such as woolen leggings and earmuffs."

"I'm hot."

"Are you experiencing the change of life."

"I have been very, very hot for two days. No."

"Do you have a fever? Let me check your head."

"Yes, a little."

"When was the last time you took Holy Communion."

"Five years. Six years."

"When was your last confession."

"Six years ago."

"What were you doing in Saskatchewan."

"I had a job. It was Wyoming."

"What kind of a job? I've heard rumors. I've heard 'lumberjack' and 'stevedore' and 'football coach.' I've heard all kind of innuendo, which I've had to go on because the horse's mouth could not, evidently, pick up the telephone and give a call."

"I was the cook at a school."

"Were you unfaithful to your husband."

Pause. "No."

"Why would you allow yourself to leave the house in a state like this, without a little eye shadow, a little something to cover."

"I don't care."

"You don't care about me? About—"

"About what a stranger says or thinks."

"Do you know how tall is your boy and what is the hair color."

"No. I am assuming still brown."

"That's right." Pause. "Don't you want to know how tall? The answer is, For a boy his age, he is titanic. Why did you never call."

"I didn't have a telephone."

"Did you forget the phone numbers of your husband and your mother?"

"*I didn't have a telephone.*"

"For how long was the time of your stay in oater-movie-land? Boise, Medicine Hat, whatever."

"Four or five years. It was Casper, Wyoming."

"Where you worked at a school during which time."

"Yes, that's right."

"Which the school had an office, presumably."

"Yes."

"Where they would have had a telephonic device of some type."

"Yes, that's true."

"Yet you did not ask permission to use this device to make contact with your husband or your mother or myself, nor write a postcard communicating the telephone number of this place where we might from time to time speak with you. You were too busy reading *Riders of the Purple Sage* and suchlike."

"I wrote with the address."

"I do not want to hear little stories which you believe to be exculpatory. How often did you write?"

Patrizia piped in, "She wrote me every Christmas."

But Mrs. Marini talked over her. "How often did you write to your husband or to the boy? I know the answer to this to be, Maybe every once in the cows-come-home."

"Not regularly."

"Why did you leave Tombstone or Santa Fe or whatever the place."

"Casper."

"Why."

"I don't know."

"Make something up."

"I had a friend, I had only the one friend, and they were going to fire her. She stole a can of potato chips, was all she'd done, and she was leaving, and she was passing through here, and I decided—"

"A moment, please. This friend."

"A woman who was the other cook."

"A friend of yours."

"Yes."

"Onward."

"And I decided I was going to come back here."

"Why."

"I don't know."

"Liar."

"I don't know."

"Turn your eyes inward toward the soul and describe what you see," the old woman said in a rage.

"I decided. That's all. I wanted to come back."

"And yet you didn't come back."

"I—I sent Enzo a telegram about Can I come home, I'll be arriving at this time and place; but he wasn't at the station and I thought that meant—"

"What telegram?"

"I sent a telegram but I thought he got it but he didn't come but I talked to him later on the phone but he didn't get it. You see. He didn't get the telegram. But I—but I could've said, I'd sent this telegram about Could I come, I will be arriving; but you weren't there, but the telegram didn't arrive, but I want to come home now. But I kept my mouth shut. But I could've. He would've come to get me. I know. But I was too afraid to ask him. Because what if he said no? But I was only in Pittsburgh by then. And I could have said please. And he might have said yes."

"I know what he would have said."

"Stop it, Costanza. Stop it right now," Patrizia said.

"And you know what he would have said, too."

"Stop it," Patrizia said.

"You would have talked him awake or driven him home yourself."

"That's enough," Lina said.

"You're a fool. I love you. You're a fool."

"Shut your decrepit mouth," Lina said.

"Why did you stay in Pittsburgh."

"I got a job."

"Coffee grinder. Monkey salesman."

"I was sewing drapes in a department store."

"How often did you write to your husband or to the boy—shut up, Patrizia, and let her answer the question."

"Twice."

"One time and then one more time."

"Yes."

"Are you experiencing the change of life?"

"Maybe, I'm not sure. My heart races."

"Why did you leave Wyoming—you know you know you know."

"Why was I in Wyoming to begin with? is what you mean."

"Unstitch. Disassemble piece by piece."

"Why was I in Wyoming."

"Why were you in Wyoming."

"Why did I take the job."

"Why."

"Why did I look for the job. Why did I stop in Douglas. Why did I sleep in the wayside in Wisconsin."

"Don't you want to know? If you don't know, who knows?"

"Why wasn't I here."

"First one foot, then the other."

"Why did I leave."

"Yes."

"It was humid out."

"And then?"

"Why did I get in the car?"

"Yes, exactly."

"It was humid and I didn't want to get in the car, which would be more humid. Why was I getting in the car?"

"Yes."

"Oh, I can *tell* you, but it isn't what you want. It was insignificant."

"It was? I bet it was."

"Yes, but it was an insignificant errand, and afterward I got back in the car and thought, Wouldn't it be nice to drive awhile with the window open? It had nothing to do with youse two or Enzo or Cheech or anyone."

"This errand—"

"It was nothing—I was making cheese, but there was no rennet left. You see?"

Silence.

"And then I kept on driving."

The plow veered onto a highway. Where they were, most of the streetlights were broken. Snow was falling. The snow cover was blue. The truck crawled up a hill. Lina's face was stiff from the cold of the window. She remembered she still had the girl's handkerchief in her dress pocket.

"How long are you staying?" Mrs. Marini asked.

"I have all my things."

"Are you *staying* staying, then?"

"Maybe."

"Nobody will beg you now," Patrizia said.

"Me, or a piece of cheese?" Mrs. Marini said.

"You can't make me ashamed."

"Shame is useless," Mrs. Marini said. "Get rid of shame."

"Okay. Sure."

"Just get rid of it."

"I'm *not* ashamed."

"It is debilitating and ex post facto and useless."

"You won't make me apologize," said Lina.

"You will, though."

"I absolutely will do no such thing."

Mrs. Marini said, "I ask that you give me that."

"Go ahead."

"Please."

"Please what?"

"Please apologize to me," Mrs. Marini said.

"*No.*"

"Good, fine, thank you. I accept. But apologies never kept me company. Apologies never tied your shoes."

Her house—rather, Vincenzo's house—looked as though it had recently been in order but then an extremely fastidious person had been directed to turn it into a pigsty. Newspapers, schoolbooks, and a table lamp formed an inelegant obelisk in a corner of the front room. The dining-room and kitchen chairs had been left upturned on the tabletops, as in a restaurant after hours. Twine strung around brass tacks in the window jambs held back the dusty curtains. The air was thick with bleach.

They found a note from Ciccio on the icebox beginning, *To Whom It May Concern*, saying that he planned to spend the night at Ricky's.

Mrs. Marini went home. Lina and her mother rolled off their stockings and got on their knees to scrub the kitchen floor. Midnight came, and it was 1953. Evidently her husband's hair had gone white; she found it on the pillow of his bed.

The next morning, the three women spread out the contents of Lina's bags on the kitchen table. A snowstorm whistled about the house. Her mother said, "Where are the rest?"

"These are the rest," she said.

"Where are the rest of your *clothes*, Carmelina," Mrs. Marini said.

"These are all the clothes I have."

They boiled water in three pots on the stove. Mrs. Marini measured the black dye powder and dumped a cup of salt into the pot for the cotton and another into the pot for the wool.

Lina had made nearly all the clothes from the leavings of the home-economics room at the school in Casper, and none of the patterns or colors mattered to her.

They did not dye her nylons or handkerchiefs.

You want a why. But there is no why. You want a depiction complete with flora, sunsets, How deep was the snow in the blizzard of '49? How was the furniture arranged in the cell where I slept in the dormitory? These are the faces of the friends I knew there; but no such depiction is forthcoming, too bad, no artifacts by which in later years to verify that I was there and my recollections are credible, no way to disprove your suspicion that I simply was, then was not, and now am again since I departed the train onto the platform. I want to be a line that extends and ravels and at length intersects itself again, a path that can be retraced stepwise, but I am not, I am discontinuous.

Another cavelike day elapsed before the snow broke and she was able to climb Vermilion Avenue to the mortuary carrying two suits of Enzo's, one of which was for the father, who was to be cremated in it and sent home in a steel urn. As she left the mortician's office, the blaze of white winter sun on the snow was like a chemical explosion that left spots on her field of vision, so that she could hardly make her way for squinting and could not tell if the commercial district of the neighborhood had decayed or been revived in her absence. Peering through a gap in her fingers, she noticed a familiar storefront, lacking a sign but evidently open in spite of the storm, and went in.

The bell on the door of the bakery tinkled, and the curtain flag of Ohio was pulled aside as the baker Rocco emerged, rattling a piece of candy across his molars.

"Tell me," he said roughly, snapping open a wax-paper bag.

"Two crescents, please. Marmalade." She opened her change purse, but there were only dimes and pennies.

Below the chalkboard where the prices were listed hung a photograph of a handsome boy, clean shaven and dreary-eyed, wearing a white military hat and smiling coldly. The photograph had been ardently colorized—the American flag in the background painted in, the lips purpled; the flush of the cheeks was girlish.

A note above it on the chalkboard read: *Prisoner of Our Enemy 832 Days Consecutive So Far.*

"Otherwise?" the baker said.

"Nothing, thank you."

"Forty-six cents, if you can find it in there."

But she couldn't, and had to ask him to put one of the crescents back.

"This is Montanero, if I'm not mistaken. I heard you had gone off to the Wyoming," he said. "Sorry that I forget your other name."

"Charlotte," she said automatically. It was her alias. She never used it again.

15

Ciccio finally spoke the word he had seen typed all over the vineyard. "I'll have to absquatulate," he said.

Exactly when he made up his mind to let his mother have the house on Twenty-second Street, he couldn't say.

Everything had gone to hell. Everything had gone to hell in a flash. Since it was everything that had gone to hell, you'd think nothing new could go there, and since it was to hell that everything had gone, you'd think it couldn't sink any farther, but not so.

Regarding the three days after the crash, he suffered from a selective kind of amnesia: He had no sensory record of that time, but he remembered ideas and emotions perfectly. He could remember feeling liberated, and not jubilant but, he had to say, happy; the calamity was a meal for the mind. But he couldn't remember what he had been physically doing, in what physical place, while he was thinking. He knew he had been on the farm; it wouldn't have been too exciting, whatever he was up to. Eventually he asked his grandmother, who told him he'd been in the vineyard, on snowshoes, tying vines sunup to sundown. He wouldn't come inside for lunch, which she had had to drive out to him on the tractor.

To be delirious from Latin was to have turned out of the furrow, as a plow.

When the record of his physical memory picked up again, he was standing in the snow in the vineyard sharpening his spring shears with a rattail file. He heard a clitterclatter in the distance; he looked up and saw his grandmother's salt-encrusted AMC truck hugging the shoulder of the highway, heading north into town. Where was she off to? Then, at dinner—dinner was bread and boiled winter squash (the physical world had returned to him, with its yellows and slimies)—he asked her what she'd gone to town for. She told him she was sending a wire to his mother. This was on the twenty-ninth of December, 1952, a date that would live in infamy. Everything had already gone to hell, and then the next morning they got a telegram at the farm from his mother saying that she was going to come to the funeral.

How amusing. Well, no, frankly, it wasn't amusing. His grandmother understood the gist of the telegram, but she made him read it out loud anyway. How was he to interpret that other than as his grandmother saying, "You're welcome to visit here, kid, but I won't take you in"?

He was a boy standing on a trapdoor.

His mother wasn't planning to rent a bed at the YWCA, like any courteous vagrant would do; instead they'd decided without consulting him that she would stay—guess where—in his house, as though it were her house. Hell was getting crowded.

No way his mother thought he'd stay in the house if she was living in it.

They were trying to put him on the street, was what they were trying to do.

There was no will. He was a minor still. His mother would get everything.

He cleaned the house on New Year's Eve while the old ladies were at the station (Ricky was with him, but Ricky was no help), stopping to touch in parting tribute the brocaded buttons of the seat cushions and the newel where he hung his shoulder pads to air them out after practice. Good-bye, number 123 Twenty-second Street. Hello, the rails.

Ricky went home.

Ciccio was alone in the house, and they were due back any minute, the women. He had to get out. He left a note saying he was at Ricky's for the night. Assuming they didn't call to verify, he had a head start of at least twelve hours before whomever they sent looking for him was sent looking (unless their plan had always been to gently suggest he make himself scarce and to send no one after him when he did).

He had nowhere to go. He had aspired to this. He was fifteen and broke and homeless. It felt like he was borrowing a bum's rags to say he was broke. A kid can't be broke because a kid isn't supposed to have any money of his own. You wouldn't say your dog was broke. But he was going to need to buy food and pay rent and he had no money for these things, so he was legitimately broke.

He had nowhere to go.

How to say: I mean this, this is a fact, this is more than what it feels like? I've packed a bag with spare socks and only one set of extra shoes because I don't know how far I'll have to carry the bag. But I have nowhere to go with this bag on my back.

There was an invisible membrane between a child's world and the world of grown people. The child's was hypothetical; the adult's was actual. The child's world was only an image. It had none of the actual machinery that made the actual world go. You didn't have to have any money. Nobody would put you in jail. Your work was school. You didn't produce anything real. You produced term papers, the graph of a hyperbola, which were pretend. Therefore the sometimes happiness of work on the farm, in which he felt the pleasing tension of labor that authentically needed to happen. The republic needed grapes for its jelly sandwiches. But he was at the farm only on weekends and school vacations. The farm was ancillary. He was somebody other than himself there. If somebody should ask him what his occupation was, he couldn't say "farmer." He was a kid, he was potential, like an egg. When the make-believe-ness of his existence dawned on him, he wanted out. But they wouldn't let him out until he'd become a nuisance to them, and then they'd forced him out.

It was late and snowing and New Year's Eve, so there was no hope of a trolley. He set out on foot. He didn't turn around to see if the house he was walking away from was lost to him yet, behind the snowfall.

How to say: I am out, I have taken on substance, I am not made of mist, I have—in fact—no place to go? Why, now that he was in the actual world, couldn't he perceive the weight he knew it had? Why did everything feel as hypothetical as before?

A teacher, Father Delano, had accused him of having a Manichean head, which coming from him was a slur, but it was true. Ciccio did his mental business as if the world was composed of two factions warring with each other. He felt them in his heart all the time. Present experience bore this out. The forces of Darkness were galloping over this town, and therefore get out, right? Here he was now, on the corner of Twenty-second and Eleventh Avenue, facing the blank-eyed concrete statue of Columbus that the K of C had erected in front of the basketball court, and there were two ways only to go—up the hill or down the hill. He chose down.

No, up.

He chose up.

He was wearing a black wool cap of his father's, a flannel scarf, the leather work gloves he used when they pounded posts at the farm, a three-quarter-length wool coat over a raincoat over a school blazer over a thermal undershirt over a T-shirt. He also wore dungarees, thermal underpants, and his clodhopper winter school shoes with galoshes over them.

The K of C had called off the New Year's Eve fireworks, said a sign slung around the great man's neck; a storm was predicted. Ciccio saw not a soul on the avenue. The wind at his back pushed him up the hill. He told himself the wind approved of what he was doing, that it was abetting his escape.

Nobody knew where he was going. There was no motion of animal life along the street for as far up the hill as he could see, nor in the trees.

Look at the snow coming down. And you might know all about its formation in the atmosphere, but when you looked up it appeared to come from nowhere, to materialize. Everything was blue, the snow, rooming houses he knew in daylight were red brick. They were the blue of snowfall at night. Something was the matter with the sky. He figured it out. It was lower, it was falling, it was enclosing this place like a lid on a box.

He had to get away.

There was this tremendous snowfall happening, this absolute blanketing, or rather erasure, of the streets. It was irrelevant to notice the swell in the snow under which he knew a fire hydrant was, or to notice any other individual thing. A mystic cataclysm was taking place. Individual physical existence was being wiped out.

He wanted to disappear.

Look, here was the snow materializing ex nihilo, what a word. And he had wanted to feel that happening to him. He'd believed that once he got on the road he'd feel himself taking on substance, becoming a thing instead of an idea. But he didn't feel that. He didn't feel heavier, he felt lighter.

He had to ask himself, What was the goal? Was it to become real, to exert force in the physical world, to have money, to be looked at instead of looked around, like people look around children?

Or was it to throw away the mirage of being real? To be looked through, to evanesce?

The snow was materializing out of nothing, and he wanted to do the trick in reverse. He was trudging up the hill, step and another step and another step, the wind pushing on his back.

He wanted to disappear into the trees. He was on top of the hill now, looking back. He wanted to leave no sign of himself. The snow kept falling. He wanted no one to remember having laid eyes on his face.

What happened was probably inevitable.

He made it on foot to the bus depot in Van Buren Heights, a distance of five miles, and fell gratefully to sleep on a bench.

He was not, once he woke up at daybreak, grateful for the wardrobe he was carrying on his body. He was trapped in an amniotic sac of sweat. Someone had turned on the current in the argon lamps overhead. An indigent struggled to topple a cigarette machine in an alcove beside the grated-over ticket window. The green air smelled of urine.

What happened was, he sat up in his sac on the bench and then a luminous angel took shape on his shoulder. The angel pointed out that absenting oneself from Ohio without warning anybody was not an unprecedented stunt and that he'd judged it severely in the past. Also, said the angel, was he really going to let his mother cast herself in the role of the respecter of the dead while he played the dead's deserter? He was going to have to go back, said the voice of virtue, and sit through the funeral, and announce his intention to leave, and then leave.

The cigarette machine came smashing face-first to the floor. The man stood cursing it. The problem seemed to be penetrating his mind that, even if he'd succeeded in breaking the glass of the face, the cigarettes were now safely entombed under the shell of the machine unless he could lift it back up again. He collapsed onto his knees and began scratching at the sheet metal. It was piteous and difficult both to watch and not to watch. Ciccio saw he was alone with this man, in the depot.

They were indoors but there was no heat.

Then the angel of Darkness appeared on his other shoulder and castigated him. Going back was a dodge, it was an excuse to let the iron cool, the more ineffectually to strike it later on. He would get comfortable, he would lose his nerve, he would betray himself.

The man had pissed himself and was scratching very delicately with his long fingernails at the back of the machine.

Ciccio pushed the depot doors into the snowdrifts and squeezed himself outside. The snow had evidently fallen all night, and it was still falling, although the wind out of the northwest had died off, so he wouldn't have to face into it. He headed back to the neighborhood and spent the day in getting there.

It was 1953. There was snow inside his socks. With every step, his guardian angel of Darkness abused him. What had taken four hours to walk last night looked like it was going to take fifteen today, and yet his strength was superhuman. He had not eaten and didn't want to eat.

There was all day through the tedium of the snow-buried streets to examine his shame. He felt it, he was ashamed. He didn't understand what it was. It wasn't the kind of shame where you're worried how others look at you. He felt shame and didn't know what it was coming from, what purpose it was serving. He had to examine it. It was a warning of some kind. It was his heart warning his will of something. That was as far as he could get with it.

In the last week he had become a grown man. The vapors of grief he may have felt before were being incinerated to power the dynamo of his long, thick, persistent legs.

By the time he'd made it into Eastpark, with two miles still to go, it was night again. The physical extremity of his circumstances started to exert its pressure. He wanted to rest, he wanted to eat something. He'd been on his feet since the previous night, with a break, to sleep on the bench, that was about half his normal sleep allotment with respect to time. He had to rest, he had to eat something. He didn't know where these things might happen.

He had mushed into and across Eastpark, mostly by way of shortcuts through the woods. There was less snow on the forest floor than in the backyards or the streets—which the plows had yet to scratch—because so much of the snow was still hanging in the trees. He sat down on what looked like an oil drum, in the woods. He needed to sleep. He wondered if he could figure out how to construct an igloo of some kind.

There was a complicated system of living things on the forest floor beneath the snow, many of which things he had formal names for or made-up childhood names for, but most of which he had failed even to notice—and the snow had erased them all. There was nothing to see here but sky, snow, and the bones of the trees. The scene was vast and clear, and he was no part of it. He felt incidental and scared. Some places were better to look away from than to look at.

He would feel better when he knew where he was going.

He had where to go? No place. The usurper would be in his house by now. He asked himself first where in the short run, then where in the long run, he could go. From olden times the death of parents had forced young men into the wilderness to make their keeps. There were still parcels of land open to homesteading in western Canada. It was two a.m., said the bell of the church, the only perceivable evidence of the neighborhood; otherwise the woods seemed to him like the aboriginal Ohio of French and Indian War days. He was trying and failing not to look at this beautiful scene, of which he was not a part and could never be a part. It was silly to look at this place and call it a wilderness when he knew it was a trapezoidal park bordered on all sides by streets, when, furthermore, he knew the names of the streets. A wilderness was by definition wild and unpeopled. This place was fenced off in order to look wild but wasn't really wild. And he—a person—was, at least materially, in it. He wanted to recede into wilderness, but there was perhaps no wilderness left. There were only places where people were and places where people had not yet gotten around to being. If there was a wilderness anywhere, it was in his mind.

At last the snowfall broke, the moon emerged, and stars. There was no suggestion of wind in the tops of the pines, and he was footsore and starved and numb of face. He gave in. There was a miserably reasonable and boy-souled answer to the question of where he could go in the short run, and he had no choice at this point. He was too cold. He was in re-treat. He descended the slope of the woods, out of the frontier, down to Chagrin Avenue, and made a right on Twenty-sixth and stole through Mrs. Marini's cyclone-cellar doors.

He tiptoed into the cellar guest bedroom, the one no one ever used, with the locked cabinets and the sink. It took him fifteen minutes to undress and hide his clothes under the adjustable hospital bed down there. Then he lay in the bed an hour or two, somehow unsleeping, composing in his thoughts the list of grievances that made it impossible for him to stay there, while his shivering slowly subsided, sensation returned to his toes, and his will to leave took leave of him.

He may have been sleeping but probably not when he heard the newspaper thump against the storm door upstairs—a thump that held out bluntly all the comforts he wished to wish to do without: routine, insulation from cold, fresh meat, people to talk to.

He got up and made the bed as he had found it and climbed the stairs in his stocking feet, his shoes in hand, dressed for a moderate trek through a winter night but having left most of his clothes hidden in the cellar. Outside her kitchen windows it was still dark. It was darker than when he'd come in. The moon must have set by now. All the lights were off inside the house.

He needed a plan. One or another of the women was going to make him account for his whereabouts the last two nights, and the truth was none of their goddamn business.

He needed a bath. There was just enough light in the kitchen that certain unidentifiable metal objects in the stove region of the room gleamed spookily. Where did the light come from? From the windows, having reflected off the snow, having shot out of stars many, many millions of lifetimes of light travel away.

It was safe to assume that if they hadn't called Ricky's the first night he was gone, they would probably have called there by now. The question was going to be, Where has Ciccio been? He was going to say he was at Ricky's the whole time, both nights. Then they would say, Oh, no, you weren't, we called, we have found you out. At which point he would say what?

He was overthinking this. They weren't going to fight with him. They were trying to put him on the street.

To get to her front door, he was obliged to feel his way along the kitchen counter. He opened the door, and he opened the storm door. He bent over the threshold and dug out the paper and mussed up his shoes in fresh snow. He was operating in near-perfect silence. He placed the snow-covered shoes on the rug inside the door. It was a crude ruse but it would have to suffice.

Now he could invite the audience into the theater.

He squared his feet on the linoleum and slammed the door shut. He banged a skillet down on the stove. He paused to listen for signs of the audience coming and, hearing none, dropped her coffee grinder on the floor and faked a sneeze.

He listened again. There was a creaking of the floorboards.

Slowly and white Mrs. Marini materialized amid the darkness of the hallway.

"Where did you come from?" she said. She was white, he wanted to say see-through, as if gaseous. Her pajamas were white and patched in a dozen places and nearly disintegrated. She wore a look of small-animal fright that he had not before seen on her.

"At Ricky's. I didn't wake you up, I hope." He had arrayed the makings of an elaborate omelet on the stove.

What strands of hair there were on her head came past her shoulders, were as thin as the fiber of a moth's tent, did nothing at all to clothe the scalp. The scalp was yellow.

And her clothes would have fit somebody three times her weight. She might as well have wrapped a sheet around herself. He would have thought she slept in a nightgown if he'd had to guess. He had never seen her wearing white clothes before. They were some man's old pajamas.

"What was I dreaming?" she said. "I can't remember. I heard the door. I thought you were someone else."

"I was at Ricky's." He was trying to get the tone of *Hello, this is my phony alibi* out of his voice and was failing. "And I came over to get the suit I left here after, after—"

"Put my egg down," she said. "Go wash your hands."

He washed his hands. She fried him some eggs and made him cut up half a grapefruit for himself and half for her. While he was cutting the grapefruit, she fixed him with a look that said, Shall I blow your cover or not, big fellow? Anyway, she didn't blow his cover.

It was the first day of the funeral.

When he knew his mother would be at the mortuary, later that morning, he went home and took a shower and got into decent clothes. The house smelled weird. Then he went to the mortuary and ate a lot of cheese and sausage.

Yes, the usurper was there, perched like a crow in the front, by the coffins. Her hair had grayed. Maybe she would die soon. She even came up to him and shook his wretched hand, trying to act like she wasn't cracked and wasn't a usurper. He didn't know who she thought she was fooling. Not him!

He fell asleep on Mrs. Marini's sofa at four in the afternoon and didn't wake up until an hour before sunrise. She had taken off his socks.

The next night he retrieved his crystal-radio set and a few pairs of

Skivvies from Twenty-second Street and stowed them in the chest of drawers in Mrs. Marini's upstairs guest bedroom, where he also slept. As long as nobody said anything, he figured he could build up a body of precedent, establish squatter's rights, and never have to have a conversation about where, in the long term, he was going to hang his hat.

In fact, that was what happened. The house on Twenty-second Street wasn't his mother's, it was his, but he'd let her have it, he didn't care. She wasn't really his mother, she was a candy wrapper blowing around on the street.

He went back to school. Months passed.

He didn't have to iron anymore or be a slave on his father's side jobs. He was hungry all the time. He was mad, all the time, an uninterrupted clenching of the jaws and fists. Beating up on somebody, or even getting beaten up on, was his only relief. When his "mother" came around, which she did far too often, with that jeering puss on herself, it was all he could do not to knock her teeth out of her head.

He was a man. He felt fifty-five years old. He didn't have to socialize with head cases. He was hungry all the time. Mrs. Marini thought three square was good enough for anybody, but he needed three cubed; he was having a growth spurt again, his stomach rumbled while he was cleaning the table after dessert. He'd discovered a topic she knew nothing about, an adolescent boy's special nutritional needs. He couldn't ask for more because what if then she got sick of having to shove so much of her monthly fixed income into his face and she made him go live at number 123? He obeyed to the letter all regulations concerning length of shower and Where do the dirty socks go? His cigarettes, he kept in a cellophane corn-chip bag in the leaf pile behind her toolshed.

He examined his shame. He poked at it. He experimented with ways of making it flare up or cool down. Where did it come from? It came from someplace in the constellation of My Father Is Dead but I Am Still Alive.

16

He wanted something to happen. He read more. It did not seem quite right to him that he should lose himself in reading, but he had nowhere else in the short term to go. It gave him no pleasure, but he didn't want to be pleased. He wanted to be displeased, to feel the displeasure of his circumstances, because it did not seem right to him, no, it did not seem right at all, that his grief had all burned off before it could produce any effect. His grandmother had made loud, pulsing screams in her bedroom, a sound from the Dark Ages, while Ciccio kneaded the dough for their bread.

The Jesuits and his lay teachers forced him to read more, and he obeyed, stupid as a mill horse, hoping that if he got lost far enough then something would happen. He didn't even care to be the agent of this thing. It was an accident that he found himself casting around in philosophy and religion for the thing that would happen. Those were the oats they were feeding him. If he had gotten into the union a few years ago, as planned, he would have lost himself in a hod or a wheelbarrow instead of in Thomas Aquinas.

During his winter oral exam that February, Father Manfred asked him, "If I told you I was both free and unfree at the same time, what would my rationale be?"

Well, said young Mazzone, we were made in God's image, and you could make the case that God was for the most part free but not entirely so, since the list of things he couldn't do was long. He could not come into being or pass out of being. He could not *not* be good. God was both free and unfree; we were made in God's image; et cetera. How about that?

But, no, Father Manfred said, God could be and not be at once if he wanted. God didn't mind contradicting himself. Try again.

All he could think of was to say: God is great. God is a mystery. God is like us and not like us.

"Yes, good, more," the priest said.

"And if you're a slave in your head? I mean, obviously you're not free to fly to Mars on your own wings. It's easy to say how you're unfree outside your head. But what if you were unfree inside your head?"

"That's it, play with that."

"If you're not free in your head—"

"Hit that. Slam away at it."

"I am working a little harder, Father, because I am afraid."

"Boom boom."

"—then you never see how little sense it makes."

"Nice. Go. Yes. Hit him. A left and a right."

"Because it's impossible that God exists, but he does. And unless you're free in your head, you can't see why it's impossible."

"And therefore look how much greater is God that he smashes even reason underfoot."

Which, okay—there was the absurdly luminous shadow of paradox, believing because it was nonsense to believe. He knew they liked that sort of thing. So did he, to be honest. It made sense to him, ha ha.

He was at an impressionable junction and knew it. Aristotle and Thomas Aquinas were beyond the edge of his understanding. Much of his thinking these days was only ingesting what the priests said and then vomiting it back up on his shirt and looking at the vomit and saying, Gee, look what I made.

His father had always told him to disregard every third word the Jesuits said. They were famous for twisting people's heads. They made vice look like virtue. They had, as an order, been kicked out of the Church for a few decades a couple hundred years ago. And yet his father's position was ambiguous, had been ambiguous. After all, he'd paid a lot of dough to send Ciccio to the school.

There was civics and there was trig, okay. You were discouraged from getting too excited about them, probably because they were relevant to the twentieth century. There was Latin, of course. There was

Latin, Latin everywhere, from *incunabulum* to *extremis*. And this year there was Greek, too. They had Ciccio trudgingly translating Aristotle in one class; reading him at length in English in another; and reading Aquinas, talking about him, in another. It was the junior-year Aristo-blitzkrieg. His defenses were weakening, but defenses against what?

"Don't let them turn you into something you're not." That was his homespun father again. Ciccio would have been far more comfortable with himself if they had just made him keep memorizing tidbits from the Baltimore Catechism—that was the method of the nuns in junior high, and he had remained mostly immune. (He had not been turned into a papist knucklehead, like so many Irish and Poles. He had maintained the cynicism of his people respecting the double-dealings of the Church.) Instead, in the high school, the priests were on a crusade to grind him into the earth with work.

It must be understood that he was a boy on a trapdoor, and the latch of the trap had been pulled, and he had fallen, and he had somehow landed in a place where old European gentlemen were razing him in order to rebuild to their specs.

The catechism was, implicitly, out. Understanding, feeling competent to discuss the assignment, were out. Clarity was out. Usefulness was out, but that was old news. Declaratives were out. Interrogatives were in. Confusion and fear. The subjunctive and the conditional were certainly in. They were the beating heart of in.

He was made to memorize what Aristotle had said about something, and then what Saint Paul had said about it, and then what Thomas Aquinas had to say by way of fitting them together. But on the exam he had to disagree with Aquinas and make a point-by-point case for the disagreement. It was another one of their dissembling SJ tricks. They knew that as a teenager he was engineered to disagree, so they commanded him to disagree, for which he had to resent them, he wanted to resist them; and where was the most obvious outlet for his resistance? Why, agreement, of course, with Aquinas. In this way they were making a Thomist out of him despite himself. Or some of them were; the others, the paradox crowd, were trying to turn him into a Lutheran, maybe.

Not that he had the first idea of what that would mean, to be a Thomist, what credo he would be following.

Is it clear why he was looking for a credo to follow? Could you maybe cut him a break for taking it all so seriously?

An untranslated eighteenth-century copy of the *Summa Theolgiae*, all dolled up in still-green lambskin, occupied seven *feet* of shelf space over the chalkboard behind Father Manfred's lectern. Now, there was no question of reading, much less of getting, this seven-foot-long idea, but there was the promise in it of a universe to get lost in. Short of joining the monastery, he was not going to read even 10 percent of Aquinas. But he'd read enough to have gotten lost in the thicket; he could say he'd read enough to have forgotten what was supposed to be the inspiring genius of the man's thought, and to be lost made him afraid, which felt righter than nothing did.

He read in the afternoons, on the hallway floor between Mrs. Marini's spare bedrooms upstairs, lying on a bath towel. It was the only place in the house free of the distraction of sunlight. Once, having fallen asleep, he woke up to her softly jabbing his ear with the toe of her shoe. The pages of his *Selected Aquinas* were folded irregularly under his head.

"This is not Ciccio who reads, this is Ciccio who lays about," she said. She pointed an accusing finger, not at him, but at the book. She said, "It escapes you whole hog, I bet."

He said, "I'll tell you what, I understand this just well enough to miss the point."

He asked Father Manfred what it would mean to be a Thomist. Would he take another name, like the nuns did? But that was a joke. Manfred said the best illustration he could think of was something he'd read in the seminary:

Picture a seascape, he said. Now picture the sky over this sea. In the deep distance it becomes difficult to tell the sky and the sea apart. There is a thin strip at the horizon, a middle space, a third space, where the other two realms appear mixed-up. This is the Thomist view of what a person is; a person is what happens when the material (the sea) and the spiritual (the sky) intersect.

Well and good, Ciccio thought. From the shore it was often difficult to say where sky ended and water began. But what did it mean that he knew that in fact the sky and the surface of the water *did not* meet, that it was just an illusion that they met? It implied that a person was either material or spiritual or neither. Sorry. It made no sense.

They were killing him with work. He didn't know what they were trying to turn him into. But he didn't know what he was, either.

March. There was the smell on the air of mud drying, of the everywhere mud of late winter drying up at last. What was the smell like? It was like the faint, bitter odor of a bin of roofing nails.

Young Mazzone was on his way to school, briskly, wide-strided, on the cusp of running. He was on the cusp of running because he had the blues, and the SJs were making him over in their image, and when they had the blues they took long walks at high speeds to purge the blood of base fluids. He was hopping a little as he went. He was the merest bit out of breath, which was good.

His route downtown, Saint Ambrose Boulevard, was the straightest shot west from Elephant Park, but it was only sporadically paralleled by proper sidewalks. Most of the way he had to toe the curb or else slop through the mud alongside, where road salt had destroyed the grass. The cleaner route took half again as long. A streetcar jangled down the median. The boulevard was asphalt in the outer lanes, brick in the inner, and gravel down the middle, where the tracks ran. Where houses remained, they were fantastic multicolored ruins with porch-roof posts that no longer reached the sagging porches, with windows busted in, each one, for sport, with scoliotic chimneys, with doorways missing the doors or boarded up, with trim that had once (you could see through the peeling white) been painted three or four carefully patterned pastel tints. Gargoyles instead of aluminum downspouts drained the gutters and spoke of the kind of money he was pretty sure didn't exist anymore. The houses did not, any of them, show the first sign of sentient life. Dark vines with showy pink buds grew up the walls and into the windows. Terra-cotta roof tiles dappled the gardens. It was a village of gingerbread houses someone had left outside to be tramped by the dog, to be eaten by raccoons, or to go to pudding in the rain.

Farther on, the boulevard veered north along the lip of a sandstone quarry and through a huddle of unpainted shanties where the Syrians had used to live; and then some colored people had lived there, but recently they had moved away, too. Then the road cut through a meadow that you could see had, years ago, been farmed—the earth was leveled out and there was a rock wall to one side where someone had piled the glacial debris. Sugar maples and scrub sumacs hemmed the meadow in, plotting its overthrow. A beech sapling grew straight out of the top of the wall.

Then, past the meadow—he checked his pulse, he sped up—the rail line forked to the south, and nearly all the auto traffic merged onto the new U.S. highway, and the road narrowed to two brick lanes.

After a hundred yards, it emerged on the lip of a great, sloping cliff.

And he had to stop here—how could he not stop here, daily, the scene sort of inflicting itself on him? Four hundred million years ago, the place where he stood was a seabed covered with a sheet of mud. The mud hardened, was covered with new mud that hardened, and so on, and became, by the time the sea receded, a vast cache of wafer-thin layers of shale beneath the surface. Then recently the river had cut it open, and then a glacier had followed the river's path and widened the gap into a broad valley walled off by the cliff. Below him, the brittle black shale lay sloppily stacked, like an enormous palisade of burned newspapers. And he could see this mud-colored river down in the valley, convolving from the southern woods into the open plain beneath the cliff, where the vast, decaying, ash-bedecked, enchanted city arrayed itself, alive and sulfur smelling, this city, his home.

He kept on walking to the school. None of the trees down here were in bloom. The shortest route into the valley was a one-way cobblestone street called Reckless Avenue. He descended the cliff at top speed. His feet were wheels.

A mist rose from the city, a slow exhalation from a great dying animal.

The yellowish morning air browned as he approached the blast furnaces on the flats, down at the bottom of the shale valley walls, and he was trying to train himself to notice things like this, perversities, that the air itself was a sort of military-uniform color, khaki, you called it. He'd discovered the color of city air on the farm, perversely, where the air was colorless. He had trouble seeing what was right in front of him. *Khaki* came from Urdu for "dustlike."

There were taverns across the street from the mountainous steel mills amid which West Seventh Avenue passed. And depending on what time he went by there he caught either the third-shift men heading mill to bar or the first shift heading bar to mill.

He cut through a brickyard and through a hospital parking lot and through the SJs' vegetable garden and then was at the school.

Nino and Ricky were waiting for him behind the boiler room.

It was 7:15 in the morning.

Nino, scratching his back on the quoin blocks, said, "Hello, Eminence."

The matinal meeting of the Gentlemen's Smoking Society commenced. They had waited for him, which he appreciated.

Nothing important was going to happen today.

He looked at Nino.

Nino had a broad, glum face. His dad was the sergeant at arms of the local to which Ciccio's father had belonged. He had a twin called Cornflake, or Corny, even by the mother, supposedly. This twin lived in a state home for retarded children, where he was visited twice weekly by his mother and brothers but not by the father. Ciccio had never seen the twin. He suspected the twin was a hoax, only Nino's was a face you thought incapable of lying. There was a theme in its construction—the eye placement that was a fraction of an inch too far toward the temples, the sharply protruding jaw, the downward point of the corners of his mouth—the theme being that he had the face of a big, guileless trout. Ciccio hadn't seen this before just now.

He looked at Ricky. He didn't know what Ricky looked like. He was looking right at Ricky and couldn't see anything other than brown hair, blue blazer, dandruff on the blazer. How long had he known Ricky, and he couldn't say what he looked like?

He was trying to notice perversities. It wasn't hard. They were everywhere. Grotesqueries. He had recently approached the bathroom mirror, tape measure in hand, in the coolest scientific spirit, unsuspecting he would find anything definitive but needing a control sample for his research into the grotesque. And he'd found, mirabile visu, and not without a certain prideful shock, that his own features were crookedly affixed to his face, that that was what was the matter with it. And he had not been aware. And he imagined that real manhood, freedom, would mean that all these mysteries that he couldn't see were mysteries because they were too close to him would reveal themselves. He would be permitted to see what had from the start been hiding right out here in the open.

They finished their cigarettes and went on into the school.

Then it was April.

Then it was May.

He needed something to happen, but that was irrelevant, his need was irrelevant. It was imperative that something should happen. No, it was manifest that something was going to happen. A substance was being held in a provisional vessel, and the vessel wanted to burst. He had been reading in the hope of dissolving himself in the substance so that once the vessel burst he'd be carried away with the rest.

He was made to write a paper on Aristotle's definition of motion. The definition was that motion, or change, was the coming into actuality of a potential insofar as it was a potential. He had gotten a grade of C-minus on the paper because he skipped the *insofar as* clause because he hadn't understood it.

Father Manfred had scribbled a pencil note on the bottom of the last page referring him to the end of book III, chapter 1, of the *Physics*, where he could find an example of what the *insofar as* clause was about. He was to be prepared to defend his understanding of the example for his oral examination that spring.

The exam took place in the courtyard between the laboratory classrooms and the SJs' greenhouse. You had to go through the greenhouse to get to the courtyard. When you got to the courtyard, you found two canvas folding lawn chairs under a tree and Father Manfred in one of them, awaiting you. He had a pitcher of fruit punch on the grass and a stack of paper cups. Yellow jackets were dive-bombing the fruit punch, and while Ciccio talked, the priest was fishing them out, crushing them between his fingertips, and dropping them into a pocket in the skirt of his cassock.

The example of a potential that Ciccio had to explain was "building material"; a block, let's say. When you were building something with it, it was in motion because you were bringing into actuality its potential to build. But, Ciccio said, if you were, say, throwing the block at a pear tree to knock down a pear, you couldn't describe it as having anything to do with building; you could say the block was in motion as projectile, maybe, because you were actualizing its potential as projectable. Then he interrupted himself.

"Whenever I think I'm getting him," Ciccio said, "him, Aristotle, right away I says to myself, That can't be right, that's so—what's the word—dumb, how could it be worth his trouble to say it?"

Father Manfred said, "No, but you're right. This is how Aristotle feels. He is observation. He has a bottom. Saint Paul also has a bottom. Now, if I were to tell you that whenever I found myself believing I understood Philosopher X, I felt a pang of dread, I knew I was about to be plunged into deeper unknowing because the teaching of Philosopher X is bottomless, then I am describing whom?"

"Plato," Ciccio said.

"Yes, and?"

"Jesus Christ our Lord."

"Yes, and?"

Ciccio picked at a mole that had recently come to light on his chin. "You want me to say Kierkegaard," he said.

"All right, but you were saying. You were going somewhere."

He tried again, but he got tangled up in the *insofar as* clause and smacked himself on his mouth.

The priest said, "Paraphrase using a different example and without using the words *potential* or *actual*."

Ciccio said, "There's a man in prison. He dreams of escaping—colorful dreams, where the authorities are chasing him. Then he wakes up. He busts the lock and starts to escape, but it isn't like the dream at all. No dogs are after him. No sirens. The guards are asleep. He's escaping, but not insofar as he dreamt of escaping." He added, more to himself than to the old man, "So, like a dope, he turns around and locks himself back up again."

"I don't follow," said the priest absently, rattling the mucus in his throat. He looked aside. In their pink and swollen orbits, his eyes floundered, tracing the path of a zigzagging object that Ciccio couldn't see.

"When the prisoner becomes free, he can't dream of being free anymore," he said. "Like as in, the dream exists only in dreaming it."

"Little blackguard thought he could sting me!" said the priest.

One of the yellow jackets had just landed on the back of his neck, where it met its death.

"You're going to have to repeat that. I beg your pardon. I had distracted myself," he said.

Ciccio repeated himself.

Father Manfred said, "The attaining of the object of the quest always disappoints, you're saying." He made a grandly sarcastic fake yawn.

"I mean," Ciccio said, "I might say to myself common-sensically, I long for what I long for. But, you know, the thing you longed for is never what you advertised. Obviously. And why is that? Maybe because you'd rather long for it than get it. Which is stupid."

"You're saying there's something the matter with the sentence, 'A potential is actualized,' because the subject of the sentence can't be what you say it is and also do what you say it does at the same time."

"Okay, then, that's what I'm saying."

"Okay, but this is not at the same time. This is motion. This is change. There are miles per hour. Time is elapsing."

"Well, I don't like it."

"I'm not trying to be rough with you, boy, but isn't that too bad? Aristotle is not your enemy, motion is your enemy."

"What are you saying, Father? I like motion." In the space between them, Ciccio erratically waved his hand.

"All of this fills you with a terrific sense of misgiving, but you don't know about what you have this misgiving. Tell me what you feel at the edge of your brain."

He looked at the priest. One of the eyes appeared to be dead, but Ciccio couldn't tell which one.

"What I feel at the edge of my brain, as in, I don't know if I even agree with what I'm about to say—"

"Yes," the priest said.

"—is bogus."

"Good."

"I feel trapped in bogusness. Every time I say to myself, Oh, look, that's real, that over there—it turns out that it isn't real, I just had an idea of a realness. But ideas aren't real. Ideas are just ideas. I feel, what, double-crossed by my mind. The more I think, the more bogus everything becomes."

"Which everything?"

"Everything. What I see, what I hope for, what I suspect."

He looked around himself. The sky was green with twilight. There was a very fine drizzle. The tree hanging over them—he knew what it was called, it was a black locust—was dropping hundreds of tiny white blossoms onto the shoulders and the lap of the priest, who noticed this and was bemused. He plucked a few of the yellow-jacket carcasses out of his pocket and bounced them idly with some of the locust petals in the lap of his skirt. It had to be the colors he was looking at, the severity of the contrast between the deeply white flowers, his deeply black garment, and the deeply yellow and glossy stripes encircling the thorax of each lifeless wasp. Every Ohio schoolboy knows you do not call this thing a bee, you call it a wasp. The priest was clean shaven. He had the exploded capillaries at the tip of the bulbous nose that you associate with drunks.

"Let me ask you something else," the priest said.

Ciccio said, "All right, Father."

"What are we making you read all this stuff for, do you think?"

"When you say *for*, I don't think I know what you mean."

"Here is what I mean. I'll tell you. Sometimes when I'm eating an ice cream, I don't care whether it's a real ice cream, or whether I'm really tasting it," the priest said. "But sometimes I care very much. Now, I am a Catholic, you remember, and I believe some pleasures are better than others. And I believe I can cultivate some desires and starve out others. So, supposing I had to choose between the great pleasure of tasting an ice cream with a brain gone smooth, empty of thought, and the great pleasure of, er . . . knowing that I don't know what an ice cream is, or what taste is, and feeling the desire to know—id est, the dreadful reaching out of my consciousness toward the force that governs the world outside it—which of these desires ought I to cultivate?"

"That's some riddle you guys made up to catch Jews in the Inquisition."

"A, B, both A and B, neither A nor B?"

"Do you want to see my horns, Father?"

"Put another way, one might ask, Is it better to feel or to think?"

"That's easy!" Ciccio said. "To feel."

17

The voice on the line was male, croaking, forthright, unquestionably Palermitano, stentorian, and sad. In the background, Lina heard someone raking gravel.

The man said, "You're selling a bicycle."

"Yes, go on."

"I have the correct number for the woman that's selling a bicycle?"

"All I do is answer the phone," Lina said.

"From this point, the transaction proceeds how, I don't know."

"You have a conversation face-to-face."

"We are who?"

"You, the person for whom you wish to buy the bicycle, the friend of mine who's selling."

"I don't get it. What are you doing picking up her phone? What kind of an operation is this? You're her, aren't you—I mean, it's your own bicycle, isn't it."

Evidently he was an outsider of the neighborhood, the accent notwithstanding. No one that lived here would have needed to ask if the bicycle was hers. "I'll talk to my friend about a place and a time," she said.

"We're discussing dollars and cents at this meeting?"

"The price is fixed. Up for discussion is whether this bicycle is a good idea in this circumstance. If your friend has been in need of the bicycle longer than twelve weeks, I'm afraid my friend can't help her."

"I might say, 'Don't worry. I have no doubts this is the right bicycle. Let's skip to the heart of the matter.'"

"I don't think my friend is willing to sell her bicycle on those terms," Lina said.

"A place and a time," said the man.

"Call back in ten minutes and I'll let you know."

"It would be helpful if the place was West Side. There is a little park someplace. There is a little park, actually, on the corner of Wisconsin Avenue and Auglaize Street."

"I'm writing this down."

She hung up the phone and rang Mrs. Marini's line.

Mrs. Marini said she could do it at ten a.m. the next day.

Lina hung up the phone, smoked a cigarette, knocked over her salt shaker, righted it, swept the salt into her hand; and the phone rang again.

"Tell me it's better if I don't attend this meeting myself," said the man.

"Sir. I pick up the phone, then I put it back down. Do you understand?"

"Well, maybe I won't come then myself, maybe. Maybe I'll go do something else, if it's all the same maybe to you, and let the girl talk to you on her own."

"That's as you please," Lina said, positioning herself in front of the opened window so that when she threw the salt over her shoulder it landed outside in the grass. She asked how her friend would know his friend.

There were some benches around a broken-down fountain, he said. And the girl would have a schnauzer pup on a leash.

The next morning, for a diversion, Lina tagged along with Mrs. Marini on the trolley ride. Wisconsin Avenue was the principal thoroughfare of a neighborhood that had used to be called Old Marsh, or the Bottom Marsh, or the Bottoms. Twice, maybe three times, as a young girl, she'd overheard a very old person on the streetcar say he was getting off at "the Bottoms" or coming from there. It was a name from a lost era. Mrs. Marini was among the last who still called it by its succeeding name, The Hague. Lina herself had always known it as New Odessa, but that name wasn't long for this world, either. When she and Mrs. Marini crossed Tooley Boulevard, they discovered that the windows of the shops on Auglaize Street were covered with pressboard, the

Cyrillic neons were shut off, and they were heading into a part of town where neither of them would have agreed to go if they'd known better.

The girl wasn't a girl. She was nearly forty. She wore a severely starched blue sundress and had tied a white mohair sweater around her shoulders. She had a pretty face, disfigured by acne scars. A plump woman about Lina's age, an aunt, accompanied her. The aunt said they'd been led to believe that Lina's friend was a colored woman. Lina replied that she'd assumed the girl herself was white. The tone of this exchange was of nonchalance, or at most of petty amusement, but it was insincere. The colored women were visibly disturbed to hear that such an immodest payment would be exacted from them. Mrs. Marini asked Lina and the aunt to excuse themselves briefly while she asked the woman a few private questions. Lina, the aunt, and the dog watched in silence, out of earshot, from the opposite lip of the fountain, which was webbed with cracks across its dry concrete basin and festooned with leaves, bird feces, and the splinters of a busted radio.

The streetcar home was a sweltering, flesh-on-flesh affair. A white woman made her son get out of his seat so that Mrs. Marini could sit down. Lina held on to a strap in the ceiling and was pressed in her back, when the car accelerated, by a man whose halitosis she smelled, although she couldn't see him. Her purse dangled in Mrs. Marini's face. Mrs. Marini muttered in Italian that when she'd asked the woman if the man in question was exerting unwelcome pressure on her, the woman only said there wasn't anything more miserable than a yellow baby.

Lina said, "Probably not."

"What 'probably'?" Mrs. Marini said testily. "Probably *nothing*."

The woman seated beside her, with the boy on her lap now, looked at Lina for a moment too long, and when she looked away, she did so with the fake lethargy of a person who has been caught paying attention and tries to defend herself by saying implicitly, I wasn't looking at you, I was looking at the empty space in front of you.

Then, with neither warning nor perceivable cause, Lina was overcome by a seizure of cramping behind her eyes. She tightened her grip on the strap hanging from the ceiling of the car. She felt a surge of pressure in her brain and a vivid intuition of homesickness and of having been permanently banished—but from where?

Then, just as abruptly, it passed.

Ciccio was a good boy. She would never tell him so, but Mrs. Marini cared for him very much. She did not need to hold forth about her feelings, like a troubadour or a knight-errant. These scenes, such as one saw at the show in which Bertha fell into Bill's embrace while they blubbered out their sweet nothings, embarrassed her.

Likewise, she had never needed to tell Enzo that—contrary to her early suppositions—she, she . . . well, she did not entirely disapprove of him. Lina was the only person to whom she had ever, as an adult, made the conventional three-word so-called confession. But that was an accident. What she'd meant to imply was, You're a fool; I love and punish you by saying it; you're a fool. Although it may not have come out that way. In any event, Mrs. Marini's behavior in Ciccio's company was testimony enough, thank you.

He was a gainful tenant, a lifter and carrier of heavy things, a duster of high corners, a painstaking washer of her Dresden china. He listened to directions. He studied these days with a high degree of seriousness. He was not given to the catatonic inbursts to which his mother had been given at his age. With the egregious exception of his demeanor around Lina, he was unfailingly civil to adults. How easy to enumerate points in his favor.

But he must have had a dim view of the adult mind and its powers to see beneath surfaces. He thought he was successfully pulling the wool with respect to cigarettes, but Mrs. Marini knew about the cigarettes, and she knew where he hid them. He even seemed to think nobody had noticed when he moved into her house, when in fact a brief, uncomplicated meeting had taken place two days after the funeral. Patrizia was going back to the farm and wanted to clarify their responsibilities.

The three women had drunk black coffee in Enzo's (Lina's) kitchen. Lina was not certain that she would stay. Mrs. Marini could use a man in the house; her fingers were stiffening. For reasons that were unclear to each of them in different ways, Lina and her boy did not get along.

So. As a courtesy, they also agreed to let him go on believing he'd orchestrated the whole thing without their permission, because to tell him they'd all agreed on it without his knowing would only demoralize him. Lina would visit regularly. Who knew. Perhaps a reconciliation could be effected. Meanwhile, sub rosa, Mrs. Marini would consult with them on the larger custodial decisions.

When Ciccio had first moved in, Mrs. Marini considered making a formal agreement with him according to which he must never come downstairs between certain nighttime hours, especially if he perceived that there were visitors, unless he heard a violent commotion. But he was too old and curious for that to work. Couldn't she, then, simply unfold the whole business to him, was he too young for that? Perhaps not. He could keep his mouth shut. This required a conference. Lina didn't care either way, but her mother was vehemently opposed. Mrs. Marini asked for her reasons, and Patrizia said, "Because no." Until now their Ciccio plebiscites had all ended in consensus, but this time Lina let her mother have her way, and Mrs. Marini was outvoted.

Mrs. Marini then let it be known that her door should not be knocked on anymore, nor should she be telephoned directly. For now, Lina was to be telephoned, a code was to be employed, and a meeting would be scheduled. When they had had business during that spring and summer, Federica obtained the use of the cellar of a widow aunt of her husband's who had indebted herself to Mrs. Marini some decades before.

However, that August, after Lina took a call from an anonymous man that eventually entangled them with a Negress from the West Side—a client Mrs. Marini should never have taken on, because one loose Negro would surely lead to a gaggle of others—they ran into the snag, which she should have foreseen, of Federica's aunt-in-law refusing to let a colored person into her house.

They had scheduled the procedure for the afternoon of the Assumption, when the neighborhood would be mad with crowd and their clients' stepping out of the trolley at Sixteenth Street would be a less noteworthy thing to witness than usual. Lina said they could use her house if they had to, except that Ciccio was always prowling around there, thinking they didn't notice, stealing his old things. His room on Twenty-second was slowly emptying, and his room on Twenty-sixth was slowly filling up. (How could Mrs. Marini not take offense at being thought so blind?) And in the warm weather, he spent the daytimes reading in the backyard of his former home, like a cat spraying the bushes. He might show up wherever they did the thing. She needed a better plan.

Before Mrs. Marini knew it, the day had arrived. She sat in the kitchen gnawing a biscuit for breakfast and jotting the letters in the tiles of the crossword with the authority of a woodpecker hammering a tree. Ciccio was still asleep upstairs. She looked at the weather forecast. It read: *Sweltering, dismal; evening thunderstorms*. But she didn't care. She felt absolutely terrific for no particular reason, or, rather, for innumerable reasons. She was rich; her neighbor's yawping dog was dead of cancer; Eisenhower had humiliated Stevenson; even the smell of the newspaper ink was divine. Everything that touched her brain delighted it. The past was dead. She was alive!

The front page of the newspaper, above the fold, showed a photograph of a beaming young veteran in a tuxedo; however his limbs had been amputated. Ghastly.

"They call it an infantry because it's made up of children," commented a Nico-ish voice, but she ignored it.

Then she turned the paper over to read the other items.

"Ooh!" she exclaimed. "I know that name!"

It was the fifteenth of August, Assumption Day.

The name she had read was Mimmo LaGrassa. Three weeks after the armistice had been reached, and one day before he was to be released from a prisoner-of-war camp, he had died in Korea. He was the son of the baker Rocco.

How dreadful.

Well, not really. She hardly remembered the dead boy. She hardly knew Rocco. She still regarded her day with blithe curiosity. Instead of invoking sympathy, reading this article only made her feel certain close-to-home affections more sharply. They were caramel affections, from which she would have liked to unstick herself with a phrase, but none was at hand. She had noted these affections before and had diagnosed them by means of an elaborate analogy:

All people, having reached a certain age, developed presbyopia. Muscles in the eye weakened over time and the lenses lost their elasticity. It was not to be confused with hyperopia, although both implied an inability to see clearly what was near. Similarly, in Mrs. Marini's experience, all people, having reached a somewhat later age, regardless of the temperament of their youths, became sentimental. In many cases the tender emotions of the later years were directed merely inward, at the old person herself. Often, however, she had found, this increase of tenderness was directed outward, toward other people or toward the visible, living world as such. According to her optometrist, all very old people who boasted that they didn't need eyeglasses (often illiterates) were faking. She suspected but could not demonstrate that this increased sentimentality had a causal relationship with the disorder, so common among the elderly, that was characterized by the slow onset of amnesia and madness, and thence eventually to death. Therefore she tried to steer clear of circumstances in which her ever more heightened faculties of pity were likely to be excited. However, with Ciccio living in her house, that was more difficult to do.

She made a good-faith effort to distract herself with the news of the day but, reaching the sports section, was distracted from her distraction. She successfully refrained from rereading the article about the baker's boy but then removed her shoes and put on slippers so as not to wake Ciccio as she climbed the stairs to his room. His door was ajar. His flattop was crimpled against the pillow. He had to sleep crookedly on the bed, with his legs folded up, because his body was too long for the mattress. (Lincoln, having been shot, was carried out of Ford's Theatre and into a nearby boarding house, where, because of his extreme height, he had to be placed diagonally across the bed in which he died.) She knew that to watch this boy sleeping was to ingest a microscopic volume of cyanide, but among her faculties that were in decay was the discipline to avoid scenarios she well knew might lead to the ruin of her mind.

At length, he awoke. His face was red from the pressure of the pillow; his eyes remained closed as he sat up; his pajama shirt was too small under the arms.

She backed out of the doorway before he could see her scrutinizing his head and descended the stairs. She went out to refresh herself in advance of the midday heat. She felt both disgusting and giddy as she paced beneath the flapping Assumption Day banners on the avenue.

The bakery was closed. Scandal! When, by seven in the morning, had it ever been closed? But given what she'd read in the paper she ought to have known it would be closed. About twenty people conferred on the sidewalk. Very soon there were twice as many, then twice as many again. She was surprised so many intended to offer Rocco their condolences. She would have thought people would avoid him. Nobody knew him well. But company loved misery, so it appeared.

Then Rocco appeared, suddenly, among them, while the clock in the church was tolling. He wore a little bowler hat that was thirty years out of date and a woolen winter suit with vertical stripes that belonged on a financier from the gay nineties rather than on his peasant self—stunted, sallow, with fearing blue eyes that were like jewels in a coal bin. He tried to tell them it was all a misunderstanding, that his Mimmo was very well, that it was a fiasco, a bookkeeping error, a fraud, a boondoggle, but no one believed him.

. . . When, while trying to solve a simple problem, such as how to distract a distractible teenaged boy for a summer afternoon, a simple solution proved elusive, the most common mistake was to entertain progressively more complex schemes. One must keep one's wits about one. One must await. First and foremost one must have one's eyes open for shifting circumstances, especially seemingly unrelated circumstances, which might contain the simple seed of the simple solution that the Fates would later appear to have had in mind all along.

She had turned away from Rocco with the rest of the crowd and pointed herself homeward when at last patience and flexibility of mind paid off.

The solution was not to send Ciccio away, but to send herself away and take him with her. Federica would have to do the procedure on her own.

All Mrs. Marini needed, then, was an occasion to tether the boy to herself from one o'clock until nightfall. It came to her. She paused, turned, and headed back through the dispersing crowd as step-by-step her quandary tied itself into a bow. She reached the baker and told him he must come to lunch at her house that afternoon. He demurred, sipping at his empty coffee cup and waving her off with the saucer. She asserted herself. At last, he accepted. She hurried back up the avenue.

Federica didn't need her anymore, she knew what she was about. Mrs. Marini's own role of late was only to keep the client calm, to coo at her sweetly, and if Freddie needed a hand, Lina could lend it as well as any other cool-witted woman. Lina was already going to be in the house; she was a quick study. And then the next time Lina could, yes, why, yes, the next time Lina could—the blood rushed in her prickling eyes—*yes*.

She could realize her forgotten ambition of years ago: Lina could succeed her.

"But, but . . . ," stammered the fraudulent ghost in the shaggy Nico mask.

"I have won!" she said, suspending her disbelief about who it really was and throwing her arms about its hairy neck. "Love me!"

"I *do* love you, Coco," it said, submitting to her kisses and elevating its monstrous brows as it said *"do."* (However, Nico would never have said that, any more than she would have said it herself. He would have simply kissed her once, hard, on the mouth, and told her to go on talking, while he sat across the table and listened intently. That was his way, to sit and listen, chewing a piece of fruit. But she was ninety-three years old, and the poor creature who was his wife and longed so much to talk to him again was imprisoned in the crevasse. Whatever she had wanted to say to him had long ago withered on its stalk, been plowed under the ground, been eaten and excreted by worms, and sprouted again in strange and unexpected shapes.)

By the time she got home, Ciccio had given up waiting on her for his breakfast and had fried his own eggs, five of them. The shells were in the sink, along with the crusts of half a loaf of white bread; he did not like seeds. She explained Rocco's misfortune. Curiously, the boy made no response and only went on feeding shamefacedly at the coagulated mound on his plate.

In order to do their share to help him, she and Ciccio would entertain the baker for an afternoon, understood? Rocco was acutely unwell and so, necessarily, in an egoistic frame of mind. Their job was to give him something outside himself to think about. Was she making herself clear? She trusted that Ciccio had no other plans for the afternoon.

He chewed, and chewed, and swallowed; he and Nino were going to go fish the quarry in Eastpark, he said, but he could beg off if it was important to her. (Here her circumspection was vindicated. "Fishing at the quarry" was what he often said he was going to do when his real intention was to read conspicuously in Enzo's garden.)

"Very good," she said. "We shall keep him talking. We shall keep his glass full. He'll get lazy and want to stay. We shall make absolutely sure he remains with us at least until five and then we shall all three walk together through the feast. What's this look of disenthusement?"

"Nothing."

"Fie on your nothing."

"Nothing, I just . . . *plop, plop, plop,* go the minutes sometimes, you know."

"What happened?"

"Nothing happened."

"Who is this other Cheech?" No, but she must resist. He was a millstone, a chore, a bacterium.

He said, "I told you, nothing happened."

"This Cheech of the sorrowful countenance," she went on, even so.

"Nothing, I just—'Where's Pop?' I ask myself sometimes, like a boob."

The big bastard. He was trying to kill her.

18

Don't look at him. Don't let any type of snoopy slinking outside the walls of his home stick its face into his bulwark of hedges and spy Eddie through the kitchen window—half-naked and hangdog, bent over in front of the electric icebox, in the house all empty but for him this Assumption morning, the appliance making its buzz—and see him poking at the wax-paper shroud of the bacon slab, wishing he knew how he might extract edible food from the package. Leave Eddie in peace to be a mopey and sweat alone. Retirement was a humbug. There were 604 individual plants in his garden out back. He had entirely routed the aphids from his cucumbers. His tomatoes consulted him before blooming. And then?

Phyllis was fed up with the feast, which was every year in the misery of summer, when who wants to eat standing up and squished in with the thousands and their foul breath on you? And the scorched-meat stench, anyway, arguing Phyllis had said, and the rabble that these days came to gape and point. Why not use the car for the purpose for which the car was intended—was Phyllis's yesterday idea—namely, for driving to Sandusky and then tying their kids to a roller coaster and letting them splash about in the poisoned lake? Um, was it not, tomorrow, a day of holy obligation? pious Eddie had asked to know. With or without, she said, their wet-blanket father. He had sired too many children too late in life.

Don't look at him in his gotchies, out of bed at the crack of eleven in the a.m., having slept through the cooler hours of garden watering and several other hours thereafter. Don't watch him, the abject, turn around and let the interior of the icebox chill his ass, failing to remember, Did Phyllis boil the bacon and then slice or the vice versa? Had the kids been made by Phyllis the Forsaker to file into their papa's room single file in the dawnlight hour, when usually he was out pruning and hydrating—except not today, which he'd dreaded this morning in his dreams all night, the house unquickened by the pitter-patter of his wee ducklings and so still, for which reason he'd slept until the heat woke him—and gently wake Papa and gently kiss his nose before they left deserted Eddie to his dozing?

What was this? Even the salami drawer was empty. How about, while packing the picnic basket, somebody thinking to leave Papa a sandwich or an olive, perchance?

Well, now, let's pull a chair to the icebox and collect ourselves. Let us observe the humid condense in droplets on the shells of our eggs and consider, levelheadedly, the limited time of our misery. Most of the morning he had already killed in bed. He was due at the church at five o'clock to hear mass, don his vestments, get blessed, and proceed with the rest of the sweepers and their brooms through the street, forcing the crowd to part so that the saint could pass. Once he returned home from his duties, the kids would be safely in the house, bouncing on the sofa, pouring into his ears their sweet noise.

Only, then, how many hours to dispose of? Six. Less than. Surely endurable.

Let us furthermore remind ourselves, as exasperated Phyllis reminds us with her daily exclamation, while circumspect us creeps out the door, kitchen knife in hand, to police the shrubs, that *nobody is out there looking at us!*

He was an ordinary Eddie, of no consequence. The palliative counsel of his Phyllis regarding how Eddie could teach himself not to see figures in the hedges that weren't really there was for Eddie to seat himself and ask himself, What was there to see in this house? What was valuable to steal? Who was pretty to be peered in on and slobbered over? Say what you would about Phyllis the Spendthrift, Phyllis who exclaimed at a high pitch at their babies; she said so often the thing he needed somebody to tell him. She thought of him. For, look! Hiding behind the milk bottle in the icebox was a pot, and tied with a length of sewing thread to the handle of the lid of the pot was a note, punctured daintily at the top so that the thread could pass through, reading, in her hand, *For Eddie.* And inside was oxtail stew.

He was an ordinary Eddie warming his stew on the stove—this she knew he knew how to do—and nobody was outside looking in. An ordinary day with somewhat less to do, was all, and somewhat fewer to accompany him.

Lina received a telephone call on Assumption morning. It was Mrs. Marini, exclaiming that she had figured out what to do with Ciccio for the afternoon. Lina didn't see why such an improbable threat merited such a tall fence, but never mind. (It was true, what they all thought, that Lina wouldn't object to seeing the back of Ciccio before too long. The others found him interesting, but she did not. She did not find him horrid, either. He did not remind her of better or worse days. He did not give her a feeling of contempt. He did not give her any feeling at all.) Mrs. Marini kept calling Ciccio "him," and "the boy," as though his name had slipped her mind, and Lina had to wonder if Mrs. Marini had at last begun to forget things.

Lina did not say into the receiver, I have been ruing your death for thirty years.

She had thrown away the outdated religious calendar that hung from the balustrade over the telephone table and had replaced it with a philodendron plant in a wicker basket. Mrs. Marini elaborated her idea while Lina admired the plant, which was somehow thriving, although she could not remember having watered it.

Soon it became evident that the plot had unspoken goals. Mrs. Marini would not be Federica's attendant, Lina would, and surely a first time would lead to a second and a third. In this way, Lina suspected, she would learn the procedure, would share in the proceeds, would grow accustomed to the income (she was now living on the last of Enzo's life insurance), and would perhaps be tricked into staying in town.

She leaned back on two legs of a chair, her feet on the telephone table, trying on the idea like a hat in a store, while Mrs. Marini schemed.

Only one element of the plot agreed with Lina right away: Federica was her kind of girl. She and Lina used to ride the trolley together—oh, it was twenty years ago, at least—from the drapery dealer's warehouse, and Freddie would make sniping judgments, in dialect, of the other passengers. She was a Siracusana, too, by way of Indianapolis, and Akron, and here.

"We shall keep him talking. We shall keep his glass full," Mrs. Marini explained.

But Lina felt she was also saying, And in so doing we shall make me unnecessary so I can die.

Federica arrived at noon with her armaments. The glinting, metallic materialness of them—an attitude of ancient authority and craft—their *hingelessness*, was sickening.

And sickeningly beautiful. Some of them (one in particular, a scoop) spoke their functions openly, in grunt words. Others suggested only purposeless, calibrated violence. But she couldn't deny there was something beautiful here, timeless and human. A collection of simple levers shaped to fit the shape of women.

The cheese they ate at lunch after the salad was an Emmentaler, imported from Switzerland, with a musky taste so subtle Mrs. Marini could pick it up only if she exhaled through her nose while she chewed. It did not really go with the peaches, but the peaches were seasonable, and, anyhow, the niceties of cuisine were lost on her guest of honor. The baker had not eaten a raw green leaf in five years, he said. She thought the caverns of his mind must be very dark and cold. She imagined they were made of sandstone and inside them, prehuman creatures clad in animal skins sat in the dirt scratching pictures of bison on the wall with sticks and sacrificing their infant children to invented gods.

Ciccio had brought the baker an ashtray and the two of them were talking about the burning of Washington by the British during the Madison administration, an event of which Rocco had never heard.

Was there any greater pleasure, she wondered, than to sit by an open window in the summertime, and drink a little, and talk?

All of a sudden Ciccio was telling them some kind of riddle.

Rocco sipped his wine and put the glass back on the table. Then he spat out the answer: "Objects descending from the clouds!"

"Oh, good, a game," Mrs. Marini enthused.

The skin of Rocco's yellow-green face had darkened from the booze and heat. He folded his arms over his bulbous stomach, as the sweat showed through his shirt, the sleeves of which were rolled above the peeling elbows, so that white flecks of him had come off and freckled his rumpled blue tie. He won another round of the game and laughed out loud. She had not heard him laugh before. It was a smoker's laugh, percussive and followed by a little fit of wheezing.

"Cry for help," Ciccio said. "Play with the rope and the bucket."

"Things to do in a well," said Rocco, and laughed again, slurping his wine.

He was a loquacious drinker, even expansive; she wouldn't have guessed. Ciccio asked how many of the states he had seen.

The baker peered into his spidery eyebrows and drummed the fingers of his smoking hand one by one mechanically on the tabletop. "Nine," he responded. Then he drew some figures in the air. "Do you know, it was forty years ago this year I arrived on our shores? It was at New Orleans, in the Louisiana. March twenty-third, 1913. Easter Sunday or the Monday following, I can't remember. The earliest Easter in a hundred years. I couldn't trade my currency because of the holiday. A city of believers, New Orleans. But I didn't stay long."

"What did you eat on the first night?" she asked. "Everybody remembers that."

"Brown rice soaked in broth," he said. "Out of a tin cup. Then I got on a train. Northbound. North-northwest. Straight into the heart of the continent—that would be five of the states right there—toward the Nebraska. I made a wrong turn coming out of the toilet and found myself in first class."

Someone in the street shouted, "Ice cream! Lemon ice! Lemons!"

"There was a woman wearing a dog, I thought it was a dog on top of her hair," Rocco said. "There was some kind of balm on the leather of the seat cushions that went all the way up my nose, and to this day if I smell it, there I am in the cabin. Midday. *Rattle rattle,* that was the tea service. Pressed copper on the ceilings. But the leather, that smell!"

The boy was mesmerized.

"Oh, it was just Newcomb's neatsfoot oil. We even used it on our shoes," she said.

"I kept a pet squirrel in the bachelor's hotel, in a city that I couldn't pronounce the name, and I went to adult education classes at the settlement house. I had an idea of everything improving. A little more food all the time, a heavier coat. My lungs were sound, my back was sound. Omaha. I couldn't say the *h,* and then I could. Every part of me was pointed to a shining idea."

"Ideas are trash," Mrs. Marini said.

"I agree," said the boy, shaking off his trance.

"Ideas aren't really there," she said.

"Of course they are. Like"—the baker paused, groping inwardly, then gestured up at the blank plaster of the ceiling—"the Holy Spirit, for example."

Ciccio looked at her, waiting to hear what she would say.

"The Holy Spirit is for children and savages," she said.

"I had a shining idea before my mind's eye," said the baker, "of the man I would become in the end."

Ciccio sat up straight. He lifted his chin from its usual evasive slouch. The mismatched features of his mongrel face seemed briefly to align. He said, "Mr. LaGrassa, I think your son is dead."

"Francesco Mazzone!" she hissed, spanking the table.

"You don't have the first goddamn notion what you're talking about," Rocco told the boy. "Or yes you have, but it's the first notion and nothing after. What is dead to a Christian?"

"Rude!" she exclaimed, but Ciccio wouldn't look at her.

"I mean, this is kind of all a charade, right?" Ciccio said. "I mean, it's kind of make-believe."

She thought the baker was about to strike the boy. He stretched himself across the table, reaching, showing the back of his hand, but he only tapped the breast pocket of Ciccio's shirt, three times confidingly with his apish knuckles. It was a gesture of uncommon, obtuse, and misplaced affection, and Ciccio might have recoiled in response. Instead Ciccio looked down at the hand with interest, even admiration, as though he were the famous dog that had licked the hand of the surgeon vivisecting it. "You have a shining idea, too, my boy," the baker said. "Everything seems to spin, am I right? But it spins around something compact in the middle. Or you're in the dark in a dream, but you're moving straight in one direction, like on a train in a tunnel. You don't see the way out but you feel there's a way out. Don't you believe you're pointed at it? I was supposed to work in steel when I got here, but the position fell through. Then I was a baker for twenty-nine consecutive years of days. I thought that was going to be the end, but I was wrong. That's fallen through as well. God is great. He has something else in mind for me, and I know what it is. Daylight waiting on the outside of the tunnel when I get there, I believe. Everything else will be stripped away. But you know what? *I will be the father of three sons.* I'd know that even if I didn't believe it."

Rather than being a birther and a rearer of sons, Mrs. Marini had been a what, a dry goose, and a snuffer-out of sons. Bluntly, a dismemberer of them. And had been one so long it was impertinent to ask anymore whether that was the glowing goal to which she was always aimed, as in Rocco's formulation, or whether instead her soul had been shaped by her work, as Rocco's hands had been shaped by his. He weighed perhaps half as much as the boy, but the hands were three times as thick.

"What is dead to a Christian?" he repeated, pointing at the boy.

Ciccio's tumid Adam's apple bounced.

"Dead is dead," Mrs. Marini said, taking the boy's side again.

"To *you* he is dead," said Rocco, "and to *you* he is dead, but to *me* he is alive."

There was a pause. Ciccio looked at each of them, inquiring with his eyebrows whether it was his turn to speak.

Mrs. Marini said, "Go ahead."

Ciccio turned to the baker. He said, "He's alive as long as you know he's alive."

"Yes."

"It's so, even while it isn't so."

"Yes."

"I wish I was older," Ciccio said, looking down at his lap. "I wish I could think better. I mean, that's a beautiful idea—"

"No, it isn't, it's disgusting," she said. "Look up when you talk."

"It's a beautiful idea," he went on, raising his chin a little, "but I just don't know how to believe it. I feel like, if I was smarter I could believe it—"

"*Were* smarter," she corrected.

"Were smarter. Or if I were somebody else."

Mrs. Marini didn't need any shining idea. That was all over. God might or might not be great. She had no evidence either way. She did, however, have ample evidence that the tempter, the prince of the silly world through which she had taught herself to walk backward, was very great indeed.

She loosed a long guffaw, haughty, at both of them. "Dead is dead is dead is dead is dead is dead," she said. Then she put some cheese in her mouth.

She breathed out, long and deeply, her lips closed, and the spirits from the bottoms of her lungs moved over the chewy mass of cheese inside her mouth and up into her sinuses, which in turn perceived the most wondrous mild, living scent. It was like the smell of a man's armpit just after he's taken a bath.

Their three places were set at one end of the grand dining-room table. The window behind them let out on the alley that Mrs. Marini's house shared with Rocco's store. Some kids were out there throwing faint, pleasant firecrackers at the pavement. Then one of them set off a toy bomb that rattled the windows in the sashes and made Mrs. Marini's ears ring.

At the table, they all three flinched.

When Mrs. Marini opened her eyes again, everything was as before except that at the far end of the vast void of the table, a figure was seated, tall, with brilliant red hair and an air of utter self-possession, as though even the table belonged to him.

Neither the boy nor Rocco, who went on talking, appeared to know that the figure was there. She looked at them both, making a little smile each to each, and glanced back to the far end of the table. The figure had not moved. It fixed her with its gaze. Its thick hair was curly, and sweat poured in great streams down the sides of its lovely face.

"That's just a better mask than the others," she told it. "I'm not so easily taken in."

It wore a sleeveless undershirt. Its legs were dapperly folded in a way that showed her one of the knees above the surface of the table, so she saw that it was even wearing the military pants—black with red trim—that Nico had worn the day of the race.

"Leave me alone," she said, her nose twisting.

The figure was out of breath. She saw that the head wasn't merely sweating, it was soaked, as though it had just been dunked in the fountain. It looked not through her but at her, a ruthless look, glib and entitled. It extracted from its pocket the playing cards she had given him for a prize.

"Go away!" she cried.

But it only looked down and shuffled the cards.

"Oh, please go away, please," she said. "I have been having such a nice time. If I—oh, please don't make me talk."

Its skin was clean and fresh and rosy, the eyebrows were trim, the mustache was blond and curled up at the corners. It dealt itself a hand of cards, panting heavily.

"Be good to me, please, and leave. Please. Oh, please. Please. Please."

Its hands began to shake as it turned over the cards. When it looked up at her again, tears beaded from its eyes. She looked to the eyes, windows of the soul, route to the brain, and felt the terrible long-lived longing in her stomach to go to them and suck them out and swallow. To go to him and eat him up and keep him. To go and sell all she had and buy him. To lay her fortunes at his feet and follow him across the world and out.

She said, "No, but I *mustn't.*"

"I thought you'd been waiting all this time so we could talk again," he said.

Her resolution failed her, but only momentarily. "Yes, I have—but this isn't the time."

"Oh?"

"The time was forty years ago."

"Oh?"

"What's the use of apologizing, Nicolo? It's unseemly. It doesn't fix anything. You missed out—I wish you had known me later on."

The radio twittered from the parlor. The baker split another peach and passed half of it to the boy.

The figure wiped the tears from its face with its handkerchief and blew its nose. As it hastily got up to leave, it knocked over the chair and bent low to right it, but the boy and the baker didn't see. The figure passed through the doorway, slow and young, its slick white shoulders gleaming.

Mrs. Marini turned to the baker. She said, "I'm afraid we'll have to be going out now."

The Forest Runner

Even today, sixteen and one half years after the fact, his sister dead, his store sold, his archive of Confederate correspondence donated to the county public library, his concordance burned, his flower garden on the bluff behind the house collapsing season by season into the lake, the house leaking rain in every room, the woman herself dead, surely— since how else has he for sixteen and one half years been denied the fulfillment that is his by right, of being called, in words spoken out loud not by himself but by somebody else, by a person living in the world out there, the thing that he is—even this afternoon, trapped in the throng of bodies in a street carnival not three blocks from the café where he had whiled away the hours, poisoning himself with sugar, ardently believing he would be found, he still casts his eyes about for the face that will know his face, for the woman who will recognize what he is and point her finger, opening her mouth to speak, and call him by his name.

The jeweler knows that the undiminished desire to be accused by name by this woman is the proof that he has failed. That gable roof with sides that are shallow in slope at the top and steeper below is a gambrel. The short sleeveless dress with a row of buttons up the spine that the little girl in front of him is wearing, against whose backside the force of the crowd is pressing his legs, is a pinafore. He has a name, too, that could save him from himself, that could turn him into a word if only she were to see him and call him by it. Then all would be lost at last. He could surrender the long-held hope to hold a thing, a thing in his hand, and leave it at that. He would no longer have a material hand in which to hold the thing. But she isn't here, surely, she's dead—the in-strument of his salvation—he killed her, surely.

He's been coming to this carnival every August for five years, but she has yet to show herself, and his hope is waning.

He has stood at the washroom mirror calling himself by the name his father shared with him, but the words only stuck to the mirror. Another person was required. Look at these people, the girl in the pinafore with her pink legs, the ten thousand others forcing him up against her; they are at least not alone in having names, like the gambrel roof, or the samovar in the café. Only he is nameless, real, among them.

At night, as a boy in the winter in Kentucky, warming himself by the potbelly stove in the cabin, his uncle showed him how to put a double bend in a saw by pushing it against the toe of his boot, and how to strike it with a hammer and control the note its vibrations made by bending it further and unbending it and striking different parts of the bigger bend. He practiced playing it at home, in the woodshed of his father's house by the lake. He taught himself to play "My Sister, She Works in a Laundry" and "The Mule Skinner's Song" and "What Was Your Name in the States?" and "Pharaoh's Army Got Drownded." And he made up his own tunes, in love, as he would never love anything else, with the queer, trembling, human sound of a shaking piece of steel, and he taught himself to bow it also, with the bow of his father's fiddle. Then his father's cousin, who picked banjo in a hillbilly band at a saloon on Saturday nights, persuaded his parents to let him go just once and play with them.

The rest of the band was standing—the fiddlers and the fellow with the harmonica and the old man they all called "Sir," whose name he never learned, were all standing while they played. Only he, the youngest, sat in a chair, while he struck the saw with a ball-peen hammer.

He had never bowed it in the presence of others. The saw played with the hammer was clothed; the saw played with the bow was naked, the sound unobstructed by the clash the hammer made. And when in the woodshed in the presence of no one else he bowed it, he himself was naked. Bowing the saw was a simple thing he had that he could do, all his own; it was the pure act, of which the other, the playing of it with a hammer, the version others were allowed to witness, was an imperfect replica.

But the men knew he knew how to bow it, and they put the screws on him. And he didn't want to. It was not for others to hear. But if he bowed it for others he might find that this was the way in, the way through, you had to expose your innermost to the outside. I address myself finally to the material world and its citizens and become part of it and one of them. So he agreed, yes, he would do it.

And the moment came, the signal, when Sir hopped into the air and brought both feet down on the stage. He slid the hammer under his chair. The others took their instruments away from their faces, and he drew the bow along the untoothed edge of the saw, knowing the audience was there but unseeing it with the glow in his eyes of the coal-oil lamps in the apron of the stage.

He was more than naked. The sound in the presence of other people ripped him up the middle, showing to the open air the wet things inside that composed him, that turned food and air into the self he was.

Then, from someplace beyond the wall of light, came the keen of somebody laughing at him.

Yet he did not stop playing or leave his seat.

When Sir clapped at last his boot on the stage, the band picked up the tune again, sewing him up somewhat, giving him some clothes to wear. They played through midnight, until the saloon closed. His cousin walked him home through the black streets. He climbed the stairs to his room.

The bishop in his miter (those two bands of cloth, hanging down the back of it like the pigtails of this pink-legged girl, are lappets) and the priests processing up the street, the young boys in cassocks, the men in long white linen albs chanting solemnly in Latin, the statue of a mulatto on a platform (a mulatto is so called because his blood is mixed as a mule's is), and this flock of crones, in black, bare-footed, murmuring over their beads (an assemblage of starlings is a murmuration), and the big, clumsy band playing so solemnly even though they are out of tune and off beat, all bring back to him the way that night in the saloon as a boy he had struggled manfully to express with the bow and the saw the solemnity he felt inside him, the solemnity of a human self, and had succeeded only in making something that was laughable. In the same way, this, the pageantry, the murmuring in a dead language, the gaudily bejeweled midget half-Negress these people are worshipping as if the icon were holy instead of standing in for something that was holy—all this is in fact solemn and in fact also mistaken, absurd, laughable.

The crowd seems to know it, as there are those among them praying, pinning money grimly to the ribbons that drag along the pavement behind the Negress's palanquin, and those also clapping and singing and laughing full-throatedly. The men carrying the idol are almost as white as he is; they are even dressed in white, they don't know that they're out of place in this place, like the idol they're carrying, like the woman whose face he is searching for in the crowd.

And it comes back to him now that, walking home through the dark streets, silently with his cousin, making his way as one used to do at night by the light of the celestial bodies, he had asked himself, Why did I keep playing, why was I, am I, *not* ashamed to have been thought mistaken, laughable, absurd?

He asked his cousin, "Did you hear that person laugh? Was it a man laughing?" And his cousin said no, he was mistaken, it wasn't a laugh, it was a woman singing along, she was merrily singing the tune he played.

And later that night, mounting the stairs to his room and hearing the *click, click, click* of his hard-soled shoes on the wooden steps and regarding even the clicking as the solemn expression of his solitude, he was struck by how solemn, in fact, it was when regarded by his own mind, and how also the very same self-solemnness when observed by the mind of another would be laughable.

But he felt a solace in this: that what is solemn to me can be laughable to you and still be no less solemn. Because the person he believed had laughed at him, or else had sung merrily along with him, was still, of necessity—he promised himself not to forget, but he did forget—*looking right into him,* apprehending the self that he felt, that his name failed adequately to name. As misery and mercy are the same, the first being what God wishes you to feel and the second the version of empathy he feels for you when you are miserable.

If she wasn't dead, she would be nearly middle-aged by now. Her face could be among the faces of the white women murmuring in their black clothes, whom he is studying one by one as they pass. The crowd is so dense, the street so narrow, that children have climbed the curbside ginkgoes and sweet gums, the telephone poles, the gutters, up there where it must be cooler and the air must be moving instead of stagnating sickeningly in the heat, as it does down here with him among the crowd. There is a bakery with little girls on the roof and a boy and a miserable-looking man in a full suit staring at the backs of the legs of one of the girls as the jeweler was doing before.

If she wasn't dead, she could call him by his name—will no one ever call him by his name again, sweetly?—but there is a crucial and mundane obstacle in the way of the fulfillment of this hope:

Sixteen and one half years ago, he had climbed up off the parlor floor, poured himself a glass of water, sat down again on the sofa, introduced himself, and asked her what her name was. But she didn't answer. And he introduced himself again, courteously, asking if she might do him the favor of repeating his name back to him—hoping this way he could be fixed, at least in the universe of words, completely, could be turned into a word so that at least, if he couldn't be real, he could be not alone. But her eyes were closed, her face was a slack red mask. And he doesn't know if she didn't repeat his name for him because she had heard but refused, or because she was already dead or unconscious from the knock of her head on the marble edge of the coffee table, in the parlor there, with an ashtray on it, and an unfinished hand of solitaire.

Night was falling, amid the mass of people and the merrily singing horns.

Solemnity is comical and comedy is solemn. As is evident from these whitish people praying to a Negress, as if she were in fact the thing she only symbolized, and from these Negroes who are, look at them, taking one another's hands to dance now in the solemnly empty space behind the band that forms the end of the procession up the avenue.

As was evident also when laughing David, dressed only in a linen ephod, danced before the solemn Ark of the Lord to the sound of the singing of the Israelites and the sound of lyres, lutes, tambourines, cymbals, and castanets. And also when Ham, the son of Noah and the father of Canaan, saw his father passed out from drinking and naked in his tent, and went out and told his brothers, thinking it was funny, but they did not see that the nakedness of their father could be laughable, too, and went into the tent backward, a cloak on their shoulders, and covered him, with their eyes averted.

The Negroes are dancing, eight of them, and there is also an old Negro man with close-cropped white hair pointing vehemently at his shoes, and at them, and at his shoes, growling, "You all stop it! You all stop it, now! Get back here, stop it!" Unseeing—the old Negro man unseeing—that the crowd was laughing and clapping its hands to the clamorous, brassy music.

Where has she gone, the girl with the pink legs and the pinafore? You call it a *pinafore*, a "pinned-in-front," although the garment, the thing, is buttoned up the back. Which is to say, the name doesn't need the thing. As the Lord God *said* there would be light; and a vault between the waters; and on the earth trees bearing fruit, each with its own kind of seed; before the things took form. So that at last, this evening if she were only to see him and accuse him by his name, he would return to the unalloyed natural state that precedes being a thing: being a word. His father was called the same name, and his father, too. His name doesn't need him.

So that at last, the jeweler having lost track of the girl, night having begun to fall, and he standing at the perimeter of the gap in the crowd in which the Negroes are dancing, a merry-solemn hope emerges from the bottom of his mind: that his name, having preceded him, will succeed him. He wants to laugh out loud in front of all these people—that should a final separation between the thing he is and the name of the thing be at last effected, then his name (the only part of him that can truly be said to be alive) will keep being alive because people, these people here, will want to know who he was, what was his name, and will discover it, and say it out loud.

PART FOUR

Cleveland

1953

. . . .

19

Gary didn't come from here. He was born in a suburban hospital on the South Side. But he loved the feast. It gave him a warm feeling. He used to come down here with his mother and dad when he was a boy. Richer people had the summer cottage on Kelleys Island; he had this, these streets, the carnival crowd.

He didn't speak the language. He knew a handful of dialect words for garden vegetables, kitchen tools, colored people; heirloom words you couldn't learn from any dictionary. His father was born in a bedroom in one of these tenements. He didn't know which, and he was never going to know because his father was dead.

Gary was a member of five formal associations: the United Auto Workers, the Veterans of Foreign Wars, the American Legion, his softball league, and the Democratic Party. He had two kids, a boy and a girl. His wife took dictation downtown. Maybe six associations if you counted the Methodist Church, but he went only on Christmas and Easter. He felt he belonged here. In Elephant Park. He felt his boy especially belonged here and needed to be taken to the Feast of the Assumption on an annual basis because they lived in an itty-bitty world of cereal and carpeting and because the boy had two names, a first and a last, one for the little self, one for the big self, the shared identity across centuries and an ocean, a name that, when you spoke it, others connected you with a clan and a place. And in this part of town, when they introduced themselves, they said the last name first and the first name last, and the priority here was unmistakable.

He would die. His daughter would acquire a new name. He wanted for his boy in the years to come to say their name and feel the completeness of self that Gary felt when he said it. He had cousins who agreed it was the least they could do to take their boys down here and watch what happened, participate instead of just hearing about, preserve this thing of ours that's slipping away from us.

Their family name was Ragusa. But some of the cousins spelled it Ragosa, so nobody really knew.

He tried to make his boy eat these deep-fried artichokes he'd just bought from a street vendor and the boy gagged, but the kid had to eat, so Gary bought him some taffy, individually wrapped in six colors, manufactured in Delaware. There were people handing out prayer cards, which were, he didn't know, in Latin probably, and the kid wanted to know what do these words mean, and Gary had to say, "I don't know."

There were all manner of different peoples down here for the feast these days. There were Slovaks and Serbs and Chinese, even. And he was annoyed because they didn't belong here like he did.

The boy groused about how crowded and how hot, and Gary wanted to explain how the boy was meant to appreciate. How they were participating now in this idolatrous thing. The men were going to carry a statue through a street with music thrumming and torches alongside and manic chanted prayers, and it was going to transport them all into the deep past.

The client, sitting on the oilcloth with which Lina had covered the bottom half of the bed, bent to remove her shoes. Lina put them on the floor, the toes under the bureau, out of the way. Then the client asked her aunt to leave the room while she undressed. Outside, a man selling fruit raised his voice over the voice of the crowds. Federica asked should she and Lina leave the room, too, and the client said she didn't know what difference that would make.

Rocco was dying in Mrs. Marini's lavatory. Maybe they'd made him drink too much and he was on his knees before the commode. Meantime, Ciccio was carrying on about Manifest Destiny and the War of 1812. They were in her kitchen in their street shoes, waiting for Rocco to finish whatever he was doing so that they could make their passage through the feast.

The boy said, "Look, it's not like we would have had to conquer every little town in Manitoba. There was no Manitoba. The game was all about Montreal. If you cut off their supply channels from the British, the other little cities to the west would have fallen off, and we would have picked them up. We could have been bigger than Russia."

A spool of kitchen thread sat on the counter. She'd used it to sew up the braciole for lunch. She opened the cupboard, intending to put it away, but then she had a better idea. "Get me a scissors," she told him.

His mouth drooped with remorse. He felt the loss of the arctic empire personally. She unwound a length of string and had him cut it off. Then she rolled it and deposited it in her pocket and put the spool in the cupboard.

The baker strode up the darkened corridor, faceless and stately in the abstracting shadows with his great shoulders and narrow hip bones. Then he came into the disillusioning light. His wavy hair was mussed. Water had splotched his coat, and his gray, uncreased trousers were roughly cuffed at the hems, as though he had shrunken since the time the trousers fit him well. He tried to grin, the little eyes blinking in the sun, his hands dripping. And they departed.

They lost him inside of two minutes. The crowd was immense. She knew they'd lose Rocco, but he was now expendable. She waited for Ciccio to get a couple of feet in front of her and then tied an end of the string around her wrist. Then she yelled at him to slow down and not to forsake her.

"Give me the paw," she said.

"Which?"

She made a wave of indifference, the string dangling, and he offered a whole arm, looking off into the crowd, as if it were help to steady herself that she was asking him for, which she was insulted that he'd presume. She tied the loose end of the string to his wrist.

"This is a leash of some kind," he said, looking down.

"As you wish."

"But I wanted to—"

"What did you want to?"

"Me and Nino were—"

"Was our plan unclear to you in some way?"

"Rocco's not with us. We lost him."

"And then?"

"And then so I thought, to be honest, I could—"

"You thought, to be honest, you could help me find him?" She knew there was no hope of finding him now.

"Okay, but we're not going to find him."

"Okay, but yes, we shall."

She should have made the string longer. Even when he put his hands in his pant pockets, all full of sullenness, he was too far from her vertically, and he had to hunch to the side to keep from dragging her after him.

The heat was such that other people would have thought to complain, could be heard complaining. She herself was unfazed.

The barbershop was not open for business, but she saw, as they passed it, Pippo in there by himself reading a newspaper, facing the window, sitting in the barber chair which he'd pumped up four feet from the floor, presumably to see the procession over the heads of the crowd outside. The flanks of his pinguid hairdo were combed up like the fins on a car.

"Ciccio will give a knock on the glass," she told Ciccio.

The barber looked up from the paper, his face awash in gladness, and pulled a lever below the armrest, descending royally to the floor, and let them in.

"We'll have a drink in the back room, then, Costanza," he said. "You, me, and the puppy dog."

"We shall, of course. Short, please. Oh, it's nice and cool in here with the fans."

"What happened to the mission?" Ciccio said evenly.

"Do you know he's not back there?" she said. "Maybe he's back there."

Pippo led them into the back room and pulled the curtain behind him and poured the whiskey into his teacups and dealt them three cards each and laid four open-faced on the table. Ciccio said he didn't have any money, so she fronted him a dollar sixty from her change purse. The game was inhibited to a slight degree by the string, but she wasn't ready yet to cut him loose.

Gary and his cousins got sick of having to listen to the heat complaint of the kids, so they elbowed their way out of the big crowds, toward the carnival rides, where there was more room to breathe. The kid was so happy on the rides. The kid was missing the point. Gary stood outside the gates of the rides with his cousins, the four of them trading their disgust that the kids refused to understand this was not a playground. This was a meaningful place.

Then there was a nun, an actual nun in the clothes they wear—how great was this?—running around to the men at the controls of the rides, evidently telling them to shut the rides off. He asked one of the ticket girls what was going on, and she said that the saint was moving—what a phrase—and she said it like it was nothing special, because to her it wasn't, she was used to this, she belonged here. They collected their kids. They couldn't see the avenue from where they were standing, they couldn't see the parade, which was the heart of the matter, and they tried to press into the crowd, but it was no use. Gary put the kid on his shoulders to see, but the kid started crying that he was scared to fall off, and anyway, he said he couldn't see anything but heads.

It was getting dark. Gary himself was thirsty and needed to use a toilet, but the parade took awhile, they'd see something, and what was the point of all this trouble if he was just going to get the kid spun around in circles on a machine and get in the car and go home?

They waited, him and his cousins and the kids, all together. The kids had quit their carping. They were looking up and pointing at these other kids that had climbed on top of every edifice. Five little girls and a boy and an old man smoking a cigarette peered down at the street from the roof of what Gary recalled was a bakery that his father used to take him to, a bakery, if memory served, that had opened every day since, like, the Civil War but had no name or sign.

The old man on the bakery roof belonged to another age, when a three-piece suit was for walking about town. Modern people were much taller, with smaller hands and solicitous looks. Not a living soul that Gary knew could have formed such a gruesome expression as the one on this man's face, the eyes utterly still, the mouth hard, the fat, lugubrious head stooped and watching.

Then the crowd started moving backward, into them, on the street. At first he thought it meant room had had to be made for the parade to move through up front, but the people started to turn around and face back.

They were trying to get out.

The purple sky behind the old man on the bakery roof buckled in the heat. Something was amiss in his dismal face. The nose was flared, in disgust maybe or contempt, but not alarm, because what hadn't he seen, this man, in his ten thousand years, standing on top of us, watching?

The kid asked him what was happening, and Gary had to say he didn't know. He asked his cousin. His cousin didn't know. The kid asked, Was there a potty where he could make tee-tee?

There were flowers tied upside down from the fire escapes.

The word he kept hearing was *moolinyans,* which he loved himself for a second, he knew what he was, how he was connected to some people and not to others because he knew this was the word for "eggplants" or "niggers," and he knew this because of his last name, because of His father had been who his father had been.

His cousin said in his ear, so the boy couldn't hear it, "Some moolie kids got into the church, like, vandalizing. Like, tipping over the statues and pissing on the rugs." And he was tied to this man, his cousin, they belonged to each other because they both knew that that word was a shortening of the other word.

Everybody was getting out, so he had to get out, too, and the kid, and his cousins, and the cousins' kids.

People were talking, it was true, but mouth to ear. He heard a man say, "Jigaboo rain dance, absolutely bare chested, while the old ladies were trying to pray." There was a deep collective hum, like trucks passing far off, that grew continually quieter until he just heard thousands of soles scratching on the asphalt and the garbage. The kid groused about He had to go to the bathroom. There was no issue of finding a way out at this point. The crowd had its own idea of direction and goal. He could go only where the crowd was taking him, feeling unmanned and stupid; and he didn't want the kid to see this in his face, so he walked in front and made the kid hold on to his belt in the back.

There was a downward pull on his pants, the kid clutching like he'd told him to do, and yet Gary couldn't shake the sensation that it was a spirit of some kind, afoot in the crowd now, something that was trying to pull his pants right down to his ankles.

He looked up at the old man on the bakery roof in the falling light. The face was never going to tell you what it saw. The nostrils gaped, the jowls drooped, the whole apparatus of his being was bent in watching. It was all Gary could hope to be and was never going to be, a hardened face, still and watching, exerting no effect on what it saw, quiet and remote.

Then the crowd threw them all around a tenement corner and the man was lost to him forever. Thrown by the current, all of them: Gary, his cousins, and his young son, named Clement, called Clem, a name his wife had read in a tabloid.

It didn't make any sense, where the crowd was headed and him with it, but they were all moving fast. The crowd went up Twenty-sixth, all the way back down Emmanuel Avenue to Sixteenth, then back toward Eleventh Avenue. He lost his cousins. His car was someplace on the west end of Twenty-second. He'd have to circle some, back up the hill. It was impossible, given the crush, to go right away up the hill on Eleventh. Everybody was headed down toward the streetcar stop. He made the boy wait with him awhile on the corner.

The whole place was emptying. A little current formed, heading back upward on Eleventh, and he yanked the boy by his hand and dove in, and they made it to Twenty-second and turned right.

East Twenty-second Street was devoid of other pedestrians, quiet under the yellow lamplight in the gloaming.

The kid, in his corduroy short pants and no front teeth, had a chance finally to ask him what had happened; what about the fireworks? And Gary had to say he didn't know—although he did know, or almost knew—because he was embarrassed to explain.

They were still in the thick of the neighborhood. There were grape arbors in the yards, and meticulously shaped fruit trees, and little devotional statues among the shrubs. Everything so tidy except for tremendous quantities of garbage in the street. The kid was unwilling to hold his hand as they made their way down the street because now there was room enough to walk separately.

A door opened. The number on the house was 123. And a gray-haired colored woman walked onto the porch and turned around and faced the doorway. Another colored woman, younger, came out, too. The younger one was unsteady on her legs. The old one took a step down and held the arm of the younger, guiding her. They descended likewise the two more steps slowly, to the lawn.

He had stopped to watch this and the kid had stopped and was watching also.

They were here, they were even here, already. They were living here. What hadn't they been given, and now they wanted this, here, too? How was he supposed to bear this? The kid was going to ask him, What are they doing here? Eventually, he would be dead. The kid would grow up and ask himself someday, Who am I?

Awhile later, Ciccio was soundly beating Mrs. Marini and the barber both and had paid her back the money she'd lent him with money he'd won from her. Certainly he was cheating. She put on a shawl from her purse so as to have a means of enshrouding her hand. It was more a tea towel, actually. She couldn't remember how it had gotten in there.

Pippo, noticing the shawl, leaned back in his chair and flipped a switch in the circuit box, whereupon the whir of the fans there in the back room and (she could hear on the other side of the curtain) in the front room faded gradually.

"Jeez, it's quiet," Ciccio said. "You can't even hear them in here."

"Who them?" she said.

"The people, he means—the masses, the craziness," said Pippo.

Ciccio smacked a card on the table. *"Scopa,"* he said again. In dialect this time—*shcoopa*—to antagonize her.

Pippo got up and pulled the curtain, exposing the front room of the shop and the broad wall of windows that looked out on the avenue. Night had fallen.

The crowd had vanished utterly.

It was an ordinary summer night on Eleventh Avenue, only less so. He unlocked the door and held it open for her and the boy. They went out to the sidewalk, looking around at the nobody, at the no trace of the thousands in the street that had been there not two hours before, no trace except that the street was white and aglow from trash, on the sidewalk asking one another murmuringly what had happened.

Others knew him as Eddie that bore the standard, Eddie that defended the faith and the hearth. Others, he knew, relied on him to speak in the voice of us, to tell us what do we do to protect ourselves. But he was also a private man with sweet feelings for private things, feelings which his position required that he keep to himself, the better to bear the concerns of others. Like anyone else he experienced uncertainty, even fear, in his heart, and Phyllis understood, and his babies napped atop him on the sofa after supper.

Oh, but he'd let everybody down, Eddie had.

He'd been so hot all day, from the minute he woke up—all day with the gastric acids scalding the holes in his stomach lining (oxtails for breakfast: a mistake). That and the heat. And the crowd! Holy Mother, the heat and crowd.

When at midday he heard on the street that the baker Rocco had closed up shop, for a few days, at least, the most exquisite notion struck him. There was an ice room in the back of the bakery. Eddie had seen it before from the counter in front. The baker had to have it for the slow rising of the pastries and the hardening of butter. So early that afternoon, Eddie crept up the alley and tried the back bakery door. Lo, it opened. The saints were with him. And he went on in and found in the ice room the bleakest, most peaceful peace of mind a man could hope to know. He took off his shirt and pants. Perfect darkness. He draped his linen cassock over a box, and sat on it, and leaned his naked back on the cold wall, and closed his eyes. Think of a sunbather in reverse. And at length, the cool and the darkness led reckless Eddie into the deep sleep of a little child.

To be discovered, and awoken, in the same moment, in such a state—this was one of the ignominies the Lord sends to a man in later middle age that seems to say, Edward, prepare thyself. Worse is in store. Thy babies shall empty thy bedpan, and thy spouse shall wipe the shit from thine ass as thou sleepest.

He was attacked by the small deranged man, the baker Rocco, and Eddie counted himself blessed to have escaped with his life and name, if not his honor, intact.

Meanwhile, having earlier that day slept through the garden-watering hours, he now had slept through the blessing of the sweepers, and the procession proceeded without him, so that he watched it among the masses like everybody else, unable to make it to his rightful place among the elect in front of the parade, and, rather than doing the pushing, was pushed himself. And the whole procession had gone terribly wrong.

He'd let them down. Oh, God, he'd let everybody down.

Homeward headed unhappy Eddie Assumption Night, like so many others, cassock in hand, thinking his babies would hear what had happened and would ask him, Was this the beginning of the end he'd been working so long to avoid?

But they wouldn't hear about what had happened and wouldn't ask him, hopefully, until tomorrow or the next day. Meantime, he would arrive at home and his babies would be there readying for bed. And the spouse. Praise be. He needed to have his Phyllis close at hand.

Like other people, he had to decide long-term what to do. Like other people's babies, his babies would not understand and would despise him.

Maybe they would have some rain again tonight. Unlike other

people, he had taken his time getting home, had paced the forsworn streets while night fell on them. Chagrin Avenue was devoid of life but for him and a skunk grazing over a sewer grate, and a wind rasped his ear. He wanted to look at this street and perceive what his babies would have perceived looking at it. He wanted to feel the significance of nightfall as children felt it.

Night, for children, was more a place than a time. For a child, to wake in the night and race downstairs toward the bed of parents was to plunge into a forest from which he might never emerge. A man could never hope to fully feel again the deep of night in childhood; he could at best recall the fact of it faintly. For a man of his age, nothing could be as vast as the nighttime of childhood except the extension of thought toward his distant past, where memory flickered, flickered, and evanesced—*My brother and I were on our knees picking the favas when a snake shot up and bit my chin; my father held me under my arms and dandled me over a well*—and the distinctness and the isolation of the flickers, the utter obscurity of what must have happened before and after, imparted to the imagined world in which they had to have taken place dimensions infinitely wider than those of the world in which he now found himself recollecting them.

And he had chosen this country, this city, this house where he was heading. And having chosen them, he might choose some other place to live. But for a child, for his children, who'd only ever lived in these six rooms, their house was nothing they'd chosen, it was a fact their father had taught them. A fact he would now tell them had never been true, had been just a useful canard. And it wasn't useful anymore.

He turned left on Twenty-second. The wind struck his face squarely. Who was going to clear the street of snow and trash when Eddie and his brood were gone?

He'd get what for the house (that there were nectarine trees—in Ohio!—which he'd made to bloom on his property, that there was not a crooked shingle or a window needing more than the tap of a finger to open or close, that there was the brickwork recently repointed by his own hand)—he'd get what? A pittance.

You know from whom we are getting the pittance, don't you? After today, after what he'd seen happen, what he'd seen those people do (almost seen), who else was going to be chump enough to buy here? Leave the trash in the street. Why not. Let them have the whole place the way they liked it.

Down the block, his doomed abode—the twin dormers, the stink pipe, the slow pitch of the porch roof—was utterly dark, was a silhouette of itself, betrayed no signs that his wife and children had yet returned.

But his mood didn't have time to sink accordingly, for who was this, and what were they up to? In the street beneath the lamp ahead was a man in a plaid shirt and dungarees, still as stone, and a boy off to his right. Just standing there. Facing Mazzone's old house that the wife had returned and was living in it now.

What was of interest that they were watching? He couldn't see. It was beyond the far edge of the pool of lamplight where they were standing. The brilliance of the lamp made what was not beneath it all the harder to descry.

It was a fox, perhaps (he went heel-toe in under the lamp, breathing soundlessly with his mouth open), an animal they were taking pains not to spook. He was in the pool of light now, he was within arm's reach of the man with the plaid shirt. There was too much light and in the wrong place, but his eyes were making their automatic calculations, attuning themselves. He saw the thing moving, a human figure, or two figures, perhaps, niddle-noddling toward the perimeter of the pool.

"But what's this we're watching?" he whispered.

The man started, not evidently having heard Eddie's approach, and made a weak-wristed gesture of incomprehension.

Eddie said in his best English this time, "What are we watching?" as the cone of light seemed to expand, and what they were watching, the figures, assumed substance, became actual, as a needle does when it pierces the skin.

"Sorry, what?"

And the man, grizzle-faced and fat, repeated it yet again, his stertorous voice lowering, an edge of impatience in it, pointing with each syllable back over Gary's shoulder at the colored women, but it was all still less penetrable than the first time.

"I don't understand you. Could you repeat? English?" Gary said.

And the fat man said it again, this time pointing at him, and then at his kid, and then at himself.

Gary pressed on the top of his hair with his sweaty hand and squinted. "One more time? Okay?"

And whatever it was, the angry fat man said it again, pointing at Gary's eyes and then pointing at his own eyes.

Possibly it *was* in English and that was why he wasn't getting it.

The niggers were getting away.

"I, my kid, here, visit," Gary said.

But the fat man loosed a long string of strident words, loud, and poked him in the chest with a finger, and said the original thing yet another time.

Gary heard a whimpering sound. There was also an odor, faintly ammoniac. He turned and looked down. The kid was crying. The eyes brimmed, and the kid blinked, and the tears popped out.

The kid had pissed his pants.

Lina looked with pride and disgust at the night's wage on her telephone table. The bills were crisp, although the dates printed on them were all from before the war. There were also three rolls of dimes bound with a shoelace.

She was standing alone under the balustrade, looking at the money, when Mrs. Marini telephoned from the barbershop. Pippo the Barber was in the room with her, evidently.

"How did your tart turn out, my treasure?" the old woman asked.

"Federica said it was fine."

"And you've washed the dishes by now?"

"The woman was resting and then she left a couple of minutes ago, and we're all cleaned up," Lina said. "Freddie's already gone home."

"Did you eat it?"

Lina thought a minute. "Yes," she said.

After she hung up the phone, she looked at the money some more.

She was unsure what to do with it. She stood thinking, her fingernail in her teeth. Then, in a wicked stroke, like a knife jabbed into the hinge of an oyster and briskly twisted so that the hidden creature is exposed to the open air, she made up her mind:

She was going to stay here. She was going to live in this house for many years to come. She was going to learn this trade and make her living from it. And she was going to take this money downtown and spend it.

She needed a coat for the winter.

Donna Costanza severed Ciccio's leash with a house key. They were on the sidewalk in front of the barbershop. Mr. Pippo the Barber said, "The Russians are coming, but where are the sirens for air raid?" The heat had broken. There was a steady wind coming from the direction of downtown, from west-northwest, and Ciccio was thinking, No, it wasn't atomical conflict coming, it was a cyclone. Wax paper and tinfoil climbed the wire fence enclosing the courtyard of the convent, and fell down, and climbed back up in the wind. North of the equator the direction of the spiral of a cyclone is unfailingly counterclockwise.

She asked Mr. Pippo if she could use his phone, and the two of them went inside, and Ciccio stayed out.

Unless he was just experiencing the humdrum cool of night having fallen. How to save the appearances? How to account for Everybody had been here and now nobody was here?

Ciccio sat down on the curb, feeling this was a brave thing to do, to settle himself, to be still and quiet in the midst of this place so many had just fled, aware of a peril on its way of which he himself was ignorant. Thinking there was a power he could have by virtue of what he didn't understand.

He was on the curb in this place of stupefying sameness that now had become an entirely other place, phantasmal, resembling in certain particulars—the shapes of buildings, the angles of streetlamp light— the place he had spent his life unconsciously memorizing, while at the same time it was nowhere he'd ever seen before. Like in a nightmare of which you say afterward, I was at the farm but it wasn't the farm.

Unless it was far simpler than that. Like, what if what he was now feeling was an impression of the place itself—what the clearing of a forest and the building of shacks and then houses and a church and the digging of sewers and the packing-in of so many people, him included, had served only to disguise? A blast might come, a firestorm. Everything alive or dead here might be burned up at any moment, and what would be left after that but a place?

And if he were somehow to survive and come back here, he would recognize it, he was sure. The eyes would have no evidence with which to confirm, but there would be no question of confirmation. He would feel in his every cell where he was.

20

The jeweler was on the bridge, at a remove of several hundred feet from the throng surrounding the parade, eating an elephant ear, wishing to talk to his sister again, examining his heart, when the throng came rushing toward the narrow bridge as though a pipe had burst. The people began to fill the streetcars awaiting them on the boulevard, clamorous to get out, now, for reasons that remained unclear to him. Night was falling. He sucked the confectioner's sugar from his fingers. He had gone to the bridge to look at the water and to get out of the crowd so that he could turn back and see it as a whole. Now the crowd was coming as though it wanted to get a last look at him up close. He stood in the bottleneck, obstructing the current of bodies. He wanted one last glimpse of the girl in the pinafore, this parting sweetness. He was summoning the concentration of hope he would need, and the concentration of mind, on this specific moment. But he was failing to do this, he was caught in two distinct present moments, as though he were wearing a pair of eyeglasses from which one of the lenses had fallen out.

For here he was on the bridge, sixteen and one half years after the fact, chewing; and also here he was gripping the rail of the bridge ten minutes before the fact, having ridden the streetcar to the end of the line, into this neighborhood he hadn't happened upon since it was the Germans who had lived here, and soon an unlucky woman with a burlap onion sack on her shoulder would pass behind him and ascend the slow rise of the hill. He wore a tawny ill-pressed linen suit, a knit tie, and bifocals; also, he wore black trousers, a lintless black double-breasted coat, sealskin sleek, on which snow fell. The day was both dates because he could not refrain from calling it both, and if only, for once, he could control the language at his disposal, then the way toward the consummation of his hope would be made plain. The August crowd might sweep him away to the boulevard. But it was also December, an arctic somnolence, the bridge empty but for him and the woman—here she was—trudging behind him, skillfully whistling a Christmas song. The creek purred, deep and black, unfrozen only up its middle. The people one after another collided with him, trying to push him across the bridge—but he gripped the rail and would not succumb, and a vigorous prestorm wind was pressing him the other way, and soon he would be blown apart by the contradiction. The leaves swam in the gale, and the branches twisted. He turned back to the crowd wanting somebody to look at him.

They were all so afraid, the crowd (as he was afraid), unknowing what they were afraid of (as he was unknowing). If he could actually touch the object of his fear he wouldn't feel fear anymore, he'd feel a fulfillment of knowing. But the fearful could never touch the thing feared. Fear was an arrow pointing at nothing. He rubbed his tongue on the wax paper, collecting the dust of the sugar and the cinnamon.

There was a dream from early youth of being pushed from a high place and falling.

He loitered on the bridge, putting some distance between himself and the woman with the onion sack, letting her pass unlucky and unsuspecting.

He turned and gripped the rail fiercely and looked down at the glittering, summer-green current forty feet below. It was from this waterway here, Elephant Creek, that the neighborhood had taken its name, although physically it was not a creek anymore but a river. Long after it had gotten its name, two other creeks had been diverted into it upstream to drain a swamp that was to become a rail yard, but still you called it a creek and not a river because the name is the soul of the thing and persists long after the thing named has passed away. He considered the name of the fried snack he'd just eaten and the name of the creek, and the coincidence here. Yet there were no elephants to be seen. The word did not need the thing it stood for. The word, being alive, had an instinct for perpetuating itself.

Below him, at the water's edge, three boys in short pants threw their shoes and socks to the farther bank, waded knee-deep, but then stopped, indecisive, seeing that the water was too deep to wade and the current far too fast for swimming. They were indecisive because they were jealous of their desire to reach the other side, unknowing that the idea was not to cross or to walk over on a bridge, but to descend into and drown.

Only, the descent was sacred, and therefore private, and so he would have to wait for the crowd and its living stink—smoky and sweat sour—to take its leave. You had to approach the house of the woman with the onion sack slowly and alone.

Where had she gone, the girl in the pinafore, with her pink legs? The pinafore was a contradiction that walked around on a girl in a crowd.

It was going to thunderstorm. The creek would turn brown and swell farther up its steep banks. Soon, privately, the water would fill his shoes. And later on somebody would find him downstream and look into his face and ask, Who was this man, what was his name? And they would print the words in the newspaper for others to read and speak.

A picture and a caption. And the caption would lay bare at last his name, age, and address.

That tree with its branches twisting was a Norway maple. No good for tapping for syrup.

He turned again and faced the unperceiving crowd. And the woman with the onion sack—six minutes before the fact, five, four—ascended the hill, whistling.

"My name is," he said, and spoke his name, haughty and shame-faced, jangling the big ring of keys in front of her face to wake her up. "Alliterative. Funny. Go on, say it."

He missed his sister. Preserver of artifacts. Kisser of soft, reassuring kisses down the despairing hours. "The clammy clown is clumsy," she'd used to say when, refilling the lamp, he dribbled kerosene on the rug in the back parlor, where they read at night before bed.

· · ·

Who would notice him gone that knew his name? Not the coal man. He only came in wintertime. Not the postman. The jeweler collected his bills from a box at the PO. His barber called him, modestly, Chief.

It was so easy to follow her from a distance of half a block and not to expose his plan of action. In fact, he had no plan. Had he intended ahead of time to climb the stoop and to open the door of the tenement, then surely, fatefully, he would have found the door locked. She went in and closed the door behind her. He saw this from the street, waiting, listening to his heart. Then he climbed the stoop, on which salt was splayed, and pumpkin-seed shells, and held the knob of the door and turned it, and the door opened. If it were necessary to any plan that he find her alone in the apartment, then the apartment door once opened would have exposed a room occupied by others. Fate required that he obey the commandments of his heart only as they revealed themselves, emerging one by one, each at the last moment, as a curb, a stray roller skate, reveal themselves to a blind man making his way with a cane. Here is a door. Open it. Here is a stairwell. Climb it. Listen. Someone has clicked on a radio behind that door, right there. So go ahead. Open the door. See what happens. See what you do. There is a woman.

People had long said, and the many books of regional history and toponymy he'd used to own agreed, that the *Elephant* of the name derived from a circus that had spent the winter upstream from here during the last year of the Civil War. A young cow had trundled onto the ice, nosing her trunk about for liquid water, and had fallen through and drowned. A painting that depicted this event hung in the foyer of the county historical society.

But several years ago he had made a discovery. He had bought a map of the portion of what would become the Ohio Territory that had been deeded to Connecticut by King Charles II in 1662, the last tract of land, as far as he knew, retained as a colony by an individual state; it was known then as New Connecticut or, as it was still sometimes called, the Western Reserve. The date under the compass rose was 1799. On it, a slim black line described a creek approximately one hundred miles west of the settlement at Conneaut, fifteen miles long, emptying into the lake. The note to the right of the creek read *La Fonte*—a little extra space between the *L* and the *a*. His French dictionary told him it meant a "melting; smelting; thaw; mixture of colors, as in painting;" or "the holster of a saddle." Or else it was someone's name. A fur trapper perhaps, Canadian, with a trading post on that site.

He held a magnifying glass in his hand. He looked up from the map. "Oh," he said aloud, "we have misunderstood."

Forgetting himself a moment, he called to his sister in the parlor. But she was dead, of course. She had been dead for three years. He was always forgetting.

Now the crowd was gone at last. Night had fallen utterly. He walked off the bridge and found at the end of the rail a muddy, switchbacking path through the bull thistle and sumacs, to the water's edge. A heap of oil filters rusted on the far bank. He took two steps into the current.

What were the worst days? The very worst? The days when he couldn't read. His eyes wouldn't stick to the words. At times a week of this. What was the sadness of weeks like these? It was the sadness of Today, in my mind, has been so void and brief, it's hardly taken place. Yesterday was only a moment ago. Other days, conversely, he lay on the parlor daybed sunup through midnight reading a big leather-bound book with gilt pages, and his sister brought in his food on a tin platter, and tea, and he got up only to empty his bladder and his bowels. On those days he felt free of the elapsing of minutes: like the long-ago preacher in Prestonsburg said of God, "He does not endure for all time; he lives outside of time." It was such a sweetness those days in the parlor, to occupy a room, a self, made only of words, the objectness of things having been peeled off and tossed aside. He said his mother's name, waking her from the dead.

If he could denude himself of his mineral self, leaving only his caption, he would become at last transeunt, transient, timeless.

There was a dream from childhood that returned to this day, a dream in which he was thrust from a precipice by an unseen person and *fell*, wheeling through the air.

The rocks beneath his feet were slick with moss. The body, even now, struggled to preserve the balance to which it was accustomed. He slipped. He fell neck-deep, his arms twisting behind him to stop the fall, to protect the head. He half-stood again, on a rock deeper down, and slipped again and fell.

Now, above him on the bridge, the nothing at which the arrow of fear pointed took shape. He glimpsed it as it became material. He saw it with his material eyes. It was as real as he was. The shape it took was of a very tall, slender male figure running across the bridge. A boy, fleet of foot, passing in the dark over and away from him.

Here is at last our end goal, the child's dream come to its fulfillment: Having begun again to fall and twist fearfully in the air, we find our will; we aim our face down; we do not say "fall," but "dive"; we watch the ground rush to meet our eyes. Here it is. We do not make landfall. We are a line intersecting a plane. We shoot through.

21

Ciccio stood up from the curb.

The Russians weren't coming. People lost track of time when they played cards, that was all.

The glut of crumpled paper cups and napkins and sandwich wrappers clogging the grates of the storm sewers was such that when the thunderstorm that was about to crack open above his head finally cracked, the streets would flood, the trash would float down to the creek and sail through the night toward its mouth and settle at last on the floor of the lake. If he stayed right here he would see the last evidence of the crowd carried off on the water. And if a cyclone touched down on this place and lifted the buildings away, and if he chose to stay here and watch . . .

Was that the choice? Were those the only choices? Whether to take shelter in the basement of a heavy building or to stay, to stay, to stay, out here and watch and risk being carried off into the air? The storm was coming, the storm was saying, Either stay here and watch me and be carried off, or take cover; either way you have to answer to me. But he didn't want to. No. He didn't want to answer it. No, he didn't. He didn't.

It wasn't until he came to a halt on the corner of Eighteenth Street to check for cars coming (there were no cars coming) that he said to himself, I've stood up from the curb and I'm carrying myself away and out. He didn't know this was happening until he described it to himself. Likewise, he didn't know he was running until he was on the bridge (the wind blasting him backward, only still he was going forward across the bridge, in the direction of the boulevard) and said to himself that he wasn't sprinting, he was galloping, that was the word, in his dress shoes through the wealth of garbage on the pavement of the bridge.

Two colored women were waiting at the streetcar stop, an older one and a younger one that only looked old, both of them laughing on the bench there. He couldn't hear what they were laughing about. It was still windier than before. The younger one was rubbing the sole of the unshod foot of the older one, who wore pearls in her ears and whose long hair was braided with a piece of ribbon and coiled around the crown of her head like a wreath.

He counted his change. There was an electric ozone odor of imminent summer rain. The smell of No more work today, time to get inside, there's a honeydew for after supper. He didn't want to go in under the awning of the trolley stop with the colored women because he wanted to feel the rain on his head when it came. For a second the wind quit squalling and he heard the older one say, "That's a coincidence. They don't call it a corn because it's like corn. They call it that because it grows out of the bone like a horn does."

Ozone was the result of electricity shooting through the air, forming oxygen molecules with three atoms instead of two, and young people smelling it were stricken with nostalgia even when they had never left home before.

Then the streetcar came and the colored women got on it, and he did, too.

Later, on the train heading west along the lakeshore, a train that was, as it happened, the last scheduled departure from Erie Station Tower for the night, the conductor asked him for the ticket he hadn't bought. Ciccio reached into the inside breast pocket of his jacket. But the ticket wasn't there! He stood and turned his trouser pockets inside out. He'd forgotten it at home! "Oh, jeez, you'll kick me off the train!" he said.

The conductor's rheumy eyes came up to Ciccio's jutting Adam's apple, and his mutton-chop whiskers grew into his mustache, so that he looked like Chester Arthur and also like a walrus. He filled his cheeks with air and expelled it pensively, looking at the loosened knot of the tie that Donna Costanza had made Ciccio put on for lunch and that Ciccio would have taken off by now if he'd had a bag to stow it in.

He didn't even have to use the weepy story about the aunt who was expecting him, who'd be pulling out her hair with worry when he didn't get off the train in Toledo. The conductor just wagged his head sadly, unspeaking, and continued up the aisle. It was a Christian country. He was a kid, there were no real punishments for the likes of him.

He woke up when the train pulled into Sandusky, then he went back to sleep.

He woke up again when the conductor was passing in the dark of the aisle toward the dim light of the gangway that led to the next car. "Mishawaka," the conductor called. "Mishawaka, Indiana, approaching. Mishawaka." The ashtray in the armrest of the window seat was stuck shut with chewing gum. It was deeply dark in the cabin. When the gangway door slammed behind the conductor's back, Ciccio stood up. He couldn't see anyone else in the cabin with him. Briefly he thought of himself, of what he might be feeling. But he figured that could only be fear, which had derailed him in the past and would not derail him now. And although he knew it was better to feel than to think, he resolved to think instead.

He thought of salmon, and bugs.

Then he thought of Father Delano, teacher of Christian Doctrine, and a game the priest had made them play in class a few months back, a kind of parlor amusement for Jesuit cocktail parties.

"Write in ink on a scrap of paper," the bumptious, shrunken, emphatic, salt white priest had said, "the deadly sin to which your character is most likely to fall prey. Don't think. Just fess up. Nobody else will see this. It's for your own reference." Ciccio wrote *wrath* and *gluttony*. Then he struck out *gluttony*. He was still growing, after all. Father Delano said, "What you have written down so quickly is ipso facto a sin you can acknowledge with ease. You are reconciled to this sin. You are clandestinely prideful of it. The ego generated this response. The function of the ego is to what? To protect the self from the world of others. Now then, being boys and being sixteen years of age, you certainly answered 'lust' or 'wrath,' all of you. I am quite assured. You even believe in the sinfulness of your sin, that it is not in fact soi-disant okay to act lustfully or wrathfully, but this is also charming. That you believe it is a sin is the source of its charm for you.

"Therefore. There is another sin, which isn't charming. A real sin. No, it is not charming at all. Write down the real sin. I give you twenty seconds this time. No one will know." When he spoke, he exposed his piebald incisors and flexed his nostrils in spasms and allowed his saliva to collect in a froth at the edges of his lips. He was Swiss, but you could never hear the accent. He had advanced tuberculosis. It was his last year at the school. They'd all heard the news that the order was planning to send him in the fall to a sanitarium in Oklahoma. But he was to die in June in his bed in the rectory, in Ohio.

Ciccio had dipped his pen. *Vanity,* he wrote in a burst. Then he looked at the word. He couldn't remember if it was one of the seven on its own or if it was a species of pride. No, it was a species of pride, the species concerned not with the insensible but with the sensible portion of the self. And it didn't fit him right.

"I want you to consider the darkness in your hearts, boys, how deeply dark it is in there. Surely what you've just written down still fails to puncture the shell of your viciousness. If it was so easy of access and if you truly believed in the sinfulness of it, you would have fixed it already. This second sin is a mask for the sin about which you cannot come clean. The ego protects the self from assaults from without but also from within, namely, in this case, from knowledge of your real sin. Your *real* sin, which is what?"

It was too dark in the cabin. The light from the gangway made it feel only darker. If he had any money at all he would have traded it away only to fall back asleep.

Wrath, he had written again, and had drawn a line underneath and circled it.

"Your sense of culpability continues unabated," the priest said, "notwithstanding that you may have meditated for many years on your sins and confessed them sincerely. Sin is layered on sin. Each layer gives the lie to a more fundamental and abstract layer. There is an *eidos* of sin, of which all these others are representations. You feel you are on the hook for something you wish you could express and cannot."

The thing to do was to keep out of his mind the desire to sleep, to eat something. To think of desires would soon lead to feeling them.

"The myths of Adam and Eve's disobedience and of original sin itself aren't postulates you must take on faith, from which postulates you derive your morality. They are allegories for something we cannot precisely articulate because we cannot precisely see it because it is so close to us.

"In fact, we have *empirical* evidence that we are broken. *Behold,* the psalm says, *I was shapen in wickedness. Behold,* as in, Look, look at it, you don't have to take anyone's word for it, you see it for yourself, if darkly. The story is a *post festum* story that we invent in order to describe mythically the supernatural source of the experience. We know in the darkness of our hearts that it is not any sinful act that condemns us but the form of sin—which is coextensive with the form of the human being—that condemns us. In our dreams we experience the infiniteness of the emptiness that awaits us, and we know it to be irrevocable. We cannot be free of the emptiness that is our fate and continue to be what we are.

"And yet our Lord promises us redemption."

And yet right now, in the cabin, Ciccio could hear his feelings, as if from a distant source; they were the ringing in the ears after a great explosion.

The priest had wiped the spittle from his mouth with his handkerchief. He said, "It would appear therefore that when we are redeemed, we shall cease to be ourselves."

Ciccio was fearful from knowing that he was hungry and knowing that he didn't know how he was going to eat again.

All his far-flung mental roads led back to a central question, and he didn't know if it was the right question, the real question, or only a question that he was tricked into asking by the flawed lens through which he had to look at things. And the question was this: In order to do what I am built for doing, must I dispose of myself?

He thought again of salmon, and of the males of so many insect species who mated, if they were lucky, only to have their heads bitten off in the heat of the act, or mated in midair and fell dead to the ground. That was the baker Rocco, whose heirs Ciccio had never met in fifteen years of passing him every day on the street. The baker was a he-wasp, built to fertilize the queen and die: The swarm he fathered would never know him or care to know him. A world would open up, but only after the founder was dispatched.

Ciccio cast his eyes about the cabin, trying to find something to take in, something physical to notice, and perceived only that it was dark and that he was alone. This was a momentous moment, the final escape— which years from now he would think of as the first escape—and he wanted something to remember it by, a perversity, like the baker's perfumed leather oil. That Ciccio could see only what was not there, no light, nobody to talk to, meant that years from now he would remember this only as a script of thinking, like the amnesia days on the farm. A wife, maybe, whose face as yet remained insensible, would ask him to tell her what it looked like inside the train when he woke up in Mishawaka, Indiana, the first time he left his home state, at night in the train that would at length lead him to her, and he wouldn't remember anything about it. He would remember only the colorless face of the dying priest who had told him months earlier that his best hope was to disappear.

Then there were stops in South Bend, and in Michigan City, and in Gary, as the morning light began to hone the edges of the shapes outside the window. He harbored within himself, despite himself, the shamefullest emotions about the country as he watched it moving by him, his home country, to which he belonged regardless of his desire to belong to it. He loved shamefully the names of the states as children love their mothers. He loved the shapes of the states. *Oklahoma,* he said in his mind, two long *o*s, two short *a*s, and wanted to know if there would be anyone to whom he could disclose, ever, the tenderness of his feelings, in all their callowness, when he said this word. There was something he wanted to say out loud. There was a word he wanted to listen to. There was a used-car lot flying past him with a hundred plastic yellow pennants flapping, and the prices were painted on the windshields of the cars.

The conductor—it was a different conductor now, but he wore the same monkey cap with the lacquered black visor—teetered by, steadying himself on the headrests of the vacant seats down the aisle of the cabin, calling, "Chicago, Chicago, Illinois, approaching. Union Station. Chicago."

He wanted to say the name of the city he came from, this word that would meanly preserve him to hear. But he screwed up his nerve and got off the train.

PART FIVE

The Present Moment

1915

. . . .

22

"I remember the weeds bending against my legs, the sun aglint on the slag between the train tracks. I had with me a bottle of water, but it wouldn't be enough, I had so far to go. I could refill it once I got to Rome, only one did not drink the water of other towns. I took three steps in the direction of returning to my father's house. I had nothing to eat. But I stopped and turned. From behind the trees, a three-tone steam horn cried out in alarm, and I heard the methodical sounding of the engine bells.

"God has not forgiven me for stepping back onto the platform. I had a suitcase made of pasteboard and it was yellow with age. The man in the ticket office looked out his little window at me, and I got on the train backward, but I kept my eyes on him so that I would not look directly up at the town and lose my resolve. I had seen him before. He was the uncle of a girl I knew in school. He had his eyes on me as a mob has its eyes on the condemned. And there was the rumble of the wheels turning against the rails, and the steam hissing. A rat dragged the rind of a yellow melon across the slag at the foot of the platform. The man opened his mouth and spoke to me. There was no one else I could see. I know that he did not say, and at the same time I remember clearly him saying, 'You have thrown your faith to the dogs.'

"I was nineteen years old. I had never left Lazio, to say nothing of leaving Europe. And I thought nothing of the fact that what he said, he said, of course, in our dialect, in the private language of our town. No, I thought nothing at all of that. But in the ear of my mind I have, as if in a phonographic recording—although I also know he did not say precisely what I remember he said—the voice of that man, Mariannina's uncle, saying in dialect, 'You have thrown your faith to the dogs.' Here is what we call a mother tongue. Think of the physical tongue of your mother. Think of your father's kisses on that tongue and how the kisses precede you into the world.

"My dear, I have never heard spoken since a word in my mother's tongue. My darling, I forsook it for the promise of you.

"Outside, I can see a wagon with the words *George D. Francesi, All Phases Building* on the side, and its mules are asleep on their feet.

"Here, I'll cut up the roast myself into the tiniest pieces and put them in your mouth. And you try to chew them.

"Of all my sins why this one? is a reasonable question to ask. Why the stepping from the weeds onto the platform and then onto the train that I knew would carry me away? After all, there are—are there not?—the spirit remains of several hundred oleaginous children in the cellar. Why not save my regret for them? I know the answer. Shall I be brutal? I saw most of their faces, most of them had faces. I'll tell you, if you eat something. Here, sit up now. Seeing as I pulled you onto the chair and wheeled you in here so you could eat properly at a table, it's the least indulgence you could grant me. I'll cut you the thinnest sliver of fat the way you like. There we go. I slip it in between your lips. You don't have to chew, just swallow it like a gull does. Listen and I'll tell you why not. You'll say it's fatuous, but it's what I think: They couldn't speak. They are hypothetical in my mind because they couldn't speak. You might think they scream, but they can't scream. No, there is only one truly permanent mistake—I have found and often remind myself—and that is when a person throws away his faith in the Lord.

"I have had only one truly permanent desire, and that has been, is, to lift the thin dark screen between me and you.

"Then there was another train, north to Genoa, and in every town where it stopped a different man boarded and pushed a cart through the corridor and repeated with impossible rapidity what I understood at first to be the words *mandarins, sandwiches, oranges, nuts.* Each man, as the train continued up, up, toward the north, said the words differently, until I was in Genoa, where I did not know what the man there was saying, and I looked into his cart and saw that it was pears and fennels he was selling. And I had to point with my lips closed, like a foreigner. I took a fennel and my empty bottle and yellow case and myself off the train. And I sat on the bench carving the fennel, ravenous and peeling off its folds. Nineteen, unknown to anybody, weeping. I could see the gulf from the bench where I was sitting, and, do you know, I had never seen the sea before. And what I felt about the sea was not at all what I'd intended to feel. I felt hopeless. As in the dreams I had as a girl in which I was a ghost among living people who tolerated my harmless haunting of them but neglected to acknowledge that I was there. There was the gulf, and the sea extending beyond it, and they were mutely real and complete, whereas I was what, was what kind of a thing? I was a fleeting thought the mind that the sea was might light upon and then forget. I was a notion. I would pass out of existence when the physical world's bleak, perpetual, unspeaking mind no longer observed me. I had had at home a provisional, theoretical persistence, and now I'd given it away, even such as it was, or killed it. There were around the buttons of my blouse the thinnest flanges of gold, and a child approached me asking for a stalk of the fennel, and as I held the fennel with one hand and tore off one of the curving stalks with the other, the child—it had no sex, its hair was long, it had no shoes—ripped one of my buttons right off me. And it ran between two cars of a train that was stopped, and then was gone.

"There were men I thought must be Arabs, they were so dark-skinned, selling chestnuts in paper cones. How ridiculous, to sell for money what anybody can pick out of the dirt!

"I remember clearly him saying, Mariannina's uncle, and also know he did not say, 'You have thrown my faith to the dogs.' This was more than thirty-five years ago, but the event resides in the center of my brain like the speck of sand in a pearl. I know it's there, but because I can't perceive it directly I can't know whether he said 'your faith,' or 'my faith,' or 'our faith.' And the difference is crucial, is it not? Other days I am convinced he did not say 'faith' at all, but 'fate.'

"Once, I dreamt that I was a little girl rinsing my feet in a river when a boy poked his head out of the current. The boy was you, Nicolo. You had a fish's tail and brilliant blood red gills on the sides of your head. You were naked in the water, and I was naked, too. You gave me a lecherous look. Then you gripped the edges of the rock where I was sitting, opened your jaws wide, and slowly began to swallow me from the toes up, in one piece; and I let you do it.

"Inside you, I felt the tingle of the bile on my skin. I touched the sleek walls of your stomach with my toes. You had reached my hips when I heard a gunshot. Then I knew it wasn't a gunshot but a door slamming and that this was a dream from which I was about to wake up. But I wanted so badly for you to finish me off. In the dream, I saw that you had been shot in your scaly back and your blood was leaking into the river. And I knew that you were about to die; and I believed that when I woke up you would be dead, so I must try very hard to stay asleep; but I felt myself waking up all the same. And you paused, severed me across my chest with your teeth, wiped your lips on your arm, and asked me with your sweet boy's voice, 'Coco, will I be dead when you wake up?' And I stroked your copper curly hair, and I felt my blood go cold.

"When I awoke I was so cold. I felt so small. In the bedroom, the darkness was a liquid in which everything was submerged. I could not find the candle with my hands. And I firmly knew that you were dead. You had taken all the useful parts of me into the grave in your stomach.

"Then I heard the squeal of the pantry door opening. I thought it could only be an intruder in the house, banging around in the kitchen— because you were dead, you see. You hadn't stayed out playing cards, and you weren't coming home and slicing a piece of cheese in the pantry to eat with a plum on the porch, as you used to do late at night, creeping courteously so as not to wake me. No, I had lost you.

"I felt my way along the parlor walls to the kitchen. I did not speak; the one I believed was an intruder did not speak either, although I could faintly see him moving about in the room. I found the lamp and the matches on the counter. I lit the wick and lowered the chimney over it, pressing the sleeve of my nightdress to my smarting eyes. I wound the wick down a quarter of a turn. I moved my trembling sleeve away from my face. The cupboards shone and were yellow and hopped menacingly in the lamplight, and I heard the intruder approach me.

"Then—as when you spy the shadow of a fish, imaginary and flat, beneath the surface of a stream; and suddenly, cracking the elemental border, the fish flings itself into the crisp and luminous air, twisting with life—from the blackened bottomless depths above the lamp, your ruddy face leapt to my eyes. And you kissed me.

"Maybe that piece is too big to swallow. Here, let me take it out. Maybe you'd like the applesauce first. I know how you like your sweet, my sweet. I'll mix in the brown sugar. You don't even have to chew. Just open your throat and lean back your head and let it slip down like birds let fish fall down their gullets. You planted the trees yourself, the apple trees. And I mashed the apples through the mill just today. There isn't a single seed, I promise.

"I had received the letter from you that I had so long awaited, but I had never heard of the place where you wanted me to go. So while the nuns were in the courtyard taking their bedding off the line, I sneaked into the library of the convent school and found the atlas page for central North America. Then I heard them coming, and I tore out the page. And I put the book back on the shelf, and I ran away. Late that night, I crept into the lemon orchard behind my father's house. The odor of the blossoms in that orchard was the ideal of sweetness. There was a high, dazzling moon. I scoured the map, but all I could find was Iowa, Iowa was right there in the middle. And I did not know you well enough to know if you would be careless about such a thing, about writing the right letters of the name of a place in the right order.

"I like this. I like how quiet it is now. You and I sitting alone in a quiet room. You don't have to talk. Just tilt back your head and swallow.

"If I met someone from my town, would I still be able to speak in dialect with him? I don't think so. You made me speak the national language like they do in the army, or, I suppose, in the king's house. I used to feel so embarrassed, like I was putting on airs, when I was first learning to talk the way you wanted. I said to you, 'For the love of God, I am not from Sienna, I am not a baroness.' But I was ashamed.

"When we were first married I was so unhappy. We had running water and two rooms to ourselves, and the coal was delivered every month to our building, into a bin in the landlady's stable. It was so much more than I had hoped for. But I couldn't bear to look you in the face. And once, you came home from the shop, and it was late, and I had put out boiled beans and fresh broccoli and some chicken necks for your supper. And you washed your hands and face in the kitchen sink, and you sat down to eat. And you watched me as you related the plain innocences of your day, but I could not look up. And you told me to look up. But I couldn't bear it. And there had been months of this. And you stood up and came to my side of the table and told me, perched enormously over me, to look at you. And I would not do it. And then you struck me with the back of your hand, hard, on the side of my head, so that I could feel my hairpin cutting me. It wasn't too hard. And you asked me why I wouldn't look at you. And I said I didn't know. And you said, 'Why did you say you would marry me and come all this way, and do it, too, marry me, if you didn't want me?' And I should have said it wasn't true, I should have said I did want you. But instead I told you the truth. I said, 'You aren't what I expected.'

"You dashed out of the apartment. I heard your feet going so fast down the shallow stairs that I was afraid you would fall. Then, in fact, I heard you stumble and I heard your body fall down to the landing. You had probably hurt yourself, but I didn't get up to see. And then I heard your feet going more slowly down the rest of the stairs. And I heard the big door come open and the din of the street gushed up to our rooms. And then the slam of the door. And then silence.

"I like to do only the one thing at a time. Today, for example, I know I should have put the roast in by three, but I had cut out the blouse pattern from the bolt of organdy, and I had told myself I would finish stitching the sleeves before I did anything else. There, done. I like to have a little box and to take everything out of the box and then put everything back in. There, done. I like to read a book from one cover to the other. I like to read every letter inside it and then close it. Therefore, having embarked on the sleeves, I did not so much as peel a carrot for supper until I had finished them. Therefore, having embarked on supper with you, I am going to stay here until you eat something.

"My consciousness is like a very bright light I shine on one thing I have in my mind or on another. Often the light is shining too directly on something and it begins to dry up right in front of my mind's eyes. There was a you I had in mind for three years, while you were in this country and I was in the other one. In the orchard, staining the map with my oily finger, I could not think of you directly. I could not see you. I could not call to mind the exact sound of your voice. You existed only along the edges of my thought and so could be beautiful. And then—it seemed very sudden—I was living in those two rooms with only you. And I did not love the you across the table. And I was looking down at my feet, trying to remember the face I had had along the shadows of my mind in the orchard, because I wanted to say to my heart, Look, they are the same man. But I could not remember that other you, that idea you.

"Everything I look at head-on, think of directly, give a name to, turns to stone.

"You were not what I had expected. It was at least as bad as you feared: You were a disappointment to me. Unless you open your eyes and tilt back your head, I will tell you something else. I will do it.

"I will do it.

"You are still a disappointment to me.

"I want to take my remorse for feeling this way and put it in a little box and close it. My darling, I have been trying to close it these many years. And yet there is the emotion, unclosed, unclosable; and there is no *There, done*, ever, there is more in the shadows sometimes, and sometimes less.

"You could say I have no right to notice my heart's feeble follies, these elusive regrets I feel for an honest confession confessed unkindly, when my conscience has vastly bigger fish to fry. I have practiced and perfected and take pride in my facility with a vicious act for which I take money. I've tried to find remorse in myself for this, but where is it? If I wanted to, I'm sure I could invent a defense, but I would only want to if I felt remorse.

"Why must everything be explained? Why must we say 'because'? We name our reasons for doing, we tell ourselves these private fables, all the time knowing they are at best incompletely true.

"Once, you were eating a pear, you were scraping the meat off the core with your teeth. You were being very meticulous, as you are. (We were walking arm in arm from the theater, where we had made a game of whispering made-up translations of the words of the play, which we had not understood.) We were talking, and I made a joke in English, my first one, that you had pared the pear to the bone. And you laughed. And then you popped the core in your mouth and chewed it and swallowed it down. And later we wondered why you had done that. What had come over you, to eat the core of the pear, stem and all? And here is what at long last, two nights later, after we had given up on the hope for an explanation, you said, snatching sense (such as it was) from the jaws of nonsense (so to speak): You said, 'I did it on purpose.' Which was not a because at all, we both knew. But it was the answer.

"My darling, my penance, my consolation, I do not love mess, as you once said I do; I only feel everything and also its opposite, and often I feel them at the same time in the same part of myself. You were falling down the stairs, and I hoped you would keep falling and also that you would climb back up to me and close the door behind you when you came in.

"I wish it would stop raining. I wish those mules did not look so piteous, asleep on their feet, the rain pelting them and also rising as steam from their gray sides.

"I return again and again to my father's house on the evening after I left it. Darkness falls. As it is October and it is early in the evening, there is a weak shower, which will pass soon. Here are the vegetable skins rotting in our garden. There are the lanterns of the last people coming off the vineyards in the hills. In the house, my mother is pulling a chain to draw a piece of wood over the window to keep in the heat. She assumes I am on my way back from my father's father's mother's house, where I told her I was going. I am late, however. I have, alas, been caught in the rain, she supposes. I am often late. (In fact, I am by now already in Rome, at the station, and the emaciated cats are slinking among the rubbish heaps.) My father and my three brothers and my five sisters and my aunts and grandfather come inside and wash the dirt out of their hands in the same kettle of water. My absence is noted without alarm. Look at them, wet and stinking, they are all already dead, and they don't even know it. They've all already been transformed into my ideas of them, as you may be someday should I outlive you. There is so little light in this room that they all of them stoop over the soup bowls to see what they are eating.

"Now, what I want to know is this: When I turned them into phantoms of my thinking, and in so doing endowed them with loveliness, did I do good by them or bad?

"You had lost the race and had dunked your head and they had carried your brother away on their shoulders when I said, 'Here,' handing you the cards, 'these are for the loser.' After that I saw you two more times. And there was always the dark screen down between us, although at moments it seemed so close to lifting, I thought my heart would burst. Then I did not see you for three years. I slept every night with your lovely ghost. And when I saw you again I was still so young, and I didn't know yet that you were not going to be my idea of you. And when I say that you are still a disappointment to me—oh, yes, I am very, very cruel, as you have said I am, but wait—I mean to say: My darling darling, you have killed the past. You have broken my heart. You have given me the present moment.

"Look at me. Open your eyes and look at my face.

"I still remember the first joke in English you made. We were walking up Maumee Avenue downtown to a musical club. We had been married a long time, and Alessio was dead. And you were pestering me, you wanted to kiss me on my ear on the street with people passing. I smacked you and was petulant, but you persisted. You called me a witch, but I was unmoved. The excrement of the horses was everywhere in the gutter. And you said, 'You wear your heart up your sleeve.' In a cage in the window above us, a monkey was screaming in a way that was so like a human child screaming that I wanted to go up there and hold it. You moved again to kiss me as we walked, and I pushed you away, and you whispered, almost touching my ear with your mouth, something as vulgar as I have ever heard you say—you remember, what you said you were going to do, the thing you said you were going to do to me, right there on the street, standing. And I said in my thoughts, wishing you could know without having to hear me say it, If you would only refuse me, I would give myself away to you.

"Or have something to drink, won't you? Won't you?

"What I wanted most to feel in those days was the exquisite suffering of you going away from me. We were unlike, you and I. You felt what you felt; whereas I, like a scientist, was always trying to know what I felt. I made experiments in my brain like a fool: If this, then how would I feel? If that, then how? My heart was hidden from me, and I believed I had to abuse it to make it give up its secrets. I wanted you, from your own disinclination, to refuse me so that I could comprehend my feelings by suffering them. But you would not withdraw from me and make a space in which I could put my thoughts between us. So I have never known, and do not know now, my own feelings; I only feel them.

"But if ever. If you should ever. Should you ever. If you were to. Were you ever to . . . then the screen would clap down forever on which ideas are painted.

"But you would not refuse me. You took my arm firmly in your brown hand. I was so skinny then and your hand so big that you could wrap your hand all the way around the thickest part of my arm and touch your thumb to your finger. And I said to myself, There is no hope. And I succumbed, was dragged by you into the club and was sat down by you, was thrown into a chair behind a low table with no cloth on it that was strewn with peanut shells and loose threads of tobacco. There were a dozen young men behind the lights on the stage playing violins and banjos; one had a mouth organ, another—a boy, seated—had a saw (a saw!) that he was bending into the shape of an *S*, and bending further, and unbending, and striking with a hammer, and making it make this human noise, plaintive, while an old man, older than you are now, with a white, patchy beard sang, and I did not know the words he was singing (it was English, only it wasn't English at all), and all of them were standing but the boy while the man sang and beat out the time by stomping his boot resoundingly on the floor, and a Negro asked you what we would drink. And you told him to bring us two bottles of beer, if he pleased. I asked myself, Where was I? I was thirty-one. We had been married ten years. Alessio was dead. I asked myself, Where was I? The boy was smashing and smashing at the saw, making it cry out under the violins, and there were the banjos and the mouth organ and the old man's yawning foreign voice and his stomping and the stout clapping of his hands. You would not let go my arm. My family were dead. I had killed them. The Negro came with the beers and poured them into glasses. I had no hope of any hope at all. The footlights threw the long shadows of the men up on the green wall behind them. I had no past or home country to return to, and no hope, only this man gripping my arm so tightly, my own hand had gone numb. The men on the stage were leaping, and the old man gave a whoop, and leapt, bringing his boots down solidly on the stage, and the others stopped playing. I saw the boy with the saw slip the hammer beneath his chair as one of the violinists passed him a bow. Then the boy bent the saw deep against the toe of his shoe and drew the bow along the blunt edge of the saw. Everything was quiet but for this. Nobody moved but this boy with his bow and the saw and the Negro carrying a bottle to a table in the front of the club.

"And the sound broke on my mind—you remember the sound, a sound of exquisite suffering with something else in it. Something I could not . . . refuse, a sound of what suffering is on its backside; it was the hopeless sound of a child's laughter.

"A minute later the old man gave a terrific stomp and they all started in again with the banjos and the singing. I could not catch my breath. And you let go my arm and touched your lips to my ear and said, 'Stop this crying.' But I did not know I was crying until you told me. I thought

I was laughing. I believed I was laughing, like the boy's saw, like a child laughing. I believed I had no hope at all. I had no hope at all. I could not stop myself from laughing. The clock over the stage read seven thirty. There was the smell of tobacco spit and popcorn.

"And if ever. Should you ever—so you must open your mouth and drink something warm. If you were to. Then—you know this, so you must help me, you must open your mouth and drink—then you would plunge me irretrievably to the bottom of the dead and irretrievable past.

"You remember, don't you? How there was a boy with fierce eyes and wispy yellow hair on his cheeks, and how you put your mouth on my ear as though we were alone, and how the old man whooped? We drank our supper. The old man, at length, climbed down from the stage, took a seat by the stove in the middle of the room, and fell asleep.

"And we stayed till eleven and listened to the lads play."

Acknowledgments

This book was written with the aid of the Fine Arts Work Center in Provincetown, the Iowa Writers' Workshop, the Michener/Copernicus Society, the U.S.–Italy Fulbright Commission, the MacDowell Colony, and the Corporation of Yaddo; and with the indispensable advice of Rick Barot, Sara Becker, Sarah Braunstein, Bill Clegg, Michael Dumanis, Tim Earley, Jaimy Gordon, Vanessa Hwang Lui, John Michael MacDonald, Fiona McCrae, ZZ Packer, Roger Skillings, Jennifer Sprague, Justin Tussing, and Emily Shelton.

SALVATORE SCIBONA's fiction has been published in the *Threepenny Review*, *Best New American Voices 2004*, and *The Pushcart Book of Short Stories: The Best Stories from a Quarter-Century of the Pushcart Prize*. This is his first book.

The End has been set in Adobe Caslon Pro,
a typeface drawn by Carol Twombly in 1989,
and based on the work of William Caslon (c. 1692–1766),
an English engraver, punchcutter, and typefounder.
Book design by Wendy Holdman.
Composition by BookMobile Design and Publishing Services,
Minneapolis, Minnesota.
Manufactured by Friesens on acid-free paper.